Five Golden Rings

and a Diamond

Marie Seltenrych

About the Author

Marie Seltenrych was born in Leixlip, Co. Kildare, Ireland. Marie attended a Vocational College and eventually became a Secretary to a Dublin MP. She pursued her acting ambition by attending evening classes, and found local fame playing the ingénue in Brendan Behan's famous play, *The Hostage*.

Marie migrated to Australia in 1971 where she met and married Henry. She lived in Sydney then Canberra, where her two children were born, then moved to Queensland. She began to write book-length stories, including *The Gum Tree Gang*, published in 1999. Marie is presently working on a second novel.

Published in Australia by
Temple House Pty Ltd,
T/A Sid Harta Publishers
ACN 092 197 192
Hartwell, Victoria

Telephone: 61 3 9560 9920
Facsimile: 61 3 9545 1742
E-mail: author@sidharta.com.au

First published in Australia 2004
Copyright © Marie Seltenrych, 2004
Cover design, typesetting: Chameleon Print Design

The right of Marie Seltenrych to be identified as the Author of the Work has been asserted in accordance with the Copyright, Designs and Patents Act 1988.

This book is a work of fiction. Any similarities to that of people living or dead are purely coincidental.

National Library of Australia Cataloguing-in-Publication entry:
Five Golden Rings and a Diamond
ISBN: 1-877059-69-2
460pp

Glossary

Shelta language:	English equivalent:
Aga di'lsa	Over this way.
Ala	Another
Alamax	Milk
Aburt	At all
Laisk my dheel and my dheel will Laisk your gilhairt	Tell me, and I will tell you again (in my turn)
Tri a gater	A sup of drink
Awást!	Away with you!
Ax!	Similar to Ah!
Axónšk	Tonight
Kam a K'ena	Son of the house.
Nid'es axiver!	Never more
Dil 'lsa axiver glori	Did you ever hear?
Agetul	Afraid
Oid	Butter
Tur an skai	At the bottom of the river.

Marie Seltenrych

I wish to note the work of R.A.Stewart Macalister's 'The Secret Languages of Ireland', Cambridge University Press 1937, Ch VI pp 174-224 and John Bear of Canberra for his help and encouragement in respect to the use of words from the Shelta language in this novel.

Common Irish words	English Equivalent
Angelus	A prayer recalling the Annunciation of the birth of Jesus which is recited by Irish Catholics at twelve midday and six in the evening at the sound of the church bell ringing.
Bamboozled	Confused
Banshee	Ghostly woman who moans at night as she combs her hair, predicting a death.
Begorrah	Mild swearword. By god.
Billyo	Go quickly
Black pudding	Product for frying that contains blood (pig's).
Buccal	Boy
Codger	A mean or strange person
Craic	Fun and laughter. A party.
Craw	Feeling irritated. Held back.
Curate	Young priest in training
Daft	Silly
Deas	Nice
Egit	Idiot
Faggot	Derogatory term for a person. Fit to be burned
Garda	Police
Gaol	Jail
Git	Bad boy. Someone base, troublesome

Granny also the Curse	Monthly period
Moron	Incapable of developing beyond twelve years of age
Niamh	Queen of the Land
Moiré	Mary
Peat or turf	Brick shaped fuel cut and dried from boggy ground.
Piddle	Pass urine
Poteen	Highly and illegal alcoholic drink made from potatoes.
Skint	No money left. Broke.
Slainte	Here's a salute to your health
Spud	Potato
Vex	Arouse one's temper. Shortened version of vexation.
Yerra:	A positive expression to indicate the hearer thinks the speaker is exaggerating. Possible shortened version of: you're raving.

Irish sayings:

As thick as a double ditch.	Hard to get through to. Very stupid.
Dei's Muire dhuit	God and Mary be with you
Guts for garters	A threatening expression against someone.
Holy Mother of God	Irish Expression of exclamation
Kettle of fish	Situation
Uische beatha	Water of life
Saint Joseph's Order	A non-existent order, which is the opposite of a convent. A term for someone who could never be celibate.
Slain leat.	Farewell to you.

Chapter one

The time is just before Maeve's wedding day! It's a cold March morning when she comes running up to me as I am walking over to McCarthy's barn. Maeve is my step-sister. Her mother, Aunty Maura, married my daddy after my mother died. Maura's husband had died a few years before that, from alcoholic poisoning, they said in whispers!

'Niamh, guess what?' Maeve asks, her face all red and glowing, like she's found some great treasure.

I'm wondering if she'll share it with me. 'What?'

'Paid's asked me to marry him. He gave me this.' She shows me a copper bangle on her arm. It's engraved with shamrocks. She smiles. 'D'you like the shamrocks? That's our secret name for each other. Sham and Rock!'

'Who's Rock and who's Sham then?'

Maeve goes all coy. 'That's for us to know and you to find out!' she says, giggling.

I giggle with her.

'Soon I'll be Missus Flynn, Missus Paid Flynn, to be exact. So they were wrong, weren't they?'

'Who was wrong Maeve?' I ask, mystified.

'They always said you were the pretty one. They said 'She'll be snapped up first, that one, with those curls and those bright eyes,' didn't they?'

'Who said that Maeve?' I ask, wondering what she's getting at.

'All the women, and the men! I even heard the rentman say it once, when we were small!'

'Is that so Maeve? Well, I always thought you were the most beautiful sister I could have.'

'Yerra go on! Well, the fact of the matter is that I'm getting married first, and Paid thinks I'm the most beautiful woman in the whole world!'

'Sure that's grand Maeve, as long as you're happy, that's the main thing.'

'I am very happy. The happiest woman in the world! You'll find out one day!'

'What?'

'About love!'

'Sure I don't want to get married for ages! I can't imagine being with one person for ever. It would be very boring!'

'You're just too immature to understand,' Maeve says, as she tosses her head, and then abruptly looks at me.

'You will be my bridesmaid?'

It's what we talked about, dreamed of. 'I will, of course I will!'

'I'll be the most beautiful bride you've ever seen,' she exclaims happily, waltzing around on the grass as though Paid is with her.

I'm thinking of the two dresses I have, this old green one with the ripped belt at the back and the fraying hem, and another navy blue dress, which is getting too small for me. 'But Maeve, what'll I wear?'

'Don't worry, we'll find something! Be happy for me, that's all I ask.' She's hugging me to pieces and crying.

'Oh God! Don't cry Maeve. What's up?'

'I'm just happy, so happy,' she says, bawling her eyes out.

In the end I join in and we both bawl our eyes out.

…

Paid and Maeve's big day finally arrives! It's Thursday, the thirtieth day of May, nineteen hundred and sixty eight. I'm standing on a bit of a hill, on the west coast of Ireland, in County Galway.

'It's a grand sight, wouldn't you say?' It's him with the black teeth, Rhonan, Paid's brother.

I have to agree, 'Tis!' I reply. We're both admiring McCarthy's Barn, an amazing structure that seems to have wound its way out of the earth into a barren landscape. Our eyes are tracing its form upwards. The steps go around and around right up to the sky, as if it's a giant ice cream cone standing upside down. Right at the top there are turrets so it looks like a bit of a castle gone wrong. Someone built it just to give the men work around these parts in the early eighteen hundreds. That's a long time ago, before we were even thought of.

'My daddy says his great-great-great-grandfather, Pat Murphy, build this barn,' I say proudly. 'God rest his soul.'

'I heard it was my family that built it,' Rhonan argues.

I remember my father's words. 'My daddy says it was his father's father's father's father, so there!'

He's eyeing me inquisitively. 'How do you know?'

'He knows!' My father knows everything, I'm thinking. 'My father knows more than your father.'

'My father is bigger than your father.' He knows that's true. His father, Billy Flynn, is a weeny scrawny low sized man who reminds me of chicken with his long face and bony fingers, which are always working with bits of wire and stuff. He makes carrying baskets, which the women love. We're staring defiantly at each other.

'Does it matter at all, at all?' Rhonan asks me, knowing I've got the upper hand now.

'No, I suppose not,' I reply.

'It's ours now.'

'Tis.' I agree with him. I feel like a great rich landowner looking at his private property.

'Do you want to go up?' he asks.

It would be something to do while we wait for Maeve to get here. 'Come on then? Let's have a look at America.' I head up, holding my long frock off the dusty steps and making my way to the top.

'God, what a wonderful sight,' Rhonan mutters from below me.

'Tis,' I reply. 'I think I can just about see America on a clear day.'

Rhonan looks straight up from below me. He's got a smirk on his face. 'I think I saw Canada as well, one day!'

'You did not,' I reply

'I did so!'

'You did not!' I reply, breathing deeply as I reach the top. 'I'd like to go axim a Skai-grut!' I use our Shelta language almost without thinking. 'They say the streets are made of gold!' I say, in awe. The grey blue waters of the Atlantic Ocean stretch as far as the eye can see, leading straight to America.

Rhonan puffs for breath as he joins me at the apex. 'Swurt a mun iath!'

'Tis. It does feel like its heaven,' I remark to his comment. 'Heaven and America must be the same?'

'They both have streets of gold. I can see them!' He's squinting into the distance.

I squint into the distance. 'You can not!'

'Can so!'

We laugh together.

'Ah, maybe we could swim there?' I suggest, immediately imagining myself flying through the water like a mermaid.

'I probably could, but you couldn't!'

'Why not?' I reply, placing my hands on my hips.

'Because you can't swim.'

'There's nothing to it. You just flap your arms around and that's all!' I retort. That's what it always looks like to me.

'Not at all! You don't know the meaning of the word. I swim every summer in the river. It's very technical. I think you'd end up tur an skai, being a girl.'

'I would not end up at the bottom of the river, just because I'm a girl!' I retort.

'No, it's because you're not interested! If you're not interested, you can't learn,' he explains.

'Are you calling me thick?'

'If you like…but you're not as thick as my brother Noel. God, but he's as thick as a double ditch,' he adds, shaking his head. Then he looks at me under his eyelids. 'I could teach you to swim… I can just see you in the nip…gorgeous!'

'Awast!' I say, pushing him with my two hands. He hardly moves.

His hand feels like a rock on my shoulder. 'You are…gorgeous. I'd love to…'

I push him away again. 'I said get away…'

'I know what you said! I wonder what you mean?' He smiles gleefully at me.

'Niamh, Rhonan, come on down. They're coming. They're coming.'

It's my stepmother, Aunty Maura, yelling excitedly.

'She's seen us now?' I say.

'Ax! One day I'll have my own horse and caravan…we can travel anywhere together…'

'Indeed!' I reply haughtily. 'We're coming,' I yell downwards.

A sudden gust of wind whirls over the turrets. I shiver.

Rhonan's long arm drapes itself around my shoulder, landing between my small breasts. 'Axónšk, I'll warm the cockles of your heart!'

'No you won't! Not tonight, or any other night!' I reply. Whenever he comes to our place my aunty Maura says, 'Here comes Rhonan, with one arm longer than the other.' I think I know what she means now!

I stick my tongue out at Rhonan as I dive nimbly under

his arm. 'I'm going down, before Aunty Maura comes up…'

'I was just enjoying the beauty of the place,' he says, grasping my arm, stepping in front of me, blocking my path.

My face is getting hot. 'I told you, I'm going down!' I wrench my arm away and manage to get past him. I yank up my dress and nearly fall down the uneven steps to the bottom. The shoe on my left foot slips off, but I hurry on down. I'm at the bottom now and Rhonan leaps down the last five steps, holding my shiny black patent shoe in his right hand.

'I think it's a bit too big for your dainty foot!' he says bending on his knee with the shoe in one hand.

I grab the shoe out of his hand and poke my foot into it. 'I'll grow into them.' I clip clop off, scrunching my toes to keep the shoes on. I'm wearing two pairs of socks, one white and the other pink. I put the pink ones on first and then the white ones, so that the white ones are seen. A bit of the pink ones is peeping out the top at the ankle as they're a bit longer than the white ones, but I'm sure nobody will notice; it's not as if they're black or brown or red or any dark colour like that, so I'm safe.

Rhonan's suddenly behind me. 'Would you look at that?'

I turn to face him, startled. 'What?'

'You've got pink socks on under the white ones. Why so?' Rhonan asks.

'To keep the shoes on, egit!'

Rhonan smiles, showing his black teeth. 'I'm not an egit, except in love!'

'Gerroff with you!' I march off.

'I hope there's no holes in them?' he calls after me.

I stop. 'Holes?'

He catches up with me. 'In your socks. Remember the story of the pigs?' I can feel my face turning pink.

'No?' I lie. I wince as I remember that story. There are

holes in the toes of my pink socks, and they keep strangling my two big toes.

'Your toes might fall off then!' he says, as though he's reading my thoughts.

…

I'm remembering the story my da tells, of someone who had a hole in their sock that was so big it strangled all the toes; one day the unfortunate man woke up and all the toes were on the ground and they had grown their own legs. That was how the story of the piggies going to market got started. The poor man had to walk on his hands after that, whilst all the toes trotted off to the market without him.

Rhonan speaks just as the story comes into my mind.

'Do you remember what happened to that poor man?'

My face gets hotter. 'No!' I trot off, leaving Rhonan behind.

'Are you trying to catch a bus?' The voice of Nell, our local fortune-teller and midwife, stops me.

She pinches my cheek. 'Ooh.' I squirm away from her, and nearly collide with Nora, my seven year old cousin, who leaps away and giggles.

'Is Maeve getting married to Paid Flynn then?' Nora asks.

'She is.'

'Will he be her daddy then?'

'No.'

'Why not?'

She's so thick, I'm thinking! 'Because she's still got her daddy. My daddy.'

'Oh!' She glances at me for a moment, and grins happily, displaying teeth as yellow as her frock. She runs off after a butterfly. She's tripping over her long frock, which has a few extra decorations stuck on the hem, bits of muck and sticks and the odd fly! She's got yellow feathers in her hair, mixed with daisies, which seem to be quite dead. She reminds me of a baby chicken after coming through a hedge, all fluffy and yellow and ruffled.

I can feel someone's presence behind me.

'Niamh?'

It's Rhonan again, always turning up like the bad penny. 'What?'

'You're wearing a new frock,' he says, grinning.

I stare at him. 'Am I now? So what about it then?'

He chews his fingernails, and then spits one out. 'You look like a statue of the virgin Mary.'

'Well I'm not a statue, I'm real, and you're…a dirty boy for biting your nails like that!'

He just smiles back. 'I am! And you're a real virgin.'

'Go away!' I run further down the slope, and then stop. I was really enjoying my dress until now.

I sit down on the grass, so Rhonan won't notice me, and think I'm a statue of the Virgin Mary.

A figure looms above me. I look up.

'What are you doing? Sitting down in your lovely dress. Get up!' My Aunty Maura pulls me up by the arms and starts brushing my skirt down. 'It's all creased now…'

'It was only for a minute!'

She admonishes me with a glare. 'Just stop where you are. Maeve is just around the corner.'

I can just see Maeve and Da jogging along the bumpy road. They've got McCarthy's billy goat pulling an open cart, as me da's piebald pony died a while ago. The women have decorated the cart with red, white, sky blue and gold fabric. The deep red and the sky blue fabric have been draped along the sides of the cart, held in scooped fashion by copper bows. The front of the cart is draped with bright white flowing fabric, held in place with painted red flowers. The seat is draped with shiny gold satin and strewn with flower petals. Da is steering Billygoat all the way to the makeshift chapel at the back of McCarthy's Barn, where a white canopy, decorated with colourful flowers, has been draped over the wide doorway.

The foreboding figure of the priest, Father Seamus O'Reilly can be seen standing stiffly in his vestments:

starched long white frock, white collar, and golden coloured scarf, as he waits with his arms folded. There's a wooden table next to him with a big book on it. There are two candles, which the altar boy has to keep lighting when the wind blows them out. There are special communion goblets for the Bride and Groom on the table. The white cloths cover the thin strings attached to them, secretly connected to Father O'Reilly's wrist.

'Come on Maeve,' someone shouts.

The crowd begin to chant, 'Get me to the Church on a goat. I'm coming in the royal float.'

The goat trots up towards the crowd, going faster and faster for some reason. Then I see he's heading for the bunch of carrots that Rhonan has in his hands. That stops him from eating the floral wreath hanging around his neck! The goat stops abruptly and the cart nearly lands on top of him, with Maeve and me da flying forward.

'Steady now,' my da shouts. He holds on to the reins and to Maeve and they fall backwards in their wooden seats. Daddy stands up and throws his legs over the side of the cart, then climbs down. He lifts Maeve over the side with a whoosh. Her white linen dress, embroidered on the hem, cuffs and neck with beautiful colours, flies in the air, revealing a blue silk petticoat. The men whistle and shout at this action. There are quite a few folk milling around Maeve and Da as many of our relatives have come here from the other side of Ireland, near Dublin, and others have come up from Cork.

'Go arak! Help your sister now.' Maura pushes me forward, forcing me to run down the slope. I nearly end up on top of Maeve, who's looking quite flustered after her bumpy ride.

'Yerra, what are you doing. Walk in front, and don't trip me up. Where in God's name is Nora? She's supposed to be here!'

'Nora!' I yell.

Like a wild horse, Nora comes galloping from somewhere,

holding onto her long dress, bunch of flowers, and a basket of daisy petals. Half the petals fly out as she leaps down the slope. She lands on her bottom.

Maeve yanks her up. 'Walk!' she shouts at Nora and me. We rush off towards the priest. Maeve then rushes after us at a brisk pace, with me da struggling to keep up with her.

'Whoa, not so fast!' I can hear me da saying as he puffs and pants barely holding on to Maeve.

We climb up the last bit of a slope. 'Stand over there,' Maeve directs Nora and me. Me da stands next to Maeve, breathing heavily.

'Who gives this woman to be wedded now?' the priest says, peering over his black-rimmed glasses. 'Sean?'

Maeve nudges me da.

'Right. Here she is then,' me da says, as Maeve steps forward and stands next to Paid, who's smile seems to be stuck in a long line on his face. He's wearing a brown suit that's too big for him, a white shirt and bright red tie. His hair is plastered to his head with hair cream.

'Here!' Maeve calls, throwing me her bunch of lavender and mayflowers, which I immediately sniff and then sneeze violently. The priest gives me a nasty stare and then blesses the couple by making the sign of the cross with his hands. He's speaking so fast we wonder what he's saying. Then, more slowly, he says, 'I now pronounce you husband and wife.' He stares at Paid with furled brows as he nods his head, mumbling gruffly, 'You may kiss the bride.'

Paid Flynn is grinning from ear to ear and licking his lips. His front teeth are black and he's reaching up, intending to plant his mouth on my beautiful stepsister's lovely sweet rosebud lips and I can't bear it. She's taller than him, by a good bit with those heels on. Someone gave her a lovely pair of white high-heeled shoes, which were a bit too tight, but like the ugly sister in Cinderella, she squeezed into them. To my way of thinking, she is Cinderella herself and Paid Flynn is an ugly prince. Maeve glows like a primus stove in the night and puckers her lips in expectation. I'm closing my eyes. Oh God, please don't let this happen to me! I am shaking like Nora's chicken feathers. It's like someone is walking on me grave. I'm next. I know it!

'The kiss of death,' I whisper to Nora, who giggles.

After that Father O'Reilly glares into the crowd and all is quite. He turns and heads for the table, praying. We kneel down now. I'm wondering if Aunty Maura will get mad at us for getting grass stains on our nice dresses? After a few more prayers he takes a golden goblet, with its string attached, and puts a round host right in their gob.

'What's that?' Nora asks, digging me in the ribs.

I whisper in reply, 'It's God!'

Then the priest holds the goblet and gives them a drink each, wiping the goblet after each one. It makes me feel thirsty.

'What are they drinking?' Nora whispers her question.

'God's blood.'

'Is he dead?'

'Yes,' I reply. 'They murdered him!'

'Murderers!' she shouts, jumping up and waving her flowers.

'Murderers!' I shout, waving my two bunches.

A searing pain rushes through my left ear. 'Will you two stop it!'

I can barely hear her words as I shake from the fright of Aunty Maura's slap. 'Yes Mam.'

I look at Nora who is holding her right ear. We don't say another word for a full five minutes. Finally the bride and groom sign the book and turn around to greet the crowd. Immediately the place is in an uproar. Things are flying through the air. As if by magic a glass and a cigarette materialise in every man's hand. 'Slainte,' rings out over the hills like a choir of angels, or more likely, a choir of devils and the choruses of 'Let's have a bit of craic!' resound through the surrounding countryside.

…

Someone is banging a bongo. Another is rattling tin spoons.

A pipe screeches through the laughter. People are jumping up and dancing. The lads have several fires going and a pot of Irish stew brewing away in one place and the smell of smoked bacon drifts from another. There are also a few chickens running around, one with its head off! There is also the tantalizing aroma of potato and leek soup wafting through the cold air. Some of the men are testing the meat by putting their forks into the boiling pot, taking out large pieces of cooked meat and devouring them. The women have brought plates of sandwiches, which are piled so high, they're toppling over onto the rough wooden tables that some of the men made. The children are lining up for lemonade, which is being poured by several women from jugs into glasses. The occasional sound of breaking glass is accompanied by curses. A bronze keg of poteen glistens from behind a tree surrounded by the men, who wait for its life giving water, uische beatha!

…

I'm sitting on a rock watching as the tempo rises and one by one the guests try to make egits of themselves. The drink is flowing, followed by inevitable dancing and ultimately by the frolicking… It always happens like this. A leg of chicken, wrapped in a piece of newspaper is warming my hands. A glass of porter sits precariously on the grass beside me. I wonder if the leg belonged to the chicken with no head? Nora waltzes past me just at that moment. She's still grinning brightly, now in the arms of our cousin Liam, who's only six, and can't dance at all. He's just kicking the ground and occasionally Nora lets out a yelp, and then she kicks him back. He lets out another yelp, and on they waltz. I can see Rhonan leaning on the shiny keg, his hand tightly grasping a glass. He's staring at me. He sways to his feet and moves forward, and then falls flat on his face. Two lads drag him back to the keg. All I can see now is the soles of his shoes, with two neat holes in them.

I look away, into the distance. The hills around here are so many shades of green and yellow, with low lying grey stone walls all around them, marking boundaries. Some of the hills look like a ton of rocks fell from above and landed here and then the grass grew over them. The sun is still visible in the sky, but I've got goosebumps all over my forearms and legs, and my teeth are occasionally chattering away, having their own conversation. Sure it's always freezing here on the west coast of Ireland. Da says it's because there are not enough trees around these parts. The few here are leaning over to one side, as if trying to hide from the west winds that come howling from the Atlantic Ocean. The wind blows past the trees and right onto the camp; that's where I live. It's not much of a place, just a bit of ground where we can put our vans. We sleep in the grass in summer, which begins on the first of June. Around six families are living here, and it's a close-knit community, especially when it comes to sharing the demon drink poteen!

As I turn around, I see Da looking at me right now under his bushy eyebrows. A dribble of some alcoholic brew is running down his chin, mingling with a few stuck-on lumps of blood, his own, which eventuated when he cut himself with a sharp razor. He doesn't shave very much these days, because his hands are shaky.

He says, 'It's time you were wedded too!'

Oh God, no, not that! He is staring at my growing breasts. My nipples are making two small bumps in my dress. They're sticking out because of the fierce cold wind. I hate this dress now. I quickly hold the newspaper-wrapped leg of chicken in front of my breasts, but it's too late! He's probably thinking of Rhonan, God help me! 'Yes Da!' I answer politely, meaning no!

'Yes indeed. There's a good girl now!' He stares at his empty glass. 'I need another drink. Slainte! The first today,' he says, holding his empty glass high and stumbling away, towards the keg.

...

Da's just shattered all my dreams of going to school and learning things that the swanky people learn - the people who live in lovely houses with biscuits and milk; and gardens and fences and gorgeous children. I want to travel and see what's in the big world out there. At nearly sixteen years of age my life may as well be over! I know he'll not stop now until he gets me wedded to Rhonan! I wish my mammy was here, she'd be on my side, but she died when I was about four. I don't know what happened. When I ask people they just stare into the distance and tell me to shush! I sometimes think I remember her, but I'm not sure about that. All I know is that her name was Niamh, the same as mine, which means 'Queen of the Land'. I had a brother, Rory, but he died a while before Mammy died. He was a tiny babby. Da ends up marrying my aunty Maura, as I told ye. After they were married, Aunty Maura told me that my job was begging. I felt very important, but I didn't like it very much once I found out what I had to do in my new begging job. She would put dirt on my face and run her hands through my hair, making my copper coloured curls all brown and sticky. She would put a ripped dress on me, which wasn't hard really, as most of my dresses were torn in a few places. She would give them another quick rip or two, and then send me to a house, to say 'Please Missus,' to the woman who answered. I remember my first job. It is as clear as day to me still: I just stood outside the door and bawled my eyes out. The woman of the house brought me inside and closed the door. That gave me a shiver of fear. I stopped in the dark hallway, staring at dark maroon wallpaper with gold squiggles. I eyed a stairs leading up to a dark looking landing. The stairs had dark brown carpet down the middle, with wooden bits each side. I stood there, shivering with the wonder of what was about to happen to me. That fearful thought only lasted a minute.

'It's too cold out there. Come on in here to the kitchen where the fire's burning,' the woman called out.

I followed her into a bright kitchen. There was a big window on one side, with a sink below. The table had a vivid tablecloth. There were wooden chairs around the table and a little glass vase with flowers. The fire was in a dark grey box, with a door on one side. 'Come over here near the oven,' she said, smiling at me.

I gasped for fear. I had heard that some people cooked children in those ovens, and I shivered, even though it was warm in the kitchen. Stiffly I moved towards the oven and thankfully she moved away. I relaxed and looked around and could see a small light coloured dresser with two doors, the drawers above them had shiny knobs, and above the drawers were shelves where lovely cups of various colours hung proudly. Behind them the matching plates stood boldly, ready to be of service to 'Missus'. There was a picture of the 'Sacred Heart of Jesus' over the table. It was a lovely kitchen altogether. Perfect! She went to her cupboard and brought out a bottle of milk and a glass. I soon decided that I liked this woman and every ounce of fear flew away as she handed me a glass of creamy milk and then put a big tin on the table. She lifted me onto a chair and I sat there, like a queen, with my legs dangling, eating off her beautiful table. She handed me the open tin. For a moment I thought she was giving me the lot, but then she said, 'Have a biscuit. Just one. I don't want to spoil your dinner!'

Spoil my dinner? I'd be lucky to get dinner at all most days! Just one? Oh God, what a choice. I trembled with excitement, wondering which biscuit to choose. I had never seen so many biscuits all lined up and ready to eat, in one place. My mouth watered as I tried to make up my mind. I finally decided on a chocolate coloured one with pink cream. I could just see the pink colour peeping at me.

'What do you say?' she said, staring at me.

I answered promptly, 'Please Missus.'

She smiled and said, 'That'll do.'

I remember how creamy the milk was, probably straight from the cow now that I think of it. I never tasted anything like that feast in my whole life before. There and then I made up my mind that one day I would have a house with creamy milk and stuck-together biscuits in it, and I would give them to girls like me. Well, that was nearly eleven years ago and I have seen inside some lovely houses since, but I have never had such a heavenly experience again. I sometimes wonder if it was just a dream, but when I remember what happened after that, I know it was real!

Aunty Maura was hopping mad with me when I came out the door. She scowled and said, 'There's white whiskers on your face. You've had something to drink'.

Then she slapped me on the face.

'Next time bring the milk to me. I'll decide who needs it.'

My lips trembled as I replied, 'Yes Mam.'

Since then I always ask to take the food, or whatever I get, back for my younger half-sister, Pauline, who died from pneumonia about six years ago, when she was eight, or my half-brother, who is called Kam a K'ena, which is 'Son of the house'. That's Diarmud, who was just a wee baby then. He's twelve now. Maeve is older than me, by a few years. Maeve and Diarmud had to go to school when they were seven, but I had a good job, so I couldn't go very often.

One time a man answered the door and I said, 'Please Missus'. I thought that was the right thing to say. He just stared at me and handed me two bob from his fob pocket and said, 'Off with ye now, I'm skint!'

Aunty Maura heard the whole thing. She was hiding behind a bush.

'What in God's name did you say?' she screamed as I came out the front gate, pulling her hair out with madness.

I just stared at her, wondering what I had done to make her so wild.

She took me by the ear and dragged me away from the house. 'If it's a man, say 'Please Sir'. Say it!'

'Ppl…' I began to cry.

'Say it, or I'll kill you!

I just blubbered.

'Get home,' she yelled, as she opened my tight fist and took the two bob from my hand.

I ran home, feeling very confused.

I remember another day when a kindly, tall woman with curly brown hair gave me a book with three pigs on the front cover and a big dog with fangs for teeth. I did a very bad thing, I didn't tell Aunty Maura about it. I told myself that if I couldn't eat it I didn't have to tell her about it. I hid it in my knickers. I used to take it out and look at the pictures and pretend to read the words. One day Aunty Maura saw me reading it.

'Where did you get that?'

I was dumb struck! I couldn't tell her. All my words were stuck inside my mouth.

'You probably stole it. Give it here!'

She snatched it from me and gave it to Maeve, who was sick with the measles. I never got it back, even when I had the measles two weeks later. I still miss that book.

Aunty Maura says I'm a 'strong willed little brat'.

...

I'm sitting here, thinking about my childhood days, hugging my knees to keep myself warm and trying to keep my breasts covered. Maybe that kind woman lives in a house around here? I could work for her. Maybe then I can meet a nice man who has a job in a factory perhaps, who would marry me and take care of me, when I'm a good bit older that is. Anyone but Rhonan!

I watch a lovely yellow butterfly flitting away until it's a small dot in the distance. I wish I were a butterfly, and then I could fly away to wherever I wanted. I see Rhonan out of the corner of my eye. He's falling over again! Down he goes, now with a glass of porter in his hand. He lies there with not a drop missing. He's getting up. He's coming to get me! My heart is starting to belt and bump so rapidly I wonder if it will fall out of my mouth soon. I'm chewing my nails until I'm eating my fingertips. From the corner of my eye I can see Aunty Maura leaping and dancing with Paid, her new son in law. Before I can think about anything else,

I'm clutching my newspaper with the leg of chicken and making a run for it.

...

The shadow is running ahead of me and the hills are calling me towards them. I'm leaping and running as fast as I can, feeling like a butterfly as I flit through the hills, until I can't hear the noise of the drumming, singing and intoxicated laughter. When I look back all I see are hills and a bit of smoke in the distance. Nobody is on me tail! My chest feels tight as though it's longing for air. I breathe deeply of the air of freedom. I can hear my heart thumping in my ears. I'm sitting down beside the stream to have a bit of a rest, and to think about crossing over.

Chapter two

The water is a good bit higher than it usually is, because of all the rain we had lately. I can barely see the slippery rocks I sometimes use to cross over when I want to get to the mushrooms growing on the other side. The water is making a gurgling, rushing sound, as if it's in a big hurry to get on down the track, over the rocks, and into the vast sea. Me da's words, *It's time you were wedded* are echoed in the rushing water. Rhonan's face crashes into my mind, 'You can't swim,' he says. I don't need to swim to cross the stream. I'll jump as far as I can. Before I can think of anything else, in one leap I'm in the middle of the stream. I'm steadying myself trying to keep standing up. The waters are roaring past my ankles, sloshing against my legs, saying, 'go on, go on', and nearly knocking me over with the force. The wind is howling by me. One more leap and I'll be on the other side. I leap. Oh God, the rocks are slippery. I'm being hurled forward and I can feel the water pouring over me. I wave my arms about in an effort to swim. I see a branch dangling near me. I try to grasp it with my fingers. I hold on to it for a second, and then it breaks away, and I'm flying backwards through the icy cold water.

Something's smacked against my head and now my head feels as if it's detached from my body. Everything's going black. Pain is shooting through my temple like millions of arrows. My eyes burst open and my feet touch the bottom of the river simultaneously. Rhonan's words come flooding into my mind, *'Tur an skai'*. Little minnow scurry over my face. I can hear myself screaming inside my head. My whole body is filling with water. I'm struggling to breathe. I know I'm calling 'Rhonan, help!' but my voice seems to be right inside my head. My neck feels like its being squeezed, as though I'm being strangled. My legs find something and I feel steadier. My head is immediately above the water. I take a deep gulp of air, but my feet are slipping and I slither off the rock. I'm back in the deep water. I'm under the water now. Different colours flash by me, black, purple and yellow. I can see my mother. I'm calling her, 'Mammy'. She's so beautiful, just like I imagined. Her long red hair swirls through the water. Her ruby red lips smile at me, exposing white teeth. She's holding her long graceful hand out towards me but I can't reach her. She vaporises before my eyes. I see a city, a bright golden city, in the distance. I move forward into its light. A dark shadow confronts me, blocking my path. I stare upwards into the face of the bogeyman with a giant shillelagh. His head is merely bones with eyes that are black holes. He throws his head back and laughs. I scream. I see the shillelagh towering above me. It's hitting me on the head, crushing me.

I look up and there's a big black hole above me! Now I'm inside the black hole, which feels like a slippery slide. I've no control over where I'm going any more. Now the whole place is black, like an ash pit where the fire has been and gone. Fear twists me into a tight ball, like knotted wool. It's grasping my arm and dragging me down, down so deep through another black tunnel with the sound of bats in my ears. Now my arm feels like it's stretching. I try to fight but I can't. I long for sleep, deep sleep.

…

My lips are pulled apart. My eyes open. I see a face, the face of some stranger. My eyelids are as heavy as copper. A river gushes out of my mouth. Stars sparkle all around my head, pretty blinking stars. I'm coughing and spluttering. My eyelids are prized open. Now a face comes towards mine and my eyes close. I can feel lips firmly on my mouth. I suck in oxygen.

A voice sounds in my ears, 'Hello there, are you all right then?'

It seems so far away. Balls of bright colour come towards me as I open my eyes. Three pairs of eyes are staring down at me. I gasp! It's the Trinity? I can't face God. 'Oh God,' I hear myself speaking inside my head.

'Hey there, don't go back to sleep now. Come on, come on now, wakey wakey.'

My head and shoulders are being raised onto clouds. Heaven? I force my eyes open again. This time I see just one face in front of me. 'Peter?' My voice sounds squeaky, like a small child's voice. It doesn't say the words correctly.

'Niall's the name. What's yours?'

'My…n…ame?' The words seem like little balls rolling out of my mouth.

'Try to drink this then.'

Niall gently helps me sit up. I sip a big mug of warm liquid. It leaves a bittersweet taste in my mouth. My stomach wants to throw it back up. I'm trying not to vomit! A basin is stuck in front of my mouth. I'm retching. My mouth is being wiped. My head is lying on a firm shoulder and there's an arm around me. I shiver with the cold running through me. A pain hurries through my head like a sharp needle.

I hear a voice saying, 'I found you in the stream; you were nearly drowned. You're very lucky you know. That bush saved your life. The hem of your frock was caught on it. I don't usually go by that way, but thank God I did this day. You'll be all right now.'

I'm sobbing hysterically, but I don't know why.

'There, there, don't cry now. You're safe here.' The person called Niall holds me close to him. I feel comforted.

'Is the girleen back with us then?' The voice emerges softly from the doorway of the room.

'She is, Missus Connor, and I think she'll be fine,' Niall replies.

'Tom is gone to get the doctor. I expect they'll be a little while yet. Has she had a drink of tea?' She scurries towards the fireplace.

'She has,' Niall says back to her.

'I'll put a bit more turf on the fire.' She turns around and looks at Niall. 'You had better get that soiled shirt off. Put it in the bucket on the verandah.'

'I'm sorry about that, Missus Connor. I didn't mean to get blood on the lovely shirt you gave me.'

'Yerra, don't worry about it. We'll get it looking great again with a bit of bleach. Thank God it was the white one! I'm just happy that the girleen didn't lose much more blood, or she might not be with us now. Can you give this fire a poke Niall? I'll go and get a bit of bread to toast for the girleen. What's her name?'

'I don't know. Do you know what your name is, girl?'

I'd love to yell out my name but it won't come. I can't think what it is! My head feels like a big ball of wool. I start to cry again.

'It doesn't matter,' he assures me. 'She doesn't know, Missus Connor.'

'She's a gift from God,' Missus Connor whispers, smiling down at me. 'I know it! God's gift to me! God knows what I've been praying for these last twenty years or more!'

I stare at her. She's not Mammy!

'It'll come to you. You had a big bang on the head.' Niall's eyes stare softly at me.

'We've bandaged your head. Can you feel it?'

He's holding my hand to my head. I feel a bandage wrapped around it.

'Good. She's got beautiful eyes Missus Connor, all those lovely colours sparkling like diamonds,' Niall tells the woman. 'She knows we're looking after her.'

'We are. We'll knit you back together again.' Her face draws close to mine. Her pale watery eyes crinkle with her smile. She rises up. 'We'll call her *Kathleen* for now. Kathleen Connor, that's your name.' Her face brightens as it comes close to mine again.

I can feel her love for me. *Kathleen Connor.* I must be smiling.

'You like that name. I can tell. Sure you'll be fine Kathleen.' She's squeezing my cold hand in her warm rough grasp.

'I'll give the fire a poke Missus Connor…'

My eyes close. The next thing I know I hear a different voice. I open my eyes try to orientate myself to the situation. It's a deep, masculine voice.

'She's suffering from temporal amnesia. The most important thing is, when she wakes up, is that she converses with you. Try to communicate with her. Different things trigger the memory, so ask her what she remembers from before her…accident. If the amnesia is retrograde she may not have remote memory. Do you understand what I mean?'

'We understand,' Missus Connor replies, staring into his eyes.

'The only danger is that she may fall into a coma. If she does, give me a call. We'll have to put her in the hospital.'

Missus Connor stares at the doctor as she asks curtly, 'So what can they do for her up there?'

The doctor takes a breath, coughs and stares for a moment. 'They can do a lot! The stitches…'

'Sure I can do that myself…' Missus Connor offers. 'I used to work with the Red Cross in my younger days.'

'Is that so?'

''Tis!'

'Right! Whatever you think is best for the child Missus Connor!'

'That's what I think is best. Here!' They walk a few paces towards the door, and then stop. 'Doctor, if she wakes, we're to try and help her to remember! If she *is* in a coma… how will we know 'tis a coma?'

'I thought you said you nursed people?' The doctor confronts Missus Connor now, whose face remains expressionless.

'I did indeed, but they were always awake,' she answers smartly.

The doctor gives a gentlemanly cough at this. 'It's hard to tell, but basically she'll be in a very deep sleep. You won't be able to wake her up.'

'Right! So, if we can't wake her up we can't get to talk to her.'

'No, because she'll be in a coma, as I explained.'

'So all we can do is pray that she wakes up?'

'Well, yes…that's correct! We do have a visiting neurological surgeon at the hospital one day…each month'

'Which day is that?' Missus Connor steps to the 'under the stairs' wall where there's a huge calendar.

'Let me see.' He rubs his chin. 'The last Wednesday of the month, I believe.'

'And today is the last Thursday…'

'That's right.' The doctor looks a bit frustrated. He coughs again. 'We just missed that golden opportunity. But there's always next month.' He seems satisfied with his remark, for he looks up and smiles. 'If there are any complications, Tom, come and get me.' He looks at Tom who's standing behind his wife.

Mister Connor nods his head.

'We most certainly will,' Missus Connor declares as she leads the Doctor into the hallway, and passes him his hat and umbrella.

'I'll come around tomorrow evening and see how she is. The bleeding has stopped, so that's the main thing. Her colour is good.'

'Sure she's a real beauty with those bronze curls and those eyes, just like…' Missus Connor suddenly seems lost for words.

'Like who?' the doctor asks.

'Just like…my sister Monica…'

His eyes narrow, 'I'm sure she is…But I didn't mean her colouring; I meant her colour!'

'I don't see any difference!' Missus Connor replies, her brows crinkling together.

'Never mind.' Doctor Cassidy steps outside, then steps back inside again. 'I hope you'll excuse my ignorance, but where has that lovely daughter of yours been stopping? I haven't seen her around these parts before. In fact, I didn't realize you had a daughter at all!'

I can see Missus Connor's face puckering up and the frown appearing on her forehead. Mister Connor shifts back from the doctor and pushes his hands so deep into the pockets of his trousers I think they might come out at his feet. He coughs and goes a bright red. Missus Connor stares straight into the doctor's face.

'Oh, I nearly forgot! Tom, go and bring that gift we had put aside for the good doctor,' Missus Connor says, giving Tom a shove.

'The gift?'

'You know! Yerra go on, in the sugar bag!'

'The sugar bag? Oh yes, exactly!' he says, marching off down the hallway.

'Now doctor I'll get back to your question about our lovely little girl. You see Kathleen was such a special girl, and our only child, so we gave her the best education we could afford, at a very expensive boarding school near Dublin. She sometimes stays with my sister Monica in Bray. She loves her little cousins; the two of them are nearly her age, Dymphna and Doreen. Remember I told you she was the spitting image of my sister Monica…?'

'Yes, I remember….You've not called me on her account before though!' he states softly.

'We have had no need to call you, thank God; that's why you haven't seen her…' I can just see her side profile, and she is smiling very sweetly.

'Of course! She must be eating an apple a day?' He laughs for a moment. 'Just one more question, if I may?'

'Well, like yourself, I was going to do the devil and all today…but certainly you may! Go ahead! Ask anything at all, at all.' Missus Connor's face is set firm as she outstares the doctor.

'How did she obtain the injury?'

Just at that moment Tom comes running in, holding a big brown paper bag. He hands it to the doctor.

'Really, there was no need…' the doctor protests as he takes the gift. He appears to know what is in the bag without looking inside.

'Yerra! It's nothing. You've done us a great service. It's a small thanks. And there's plenty more where that came from!' Missus Connor says happily, giving the doctor such a nudge in the ribs that he almost loses his balance. There is a silent pause after that. Missus Connor is urging the doctor towards the front door. The doctor turns towards the door then back again.

'So, how did she injure herself?'

Missus Connor takes a deep breath. 'I thought you already asked that question?'

'I did, but we were…interrupted,' the doctor replies, holding his hat to his heart.

Missus Connor takes a deep breath, then replies, 'She was horse riding; you know what young people are like, fearless! They rush in to places where angels fear to tread.'

'Horse riding?' Tom Connor exclaims.

Missus Connor stares at him. 'Kathleen's fall!'

He moves back a pace. 'Oh…right!' Mister Connor replies as though he's forgotten what happened already. He folds his arms and goes into deep thought, then suddenly speaks. 'She was racing over the hills and jumping walls, and I think she overdid it somehow, and fell off…and there… there you…you…have …have it!' His speech is suddenly stuttered and his face is coloured bright red. He pauses to catch his breath.

'She hasn't got a psychotic problem at all?'

Mister Connor stares at the doctor with his mouth open.

Missus Connor butts in at this point. 'I wouldn't be surprised at what's going on in that pretty head of hers. She's psychotic all right.'

'Anything specific bothering her that you know of, such as problems at school?'

Missus Connor interjects with an answer. 'Nothing that won't work itself right with time! It's her age. She's a bit wild at the moment, with all those hormones working day and night! You know, like the birds and the bees? Can you remember when you were that young and carefree, or careless as the case may be? Wild oats being sown and all that?' The doctor quickly steps away as Missus Connor raises her elbow for a big nudge again.

Mister Connor is just standing with his mouth open. The doctor steps a few paces away from the Connors. 'Well…you might be right there!' Doctor Cassidy reflects for a moment. He is smiling. 'Sure, she'll probably grow out of that wild stage, that's what'll happen.'

'I'm sure you've hit the nail on the head Doctor Cassidy, as always,' Missus Connor says most agreeably.

'I'll bid ye good evening then.' He tips his hat. 'Call me if there's any further repercussions before tomorrow evening.' Doctor Cassidy steps through the front door once more and heads off into the wind, the door following on his heels.

'That was close,' Missus Connor says softly, leaning on the closed door.

'You made me feel like an egit!' Mister Connor says curtly.

'Well, I thought you did right well. That was a great idea about Kathleen jumping over walls!'

'Lies, all lies. Why did you have to bring your sister Monica into this? You haven't spoken to her for years.'

'Well, I'm not telling her about Kathleen until I'm good

and ready. I don't want her going to the garda, nosey parker that she is.'

'That's a good subject Kathleen. Tell me what's going to happen if someone comes looking for a missing girleen? What are we going to do if the garda come here?' His voice is low and harsh.

'We'll cross our bridges when we come to them.'

'I hope you know what you're doing woman! And what about you telling the good doctor that there's plenty more from where that's come from?' he says, mimicking Missus Connor. 'That was my last drop!'

'Don't be like that now Tom. There, there now!' she says comfortingly, kissing his cheek. 'You can go and see your man about some more. You were always able to do that until this minute.'

'But woman, this is serious business. We don't know who the girleen is. What if she's escaped from some mad house? What if she's psy... whatever he said.'

'Psychotic! Not at all! You're a worrywart man. Can't you see she's been sent as a gift because we can't have our own children? Are we going to fly in the face of God?'

'You're raving mad, woman,' Mister Connor says to this remark.

'I'm not mad. I've come to my senses, more like it!'

'You don't make any sense to me Woman,' he shouts at her.

'Keep your drawers on. I don't give a tinkers' curse what you say. She's mine, and that's that!' She rises to her full height and places her hands on her hips.

'Don't vex me Woman,' he snarls.

Missus Connor ignores his snarl. 'I won't vex you at all if you just co-operate.' She stares at him and smiles sweetly. 'I'm off to make a cup of tea, would you like one?' she says, changing the topic.

'And what are we supposed to do with a sick girleen? I didn't understand one word the doctor said.'

'Don't worry about that. I understand, perfectly.' Her

chin lifts as she continues, 'Remember I was in the Red Cross.'

'As a cleaner.'

'There's nothing wrong with being a cleaner. I'm proud of the job I did for them. That place was always spick and span! I learned a lot of education there.'

'All right! I'm sorry Kathleen; I know you did a grand job there! I'm totally bamboozled by all this. I don't know why you didn't want her to go to the hospital. That's where she should be.'

'You go to the hospital to die!'

'You're a stubborn woman!' Mister Connor marches through the hallway into the kitchen and out the back door. I can hear his footsteps as he stomps away.

It's my fault they're having all this trouble. Missus Connor seems to really care about me. I wish she were my real mother! I know my mother was someone with red hair! I remember that! My memory must be coming back. Missus Connor has curly brown hair, so it can't be her. She's a lovely woman. I know she loves me. Maybe she's my God Mother! I heard her say something about God! That's grand. I love being with my Godparents. Kathleen Connor, that's who I am now, and I don't want to know who I was before! Oh, God, I'm praying, don't let me come between Mister and Missus Connor. I like the warm fireplace and the smell of toasted bread.

…

My head is throbbing. I'm turning over on my pillow and facing the fire. From my sitting room sofa bed I'm staring into the flickering flames. I'm watching the funny flame shapes form and leap up, changing colour from red to orange then yellow. Then they turn into a plume of smoke…. twirling upwards into the black chimney cavity. I must have fallen asleep after that, because the next thing I know, it's morning. Missus Connor is holding a nice hot cup of tea under my nose.

'My, you look better already, Kathleen. The fire's dead! I'll just give this peat a bit of a poke. It'll warm the cockles of your heart in no time.'

'Thank you…Missus.'

'Call me 'Mam! Niall,' she says, turning to Niall who is suddenly nearby. 'She sounds like a little child. My own baby that I've prayed for.' She sniffs and wipes her eyes. 'The smoke's in me eyes. Can you have a little chat with her? I'll go and feed the chickens…you can check Finn McCool later.'

'I gave him his nose bag already Missus Connor. And I'd love to talk to…Kathleen. What will I say to her?'

'Ask her what she remembers from before her fall, but,' she pauses, 'we'll keep it to ourselves for now!'

'Right.'

…

Niall spends an hour every morning and afternoon with me from then. He's been asking what I remember. I find it very tiring, and can't seem to remember hardly anything from before my accident. My speech is returning quickly though. The doctor says I am making good progress. I want to cheer Niall up by remembering something important. I squeeze my mind with all my might, but nothing comes to mind, except Missus Connor poking the peat.

After two weeks of intensive care, the doctor says I'm now well enough to visit him if I need to, at Missus Connor's discretion. Around this time, Niall sits down next to me as usual. 'So, how are you feeling today, Kathleen?' I open my eyes. 'I think I'm getting… better,' I lie.

'You're looking grand. I think you could do a jig for me!'

'Jig?'

'That's a dance! You're a dancer! Remember I told you that you had one lovely hornpipe shoe on when I found you?'

I stare at Niall. 'Dance.' Somehow that word seemed to tumble through my mind like a huge drum. Niall takes my hands in his. I can feel his warmth. It's like an electric charge, giving me strength. I'm closing my eyes. 'Niall…I remember playing…with other children in a…circle. We are dancing. Someone is saying, 'let's… dance…all the day.'' I say slowly, and then open my eyes.

Niall's face is bright with expectation.

'That's great. Can you see the people you're dancing with?'

I'm closing my eyes. 'There's a girl with long...light brown hair... tied back. There's another girl with short dark hair. She's...smaller.' I open my eyes. 'They're gone.'

'It's coming back. You're doing great. Are you tired now?'

Niall seems to sense my frailty so well. 'I am...a bit.'

'Well, I'll tell you a story. It's about three pigs...'

'Three pigs! I remember three pigs.'

'Oh God, but you're a marvel. Your memory is working again!'

I giggle. I'm really enjoying Niall's story telling. He sometimes tells me jokes that I don't understand, but he makes me laugh anyway.

Seeing those children dancing in a circle has started something happening in my mind.

The following day I am really feeling much better, so I tell Niall that. I don't have to lie any more.

My memory is coming back.

'You know, Kathleen,' he whispers, 'it won't be long before you'll know exactly who you are.'

Maybe I was beginning to do just that. 'Niall, I can re-member...being in a white dress...and a veil,' I tell him excitedly.

'Oh God, you're married! No, you can't be. You didn't have a wedding ring on when I found you!'

'There are lots of other girls...in...white. They all have... veils on their heads,' I whisper.

'I know,' he says excitedly. 'Your first communion! All the girls wear veils and white dresses. You're probably a Catholic.'

'A Catholic. Is that bad?'

'No. Unless I was a Protestant!'

'What's a...Protestant?'

'It's just a name for a religion. Never mind that now. Can you remember a big building? A church?'

'I'm not sure.'

'What about someone saying your name?'

'No. But I remember calling someone…May…no… *Maeve*. She's my age, or maybe a bit older. She could be my friend, or my sister?'

'What about her last name?'

I shake my head.

I can't imagine any other place on earth where I want to be. Niall is one of the reasons why I'm happy here! He is so handsome he makes my heart flip over every time I catch a glimpse of him. He's a lot taller than me, with dark wavy hair, with a strand falling forward like a small boy. His deep-set brown eyes pierce into my soul and make me feel weak at the knees. It's an exciting feeling and I'm enjoying it as much as I can. He is the farmhand around here. He has come from Dublin, and he tells me he lived in Kildare as well, so he calls himself a bit of a wanderer.

I often re-live the first time I saw him when he was kissing my lips and giving me his breath. It makes me feel tingly all over to think about that. I wish I'd taken more advantage of the opportunity and said something nice to him. It makes me blush like a beetroot when I think of him kissing me, and I'm not exactly sure why! I notice he's always looking at me. Now that I'm recovering, and the bandage is off my head, I've been allowed to join the family for meals. When we're at the dinner table Niall keeps staring at me, then looking down and burying his face in his dinner; I think I saw him looking like a beetroot too, a few times!

One evening about six weeks after I've been living here, I'm busy with a stiff brush in my hands, shining up Finn Mc Cool's coat until it glistens. He's a beautiful chestnut coloured horse with a white stripe down his slender face. I was a bit afraid of him at first but Niall makes me feel completely at ease with the Connor's favourite horse. I think I'm just happy to be near Niall. As I'm stepping back to admire my work, I trip over Niall's big feet. I'm falling over. He's catching me by the elbows and somehow I'm falling into his arms. His arms are around me. His hand holds my left breast for a moment. My heart pounds in response. He quickly moves his hand away and holds me by the shoulders.

'Steady there. Are you all right?'

'I'm fine,' I'm saying, weakly. I feel my face turning into a beetroot so I'm spinning away to pick up the stiff brush. I'm grabbing it and then dashing off to the house. I'm rushing up the stairs, holding the stiff brush tightly. I don't even realize I'm holding it until I sit down on my bed and gasp for air. 'What's happening to me?'

I push the brush under the bed with my foot, and then I hear Missus Connor calling, 'Kathleen, dinner's ready. Wash your hands and come on down before it's cold.'

I'm coming slowly down the stairs and now I'm standing in the doorway to the kitchen.

'What's up with you Kathleen? You look like you've been struck by lightening.'

'I'm not feeling very hungry. Do you mind if I just go to my room and rest?'

'Niall, help her to her room. I don't want her falling down the stairs.'

'No…it's fine. I can go by myself. I just need a rest.'

'All right! Go and have a lie down, Kathleen! I'll take you up a bit of tea later. Would you like that Alanna?'

I smile weakly. 'I would.'

'Right. I'll do that then. Off with you now and rest your weary head.'

Missus Connor's best cup with golden brown tea sits on the little table in my room. Thinly sliced butter toast sits up in triangles on her best fine porcelain plate. I can't bring myself to drink or eat. My hand is resting on my left breast. All night long I feel the imprint of his hand like I've been branded with a hot iron. 'Niall!' I whisper.

That fateful night brings with it a sword that cuts my soul into two people. One is a little girl playing with a happy boy, whose face looks like Niall's. The other is a tormented woman who screams as monsters come to destroy her with giant shillelaghs and pitchforks. Every night now I'm waking up with horrific nightmares. Faces from my past life are beginning to materialise. They are the faces of killer monsters that seem determined to destroy me. I don't know who they are, and I don't want to know.

I'm trying to forget the nightmares and think about Niall as much as I can. I wouldn't even dare tell anyone what is happening to me at night. The Connors might really think I'm 'psychotic' and lock me up if they knew how I'm now spending many hours at night staring out the window into the dark night, with its weird shadows and shapes. My mind seems like the shadowy dark night, with its terrifying shapes banging on the door of my memory, trying to get back into me. I can shut the window and draw the curtains on the dark shapes of the night, but not on the dark shapes in my dreams. The windows of my mind are getting harder to close. The monstrous shapes and faces are beating my doors and windows down. I know that. I'm feeling weaker as they return every night, slithering through little cracks in the windows of my nightmares, plastering themselves to my mind like wallpaper to a wall.

…

One evening at the beginning of August, about two weeks after my nightmares began, I'm sitting on a chair gathering the last of the heat of the sun. My eyes are half closed as I'm enjoying the laziness of the feeling. The soft summer sun is warm and friendly. I'm thinking of Niall and me playing games together, like two children.

'Lovely evening.'

Niall's voice startles me.

'Sorry, I didn't mean to frighten you.'

'That's all right. I'm fine. I was cat napping. It's such a beautiful evening.'

' 'Tis. Beautiful,' he says. I know he's staring at me as he says the words.

I know I'm blushing like a red rose now.

'Kathleen,' he says, after a pause, bending on his knee and taking my hands in his.

'What is it?' I sit bolt upright. My hand feels like a wet chicken after being plucked.

'I...I wanted to tell you something.' He stops.

'Tell me,' I whisper. I think I've got instant laryngitis. I can hardly speak. His look takes my breath away. I'm trying to think what else to say.

He's as shy as me. He's got his mouth open. I know I want to hear what he's wanting to say, even though I don't have any idea what that is! I wish I could squeeze the words out of him. Beautiful words. I look into his eyes. I'm begging with my eyes. He's looking away. He's weakening. His knee is shaking like there's an earthquake.

'I...think the dinner is ready. We have to go...' He's getting off his wobbly knee and releasing my hand.

'Niall!' I'm leaping off the chair and holding my hand out to him, and he's taking it again. I'm staring at him. I'm lowering my eyelids. I can't let this opportunity go. I'm holding his hand tightly. Maybe if he holds me the nightmares will go away. He's the key to my happiness, I know that!

'Sure is that all you want to say to me now?' My words feel like creamy butter, smooth and rich. I'm surprised at myself. May God forgive me!

'No.... Look Katheen, you're too good for me. I know that. I'm just a farmhand with very little to offer. You're probably from a very rich family. You know what I think?'

'No,' I reply, my eyes fixated on his.

'I think you were locked in a tower, like Rapunzzel, and you got out, so they tried to drown you, and now you're here, with us! I don't want them to come and take you away, because...'

He suddenly stops.

'Niall, please don't stop! I'll be what you want me to be!' We're standing close together now. I want him to fill my mind, night and day. I can feel the heat from his body radiating to me. 'You're the most...kindest man I ever met, if I ever knew another man, but I can't remember... I can only remember... monsters!' There, I've said it. I stare into his face.

'Kathleen. You've been through so much. But I'm here for you now!'

Somehow he's holding me in his arms and I'm weeping into his clean shirt.

'You saved my life.' Liquid from my nose is mingling with my tears onto his shirt. 'Sorry!' I whisper.

He doesn't even notice.

'Oh, Kathleen, I can't stop thinking of you, night and day. I love you to distraction. I want to marry you. Please marry me. Everything I have is yours. Please say yes.'

His eyes stare down into mine. The desire to kiss his soft round lips is coming upon me. I can barely say the next small word. 'Yes?' I whisper.

'Is that yes with a question, or just plain yes!'

'Yes, plain yes! A thousand times! Yes, I'll marry you.'

'Oh Kathleen, I adore you. I'll give you…the whole world.'

He's grasping me in his strong arms and lifting me into his strong chest. His lips are bending to mine and we are pressed together. I cannot remember having felt such a belonging kiss before. I want our kisses to last forever…I feel like a little bird being whisked away from the monsters by its mother and flying through the sky. His cheeks are wet, his shirt is wet, my face is wet, but I feel like I'm being washed of my fears. They're all being washed away with our love.

…

That night, as I'm climbing softly to my room upstairs, I overhear Mister and Missus Connor, 'So, now they want to get married, what are we going to do?' Mister Connor poses this question to Missus Connor, who is sitting, knitting away at a huge green jumper for Mister Connor.

'Let them get married. They're in love.'

'In love,' Mister Connor sneers.

Missus Connor pauses and stares at her husband. 'They love each other.'

'But she's only a girleen.'

'She's at least seventeen or eighteen years old. I was married at seventeen, if you can remember back that far.'

'You were so young! I was a young strapping lad myself then. God be with those days.' He fills his pipe and stares into the fireplace at the smouldering embers. 'I still think of her the day Niall found her. She was wearing children's socks, like a little girleen.'

'But, you may or may not have noticed, the girleen has become a young woman since she arrived here.'

'You know, Kate, you're a very observant woman. You're right. She is looking more….' He's scratching his balding temple trying to locate the right word here.

'Womanly?' Missus Connor finishes his thoughts.

'That's the word. Yes, womanly.'

'Right! She should be married if she's a woman. The time is right.'

I'm shocked to think they've noticed such personal changes in me. But Missus Connor is right. Since I arrived my breasts have become rounder. In fact I'm rounder all over. I have become a real woman in just a few months! I thought it was just the good cooking Missus Connor does. I'm blushing when I think of my big breasts. Missus Connor kindly left two brassieres on my bed a few weeks ago, which I'm wearing all the time. Now my breasts don't bounce when I run.

'So, are you ready to give her away in marriage?'

He bangs his pipe on the fire grate before he replies. 'I hardly know her. She doesn't even know who she is. How can I do that?'

'You're her father. It's your job.'

'Her kidnapper…we'll could both end up in gaol for this.'

Missus Connor stares at him. 'Don't say such a thing! Think of yourself as her Stepfather. To the outside world you're her real father. Put that in your pipe and smoke it!'

'All right! Have it your way! But if the priest asks for her birth certificate, what are we going to do?'

She smiles with her eyes, above her knitting. 'Don't worry

your head about a thing. I'll fix it! Everything will be all right, you'll see.' She pauses from her knitting and stares at Mister Connor until she catches his eye. 'Tom, all you have to do is walk down the aisle with herself on your arm, and when the priest asks who gives her to Niall, you say, 'I do'.'

'I do?'

'Yes, 'I do'.'

'Is that all?'

'No.'

'What else?'

'Get in the spirits for the wedding. You know what I mean?'

'I do.'

'Right. Do you want a cup of tea?'

'I do. No, I mean… I don't want a cup of tea. I want a bit of peace. I want sanity in this house.'

'Are you sure you don't want a cup of tea. You'll feel better then. It's no bother…' Missus Connor acts as if a cup of tea will bring peace and sanity to the house, even to the whole world if necessary. She's rolling the wool into a big ball, and then plunging the knitting needles right through the centre of the wound ball. 'Right! I'll go and make us a cup of tea anyway.'

Chapter three

I'm quietly racing up to my bedroom, two stairs at a time, and plonking myself on the side of the bed. I'm in love! I know it now! It's a wonderful feeling! I know Mister Connor will be a grand father for me on my wedding day. Missus Connor will see to that! I'm gazing around my room. It's a lovely room with beige wallpaper with tiny pink roses splashed all over it, a little wooden dresser with a mirror, and a tall wardrobe with a long mirror inside. That's also where I hang all the nice clothes the Connors have given me. This room has been my haven of refuge and my battleground for the past two months. My eye is wandering to the window on one side with soft pink curtains. They blow in the breeze when the window is open. Like it is now! I see Niall walking across the yard, his shadow long and firm in the evening light. My heart is leaping. I can't stop staring at his attractive stature as he strides along. He looks happy, like me! I'm staring until he disappears through the barn and into his own room at the back. That is the picture I want to keep in my mind forever, and not those awful monsters that are coming to get me at night!

I'm having a quick wash with my little jug of water and

washbowl, which sits on a small table in the corner of the room. All the time I'm thinking of Niall. He fills my whole mind. Missus Connor says I should brush my hair a hundred times to get the hair growing faster and make it shine. I pull my flannelette nightie over my head, drag the soft brush through my hair, counting quickly, 'One, twenty, forty, fifty, ninety, one hundred? They're all the numbers I seem to be able to remember, so that's how I do it! 'Ouch!' I've hit the sore bit. I'm rubbing the spot with my fingers. A pain is shooting through my head for a moment.

I'm climbing slowly into my little bed. I'm pulling the crisp white sheets over me, and then the warm fluffy blanket. 'Thank you God,' I'm mumbling as the pain dies down. I'm drifting into sleep, the first pleasant sleep I've had for ages.

…

I wake up feeling like a new person; all bright and happy like the sparkling sun coming out from behind a black cloud.

Missus Connor goes into action straight away. She has Tom Connor running off to find an old friend who is a priest. Two weeks later, a woman called Missus Brady is bustling into the sitting room carrying a big tissue wrapped package. 'So, you're the lucky bride to be, Kathleen?'

'I am!'

She stares at me. 'I don't know why they've kept you hidden for so long, you're a real beauty!'

She immediately unwraps her parcel on the wooden table at the side of the room.

'We'll see how this fits.'

'What is it?'

'It's your wedding dress! Step into it and pull it up over your hips. That's the best way to get it on. I'll squeeze you in!'

I'm wondering if she expects me to take my clothes off here. I blush, just thinking about that. 'I won't need help putting a dress on. Do I have to do it here?'

'God but you're shy. You can go up to your room… Go on. Then come straight back down here.'

She places the dress in my outstretched arms, and then

folds the end over, so it doesn't trail on the floor. I'm carrying the gown with the fear that I'm going to fall over or even worse, step on it. I'm thinking, maybe I should just bare all and try it on right here. No, I said I didn't need help, so I'm heading up to my bedroom. Climbing the stairs is a new nightmare. I trip up and fall into the bundle of fabric. Missus Brady shouts, 'Don't ruin it! Turn yourself around, it's easier that way.'

'I'll try that!' I reply, moving my feet in a semi-circle, ever so slowly.

'Stop there,' Missus Brady yells when I am facing the way I usually come down the stairs.

'Now move backwards up the stairs,' she instructs. 'I'll take the end for you.'

'It works!' I call out. We eventually enter my room without tripping up again.

'Well, I'll leave you for a minute,' she says, leaving the door slightly ajar.

I never saw such a dress! It's got bones all down the front and back bodice, and no matter how I twist my arms I can't get the back done up. I'm not even sure I'm putting it on the right way round. I'm having a private dressing nightmare for a few minutes. I'm puzzled about this big lump around the back. It's all twisted up. Maybe it comes off and goes on me head!

'Missus Brady,' I'm calling.

Immediately she's beside me in the room. 'Sure, you're all twisted up.' She yanks the sides of the bodice and pulls my brassier strap up a little higher. 'Brings up the bustline, that's what it does! Flattering!'

My breasts are staring me in the eyes as I'm looking down. They're just under my chin. The neckline is a 'v' shape and reveals my cleavage. I can feel the blood pouring into my face. I don't know if it's from embarrassment or the tight dress.

'It's a bit…low,' I venture to whisper.

'Voluptuous you mean. Sure, you've got a great shape.

You won't always have that. Flaunt it while you've got it, that's what I always say!'

After an arduous ten minutes of Missus Brady's bustling around me, tucking bits in here and there, she says: 'Hold your breath now. I'm going to lace you up.'

I hold my breath and she pulls at the hooks in the bodice. I feel like I'm being squeezed to death, and wonder why my ribs don't break? I'm gasping for air.

'Take small breaths, or else the hooks will burst asunder!'

I'm trying to breathe quietly.

'Now, hold your breath again. I'm going to zip you up.'

I'm holding my breath.

'Pull your shoulders back. Stand straight, bottom tight, stomach in.'

She's roaring at me, while the zip slowly inches its way up my back, going up higher and higher, like a train winding its way along a track uphill. She is holding her breath during the last six inches of zipping. She's letting out a gasp.

'Done. Wait a minute. There, now turn around and see yourself.'

I'm turning towards the mirror that hangs in the inside door of the wardrobe. It's almost a full body length mirror. Is it really me? I'm staring at this lovely 'antique' white dress with pearls all over the front.

'It's a beautiful frock,' I say after staring a while.

'Frock! It's a gown. A gorgeous gown,' Missus Brady says tugging at the waist.

'It is…' The bust is a bit high for my liking, and the neckline too low, but the overall picture is of someone I don't really know.

'You're a real picture, that's what you are! What a figure! A film star in the making,' Missus Brady says, completely flattering me, or that person in the mirror.

I'm placing my hand at the neckline, trying to cover a bit of skin.

'It is a bit bare at the neck. But don't worry about that because Missus Connor says you can wear these pearls.'

I am dumbstruck with awe as she opens a box with layered strings of beautiful creamy-white pearls. She's standing close to me, being careful not to tread on the hem of the dress. She's hanging them around my neck. Four rows of glistening pearls extend just to the apex of my bustline.

'That should draw attention away from your cleavage, without detracting from your feminine beauty.'

I cannot get my eyes off those shiny, shimmering pearls. 'They're lovely.'

'Lovely! They're glorious!' Missus Brady insists.' There you are now!' she exclaims, standing back and admiring me as though she had just carved me from ivory.

I'm staring into the mirror again. The bodice glistens even in the dimly lit bedroom. A ray of sunshine bursts into the room and I light up like a crystal.

I'm turning slowly viewing the cut of the dress from every angle. The bodice is very tight, sloping towards my waist into a 'v' shape just above my hipbones. The sleeves fit tightly on the edges of my shoulders, and cling like skin to my arms, making them look sleek and long; with a 'v' shaped piece hanging down near my wrist, and a tiny pearl on the tip at the end. The twisted up lump at the back miraculously turns into a 'bustle', as Missus Brady calls it. It makes my bottom look like a duck's, sticking out behind me as I walk. The fabric is tucked into rolled layers and leads the eye to a long train of soft silky material. There's so much material trailing behind me you could've made three dresses with it.

'It's our own fabric. Made right here in Ireland,' Missus Brady declares, as if she wove it all herself.

'I'll just tidy this a bit.' She is fingering the bustle.

How do you tidy a bustle! 'It's a bit…duckish!' I stammer.

'The more duckish the better! That's what I say! Bustles have to be like that. They're all the rage around here again!'

'Did you make the dress?' I ask timorously, hoping it is the right question to ask.

'I did indeed! It's a long story!'

I stare. I'm not sure I want to hear the long story. 'Right.'

Missus Brady stares at my face in the mirror. 'You remind me a bit of my Angel.'

'You saw your angel?'

'Angela. I made the dress for her. She was only nineteen, around your size. She never got to wear it. I hope it brings you luck.'

'Luck…so, what happened to…your daughter?'

'We adopted her when she was five,' she begins.

'I'm sorry,' I say haltingly.

'Don't be. It's not a secret. She was a beautiful, angelic child. That's why we called her Angela. Her real name was Veronica.' She pauses and takes a deep breath, as though recalling a precious moment with Angela. She's shaking her head. I can see tears in her eyes. 'She met this pilot. Fine young fellow. Raphael Gilmore was his name. Raphael and Angela, two lovely angels. They were madly in love.'

'So did they…marry?'

'They flew away and never came back. Like angels in the sky.'

'Where did they fly to?' I question. I mean you had to fly somewhere, to another place.

'Their 'plane was found two days later, all smashed up, nothing was left. Their bodies were found, wrapped around each other, like two little black babes.'

'They died?'

'Two days before the wedding.'

I shiver. It's two days before my wedding!

Missus Connor appears in the doorway. 'Oh, she looks just like Queen Mary!'

'Begorrah, you're quick off the mark Kathleen! The gown is a copy of her wedding gown!'

'Sure I know all about the royal family…I have a bit of royalty in me. I believe we're the descendants of King Rory O'Connor!' She wanders forward as she speaks. 'Alice, you've done a great job.' She has a handkerchief in her hand. 'My little princess Kathleen is all grown up now…nearly eighteen. The dress fits like a glove.'

'It does. Maybe it was meant for your Kathleen?' Missus Brady discretely brushes a tear away and stands a couple of steps away. 'You'd better put your high heels on too. It's a bit trailing. You might trip up.'

'I happened to see these perfect white satin shoes the other day. They were just staring at me from Lynch's shop window, so I bought them. I'll get them.' Missus Connor hurries to her own bedroom and triumphantly arrives with a box filled with tissues and pearly-white satin court-style shoes with a huge pearl at the 'v' shaped front.

'Try these on for size.'

I hold on to Missus Brady as Missus Connor huddles down at my feet and places the shoes on my bare feet. 'God but your feet are as rough as sandpaper. Push.'

I feel myself rising up like the sun.

'You'll have to get those feet softened up, and then you can wear silk stockings! They fit like a glove, Kathleen child,' Missus Connor says, clambering to her feet. She glances at Missus Brady. 'A mother's instinct!' she sighs, and then hugs me, 'Alanna. You remind me of my sister. The image of her!'

I respond like a daughter, 'Thanks Mammy.'

She stands a little away from me, smiling smugly and holding my shoulders, then running her eyes down my form from head to toe where her gaze rests. 'We'll use the pumice stone and get those feet as smooth as a baby's bottom!'

I wonder what a pumice stone is, but instinctively can almost feel the pain I am about to endure.

Missus Brady heads downstairs and brings up her large bag filled with bits and pieces. She extracts a pincushion with pins. 'Breathe in.'

I gasp in fright and hold my breath.

'Don't worry, I'm just sticking pins in the dress, not your-self!' she mumbles through a mouthful of pins. 'Out!'

Relieved, I relax.

'No. Not that much.' She glares at me and I breathe in a bit and hold it.

'For the next two days just stay away from apple pie and custard! You can't afford to put even one ounce on. Do you understand me?'

'I do,' I whisper.

I have hardly eaten at all for the last two days, for fear of 'bursting asunder' in my tight wedding gown. It's been hard to resist Missus Connor's hot apple pies with lashings of custard made from fresh milk and eggs, which has become one of my favourite foods these past months.

Missus Connor asked Noleen, a young hairdresser, and beautician, to come and do my face and hair.

'Sit in front of the mirror, Kathleen.'

So here I am, sitting down in front of the mirror and she's working on me as though I'm a masterpiece. She places a white elastic band around my head, holding the hair back from my face.

'First, you need to cleanse, tone and moisturise, that's the latest technique.'

She begins to rub my face with a cream. Next she uses a soft cotton ball and cleans my face again. Then she rubs cream all over my face and neck.

'I'm just going to put a first foundation layer on now.'

I watch as she rubs some skin coloured stuff all over my face.

'Do you think I look a bit pale?' I ask.

Her eyebrows frown. 'Hold your horses, I'm not half finished,' she snaps.

'Sorry,' I whisper.

'Never mind.'

She removes the white band and tugs at my hair as she pushes a thick brush through it. Next she divides my hair and some falls in front of my eyes. I don't move in case I upset her. But I can hardly see a thing.

'Did you want curls towards the back?'

I nod.

After some time she begins to work on the front pieces.

I look into the mirror. She has some of the hair piled

high and curls hanging down the back of my head to the nape of my neck. She's rolling some of the hair from the front under, so it looks like a sleek sausage shape on top of my head.

'Your hair seems a bit thin on this side, where there's a nasty scar.' She looks at me in the mirror and I catch her eye. 'What happened?'

'I fell off the horse,' I lie.

'When?'

'A while ago now…' I reply.

'It still looks sore,' she adds as I squirm when she brushes the spot.

'Just a bit.'

'Well, I'll cover it with makeup and then let the hair come softly over it.' She cocks her head from side to side, moving a piece of hair as she works out her plan. 'There! Nobody will notice anything,' she says, dabbing something on the scar and gently easing the hair over the mark.

'Magic!' I exclaim, peering into the mirror to try and see the scar. 'It's gone!'

I can see the big smile on her face. 'Yerra, it's not gone. It's not gone at all. It's just hidden.'

'I can't see it at all. You've done great,' I say amazed.

'It is my profession. I am happy with that though!' She sighs and admires her work in the mirror.

'Now keep still. I want this to look straight,' she says, placing a gold crown that she places right behind the rolled piece of hair on my forehead.

'I look like a real princess,' I say exuberantly.

'It's not real gold, just plastic coated!' She smiles in amusement and delight at my astonishment. 'I'm glad you like it,' Noleen replies. 'I didn't think a floral wreath would suit that gorgeous gown you're wearing. You have a real royal look, that's why I suggested the crown.'

I just smile.

She opens a shiny black box to reveal a row of colours.

'But, the magic transformation is not quite finished,' she announces. 'This is my secret to success in my business. I'm going to put another layer of foundation on.

'Do you use this every day?' I ask inquisitively.

'I do. It doesn't take me very long now!'

'How long?'

'Fifteen minutes! That doesn't include my hair…'

'That's quick,' I remark.

'I know, but it gets easier with practice. I've been doing this for a few years now.' She stops plucking at my hair and looking intently at my face. 'You should be doing something with your skin now. The climate in the West is not the best for our fair skins. You can get wind burn very easily.'

I smile.

'I sell beauty products at the shop. Come on down and have a look. Your skin could really do with a good beauty routine. Now that you're getting married you need to keep yourself looking great. I don't believe in letting yourself go, just because you're married. You need to keep your husband interested.'

'Right,' I reply, wondering how on earth I ever got Niall interested without any of this stuff in the first place.

She selects a box with face powder and dunks a big fluffy powder puff into the contents. 'So, what school did you go to?' She dabs the powder all over my face as she speaks.

'School?'

'You did go to school?

I breathe deeply. 'Mm' I mumble.

'I never saw you there.'

'Where?'

'The local school!'

'I didn't go there…much.'

'Did you go to Dublin?'

'Mmm,' I say behind the makeup.

'I suppose you have the money, that's the thing!' She finishes her dabbing process, and takes a big brush from her box. 'Close your eyes.'

I close them.

'So what were the lads like there?' She gently flicks the brush over my face.

I wait until she stops to reply. 'I think it was an all girls school.'

'How do you mean, you think it was an all girls school? Don't you know?'

'Well, it was, except for some of the teachers!'

'I see. What were they like?'

'Who?'

'The male teachers?'

'Oh, they were very old. Really old, like ...my daddy, Mister Connor!'

She pauses for a moment. 'You don't have to tell me who your father is. He is a bit of an old goat! Sorry, I didn't mean to insult you...'

'He is.' I laugh to hide my nervousness, the fear that I'll let the Connors down and she'll discover they're just my step parents, my God parents really. 'But he's a wonderful father. He's always giving me things...'

'Not like my father! Never mind about that! Tell me about the rest of the time in the all girl boarding school? Did you go to any of the Dublin clubs or that?'

'Clubs?'

'Surely you weren't locked in the school all the time?'

'I was...'

'That's awful. Then where did you meet Niall?'

'Here!'

'I see! Now keep your eyelids down. Did you want eyeliner?'

'Whatever you think...' I reply immediately.

'It's highly fashionable now, and mascara,' she adds. 'I'll use the dark brown to give a softer touch. Don't blink. Hold it there.' She moves along my lashes with a tiny brush.

'Now for the lipstick.' She holds up a bright lipstick.

'It looks a bit bright,' I mumble.

'You can wear it, with those lips,' she states emphatically. 'Say 'aw'. Great!'

'Now, we'll just attach the veil. There now. Finished!' She lifts the veil over my face. 'Have a gander!'

I open my eyes and stare. I make a face in the mirror to make sure it's not a picture of another person. It's really me!

'Don't you like it?'

'I do. It's grand. I just wondered if it was meself.'

'Now smile.'

I smile widely.

'Less.'

I move my lips closer.

'More.'

I move my lips out a bit.

'Great! Hold that smile there.'

I try to retain the smile as she speaks.

'Now that's the one you want when you walk down the aisle. Get the feel of it. Keep that smile, even when the veil is over your face. You can relax now. But remember not to cry! You'll ruin all my good work! I'll just do your nails. Spread your fingers and keep them stiff.'

Noleen sits down on a chair beside me and places her nail kit on the dressing table. 'Good God!'

'What?'

'Your nails!'

'What's wrong with them?' I ask, staring at them.

'I've never seen such neglected nails. Do you bite them?'

'Sometimes.'

'I can only do my best. Do not bite these again until after your wedding, or I'll come and haunt you when I die.'

'I won't,' I reply, suddenly feeling terrified at the thought of Noleen coming to terrorise me at night with all the other monsters.

'Promise now!'

'Promise!'

'Good.'

'That's today! Oh God! What are you doing now?'

'I'm going to give you some long nails. These are fake.'

I stare at the row of nails. I never saw such a thing before, but I say nothing. I decide to ask her a few questions before she asks me too many questions I can't answer.

'Is this what you do every day?'

'It is. I've been working at it since I was fourteen. That was when I bought my first lipstick.'

'Now you have so many lipsticks!'

'I've earned them, I can tell you that. But it costs me a bit of money. Everything costs money these days.'

I smile.

She glances up at my face. 'You don't have to worry about things like that!'

'What do you mean?' I ask, wondering what she's getting at.

'Money.'

'Me? No, I never worry about money,' I say lightly.

'I never stop worrying about money, ever since I've been married.'

'So, you're married already are you?'

'I am.' She holds up her left hand. 'See!'

'It's lovely,' I comment, admiring her wedding ring.

'You probably thought I'm too young. Is that right?'

I never thought of that! 'I did… You look very young.'

'Everyone says that! But I'm very mature for my years!'

She probably is, I'm thinking. 'You are!' I exclaim.

'You look young yourself,' she says, moving her eyes from my fingernails to my blushing face in the mirror, just for a moment.

I smile. 'Thanks.'

There's a pause. Then I think of another question. 'So, how long have you been married?'

'Over a year now.' Suddenly her face becomes bright pink, which I can detect even under the double makeup. 'Expecting our first. Can you notice?'

'What?'

'My bulge?'

'No!' I answer truthfully. I'm not sure what she is talking about, but she pats her stomach as she says it, so I know it's got something to do with the stomach.

'Vincent says I hide it well.'

'Vincent?'

'My husband.'

'He's right, you hide it well,' I say, not sure what she's keen on hiding. That seems to please her.

'Well, what do you think?'

'About your bulge?'

'No, your nails?'

I stare at my spread out fingers. My mouth drops open. 'How did you do that?'

'Trade secret! If you want refills you'll need to visit the salon. They're half price until December twentieth.'

'They're so…pearly and…long! Like cat's claws!'

'The longer…the lovelier, that's what I say. Just don't move them for fifteen minutes, 'till everything sets.'

'I'm finished Missus Brady,' Noleen yells as she starts to pack up her beauty products into their special places in her black box. 'I'll give you a hand with the dress.'

'What a beauty queen,' Missus Brady says, bustling into the room carrying a small flat box.

Together they pull my dress over my slip and into its strangulating position. 'She's got a great shape,' Noleen says, lacing the dress at the back.

'She won't always have this. Not after a few buns in the oven,' Missus Brady remarks. They both laugh as though I'm not here.

After an allocated fifteen minutes on Noleen's instructions, wrist-high satin gloves, with the fingers removed, are taken from their flat box and pulled over my hands. A bouquet of fresh apricot coloured roses and forget-me-nots, trimmed with sweet-smelling lavender, created by Missus Connor, is placed in my hands, the smell of which keeps wafting to my nose and making me sneeze.

'You're not allowed to sneeze. Look at the light if you feel one coming on,' Noleen instructs at the last minute. 'God bless you now!' She leans forward and kisses my cheek, then rubs it. 'Lipstick. I wish they'd invent one that doesn't leave a mark!' She smiles and rushes off. She has to be at her work by nine o'clock, so leaves before the ceremony begins. I noticed Missus Connor giving her a fat envelope as she leaves the house. I just catch a glimpse of her from my bedroom window. She's opening the envelope and glancing back as she walks towards her bright pink car, a huge smile on her face. She jumps inside and away she goes like the wind. I wish I could be so modern and confident.

The wedding is in the rose garden next to the house. Mister Connor has been keeping all the open buds for the last two days.

I've seen some of the guests arrive in the last few minutes. There's Mister and Missus Connor, all dressed up to the nines; the priest, Father Patrick Buckley, a sombre looking man who used a walking stick to walk up the footpath to the house. He takes a full ten minutes to go ten yards. As soon as he arrives he's lighting his pipe.

Then there's Missus Brady who brought the dress. Missus Kearney is here to help with the food preparation. With Missus Brady's help I travel safely to the bottom of the stairs and enter the sitting room. There's a young woman standing, staring out into the garden. She turns around as I enter.

'Now, have you got something old, something new, something borrowed and something blue?' Missus Brady asks.

'I don't know?' I reply.

'The dress is borrowed, the shoes are new, the pearls are very old…Oh God, this is a disaster.' She looks as though she might faint. She cups her hands over her face. 'Nothing blue!'

'I have!' I suddenly remember as I extract a blue handkerchief from between my bosoms. 'Mammy gave me this. And I have these,' I point to my forget-me-nots.

'God bless her, thank God!' she says, almost swooning with delight. 'Have you got your horse-shoe?'

'I have,' I reply, raising my left hand to show her the newly crafted silvery shoe dangling on my arm.

'You'll have great blessings and good luck then,' she says, completely satisfied. She's all yours now,' she says to the girl. Then turns to me. 'This is Bridget. She's your brides-maid,' Missus Brady announces. We smile at one another. Bridget is about my age, a little shorter than me, and with short brown hair. She's wearing an ankle length pink frilly frock and a wide brimmed bonnet trimmed with pink roses. She's wearing white gloves and holds a small bouquet of pink roses and lavender. 'She's Missus Kearney's daughter,' Missus Brady explains. 'You probably know one another?'

'Probably,' I say, feeling hot under my makeup. I can't remember her at all.

Bridget stares at me and smiles, exposing her giant teeth and pink gums. She shrugs her shoulders.

'Where is Tom?' Missus Connor rushes through the double doors, and stops when she sees Bridget and me. She cups her face in her hands and shakes her head. 'You're beautiful. You too Bridget!' With that she dashes outside looking for Mister Connor. The window next to the double doors is wide open, so the guests can see me if they turn around. Through the nylon lace curtain I can just see them waiting nervously in the garden, sipping drinks. There's Nancy Crowe standing near the rose bushes, looking like a rose bush herself. She's dressed in a large-print floral suit in pink tones, with a huge pink, brimmed hat, which keeps bobbing as she talks. A brighter pink ribbon is wound around the crown of it and there's a bunch of plastic looking snowdrops stuck on one side. She is wearing high-heeled black shoes and stockings that glitter when she moves. She is checking them now for snags. I think she should move away from the rose bushes. Pink gloves and a black patent handbag complete her outfit. She has bright pink lipstick on her lips and her cheeks are very rosy. She keeps blowing kisses to Ned, who's standing near a table with decanters filled to the brim with varying coloured liquids. Ned keeps raising his eyebrows in response. He is dressed in his best black suit in a bright red cravat with flowers on it. Ned is our part time stable hand, and is Niall's Best man today. He has been courting Nancy for over twenty years, so Missus Connor says. Missus Connor rushes in through the front door, and gasps for breath. 'He's on me heels,' she calls to me. She seats herself at the ivory keys. The high backed piano shines like brand new from polishing. We can hear Mister Connor's cough as he comes through the sitting room door. I turn around and his mouth drops open.

'Get over there and take her arm. Hurry on now. Remember, she's your only daughter!'

'Right.' He staggers towards me, his mouth still open. I place my arm in his. He just keeps staring at me.

I beam at him.

'Doesn't she look a picture?' Missus Connor says, swivelling on her piano stood, squeaking and beaming at once.

'A real picture,' Mister Connor agrees, 'a film star.'

'Open the double doors,' Missus Connor instructs Missus Brady, waving her arms out and back again. 'We're ready!' A note is sounded on the piano. I step through the double doors. The sounds of 'Beautiful,' reach my ears.

I'm suddenly feeling nervous and shake for a moment. I stare straight ahead at the priest.

Father Patrick Buckley grunts like a pig. He's wearing his long white surplus and scapula. He's got his arms folded and if we didn't start moving I think he might have fallen asleep. He's placed his pipe on a little table. It's still emitting whirls of smoke. It's a fine sunny day, with a little breeze, which makes my veil flutter like a little dove. Where's Niall? For a split second I feel panicky as I'm thinking 'he's not here'. Suddenly my hero appears from behind the bushes at the side of the house. I breathe a sigh of relief. I walk towards Niall, who is now standing at the end of the garden near the spot where he proposed to me. I'm treading cautiously along the little stepping-stones. With the long gown and the high heels to manoeuvre I feel like a giant on stilts.

I suddenly feel a bit giddy. I'm slipping on the smooth stones. For an instant I can feel water running over me, all icy and cold. I shiver. Mister Connor steadies me and we keep walking. Missus Connor is playing, 'Da, da, da da, da, da da da', something like that, hammering the old piano. The music flows into the garden. As we get closer, Niall's eyes bulge out of their sockets as he stares at me. He looks ten feet tall with his hair black and shiny, slicked down with hair tonic, and his fine black suit and apricot coloured cravat. His white straight teeth sparkle from scrubbing. They match his brilliant white shirt, freshly pressed by Missus Connor and starched so that it could stand all by itself. My mouth is automatically smiling in return, hidden under my veil. My heart throbs. This is the pinnacle of my life. Nothing will ever compare to this splendid moment. I am a queen for a day! Niall's queen!

The priest moans in prayer. 'Join hands' he instructs us. He then asks Niall if he takes me as his wife.

'I do,' Niall replies, his eyes shining.

Then the priest turns to me. 'Do you, Kathleen Mary Connor, take this man, Niall Finbar Dempsey, as your lawfully wedded husband...?' His voice moans on. The priest is staring at me, mouthing *I do*.

I say, 'I do.' That wasn't too hard. I feel more relaxed now.

Then we have to repeat everything Father Buckley says, which all seems like a dream to me. Then Niall gives me a lovely ring, just the right size for my finger. Then the priest says, 'You are now husband and wife.' There's a slight pause, then gruffly, he says 'You may kiss the bride.'

Niall raises my veil and our faces meet for the first time as man and wife. His face is glowing with happiness and I can feel mine reflecting his joy.

'Wait on there!'

Just as our lips merge, Ned Smith has the camera out. 'Just hold it there for a tick.' We hold our mouths together for several minutes whilst he adjusts his settings. We start to laugh. 'Ready steady, hold on. Hold on! Can the priest move in a little bit closer, just between the two?'

Father Buckley grumbles as he shuffles a few feet to the left behind us. 'Great, that's great. Now keep those lips puckered together. Right!' He finally clicks his camera.

After a few more snaps with Mister and Missus Connor, and one with the guests, we head to a table in the hallway where an open book lies atop a clean white tablecloth sticking out like a ballerina's dress. A pen with a quill attached awaits our capture. I have been practicing my writing for the last few days. I seem to have forgotten how to write! Niall has been helping me form the letters again, but it seems so hard that I don't know if I'll ever be able to write properly again, or read for that matter. Niall places his hand over mine to stop me shaking as I write. He guides the pen over the parchment. 'That's grand.'

He then signs his name and I lovingly follow every move of his fingers with my eyes. He has beautiful, strong, manly hands. Father Buckley has just gone outside to light his pipe that must have gone out. He returns and peers at our signatures. 'Right.' He signs his wobbly signature and the date of our marriage as Wednesday, 21st August nineteen hundred and sixty eight.

After the signing ordeal, I am determined to enjoy myself. We walk through the sitting room doors together, as husband and wife. A loud cheer greets our ears. Bridget is following behind us, holding up the train of my dress. Missus Connor goes into loud mode on the piano, and she's belting the thing and hopping off her chair with the force of her hands and arms. Her whole body is rocking with the rhythm all the time. Now we're all kissing each other and being real friendly. Nancy Crowe is sniffing into her pink lace handkerchief, and Missus Brady is wiping her tears with a white handkerchief. Why do people cry when they are so happy? It makes me want to cry, but I'm afraid to cry with all the makeup on my face, like Noleen warned me about. There's a mountain of food spread on Missus Connor's table, plates of neatly cut triangular sandwiches, a bowl of sausages, sausage rolls, meatballs. There's a beautiful iced wedding cake, with a little figurine of a man and a woman getting married on the top. Her best tablecloth is stiff and starched, but you can barely see it for the food. There's a silver pot with tea in it and cream in the jug. On another side table there are jugs of orange juice and bottles of porter. There are also unidentified bottles of a clear liquid that I thought was water, but after taking a mouthful realized it has a burning action in my throat that takes my breath away. I believe it's the poteen. There are also a few bottles of whiskey and brandy with little glasses by them. From the kitchen we can smell the aromas of boiled corned meat, roast beef, roast ham and roast chicken, and roasting potatoes. Missus Kearney is busy preparing the food, with a couple of helpers. Missus Connor has her best china and polished silverware on display on the grand dining table. We all sit at the table and Missus Kearney and the two young lasses pass the food around. The wedding cake is taken away after Niall and I cut it together. I'm told that the top tier is reserved for our first child. We finish our meal with a small sample of the wedding cake, which is a whiskey fruitcake.

After that Mister Connor rises up and says, 'God brought us our little girl, Kathleen. We love her and hereby give every blessing in her new life with Niall.'

Ned then gives a talk, complimenting the bridesmaid and those who helped to make this day possible. He tells us all about Niall's excellent character traits, which I know already.

Next the table is cleared and made smaller, then pushed into a corner. Niall puts on the record player and we all jump around dancing. It's a grand day altogether. I end up dancing with all the men at the wedding, including Father Buckley, who is very lively after a wee drop. I'm nearly 'bunched' by the time evening comes.

The Connor's have given us the 'guest room', a room

outside the kitchen and to the left. It's got its own entry, like a little house in itself, but it's just one big room. It has a little table and a jug and bowl for us to wash in. Mister Connor has also placed an old enamel bathtub in the middle of the floor, which we can fill up and have a bath together! Everything is heavenly. The bed has a soft mattress filled with feathers. Niall and I just feel like staying here forever, our skin touching each other, being 'one flesh' in obedience to what the priest said at the marriage. Then he glared at us with his red eyes. I go red meself when I think of it, but when I'm with Niall it feels like it was meant to be and we don't feel like beetroots at all. I'm thinking this is what heaven must be like.

…

Two days after the wedding, Mister and Missus Connor look really downcast as they sit in front of their laid out bacon, eggs, black pudding, sausages, tomatoes and fried bread. The food is on the kitchen table, next to the radio. They turn the volume down as Niall and I arrive. Niall gives me a quick kiss just before we walk in the door. He squeezes my hand in his. I give him a special smile. My heart is over-joyed with love for this wonderful man. Nothing will ever change that.

'What's the matter?' Niall asks Mister and Missus Connor. 'You look as though someone's died.'

Missus Connor stares at Niall. 'How did you know?'

'Know what?'

'Someone's died.'

'So, who's died then?' Niall picks up his fork and plunges it into a plump sausage.

'Not Finn McCool?' I ask stopping my bread buttering action.

'Not Finn McCool! It's Father Buckley!'

'Thank God,' I say spontaneously. 'Sorry, I mean…'

'Good God! What happened?' Niall asks.

'He's dead!' Mister Connor advises sombrely.

'But, he was dancing with me a couple of days ago. He was a good dancer and all!' I exclaim. I notice I have dropped my butter knife.

'He's dancing with the angels now,' Missus Connor says, shaking salt vigorously over her eggs. 'He was a grand old priest.'

'So when did this happen?'

'Some time through the night! He was found in his bed this morning. He was supposed to take the morning Mass and the new young curate…what's his name? Father Oglvie I think. Well, he found him still in his bed. Stone cold dead! We heard it just a few minutes ago on the radio.'

'Well, may God rest his soul. Would you like a cup of tea?' Missus Connor picks up the teapot, which is covered in a colourful blue and red tea cosy with black eyes each side of the spout.

'Thank you, that'd be grand.'

'We'll have to go the wake, then the funeral Mass at Lisdoonvarna on Friday. So, we'll leave the both of you to look after the place for a few days. Did you ask Ned to come over on Friday Tom?'

'Yesterday he said he might see me on Friday, then he said he mightn't.'

'Right. Well, if he does come, make him a bit of lunch, Kathleen Mary. Will you do that for me Alanna?'

'I will,' I reply, wondering how many more names I have.

Niall and I eat our breakfast in silence after that. We just don't know what else to say.

Chapter four

Two weeks after our wedding, I am being persuaded by Niall to climb on Finn McCool, and have a ride. I feel excited but fearful at the same time. Anyway, I'm finally sitting upright in the saddle and my fear is gone. Sure Niall can persuade me to do anything!

'It feels grand. I love it!'

'I knew you would.' Niall is smiling and his eyes are like stars.

Suddenly, Toby the dog comes running after the ginger cat and they come right up to Finn Mc Cool's front legs. He makes a neighing sound and leaps into the air. I fly through the sky and land in the mud.

'Kathleen.' Niall shouts my name.

The sound is far away for a minute, and then I can hear him all right again. 'I'm all right.'

He's lifting me up, very gently, cursing the dog and the cat at the same time, and apologizing profusely to me. He's taking me inside and laying me on the bed. My head aches.

That night I wake up, screaming. I can see monsters coming to take me away again. One face belongs to someone I remember! I know who the monsters are! I remember who I am. I scream. Niall wakes up.

'I'm not a famous pam....pampered dancer living in a tower. I'm a...they call us…Tinceard…Oh Niall, what would you want being married to me?'

'Sure I'm totally in love with you Kathleen. I don't care about all that class distinction stuff. You're the most wonderful girl I've ever met, and the most gorgeous! The important thing is, can you remember your name then?'

'Niamh. That's my name, Niamh Murphy.' He is holding me tightly and I'm pouring out the things I remember and relating my dream to him. 'What would the Connors say if they knew I was a tinceard?'

'Don't worry; I won't say one word to them! This is between you and me and God! And you know, whether you're Kathleen or Niamh, you'll always will be a famous dancer, and my queen. Begorrah, we'll get away from this place. Listen to me now Kathleen Niamh!'

Somehow he makes me look into his face. He kisses my forehead and continues, 'I have a bit of money in the bank. Just let me sort out a few things, and then we'll go far away from here. We'll just ride off into the sunset.'

My crying and trembling stop as I lie in Niall's comforting arms the rest of the night.

'Niamh Kathleen,' I hear my name and struggle to open my eyes. Niall's face is close to mine.

'My one true love, do you mind if I move my arm.'

'I'm sorry!' I raise my head.

'It's as stiff as a dead cat,' he moans.

'Oh Niall, I'm sorry. Are you all right?'

'It's going all pins and needles, so it must be still alive.' He turns to me, rubbing his strong, hairy, arm. 'But you're worth having pins and needles for any time.'

He kisses me softly on the forehead again. I throw my arms around his neck and we indulge in a very passionate kiss. For a long moment we lose ourselves in each other. After a while we both need to breathe again. I can't help smiling.

'I feel better, much better…after that terrible dream. Niall, don't ever stop kissing me like that!'

'Don't worry, if I live to be a hundred I'll always kiss you like that. Niamh Kathleen, I think everything is going to be grand.' His lips find mine once more.

…

Later that day, I'm busy in the kitchen, rolling pastry for Missus Connor. She's just gone outside to sharpen a knife on a stone. We're making apple pies.

Niall comes in and speaks quietly in case Missus Connor hurries in unexpectedly. 'Listen, Niamh, Tom wants me to go up to Dublin with him. He's got a good tip on a fine racing horse. He wants my advice. While I'm up that way I'll get the money.' He gently squeezes my shoulders.

'Oh Niall, please don't leave me.' I grab his arm.

He holds me tightly and flour is going all over his shirt. He's kissing my forehead and hair.

'We'll be back in less than a week, I'll make some arrangements while I'm in Dublin.'

'Take me to Dublin with you.'

'I will. We'll go there and be happy ever after. Right now, you have to stay here. Missus Connor will be good company for you. I'll be back in no time at all.'

'Take me now, please!'

'I wish I could, but I can't! I promise I will take you there in a week or two!'

'All right then. Remember, you promised!' A thought comes to my mind right then. '*What must be must be.* My Aunty Maura used to say that! I can remember so much. Oh Niall.'

'Your Aunty is right. I'll come back to you. I will, cross my heart and hope to die. We'll dance all night in Dublin, that's a promise!'

'Oh Niall, I keep getting horrible visions, even during the daytime now! I can see my drunken father, falling over me in a shed. Then my Aunty Maura is having a stand up fight with him, banging him with a brass pot or a stick to stop him doing something bad…' I gulp for air between my words and tears.

'Now now, 'tis going to be all right. These thoughts will go away. They're only in your mind.'

'I can't bear them…I can see Maeve and me huddled together. We're frightened to death by the cursing and swearing of my da…'

'It must have been terrible for you. But you're safe with me now. I'm your very own man, your husband.'

'Hold me Niall.'

'It's all right.'

I keep talking as I lean into his breast. 'I am always shivering and hungry in my visions. I can see myself going from door to door asking for a bit of bread and my stomach turning itself into knots with the growling and groaning. I hate the life I had and now I want to keep the life I've found. You know something, Niall?' I look up into his concerned face.

'What?'

'I wish I never got my memory back. But then, I'm glad because now we'll get away from this place forever.'

'We will, we will. I promise, if it's the last thing I do, I'll take you away from here.' He bends his mouth to mine and we indulge ourselves in a long passionate kiss…

'A hem…well now, I think Tom is getting anxious to be off…' Missus Connor tries to be discrete as she comes in the door.

We pull our lips apart from each other. My mouth tingles from the passion of Niall's kiss.

'Sorry Missus Connor. I'll be off then.'

I smile at my beloved Niall as he shyly lowers his red face and hurries off. At the door he turns and looks into my face once more, his eyes betraying the deep passion in his heart. In that instance it seems that our hearts leap from our bosoms and fuse together. Suddenly, he's gone, leaving me with only an ache where my heart used to be!

…

Niall and Tom Connor have been away for two days now and I'm kept right busy with all the extra work around the place. Each night I'm waking up in a sweat, my da's face in front of me; him with a pitch fork in one hand and a bottle of the drink in the other. He always says, 'You need to be wedded now.' His face comes right up to mine. His face is cut and blood drops onto me. His eyes are red as though they've been roasted in the fire. His teeth are clenched and coloured brown. His face is imprinted with blue and red lines, like streaks of lightening zigzagging across his cheeks and nose. His nose is red and huge, like it's a Christmas light. Long whiskers poke out of his nostrils, which move in and out like a bellowing bull. Spittle drools from the sides of his lips. His tongue is green and red and has lumps on it. He holds the huge rusty fork in his rough hands. The long prongs of the fork are held against my neck. I wake up at this point, trying to scream, but I can't because of the prongs on my neck. My forehead is always dripping and my heart is nearly leaping out of my bosom with fear. Through the day I repeat what Niall said, 'Everything is going to be fine!' Then I feel better.

'Kathleen, I need to go into town today.' Missus Connor announces as we sit down for breakfast at seven on the morning of Wednesday 13th September.

Her words bring a strangling fear to my chest. 'Why so?'

'I want to get a bit of wool,' she says slowly, looking away. 'I've got nary a bit left. I think we might be needin' some little garments in the not too distant future, the way you and Niall are ... carrying on.' She looks sheepishly at me.

I stare. What on earth does she mean? I'm thinking.

Suddenly my face feels hot. I bury my head and stare at my sausages, black pudding, fried eggs, tomato and bacon. My stomach heaves just seeing the food. 'You don't mean...a babby!'

'Well, you never know. I'm very hopeful. I've never been a grandmother. I think it would suit me fine.'

She's very hopeful! What about me? I never even thought of such a thing happening until this minute. 'Excuse me…'

Before I take a mouthful of food I feel so sick I have to run outside.

By nine o'clock she is all spruced up in her best jacket, her light grey; the one she wore at our wedding, with her dark grey pleated skirt and light grey hat with flowers on the brim. She even has stockings on. She's wearing her deep pink, double frill blouse, which gives her an enormous bust. Her lips are bright red. She looks really strange climbing into the old rusty truck. Toby leaps up beside her before we can stop him. She tries to shoo him away, but he is stuck to the seat and won't budge. He whines and looks sad.

'He can come for a spin,' she says.

I notice that her face is as pink as her double frill blouse.

'You're all right now?'

'I'm fine thanks,' I reply, smiling as brightly as I can. 'I think I just overate.'

'Sure you need to keep your strength up. You take care of the place now, won't you Kathleen, mo vhoirneen? The fowl need feeding and the pigsty needs a bit of a wash down. Keep yourself busy. Idle hands are the devil's work.'

'Yes Mam!'

I'm keeping very busy cleaning up the kitchen, then feeding Ginger the cat, then the chickens; then I'm filling a bucket with water and carrying it across to the pig sty. I wish they put the pump a bit nearer the pen. I don't particularly like the pigs, but they remind me of my pig book, so I put up with their honking. I am not sure how to clean their home with them in it. Tom or Niall, and sometimes Ned do this job. Maybe, I'm thinking, I should take the pigs out and put them on the grass, and then put them back in. But what if they run away? My thoughts are interrupted by the sound of voices.

'Thank God,' I say aloud. I look up hopefully, expecting to see Niall and Mister Connor coming back early; but there before my eyes I see a band of men, yelling and howling. I remember my nightmares, and then I'm making a run for it. I can see me da. He's lagging behind the front-runners. I can see his grey jacket flapping in the breeze. He's got some weapon in his hand, a pitchfork! I'm looking for a place to hide. I jump over the pigsty wall in one leap. The pigs are a bit startled and back off as I crouch down behind them. They stink and make noises like sirens and I tell them to *shush*. I'm grabbing one of them and trying to hold it in front of me, but he's making a terrible screaming sound. I'm letting him go and lying as low to the ground as I can. He's burying his snout in the ground and sticking his curly tail in my face. *Niall, Niall,* my heart is crying… but he doesn't hear me! The next thing I know, Jack Sullivan is peering over the pigsty wall.

I'm looking up from behind the fat bottom of Squealer. He's pink, hairy and obese, shamelessly wriggling his obnoxious rear end in my face, as though he's saying he's proud of being porky. He squeals in fright as a face peers into his. He steps back, bowling me over. I let out a yelp! The face peering at me is pink, with rough grey stubble draped around brown-spotted lips, which open to reveal a dark mouthful of broken, greenish-yellow and occasionally black teeth. Grey whiskers curl from flailing nostrils. The deepest eyes, shaded by black and white peppered thick bushy brows, rise to allow round dark beady lenses to penetrate the recesses of my eyes. My mouth opens and the words jump out, 'Jack Sullivan!'

'Begorrah, ala!' Jack's neck stretches like a turkey's as his face comes even closer. 'A pig that knows my name?' His mouth hangs open. I can see red zigzagged maps in the whites of his eyeballs.

'I thought it was me own sow!' He chuckles as he ogles me, revelling in his peculiar sense of humour. 'The wife!' he says, by way of explanation.

I'm sitting on my bottom with Squealer in my lap. 'Shush Jack,' I'm pleading, as I try to heave a thousand pounds of bacon off me.

'Begorrah! You can't fool old Jack. You're not a sow!

You're Niamh Murphy.' He's beckoning my father who's close by. Suddenly he bursts into excitable shouting, mixing his Shelta language with English. 'Aga di'lsa, over here Sean!'

Squealer rolls off me with a final shove, ripping my skirt in the process. I leap up, vault over the pigsty wall, and make a run for it. I know I'm a good runner. I'm a good dancer and a good runner! I'm glancing back to see if they're on me heels? 'Oh God, they are…' I'm falling over in the high grass.

'Oh, Mammy, mammy…' My leg is aching, but I'm up as quick as a flash, ignoring the pain. Oh God, I'm stumbling all over the place. My leg's bunjaxed. 'No…' I scream as the thunder of heavy breathing encompasses me and I'm tackled to the ground. I close my eyes. 'Just let them kill me,' I pray. I'd rather die than go back to the tinceard's camp!

Voices clamber for fame. 'She's down. Come on lads. Get her arms, quick!'

'I've got a leg.'

'Me too!'

Two lads have taken hold of my left leg. 'Not this one, ye egit. I've got it. Get the other one, Dan, be quick now.'

'This one?'

'She's only got two, ye Moron!'

'Get her arms someone. The two of them!'

My arms are squeezed. I'm kicking and wriggling with every ounce of energy, but 'tis no good, they've got me cornered. The pain in my leg is excruciating, but easier to bear than the burning humiliation I'm suffering as they haul me away like a rabbit, legs first. I can see Jack Sullivan and Dan O'Brien holding my legs, romping along at the front. Seamus Creen and Dennis Buckley have me by the arms. They're like a pack of dogs when they gang up. Every step is a jabbing, searing pain in my leg. 'Gits' I yell. 'Let me go. Jesu Criosta. Oh Mother of God!' My skirt blows above my knees, but I can't move my arms to push it back down again. They're probably hoping it blows right up over my head! They'd love that! I'm glad I've got knickers on me. Thank God for that! I can just see that ugly Jack with his red eyes, stubbly chin and cheesy grin trying to have a good look. 'Stop gawking at me…' I'm yelling at a couple of other fellas with scarves over half their faces. I don't know who they are. 'Cowards. Yellow livers!' I sneer.

'She's a whore!'

'Like her mother!'

I shout 'Leave my dead mother out of this.'

They keep making indecorous comments as they run alongside me. I'm spitting in their faces and cursing and swearing at them. Now I hear different noises, which flood my mind with old memories. I can just see the campfires in the distance. I can hear the shouts of people coming closer to inspect their prize, me!

'We're here thank God! She's like a ton of spuds! Throw her over there lads!'

'Don't call me a sack of potatoes!' I shout, as I land, bottom first, in the dirt.

'What can we call you then, whore?' Aunty Maura's voice bellows out before I can see her face. I turn my angry countenance away from her face. I pull my skirt down over my knees.

'You know my name!'

'Stand up when I'm talking to you!' she orders. She pulls me by the arms.

'Gerroff!' I scream. My arms are all red and nearly blue, and soon will be black. My right leg is throbbing and looks bigger than my other one, the left leg, that is! I'm not even trying to stand up, but just sit as cool as a cucumber in the damp grass, staring straight ahead, resisting the tears pressing on the back of my eyes.

Aunty Maura lets go and stands above me, frowning. 'She's become a real little trollop altogether! *Nid'es axiver!*' she roars as she hits me across the head.

'I never was one! *Dil 'lsa axiver glori* the truth Maura…'

She scowls at me. 'Don't worry, I know the whole truth.'

'Nobody asked me what happened…'

'You always were a bloody liar.'

I stare at her. 'I must have learned it from you…'

She stares back at me, dagger for dagger as her right hand rises to clobber me. 'You'll be the death of me!' She grits her teeth as her arm stiffens in mid air. Her bright blue eyes in her white face are cold and unfeeling. 'Thank God I'm not your mother.' She flips her hand hurriedly to her forehead, chest and shoulders as her own blessing falls on herself. Her eyes soar into their sockets skyward for an instant, then back to focus on my face. I stare at her in disgust. Her dark hair is uncombed and blowing across her face in the wind. Her mouth is a thin rust-coloured scowl with a few bits of egg yolk around the edges. She is hugging her old brown and red tartan rug close to her chest. She's wearing a long grey skirt and dark brown brogues on her feet. They look like two left shoes to me from this angle. She has no stockings on. I can see her dark varicous veins winding up her legs like the branches of a tree.

'Thank God. Amen!' I reply. 'You've got egg on your face,' I add maliciously.

'Shut your gob,' she sputters in reply, pushing my head with a fist filled with hatred.

'Is this how you welcome your own flesh and blood?' I say, covering my head with my fists.

'You belong here, under my care, God help us all! You think you can come and go as you please, without leave or reason? You're very much mistaken you little trollop!'

'And what have ye all been doing all your life? Going from place to place?'

Her wild eyes come close. 'Don't back answer me! You've disgraced your father and me, running away like that! Your not Irish *ar burt*'

'I'm as Irish as you are. I'm not *agetul* of you!'

'You should be afraid, you faggot!' Maura screams. 'Give us a bit of hand, Betty, Alice, Mary!'

Three wiry women, who are standing in a huddle, leap

into action, taking an arm or a leg. Now I'm being dragged to an old van nearby. Somehow they squeeze me through the narrow doorway, and hurl me onto the floor. Heavy breathing is the only sound I hear for a moment.

Betty stands in the doorway. 'That'll sober her up!'

I'm curling my fingers like claws. 'Yerra, gerroff,' I scream and shake my head, so that my mop of wavy red hair flies all around my face. I snarl for added effect.

Alice pushes Betty out the door, almost knocking Maura over on top of me. 'She's a bloody witch, that's what!'

Betty and Alice run off, screaming, 'I think she might be a Banshee! Oh God help us!'

Maura steadies herself and scurries out the door after the other two.

'She's mad! She's insane!' 'Lock her up *axonsk*,' Mary screams, leaping out the door on top of Maura.

I make a growling sound. 'I'll put a curse on you!'

'Mary's right. Lock her up tonight. Quick! For God's sake lock her up. Hurry up!' Someone screams hysterically.

The door bangs shut and a bolt is secured. I can hear their voices mingling in high-pitched animation.

'At least I bring a bit of excitement into your miserable lives,' I shout after them.

I lie down for a few minutes, 'How in God's name have I come to this?' I wonder.

My leg is aching so much I'm feeling faint. Alice and Mary are back again, peering through the foot square, dirty window. I prop myself up. 'Stop gawking at me, you pair of witches!' I yell.

Their eyes grow large for an instant, and then with a yelp they disappear.

That suits me fine! I lie back cautiously on the splintered ridden floor and stare around me. The van has been stripped bare. All the cupboards have been pulled out, leaving broken walls behind. There's a piece of snapped wood nailed to the floor where a bench used to be. My right foot rests in a space where the floorboard has been removed. I can see the dark green grass below in parts where boards have disappeared, probably for firewood, I muse. The wind is blowing through the holes, making goosebumps rise on my skin. I tug at some of the broken boards, but soon my hand is filled with splinters. I suddenly feel exhausted and the pain in my leg seems worse, and a pain lands on my head like a brick. I try to pluck the splinters out of my fingers, and realize I've got my wedding ring on. I pull it off, pull up my dress at the back and tuck the ring inside my elasticised knickers. I can feel the cold ring safely inside my drawers. That gives me some satisfaction. I'm closing my eyes and the tears are accumulating around my eyelashes. I'm allowing them to find their course down my cheeks and over the tip of my nose and into my hair. I'm falling into a restless slumber… darkness …light…I escape my pains for a time.

It's some time later and now I'm fully awake! I'm on the cold floor, in the little van where the four women dumped me. There's a horrible cold draught rushing at my face from beneath the van. It's getting dark, so I must have dozed for a number of hours. I curl up to try to stop the shivers going through me. There's a gap of about an inch under the door, and I can see a bit of light under it, but any cockroach can come walking in. I close my eyes, as I'm still feeling too tired to care if a thousand cockroaches come and crawl all over me. I shiver at that thought. I wish this was a nightmare, but I know it's not because the pain in my leg is fierce. I can hear someone banging on the door of the van. 'Oh God, let it be Niall, please.' Then the door bursts open! It's Nell Doran and my step-sister, Maeve.

'Maeve, Nell, thank God you're here. I think my leg's broken.'

'Serves you right, running off like that!' Nell says, tut tutting beside me with her hands on her hips. She's swaying back and forth. She smells like a brewery.

I'm holding my nose. 'You stink!'

'Pig! You stink yourself!' She almost falls on top of me.

'You've caused more than enough trouble Niamh. I'll go and get something.' Maeve rushes off, leaving Nell and me. We stare at each other for a time.

'So, are you going to run away again then? Going back to your pigs, or your buccal?'

'What do you mean, my buccal? '

Just then Maeve rushes back in the door, carrying an elastic half stocking in her hand.

'I found this. It's Mam's, for the varicose veins. She doesn't use it. Here, put it on. It might help a bit.'

She pulls the thing over my foot and proceeds to yank it up over my leg. 'Where's it broke?'

'Ouch. Easy on. The pain…it's everywhere. I think it's near my ankle, maybe about there.' I point to an area, which is sore to touch just above my ankle.

I'm on the verge of screaming as she pulls the stocking over the area. I have to hang on to her arm to keep myself sitting up and not to faint.

'You always were such a baby! I'm doing my best for you, and you're just ungrateful!'

'I know. I'm sorry for complaining Maeve,' I reply.

'I can get you something for the pain,' Nell says, swaying and peering at my leg.

'What?'

'My secret recipe… I'll be back.' Off she stumbles through the door, disappearing into the darkness.

She returns a few minutes later with something wrapped in newspaper. After she unwraps the layers of newspaper, there's a tiny amount of green powder sitting in the middle of the large page.

'Try some.' She pinches a little with her finger and puts it on her tongue.

'I don't know Nell. It might kill me!'

'It didn't kill me!' She pops her eyes wide open at this remark.

'All right.' I pinch a little between my thumb and forefinger and place it on my tongue. It tastes bitter, but bearable, like a piece of lemon skin.

'Have a bit more,' Nell coaxes.

I take another pinch. I can still feel the pain in my leg. It has become a throbbing, low, burning sensation.

'Give it a bit of time. Now we want you to come for a bit of craic, mo chaileen ban.'

'What's the occasion?'

Nell turns to stare at me, her eyebrows raised.

'We've decided to celebrate your homecoming. You've come back from the dead to us.' Nell explains in her 'mystic' voice.

'From the dead?' I say.

'That's right Niamh. We thought you had drowned. Someone found one of the shoes you wore to my wedding,' Maeve informs me in a low voice.

'So, if you thought I had drowned how did you know I was alive?'

Maeve moves away a pace. 'It's a long story. Come on! Everyone waiting for us.'

'Give us a hand up then.'

Maeve and Nell come on either side of me and we hobble and wobble as we make our way down the step of the van and move slowly towards the campfire. I can see the flames flickering in the dark night, and hear the rumble of voices as we come closer. A few people call out to me. 'Y'are back?' 'There you are!' 'You're looking great!' I try to smile, but I just don't feel I belong here any more.

About twenty people are sitting around the fire, roasting chestnuts. They smell good enough to eat! I realise I am very hungry. We sit down and Maeve hands me a stick with a chestnut on it. I lean forward and put it into the bright flame.

'She's back. Our queen is back.' Jack Sullivan's sarcastic voice rises up in the darkness near me.

'Treason!' someone else shouts and throws a chestnut at me, laughing. It hits me on the arm.

'Witch,' another voice shouts and suddenly I am being bombarded with chestnuts and other stuff.

'Deserter,' someone else shouts. A number of voices rise

up in reply, 'Deserter, not good enough for you now!' A barrage of stones and chestnuts are hurled at me. Maeve and I cover our heads with our arms.

'Get her lads!' Suddenly, two lads take my arm and drag me away from Maeve, towards the fire.

'Stop, it's too hot.'

'You'll burn in hell. Get a taste now.' It is Jack again, and his drunken friend, Seamus Creen.

I heard some lad shouting from the shadows. 'Burn her, she's a witch!' I can feel the heat of the fire on my feet and face. They push me closer to the fire, and then stop.

I recognise Nell's sneering voice, shouting, 'She's a traitor. Queen!'

Mixed voices shout, 'Burn her. Burn the Queen!'

I turn around and see the group coming closer and closer, shuffling their feet as they draw near. They draw close to one side of me. The fire is on the other side. O, God, help! I'm crying. A spark flies out and hits me on my skirt, singing a small black hole. I quickly brush it away.

'Put more wood on the fire,' someone shouts.

The flames lick close to my legs. Someone starts pushing me by the shoulders. I fall to the ground, holding on to the grass to stop myself being pushed right into the fire. 'Help me. Somebody help me,' I scream as a spark strikes my hair and I can smell the burning lock. I can see the feet of the crowd getting closer, and they shuffle a jig in unison and cry out, 'Burn her!' Ara go on, we're only joking. Ara go on, go on, go on, we're pulling your leg.' Someone throws a half burned stick, which ignites my skirt for a second. I stamp it out with my hand. 'You're all mad!' Suddenly I feel a great anger rising up in me. 'Get away. Get away or I'll put a curse on the lot of you,' I hiss. I begin to rise up, kneeling on my right knee, the bad leg, and placing my left foot in front of me. They stop moving.

'She's cursed,' Nell yells, pointing at me.

The crowd scurries towards me once more. I pick up the half burned stick and stand up on both legs. I glare at the crowd, waving the burning stick towards them. The backs of my legs and bottom feel like they're being singed.

'She's just like her mother.' The voice is Nell's.

'Stop it, the lot of you!' a voice roars loudly behind the crowd.

It's my father!

'She's my girleen. Leave her alone or you'll get no more drink…'

Instantly, the crowd is breaking into two groups, one on either side, leaving him a clear walkway.

Maeve rushes to me. 'Egit, be quick, here's your chance. Get out.'

'Get a new queen,' Maeve shouts. 'Nell!'

A voice calls out 'Nell is our queen.'

'I'd be proud to be your queen,' Nell's voice roars. 'I'm very obliged to you all.'

The crowd shouts, 'Let's drink to Nell.'

Maeve and I head through the break in the crowd towards me da. He's coming towards us. The crowd close as we move through. Father places his hands on my shoulders and the feeling of total relief sweeps over me. I cling onto him as the three of us stumble back to Maeve and Paid's van.

'I'll get something to cover the sofa. I don't want you marking it with all that black stuff,' she says, hurrying into the adjacent room and bringing out a white sheet. She throws this over her bright yellow sofa, with purple dancing flowers, her pride and joy.

We sit down. 'Where's Paid?' I ask.

'Why do you want to know that?'

I shrug my shoulders, 'Why shouldn't I. I like Paid.'

'I know that right well. But I'll warn you now, keep your hands off him!'

'What?' I ask wondering what she's getting at.

'Nothing! Don't worry! He's working hard if you must know! He's in county Mayo, helping with fencing a very big farm property.'

My teeth are suddenly chattering. Maeve immediately seems concerned for me.

'You look like death warmed up. Did you burn yourself?'

'I'm not sure. My foot…' I say, pulling my black left foot up for inspection.

'Ax, it's only soot. Sure I think I got more singes than that.' She gets up. 'I'll put the kettle on and we can have a nice cup of tea.'

My da just sits. 'Thanks da. You saved my life then!'

'Don't worry about it…'

Now that I have got his attention I ask him 'Why did you bring me back da?'

Da furls his lip under. He looks at Maeve.

'He wants you to be wed,' Maeve says, as she finishes pouring the tea.

The words to explain that I am already married are stuck in me craw.

'Maeve's right. Sure now he's a fine fellow, from a grand family.' Da smacks his lips to show his satisfaction.

'But what about my choice?'

'Me and your mother know what's best for you…'

'My mother's dead,' I retort.

He stares at me with red eyes. 'I loved your mother too! Your Aunty Maura has been more than a mother to you since she died. God damn it girl, but you're an ungrateful wench.' He suddenly rises and marches out the door.

'What about your tea?' Maeve calls after him.

I stare at the door rocking back and forth in the breeze.

'Don't just watch it, shut the bloody door Niamh!'

I feel too numb with fear to move.

'I'll do it myself.' She rushes over and bolts the door. 'Nobody can break in now!'

She hands me a cup of tea in her best cup, sitting on a saucer that doesn't quite match.

'It's lovely Maeve, just the way I like it, hot and sweet.'

'Sure I've always spoiled you rotten.'

After a few minutes I ask a question. 'Maeve, why did they try to burn me?'

'Take no notice of them at all. They just got carried away. They've been drinking the poteen since this morning! They won't even remember it tomorrow.' She stares at me. 'Do you think I enjoyed it? Look at me arms!' she says, showing me a red patch. 'I got burned too you know.'

'I know,' I reply. We're silent for a minute. 'What's this about me getting married?'

'You're safer being married. At least you'll have a husband to protect you.'

'I am married!'

'Ah, go on, you're pulling my leg. Sure you've only been gone just over three months.'

'I can prove it,' I say. I pull the ring from my drawers. I tell her about Niall and me and our secret marriage. She stares at me as I relate the whole story.

'If you value your life, don't say one word about this to Sean.'

'I have to Maeve?'

She comes close to my face. 'You aren't married at all!' she says viciously. 'You can't get married if you don't know who you bloody well are!' She stares at me. 'Now, you made me swear!'

'I'm sorry Maeve, but Niall loves me. We're going to run away…'

'It's no use running away all your life. Da's made a grand match for you now. You belong with your own kind. Once you've been back with your family Niall won't want you any more, you know that, don't you? The country people are all like that. Sure if Niall and Sean ever met, there'd be fireworks all right. Your da can kill a full-grown sheep with his bare hands. Niall would be like putty in his hands.'

'Niall is very strong too, and he loves me.'

'And your new husband will love you.' She speaks more softly to me now. 'Listen to me Niamh, for I know what's best for you. Just obey your father, that's the fourth commandment! Then everything will work out just grand. Not another word about this now. All right? Niall is better off with his own kind, someone educated! Get him out of your mutton head.'

I'm shaking all over with fear and confusion. Her words sound right, but I know that I love Niall and he loves me. But reason tells me that I have to get him out of my head, for his sake as well as mine. She's right, Niall is better off with someone educated, not a muttonhead like me!

She hands me one of Paid's hankerchiefs. 'Blow your nose. There now. Let the rivers run dry.'

I blow my nose.

'That's settled then. Promise you'll not run away again?'

'I promise.'

'Would you like a biscuit with your cup of tea?' Maeve takes a small tin out of the cupboard. She opens it and hands it to me. 'They're only wheatmeal. Do you want a bit of oid on them?'

'No thanks Maeve. I've been feeling sick at the sight of butter lately.'

'You'll feel better axaram! Go on, have one biscuit. Go on!'

'Tomorrow never comes Maeve!' I accept one of her biscuits. My love for Niall is pressed deep into my heart, even if my mind forgets him, which doesn't seem possible right now. I bite into the biscuit as I'm thinking of him. I nearly bite my finger. 'Ah!'

Maeve is keen to change the topic now. 'This reminds me of when we were small, and I saved that chocolate wheaten biscuit until we went to bed.'

'I remember,' I reply. 'You kept it in your drawers and it melted.' I suck my sore finger for a moment.

'We ate it anyway.'

We sit silently together. In the background we can hear a bit of yelling and laughter at the campfire. I shiver. I never want to sit at a campfire again after tonight. I crunch on the wheatmeal biscuit, and try not to think of Niall.

'You give yourself a bit of analken, and get some rest.' She places a little basin of hot water on the chair in front of me. 'Everything will be all right in the morning, you'll see. Goodnight, sleep tight, don't let the fleas bite,' she says lightly. She pulls a curtain across, behind which lies her and Paid's bedroom. A moment later, she emerges holding a green and brown tartan woollen blanket. 'I'll let you have me best spare blanket. But make sure you wash yourself before you soil it.' She folds it and places it on the sofa.

'Thanks Maeve!'

After I turn the clean water into a black mess, I feel too fearful to throw it out the door. I can't stand on me leg, so I hop to the little table and leave the basin with the black water and the now blackened soap there.

I lie on her couch until morning, glad to be alive and clean. Even my bad leg doesn't seem so bad now. Even though I said I would forget Niall, I'm thinking of him all night long. He's going to think I ran away again, and Mister and Missus Connor? I can't go back and tell them I was taken from them, because then the Connors will know I'm a tinceard and they won't want me then. Now I'm wondering what Nell insinuated when she said, 'Just like her mother?' Nobody ever told me why she died. I thought it was the consumption, but now I'm wondering about the truth of that. It's almost dawn when I pull the soft blanket over my head and drift into a restless sleep. I awake shortly after, thinking the bed is on fire.

Every day I long to run back to the Connors, but my head tells me that will only bring more trouble on everyone, including Niall. My leg is too painful to walk on, let alone run anywhere. The women have been visiting me, talking excitedly about my forthcoming marriage. You'd think they were all getting married, not me.

'God has let you have a broken leg so you can't run off this time,' Nell says, laughing as she passes by the van a week after I was brought back.

'It's not broken. It's sprained!' I retort.

'He's dead you know, R.I.P,' she says through the window.

'Who?'

'Buccal deas fell off a horse. Slean leat!'

Later that evening I question Maeve. 'Nell talked about someone falling off a horse?' I say. 'Do you know anything?'

'Don't take any notice of Nell. She's raving mad, you know that!'

'She might be, but still, where there's smoke there's fire. Did someone get killed around here?'

'Maybe.'

'Who? When? Where?'

Maeve is fussing over a petticoat she's hand sewing, and doesn't even look up. 'God, you're full of questions. I don't know who he was. All I know is that a man fell off a horse near Bealanbrack River and they thought he was killed.'

'Maeve, it might have been Niall.'

'Sure I told you to get that name out of your mind. It was probably a stranger in these parts.'

'What if it was Niall?'

'Niamh, I won't tell you again, I don't know! I just heard it from Jack and Sean.'

'Niall is a great rider. He wouldn't fall off Finn McCool. Tell me it wasn't him, please Maeve.'

'God, you get on me goat! I have to go and see Mary.' Maeve folds her petticoat up, stuffs it in a crocheted bag and leaves.

I know it was Niall; otherwise they'd say who it was. I feel suddenly faint. I lie down on Maeve's couch and close my eyes. The hope of ever seeing Niall again fades in my heart.

On Thursday, 26th September, nineteen hundred and sixty eight, just two weeks after I was brought back to the camp, I find myself standing on my painful leg, wearing the dress Maeve wore on her wedding day, in the same place that Maeve and Paid were wedded, near McCarthy's barn. This is where I'll meet my new husband. Maeve is my matron of honour. She looks great in a lime green coloured dress down to her ankles and a halo of the last of the wild roses on her head. She's got two wild roses tied together with lime green ribbon in her hands. The same wild roses are made into a little bunch and I'm carrying them. It's now autumn, and it's freezing cold. Maeve bends over behind her posy, and whispers, 'Would you look at the get-up of him.'

I see Rhonan standing proudly, all spruced up in a suit. He's got a black suit and brown shoes and a red bowtie. His hair is slicked down with grease. He's grinning from ear to ear. His teeth are not black; they're not there at all. He's gummy!

'What happened to his teeth?'

'He had a fight. I think it was over you!' Maeve whispers back.

'Oh God,' I moan.

'But he didn't win!' she adds.

Just at that moment, from the corner of my eye I see a young man coming out from behind the barn.

'He was having a piddle,' I hear Nora, my bridesmaid, whispering to me from the other side. She giggles.

I am so relieved I almost drop my bouquet. I'm viewing him through the misty outlook of this veil.

'It's him!' Maeve says excitedly.

'Who?' I ask.

'Your man!'

I hold the veil still as I take a good look. He's quite tall, with sandy coloured hair and a tanned face, which has a flush of pink on it as he walks towards the wedding party. He's grinning from ear to ear. He seems to have all his teeth in place. It's Jimmy Farrell! I remember him from a few years ago when he did some work in these parts. A shiver suddenly creeps over my neck and arms.

'Are you cold?' Maeve asks.

'A bit,' I whisper back.

'You'll soon be Missus Farrell, and then he'll warm you up. He's a fiery one that fellow,' she whispers.

My hands suddenly feel clammy. 'You make my blood boil!' I whisper back.

'You're warming up then?' she says cynically.

I glare at her through my veil, but she looks straight ahead.

I'm now going through the ritual with the same priest officiating as Maeve had, Father Seamus O'Reilly. He talks so fast and low that I don't know what he's saying at all. I catch words like worse...poorer... sickness...death, then I'm repeating something after him, my own voice seeming to speed up, saying, 'I do,' at one stage, as though we are all in a hurry to catch a bus. I'm nearly saying 'I don't, but he interrupts at I do… Even as I say the words, I look around, wondering if Niall will come back alive from heaven itself and gallop through the throng on Finn McCool. We could fly away to Dublin. That would be grand!

Now I'm getting a lovely bright gold ring on my finger. I never saw such a ring in my life before. It's very wide and made of very shiny dark gold. I can hardly believe that this is my second wedding ring, and my sixteenth birthday is not until the thirty-first of October. Everything is going according to plan and the next thing I know, I'm Missus Farrell. I don't know how to write the name Niamh Farrell, and I realize that I have never learned how to write! Niall did teach me how to write 'Kathleen Connor'.

'Put an X there,' the priest shouts and points to the spot where my name is written as *Niamh Murphy*. I just sign an X there. Jim does the same with his name. So, there we are, mister and missus X.

'It's a grand ring,' I tell Jim a little while later when we get a chance to say a few words to each other.

'I made it myself. I'm pleased you like it. The gold is very soft, so you'll have to take good care of it.'

He looks into my eyes. 'I know you will,' he says quietly, giving me a kiss on my lips.

I let him kiss me for a moment, then gently ease myself away. 'So', I ask, 'where did you get such grand gold?'

'Niamh, I can't tell you that. That's my own business.' He holds me tightly by the shoulders and stares into my face.

I gasp as his hazel coloured eyes meet mine. His eyes are reflecting the fire the lads have lit to cook the meat and to keep us warm. 'I don't ever want you to question what I do. I don't want you to be one of those nosey, stupid women with nothin' in their heads but wild stories. You're my wife and you have to obey me, or else. Do you hear me now?'

A cold fear creeps over my skin. 'I do. Whatever you want. Let me go, you're hurting me!'

'Sorry!' He lets his grip go. 'You seem cold. Come over to the fire,' he says more gently. I follow him to the bon fire.

Jim is very devoted to me for the first month or so as I've been feeling sick nearly every day. He brings me lovely flowers, which he picks on his way home from work. Sometimes they look more like flowers from someone's garden, or even, God help us, from the graveyard, but I never say a word about that! I'm trying to respond to him as a wife but my heart is not in it. I feel like I'm just doing my duty as a wife. I think I know more about the bedtime things than he does, but I can't let on, or he'll find out I've been married before! I try to act like an egit, which suits him, as it makes him think he's better at husband and wife things than me. Winter is nigh, and it's freezing cold here in the west now.

…

Jim has a job as a labourer with the local county council, mainly doing roadwork. He has a trade of making pots and pans, but there's not enough money in that to keep the clothes on our backs and food on the table. One night he comes home looking happier than usual. After we have eaten our simple stew comprising boiled potatoes, leeks, bacon and parsnips, he sits down beside me.

'You're looking happy!' I say, being careful not to ask why.

'I am. I've got the most beautiful wife in the world, and a good job. What more could I want?'

'A child?'

'A child of my own.' He bends over and kisses me gently.

The next thing I know, he's carrying me into our small bed. I try to enjoy his rough lovemaking by closing my eyes and remembering Niall. Jim seems to be enjoying it anyway, and doesn't even notice my eyes are closed the whole time.

Afterwards, we lie there. My eyes are opened now and we're staring at the brown stained ceiling of the van.

'Did I ever tell you about my father?' he asks, turning to me. The light falling on his face gives him a chiselled, almost handsome look. Some would call him a 'fine fellow'. Maybe I'll get to love him one day, when this ache for Niall goes away from my heart.

'I heard he was a great one for the pots and pans. A real artist and all!'

'He was that.'

'He also was a great 'poteen' maker. I think it killed him in the end.' He pauses.

'Go on!' I urge him.

'It's true. Do you know what happened when he died?'

'No, what happened?'

Jim sits up and leans on his elbow. He runs his finger down my cheekbone as he tells me the story of his da's demise.

'The people who touched him after he died had a drunken party on the spot, without drinking a drop.'

'Go on!'

'Tis true! They say the smell off him was so intoxicating that the priest fell into the hole in the ground when they went to bury him.'

'Was it Father Buckley?'

'Don't interrupt me Niamh. The name of the priest doesn't matter. The important thing is that it was a priest. Now I don't know where I was.' Those flames of fire suddenly flicker in his eyes again.

A fear creeps over me. 'I'm sorry. They went to bury him…'

He relaxes and the fire in his eyes is snuffed out. 'Right.

They went to bury him, and the priest fell in the hole. They tried to haul the priest out. He was laughing so much that the people hauling him fell in too, and were laughing at the bottom of the grave for hours. In the end they had to throw buckets of cold water on top of them to sober 'em up. Then they all nearly drowned.'

It sounds like an exaggeration to me. 'Yerra, go on!'

'It's as true as the nose on your face.' Jim smiles and the corners of his mouth make these deep creases in his face. His hair tumbles forward, giving him an impish look, like a leprechaun, I think. I smile at my own thoughts. 'You're full of the Blarney,' I exclaim laughing.

'I'm just like me da, that's what!' he says. He lies on his back and stares at the ceiling. 'He was a good man… C'me here to me.'

He pulls me close with his strong right arm. My head lies comfortably in the nook of his armpit, near his almost hairless chest. We lie huddled together all night long.

Through the night I wake up in the middle of a dream. Niall is so real in my dream. He's smiling at me.

'Niall,' I'm calling his name when I wake up. I'm still lying on Jim's chest, so I try to move away by gently lifting his arm. Jim suddenly sits up, giving me a shocking fright.

'Who's Niall?' He shouts, shaking me by the shoulders.

'Nobody. It was just a dream.'

His voice rises with anger. 'Why did you call him?'

I start to tremble with fright. 'I don't know why!'

'Why are you so frightened? You're hiding something!'

'No I'm not!' I reply.

'Niamh, I know you well. You have to tell me who he is.' He suddenly drops his voice and says threateningly, 'or I'll kill you.'

'All right. If you must know.' My mouth feels dry. 'I… used to play with him when I was a child.'

'So where is he now?' he asks quietly.

I shrug my shoulders. 'He died!' I say quickly. At least that's true, I'm thinking.

He sits up and his form looks fearful in the moonlight. 'I can't remember a Niall around these parts...'

I feel very cold all over as I try to calm him down. 'You didn't live around here then ... I think it was a nick name anyway.'

There's silence for a moment. Jim gets out of bed and stands. I can see his silhouette in the light. 'You wouldn't lie to me, would you?'

I swallow before I speak. My breath is shallow. 'No,' I whisper.

He leans towards me. 'Niamh. I'm your husband. You can't lie to me.' He takes my wrists and pulls me up to him.

I know that he's too strong for me. 'I know that!' I reply.

He throws me onto the bed. He looks at me, and then suddenly falls on top of me. 'You're my woman!' He kisses me roughly, and then hits me in the face. 'Don't do the wrong thing by me, or else... Ah!' he says in a controlled voice. I curl up in a ball and hold my hands over my head. There's silence for a minute, then I feel a blast of cold wind as the van door opens. It creaks on its hinges. I breathe a sign of relief as Jim stomps out the door.

...

It's three days after that incident. Maeve comes over that afternoon with an apple tart she baked in her new gas oven.

'What do you think about that?'

'Maeve, it looks delicious. Can I have a bit?'

'You and Jim can have it all. Happy birthday! And we want to give you this.' She hands me something in a red wrapper with a gold bow.

'What did you get me?' I ask, hurriedly removing the wrapping.

'Don't tear the paper. You can use it again,' she reminds me.

I unwrap the gift. 'It's lovely. I haven't got one.'

'Paid made it himself,' she says happily.

'I'll go around and thank him later.' I stare at Maeve. 'Honestly, I forgot about my birthday.'

'Well I didn't. You're sixteen now, a real woman. But remember it's also Halloween!' She looks at me, smiling happily. 'Paid brought me this big bag of flour and a bag of crab apples and two pounds of sugar. I learned this great recipe and I wanted to try it out. Every tart was a success. Tell Jim to get an oven like mine, and then you can bake things for him. That'd put a smile on his face.'

'You've noticed then?'

'Noticed what?'

'Jim and me. We haven't been talking.'

'Well, now that you mention it, I have noticed Jim's not himself at the moment. What did you do now?' She sits down.

'Why do you think it's always me?'

'I know you Niamh. You're a born troublemaker. What happened?'

'We had a falling out. He heard me calling Niall in my sleep.'

'No wonder he's down and out! Niamh, that fellow is well and truly gone by now! Don't keep bringing up his name and you won't have trouble.'

'Maeve, I was asleep. I couldn't help it! I know Niall's dead.'

'Here you are, talking about him again.'

'I'm just telling you about my dream!'

'So, go on, what happened after that? After your dream?'

'Jim won't speak to me now. It's like being a nun in a convent.'

She sniggers. 'Well, you'll never be a nun! Only in Saint Joseph's Order - two heads on one pillow.'

'It's serious Maeve. Ah, I don't know what to do.'

'You're his wife aren't you?'

'I am! So, how does that help?'

'Come on Niamh. You know!'

'No. I don't know!'

'And you think Rhonan is thick!' She shakes her head in despair. 'Be nice to him. Give him love!'

'You mean sex!'

'Well, whatever vulgar name you want to call it. Matrimony is a sacred state! Just encourage him in your matrimonial duties!'

'So, what'll that do?'

'You'll see. Awast! You're sixteen - and you've been married a month now!'

'Maybe I can try.'

'It's your birthday. Give him the gift of yourself!' She places the tart on the small table and brushes flour from her skirt. 'I'm off now. Paid is coming home today, so I want to prepare myself for him.' She steps out the door.

'Thanks for the tart!'

She turns back. 'Awart! Sure that's what sisters are for. Promise me you'll put Niall out of your head and comb your hair before Jim comes home!'

'I promise.' I immediately search for my hairbrush, and drag it through my knotty hair. I run a sticky bright red, broken lipstick over my lips. I found it on the road one day. I stare into the lovely mirror that Maeve has just given me for my birthday. I press my lips together, and decide I look like a bit of a tart! Maybe Jim will like that! I rummage in my clothes box and find a purple coloured blouse, which someone gave me. I pull it over my head. It's loose, with gathers around the neckline. My skin looks so white. The neckline is quite low, so I can see the tops of my breasts. 'I hate it!' I mumble and pull it off, over my head. I stop as I hear the door open.

'Jim.' I quickly pull the top back on.

'You're all dressed up and wearing lipstick. What for? Are you off somewhere?'

I force a smile. 'No! I just wanted to look nice for you. It's my birthday.'

'Niamh, you're beautiful without lipstick. Come here to me.'

He pulls me into his arms and kisses me so hard my lips are stinging.

'I'm trying to be a good wife…'

He's quite for a moment, and then speaks. 'Every man is jealous of me. I'm so worried about someone taking you away from me.'

'Nobody will do that!' I say instantly, remembering that Niall is dead!

'I'd kill them if they did!' he replies emotionally. 'Let me give you something special for your birthday,' he says, lifting me in his arms and taking me into our tiny bedroom to give me his love.

The next day, Maeve comes running over. 'Jim looked happy this morning. He was whistling on his way down the road.'

'I know. We're pals arirt. Thanks for your good advice Maeve.'

'I told you it would work. Yerra, you'll be all right now!'

Chapter five

It's about three months since Jim and me were wedded and we haven't had a row for a month.

'You're not still in bed, you lazy lump,' Maeve says, peering behind the curtain separating our small bedroom from the rest of the van. 'I made lovely fresh soda bread! What's up with you now?'

'I feel terrible,' I say, pulling myself into a sitting position.

She comes closer. 'You do look a bit pasty. When did this come on?'

'I've been feeling sick on and off for months!' I pause before saying that I think it's because I'm sick with longing for Niall. 'But this morning I collapsed in a heap while making Jim breakfast. He carried me back to bed and left me here.' I suddenly cough. 'I've probably got consumption. It's a slow death they say.'

'It's not an infection from your sore leg, is it?' Maeve asks, pulling down the blanket and lifting my nightie. 'It still looks a bit red and swollen.'

'It feels all right.'

She pulls the blanket over me again. 'It's the low tops!'

she says sternly. 'You've probably caught a chill going around half naked.'

'How do you mean?'

'You know what I mean!' she says curtly.

My face feels red. 'I only wear them when Jim's coming home!'

'I hope so!' she retorts. 'Will I make you a cup of tea?' she offers in a kinder tone. 'You can have a bit of soda bread as well.'

'I'll try.'

She pulls the bedroom curtain over and moves to the kitchen table. I can hear her striking a match and lighting the primus stove. She pours water from a jug into the copper kettle and places it over the flame.

'Jim's asked Nell Doran to come and see what's up with me…' I call from the bedroom.

As if she heard me Nell's voice sounds in the doorway. 'The top of the morning to you!'

'Come in Nell,' Maeve says. 'I was just making a cup of tea. Would you like one?'

'I would begorrah! It's chilly today!'

She pulls the curtain on the bedroom over and stares at me lying on the bed. She walks back and forward in the tiny space, smacks her lips and mumbles something that sounds mysterious. She likes to think she has magical powers.

'I can see a tiny baby in the distance,' she says, with her eyes closed and her hands touching her forehead. She opens her eyes and stares at me, 'You're going to have a child, that's all.'

'I am?'

Then she turns to Maeve, who is now standing behind her, holding the copper teapot that Jim made me.

'I'll let this draw for five minutes.'

I'm sitting up, staring into the kitchen, happy. 'I'm going to have a babby Maeve!'

Maeve nearly drops the teapot. 'Glory be! I don't believe it!'

Nell speaks to Maeve, 'So, Maeve, have you been feeling all right?'

'I have. I'm feeling on top of the world.'

'You're going to have a child too!'

'Is that right? Are you sure now,' Maeve questions, taking a couple of cups off the dresser, and pouring the tea. 'Sugar and milk?'

'That's right. Two lumps, maybe three!' Nell replies, sitting down on a rickety wooden chair that Jim is going to fix.

'Would you like a piece of my freshly made soda bread Nell?'

'Begorrah I would, with jam. Can I have the teapot too!'

'Niamh, she wants the teapot.'

I get out of bed, drape the blanket around me and stand in the doorway. 'Jim made it for me.'

'Have you got money then?' Nell asks. 'Ain punt.'

'No, I haven't. Take the teapot!' I moan. Anything to keep the peace.

After she finishes her tea, Nell hurries off carrying my shiny teapot as if she won a great prize.

I sit on the rickety chair. 'What's he going to say Maeve?'

'He asked her to come. He can make another one!' Maeve stares out the door. 'She took the tea and all! And I didn't even get a cup myself.'

'Here, have mine,' I encourage Maeve. 'I don't want it now,' I say.

'What's wrong with it?'

'Nothing. I feel sick,' I say, pushing the cup and saucer towards her.

'Well, I wouldn't want to catch anything!'

'I'm going to have a babby Maeve, not the mumps!'

'I was married long before you, so I'm the one who should have a babby first,' she says, sipping the tea I gave her.

'But what if God gives me one first?'

'Well, you don't deserve it. I've never seen you saying the rosary. Paid and I say the rosary every night hoping for a child. You are a bit of a lazy lump too,' Maeve assures me. 'It just wouldn't be fair, that's all.' She sits on our wooden stool reflecting.

'So you don't think she's right?' I ask.

Maeve gets up and puts the cup in the little basin and drains the tea dregs out. 'Ax! I hope you're not going to have one before me, that's all.' She stares out the tiny window. I know she's going to ask something very personal. People here don't usually talk about personal things easily. 'When did you last have your granny?'

I feel my face turning red as I reply, 'Not since I was at the Connors.'

'Not a spot?' she inquires, turning towards me.

'No. I only got me granny once before that anyway, remember I told ye, just before your wedding, and then once before I got married…' I add. 'I didn't like having it anyway.'

'Niamh, you're a terrible egit when it comes to these sorts of things.'

'I am!' I reply. 'I remember now. Missus Connor told me it would come every month…but it hasn't…'

'It stops when you're going to have a babby. For nine months! You're so thick Niamh.'

She stares into the cup. 'I think I see a babby in here!' she exclaims. 'Look!' she holds the cup with tealeaves stuck to the sides. 'There, it looks like a child's hand.'

'Maybe that's the sign?' I say, thinking I might be having a child after all and that's why I've been so sick every day for months.

Maeve smiles brightly. 'It could be. I drank the tea, so it must be my child. Oh God I hope so! Me Granny's not due for another week. I'll know for sure then.'

I just stare at her. It was my cup of tea, so I don't know what to say. I try to look happy.

She gives me a more compassionate look. 'I hope you do have a child one day, but not before me!'

'I think Jim would love a child,' I say.

'It's Paid's dream, to be a daddy!' she replies brightly. 'Do you mind if I take this cup home and show it to Paid?'

'No, go on, take it!' I reply.

'I'll wash it after that,' she says. 'Now I'm off to scrub the draining board, and the floor.' She marches out the door of the van, humming to herself.

…

Before I see Jim Nell has spread the news that Maeve and me are having babies. Jim promptly goes off with the lads for a drink after work. He comes home in the early hours of the morning, singing at the top of his voice, 'Oh, Father dear, now do not fear, for your babby is nearly here…' and then he falls down on top of me and begins to snore. I shove him off me and he rolls over onto the floor with a bang. He sleeps soundly on the floor, until half-eleven the next day!

Since the news has gone around that I'm going to have a child, Jim has been staying away every evening, drinking. I wait up for him, to make sure he does come back home. I usually pretend to be sleeping. I'm getting a bit worried about him as he's been sleeping in the daytime and not going off to work regularly like he did before. He seems to be drinking through the day as well lately. I know that, because whenever I've gone over to Maeve's place for a while and then come back, I can smell the sour smell of alcohol in the place, and fried sausages. Jim always has fried sausages and black pudding fried in lard when he's had too much to drink. The smell is enough to turn my stomach.

Maeve is definitely having a child too, just like Nell said. The snow arrives, just after Christmas, and I'm not feeling sick any more, which makes me feel happier. Jim found an old kerosene heater on the dump and got his pal Kieran to fix it. It's nice and warm in the van now. The world outside the van is white and frozen, even the washing on the line that Jim set up for me freezes in half an hour after hanging it up. Jim finished with the council job and has been spending his time hammering bits of tin and copper. He's making a shiny copper teapot that is even nicer than the one Nell took. He is also making little cups and plates for the baby. At least it's keeping him occupied during the cold weather. Food is scarce, and we have used up all our tins of food long before spring comes. All we can afford to buy is an old frozen rabbit or a bit of mutton or tripe for dinner. Sometimes my da comes over with a bag of bread or a cake. He has a knack of finding food when times are hard. Jim isn't like that. He expects everything to suddenly appear as if by magic. I've been knitting with some wool and needles Maeve gave me. She showed me how to follow a pattern for a baby's dress and cardigan, so I'm working on that with this soft blue and pink wool. I've decided to put both colours together, so then it can be for a girl or a boy.

The first day of spring, March first, is finally here and I've finished knitting the baby's dress, cardigan, bootees and a bonnet, so I'm well pleased with myself. When I gaze out the half-frosted window the sun is finally reappearing from its wintry hibernation and melting the crisp snow. Small puddles of melted ice dot the land like saucers of water to give the birds a cool drink. Other melting ponds are turned into brown slush by human footprints. In other places fresh green tufts of grass are appearing; beautiful snowdrops, buttercups and cowslips are popping their heads up, as though they have been in a deep sleep, and now they are stretching upwards as they awake. The most delicate of flowers, the velvety violets push their way through the hard ground and suddenly spruce up the dull corners of the bush undergrowth, like beautiful royal jewels.

The lambs are arriving too. Yesterday I saw a couple hopping around on their four legs as though they had springs in them. My baby seems to know that spring is here and it's time to leap and jump for joy. Little angular shaped bulges suddenly appear and are gone again. I can hardly get around the van without bumping into things.

I can see Maeve coming along the track to the van.

'Come in Maeve.'

'It's hard to believe it's Spring,' she comments, taking

her shawl off and hanging it on a nail at the back of the door.

'It's a bit warmer,' I say, turning up the heater a bit.

'Turn that thing down a bit Niamh! What I meant was, Spring comes quickly when you're happy, expecting.'

'I suppose so,' I reply. 'Maeve, I finished these yesterday,' I say, proudly displaying my baby garments.

'Is that all?'

'I thought it was tucks,' I reply.

'You'd better get a move on. I've got ten times that much done already.'

'But Paid has been getting the wool for you,' I say lamely.

'That's no excuse. I said I'd give you as much as you want. You're like Lady Muck, hardly moving a finger.'

'I did me best Maeve,' I reply.

'Well, anyway, I came to tell you that Paid said there's work at the glass factory if Jim wants it.'

'He's gone off with Kieran,' I reply.

'If he's ready at six in the morning he can go with Paid.'

'I'll tell him.'

'Niamh, your job is to make breakfast for your husband, and get him ready. Can you do that tomorrow?'

'I'll try, although I have been sleeping in a bit lately.'

'I know. I've knocked on your door at ten o'clock and you've still been in bed. You'll have to get out of that lazy habit if Jim has to get up for work.'

'I'll try, but we don't have a clock, so it's hard Maeve.'

'Well, just for once, I'll come over at five and give you three knocks on the door.'

'Five? But it's freezing then, and dark.'

'That's when Paid and I get up every day. If we can do it, you can.'

For a whole month I have been getting Jim up at five in the morning. Maeve gave the knocks on the first morning, but after that I have been staying awake most of the night, waiting to see the little lamp going on in her van. It lights up at five every morning. I go back to bed after Jim and Paid leave around six.

…

April turns into beautiful May, followed by a dazzling June, and the onset of Summer. It's a year since Maeve got married and I ran off. On the breezy sunny Wednesday morning, the 4th June, nineteen hundred and sixty nine, after a few days of rain, at around eleven, Maeve turns up at the door, wearing her warm shawl and holding a copper bucket that Paid made. 'Are you up yet?'

'Of course I am,' I reply. I've only just got out of bed. I smother a yawn.

She comes inside. 'Do you want to pick mushrooms? There's loads down the fields, so Paid said.'

'Surely, I'd love to Maeve. I feel great these last few months. I'll just take a warm shawl with me.' I feel excited at the thought of getting out of the stuffy van.

'I can't wait to get a bit of exercise,' Maeve remarks as we step out of the van and stroll off with our empty buckets and our rubber boots. 'I've been feeling on top of the world. Ma says having a confinement suits me, and I think she's right!'

We head off in the bright sun, which gives a nice warm feeling on our faces.

'I can hardly believe we're both 'expecting' at the same time. I hope mine comes first.'

I catch my breath at the sudden pain across my bulge.

'Are you all right?'

'It's a cramp.'

'God, I haven't seen you standing for a month. Begorrah you're as fat as a pig that's ready for market,' she says, staring at my monstrous sized bulge, comparing it with hers.

'I know!' I reply.

Maeve stares at me. 'It's all that porridge you've been eating.'

'It's supposed to be good for me,' I reply.

'Not if you eat too much! I've seen you gobbling up a whole potful!'

'I think I've been making up for all those months when I could hardly eat at all. I feel so hungry in the mornings!' I say lamely.

'You still have to be careful. I only eat cornflakes now, with tinned fruit!' she says smugly, as she moves swiftly through the fresh dewy green grass. I try to keep up with her.

We soon run into a whole field of mushrooms. We start picking them by the stalks.

'Would you look at the size of them,' she says, holding one in the palm of her hand.

'It's like mushroom heaven,' I comment.

We spend the next three or four hours together, laughing and talking, and picking buckets of mushrooms. Whenever we feel tired or hungry we sit down and eat a few mushrooms and drink fresh water from a stream.

'There's nothing like the spring fresh water running in the west,' I say as the cool water dribbles down my chin. 'It's really sweet today.'

'Tis,' Maeve says, scooping up a handful of fresh water.

'Maybe we should bottle it and sell it?' I suggest.

'Now that's a grand idea. We could get Paid and Jim to blow bottles and we could fill them.'

We're laughing about everything. I am bulging so much I can hardly lean into the stream to get a drink.

'Oh, the cramps again.' I'm holding my breath.

'All this water is making me want to do a wee wee,' Maeve says, running off behind a bush a few yards away.

I can hear the faint rustling of Maeve as she relieves herself. That makes me feel the need to go too!

I head in the other direction by a few yards. It is then I notice that I am very wet. I dry myself off with one of Jim's big hankies.

Maeve and I decide to have a bit of a rest then. We're sitting with our backs against a rock and our faces towards the sun. After a while my cramps are coming again. I'm breathing heavily. Then I feel myself relaxing. Then I feel the cramps again. They seem to be coming every five minutes or so.

Maeve has her eyes shut. I close my eyes too, trying to ignore the pains. I open my eyes and then I see a most wondrous vision. I rub my eyes and stand up to take a good look. 'Maeve, I know that place!'

'Too well, I should think!' she mumbles, with her eyes still half-closed.

'You knew I lived there?'

'Where?' She's awake now! Her face is pink.

'The Connor's farm! Maeve, did you know where I was?'

'Of course I did!' she replies harshly. 'We all knew.'

'Did you tell me Da?'

'For God's sake Niamh, I had to tell Sean. We were out of our wits with worry. What would these people do with you if they found out you were a common tinceard? You know how these gentry feel about us?' She stands by me and places her hand on my shoulder.

'I was very happy there.'

'Because they didn't know who you were. If they knew they would have sent you back to where you belong. But surely you're happy now?'

'No!' I reply curtly.

'You don't know what's good for you. Here you are with a loving husband, a place to live and a bouncing baby on the way. You should be over the moon!'

'Maeve, I'm not over the moon as much as I was then.'

'You always want more. Greed should be your middle name. Well, there's no more!' she says, pulling me around to face her.

I push her away. She stumbles and nearly falls over.

'I'm sorry Maeve.'

She steadies herself and brushes her skirt. 'Are you trying to kill me now?' she asks curtly.

'No, but I do have a crow to pluck with you.'

'What?' She sits down.

I stay standing. 'Did he give you something?'

'Who, what?'

'Da. Did he give you something for snitching on me?'

'I told him the truth. I didn't snitch.'

'So, he did give you something. You and Paid?'

'We didn't take any of the drink from him. Paid doesn't drink any more.'

I sit in the grass beside her feet. 'So, he gave you all drink?'

'No. It was for the wedding. The lads were given some for bringing you back.'

She looks at her feet for a moment, thinking. 'All right, I'll tell you the truth. Sean had an offer.'

'What kind of offer?'

She plucks a piece of grass. 'If you married Jim Farrell, he could have a keg of poteen from Jim's uncle on the Aran Islands. He gave them a hundred pounds dowry for you. That was the night of our wedding. He was drunk. When you went missing it nearly broke Sean. He was devastated when he thought you were drowned. When I saw you at the Connors' he was so happy he did a jig on the spot!'

'So, he had to get me back to get the poteen!'

'They're very cunning, the Farrells. They wouldn't give him the drink unless he could guarantee the wedding was going ahead. He had to get you back.'

'Or he'd lose the money.'

'I don't know what would have happened because we found you and the wedding went ahead as planned.'

'So, if you didn't get poteen, what did you get?' I grab her shoulders, tightly.

She lifts her head. 'It was only money!'

'Money? How much?'

'Niamh, it doesn't matter now. We wanted to have you back with us…'

'How much?' I squeeze her shoulders.

Her face turns white. 'Fifty.'

'Shillings?'

'No, they're not shillings any more now, egit! It was fifty pounds.'

My rubber boots feel heavy as I move, so I pull them off and leave them with my bucket of mushrooms. I can move more quickly now. They only wanted the money and the drink. I can't see for the tears in my eyes. Maeve bought me with fifty pounds! Da never gave me even five shillings! I always had to beg for everything. My heart suddenly burns with fierce hatred for my father, and Maeve…

'Stop running away. I'm telling you stop!' Maeve screams at me.

I keep going until the pains in my stomach make me stop. I double up in agony. 'Niamh, come back,' I can hear Maeve's voice coming closer, shouting my name. Suddenly she's kneeling beside me, breathing heavily. 'Honest Niamh. I didn't really do it for the money.'

I stare at her. I can't speak.

'What's the matter?' She crouches down beside me.

Tears are running down my cheeks. 'My stomach hurts. It must be the mushrooms. Maeve, I feel so awful.'

'Lie down for a minute.'

I lie down and stare at the blue sky with wispy clouds scurrying towards the east. I close my eyes as pain sweeps over me. Everything is going quiet and blank.

I can hear Maeve's concerned tones. 'Try to get up now. You're just upset.'

The pain stops as suddenly as it started. I feel really calm. I sit up. 'I think they're gone.'

'Thank God,' Maeve says. 'Come on, we'd better get on home.'

I get up on my hands and knees, and then crumple into a ball, breathless. I look up at Maeve's worried expression.

'I know what it is. You're having the baby! But it's too soon! You're supposed to be due after me!'

'They've stopped again,' I say, relaxing again.

'You just lie here. We need boiling water. I'll go to the house! Maybe they'll help…'

'Please don't go...not now! Remember you said the country folk hate the tinceards? I don't want them to know where I came from.' The pains come back. 'Mother of God!' I'm grasping Maeve's arm.

'I'll not leave you then. Come on, I'll help you home.' Maeve tries to lift me under the arms and help me to get up.

'It's too late! I can feel it. It's coming. Oh God…' I gasp.

Maeve gently lowers me to the ground. She pulls my skirt up. 'I'll have a look. I helped deliver Sheamus, remember? I know what to do…. It's dark up there,' she says, pulling my skirt down again.

'Maeve…' I gasp again.

She looks again. 'I still can't see anything, except your navy drawers.'

The pains stop again. 'I'll help you get them off,' Maeve says, catching hold of the elasticised legs of my drawers and pulling them down. She kneels up. 'Mother of God, blood! You're bleeding! It's a sign!'

She lifts her own skirt and pulls her white half-slip off and places it under my bottom.

She looks at me. 'Jesus, Mary and Joseph…' she says, her voice trembling. 'Niamh, it's a baby!'

'A baby!' I exclaim, though what else could it be?

'It's nearly here. Bear down. Push, come on, one more,' she urges me.

I lean forward, and suddenly I hear a loud cry as the pushing stops. I gasp for air and look at Maeve.

Almost magically, she's holding a little black haired, pink coloured baby. Its arms are waving and it's crying boldly. Maeve gently wraps it in the white petticoat and takes it into her arms.

'A little girleen,' she says. 'She's perfect. Then she stares at me. 'So, it hasn't turned out the way we wanted. You had to have your baby first to spite me!'

'No Maeve.' I feel cramps again.

'Well, you're lucky to have me with you today. Here hold on to her, while I go and get a sharp stone to get rid of that

cord thing. Nell said you have to do that! I remember now!'
She's placing the warm baby across my body. I hold her with
one hand and prop myself up with the other. 'Hello there?'
I say. She's looking at me and twisting her mouth. 'You're
beautiful. Look at your lovely dark hair. You're a picture!'
I stare into her small pink face and another face comes to
mind. 'You remind me of… dearest Niall.'

'Niall?' Maeve suddenly says, looking up from her kneeling position between my legs. She has pulled my skirt just
over my knees, so I can't quite see her. She is busy cutting
the cord thing.

'You have to wait until it stops beating, so Nell says,' she
explains, chopping steadily. 'Then you clamp it. I'll use a
strip of this.' She tears a strip off the petticoat.

'Your good petticoat is ruined.'

'I've made another. Remember I'm a diligent person.'

'I'm glad you're with me Maeve.'

'Finished!' Maeve says, her face appearing above my
knees.

'Here, let me wrap her properly,' she states, taking the
baby from me and rearranging the white petticoat.

'You need something to lie on.' She pulls off her jumper,
folds it and puts that under my head.

She shivers in her thin blouse but her gaze is set on my
face. 'Now I understand.'

'What?' I ask.

'Niall's her father, isn't he? But you said you got your
granny before you were married…'

I nod my head. 'To Niall!'

'You lied to me. I thought it was your marriage to Jim.
That was a real marriage.'

'Yes Maeve, but what will Jim say if he finds out it's Niall's
child?'

'Well, I'd say you're in for trouble. She's not a bit like
him. And she's early by about a month!'

'Jim won't know that! Sure he doesn't even remember
which day is what! He got up to go to work one Sunday,
thinking it was Monday.'

'He'll find out.'

Suddenly I scream. Maeve turns back and kneels next to me. 'What's up now?'

'Pain…' I gasp.

She takes the baby from me as I lean forward with my head almost touching my knees, hardly able to breath.

'…Something's wrong.' I gasp the words out. 'I think my guts are coming out…'

She takes the little girl and places her on the grass. She lifts my blood soaked dress.

'Jesus, Mary and Joseph! I'll have to get a doctor…'

'Maeve, I'm a-dying.'

Suddenly her voice changes. 'Wait on a minute! Ala! It's another one!'

'Another baby?' I say in amazement.

'Ala! That's why you're so fat!'

'Maeve…'

'Push! One good push, don't stop.'

I've got such a shock I'm sitting up straight away, pushing the little flat blue slimy package out into the wide world. It comes out like a fish in a waterfall. Maeve catches the tiny living creature in her arms.

'Mother of God!' I stare at the flat blue-grey infant. I hardly notice my first baby screaming beside me.

'It's a boy.'

Maeve quickly removes something from his mouth and turns him over in her hands like turning a pancake. The little flat blue-grey bundle suddenly makes a loud cry, and miraculously becomes a round pink wiggling baby in an instant. The pair of babies are crying loudly now.

I smile at Maeve. She scowls back.

'I don't believe it. You've had a boy and girl on purpose. You had to be better than me.'

'No Maeve. I thought I was only having one, honestly.'

'What am I supposed to wrap him in. I've given my pet-ticoat.'

'Here, use my shawl.' I throw my warm shawl towards her. She grabs it and places it under the baby's tiny form.

'Maybe there's more?' I say as Maeve wraps the little baby boy.

'There's too many already, so stop raving Niamh! Just hold him while I cut the cord thing again.'

I gaze at the tiny pink bundle lying on my thigh. He looks like me with his pink face and hair so light he looks bald. He has little reddish coloured eyebrows! He cries loud and sharp.

I stare down at my babies. 'So, what do we do now?'

'You'd better feed them, egit!' She picks up the baby girl and places her on my right side.

I pull my jumper up and my little girl turns her head and makes cute shapes with her mouth. I don't have a brassier to fit anymore, so I just haven't been wearing anything these last few weeks. She sucks hungrily. 'Oh, that hurts,' I say as I feel pinpricks around my breast.

Maeve picks up the baby boy and places it on my left side. 'You'd better get used to it. Here comes alamax!'

'I lie back on Maeve's woollen jumper and try to relax. I can't believe I've suddenly got two babies, one on each breast, feeding hungrily. I wonder if the milk tastes like mushrooms. I stare up at the sky. Maeve's face appears in the picture, framed by the misty sky.

'You still have a big bulge down there.'

'Do you think there might be a third?'

'I think it's fat!'

'You're probably right. Remember all the porridge?' I say lightly.

After a short few minutes, Maeve looks restlessly towards the Connor's house.

'I still think I should go to that house and just ask for some clean water to analk in. Unless I go back to the stream. But it's a fair walk…I'm very tired.'

'Maeve,' I say quietly.

'What?'

'Would you do something really special for me?'

She replied instantly. 'I've given you my petticoat, what else can I do.'

'I have an idea. If I give this child to Missus Connor, she'll have a grand life. She's been praying for a child for years.'

'Well, you take the cake Niamh. You can just give your own child away like that?'

'I can, because it's the best thing for Kathleen. Jim won't see her, and he'll be happy with a boy who looks like me. He won't ask questions. I wanted a life for myself there, but I can't have that now. Kathleen can have a good life instead.'

'I never heard of such deception in all my life! But you have a good point there. At least Jim won't be suspicious. And I think one child is enough work for a lazy mother such as yourself.'

'That's right Maeve. If I have two babies I'll be asking you for help every day.'

'You're right. Missus Connor will probably make a better mother for her than yourself.'

'She will indeed Maeve. I know that!'

'I'll do it! But on one condition.'

'Yes Maeve.'

'If ever you tell anyone about this I'll tell Jim it was your idea, that you gave the child away.'

'That suits me fine. Can you take her now?'

'Give her to me.' She snatches the little bundle in her arms. 'She's not one of us anyway! What'll I say?'

'Leave her in the big fuel bucket at the back door. It'll have peat in it. Yell out her name… Kathleen, then make a run for it. Make sure she doesn't see you, or she'll know it's a Tinceard's child!'

'Kathleen?'

'Yes. That's her name. Please hurry Maeve, it's getting cool.'

Maeve gives me one last look and then races off like a greyhound, (a fat one).

I can hardly believe I've just given Kathleen away, but I believe it's for the best. I'm staring at my little baby boy, 'One day I'll tell you about your lovely sister.' I watch the horizon for Maeve, counting every minute, willing her success! Suddenly she's coming thought the high grass over the hill, just as the sun starts to dip its rays beyond it. 'Thank God!'

She pants for air as she flops down in the grass. 'Mother of God that was no joke. I'm exhausted now. Someone was coming as I ran off. I don't think they saw me.'

'Maeve, you've done really well. A thousand thanks Maeve.' I pause and stare at my little boy. 'He's getting cold.'

'I'm hot!' she replies. 'Here, have this,' she places her shawl around my shoulders. 'I'll go and get the lads.' She heads off again. 'I'll be back in the twinkling of an eye.'

'Thanks!' I follow her with my eyes as she disappears in the other direction now. Then I look towards the Connors' house and find myself praying that they'll find Kathleen. What would happen if they didn't find her until morning? No, I assure myself as I notice a whiff of smoke spiralling upwards from their chimney. They'll be bringing in extra peat now. In my mind I can see the lovely sitting room with the warm fire burning and the room all neat and tidy, with the soft carpet on the floor. Mister and Missus Connor would be sitting down now, wondering how God sent them this beautiful girl, delighting in having their very own baby at last!

…

It seems like a long time passes before I hear voices coming over the hills. I see a figure hurrying towards me.

'Niamh!' he calls.

'Jim!' I call back as loudly as possible.

He sees me and runs towards me.

'Our son,' I say to him as he nears me.

'You shouldn't be going walking so far.' His face is bright with happiness, even thought he is scolding me. He kneels on the grass beside us and places his large finger into the little boy's hand, which grasps his finger tightly. 'James, our little James, after me da,' he adds.

Maeve comes running from behind Jim. Behind her is Nell, carrying a bucket of water and some towels.

Jim puts his arms around us both for a moment. Then he holds the baby as Nell and Maeve try to clean me up as discretely as possible. Nell's eyes grow large as she notices the bloody mess on the ground. 'Such a lot of blood.' she exclaims.

Maeve looks at me and then at Nell. 'Tis!' Maeve agrees and then tries to divert her attention from the messy scene. 'Nell, do you know that lovely brass vase you like. The one near the window of the van?'

'I do. What of it?'

'You can have it, if we get Niamh cleaned up quickly, before nightfall.'

Nell's eyes bulge with delight. 'Right so!' Nell briskly wipes my legs and places a towel around my bottom under my skirt. She is very discrete and suddenly speeds up her actions.

'I knew it was a lad?' Nell exclaims happily.

'You're always right' Maeve remarks, glancing at me.

'And you're a really great nurse,' I add.

'Yerra, go on now. I'm just doing what any woman would do,' she replies humbly. Her face beams with pleasure.

'I'll take James,' Maeve says, lifting the child from my arms, and hugging him tightly.

'I'll carry you Niamh,' Jim says, gently lifting me into his arms.

I feel as though I'm as light as a feather. For a moment my head rests on his shoulder. I wish I could be more open with him, but I can't share the truth about Niall's children, or he'd surely get so wild he'd throw James and me in the river. This time there's no Niall to rescue us! I keep my eyes closed as he marches through the high grass. He carries me all the way back to the camp. Maeve follows close behind with little James in her arms, crooning away to him. Nell follows behind her, with the bucket and towels over her arms, singing happily, 'I can cook and I can sew. I can keep a house right tidy…'

…

When we arrive at the campsite Maeve and Jim boil up some hot water on the stove, to make a nice hot bath for James and me. Soon I am sitting in our copper bath, made by Jim. Maeve bathes James in a large copper pot, which is just the right size for his tiny wiggling body. She finds some clean things to put on his fine silken skin, a muslin nappy and a flannelette nightie with a little blue ribbon at the neck. She puts some little socks on his red feet.

'It's a good thing that I had some spare clothes Niamh. You ought to be ashamed of yourself, not being prepared for this.'

'I did try Maeve,' I reply.

'I don't know what you'd do without people to help you. You're a hopeless case.'

'I'm sorry if I am a hopeless case Maeve, but isn't he a lovely baby,' I say, gazing at my beautiful son.

'He's a fine fellow,' she agrees.

'Maeve, you look exhausted, you should have a rest now,' I say, noticing the dark circles under her eyes.

'You're right! I'm very tired now, so I think I'll be off.' She hurries out the door. 'And we'll have to go looking for your boots and bucket in the morning, before some codger nicks them. The mushrooms in the bucket will be rotten by then.'

'I'm sorry about that Maeve.'

A few minutes later there's a knock on the door. It's Nell.

'I made a nice pot of tea.' She's clutching the teapot she demanded when she announced that I was expecting. She beams with happiness as she pours me a cup of strong tea and puts four lumps of sugar into it.

'Thanks Nell,' I say, sipping the sweet golden drop.

She makes sure she doesn't forget to take the teapot back with her when she leaves.

…

James is three months old now. Maeve comes over to see James and me, just before lunch one day.

She's moaning. 'I've been awake half the night!' She

holds her back. 'I've got pains all over, in me back, and terrible stomach cramps for the past six hours.'

'Have you been eating too many blackberries?'

'Yerra no! I think the baby's arriving, egit!'

'Oh Maeve, that's wonderful! What can I do, pick mushrooms, boil the kettle?'

Maeve laughs. 'At least I'm ready, not like someone I know. I'd love a cup of tea.'

'I'll put the kettle on,' I say, reaching for the jug of water and pouring some into the kettle. I strike a match and touch its sizzling flame to the methylated spirits in the primus stove. Instantly the bright blue flame leaps around the element. I place the copper kettle on top.

Maeve sits on the chair that Jim has fixed. 'I'm hoping for a little girl. That's what Paid wants anyway.'

'What if it's a boy?'

'I'd rather have a girl, seeing you were the first to have a boy. That way we can both have a first!'

'But I had a girl…'

'Yerra, stop that now. I don't want to hear it! So, how are you and Jim getting along?'

'All right… since James arrived. He's a great little lad, always sleeping his head off.'

'You're very lucky to have such a wonderful baby.' She suddenly gasps for breath, bends over and holds her stomach for a few minutes. 'I'd better call Nell,' Maeve says, as she stands up. 'The baby's due the first week in September, which is this week!'

'You're such a clever person Maeve, working all that out.'

'I know! I was always good at counting!' She smiles smugly. 'And organizing things. I've even made Paid's tea for today, a few extra apple tarts and a blackberry tart yesterday!'

She suddenly holds her breath again. 'I'm off then.'

'I'll come with you,' I say. 'I'll call Nora and ask her to keep an eye on James.'

Moiré arrives four hours later, on Monday the 1st September. Maeve skilfully delivers a perfect little girl, around six pounds weight, helped by Nell, Mary, and Maeve's mother, Maura, who came back from praying at the chapel in the nick of time to see the birth.

'Do you hear that?' Maura asks as she gazes at her grandchild.

'What Mam?' Maeve asks.

'The bell is ringing. We should say the Angelus!' She suddenly bursts into rapid prayer for a few moments.

'God must want you to call her Mary,' Maura says.

'You mean because the Angelus reminds us about Mary's visit from the angel, when Jesus was conceived?'

'That's right. I think it's a grand name for our very first granddaughter!'

'It is Mam!' Maeve agrees, casting a glance at me that says, '*Don't ever mention your daughter!*'

Paid and I wanted to call her Moiré.'

'Would you believe that now! Sure that's the Gaelic for Mary. That's my name in Gaelic too,' Maura says happily. 'She is the most beautiful child I have ever laid eyes on,' she adds.

'She is a very beautiful child, your granddaughter! We thought Ellen would be a good middle name, after Nell!' Maeve replies.

'That's a grand name altogether,' Nell says, picking up the bucket with soiled lined and taking it outside.

'Sure, here's Paid now,' Maura says, meeting Paid outside on his way home from work.

'Paid, you're the father of a lovely little girleen, our first granddaughter!' Maura says. Congratulations! I'm back to the chapel to offer a few prayers to God.'

Chapter six

Winter comes suddenly in October, with snow, sleet and rain arriving together on my birthday, the 31st. After that I hardly go out at all because of the pelting rain and cold wind. I try to stay in the van with James, so that he doesn't catch a cold. I do take him to Mass at Christmas and show him the little stable with Jesus and Mary, Joseph and shepherd statues there, with some animals. I'm taking a bit of the straw to keep. It's supposed to bring good luck. The Saint Vincent de Paul people have come around, bringing gifts for all the children. James loves his little ball and bag of sweets. They also give each family a box of lovely food. We have a lovely dinner together, the whole lot of us, with roast turkey, ham, Christmas pudding and even custard. Me da and Jim and Kieran manage to get a bottle of poteen and the three of them are drunk by the afternoon. After the Christmas celebrations I'm feeling sick in the mornings. I am expecting Jim's child, that's a certainty!

Two months later Jim comes home late. James is sleeping and I have been dozing, waiting for him.

'I want you Niamh,' he says, pulling me towards him.

'Not now Jim. I'm sick.'

'I need you Niamh. Now!'

'No, Jim, you're drunk!'

'You're my wife, damn you!' He violently tries to force me to have sex with him, but in the end he collapses in a heap on top of me. I climb out from under him and sleep in the chair the rest of the night.

The next morning I feel sick again. I get up and eat a piece of dry bread. That helps. I feed James.

Jim is sleeping his head off. 'Get up. Aren't you going to work today?'

'Go away!' He rolls over and closes his eyes.

Maeve comes over a few minutes later with some fresh bread. 'Moiré is sleeping, so I thought you could use this!'

'Can I come over to your place,' I whisper. 'Jim's not well.'

'As long as you're very quiet, come on!'

We walk to her and Paid's van. 'We're sorry to hear about Jim,' she says kindly.

'He's just had too much to drink. He'll be at work to-morrow,' I explain.

She turns her head sharply towards me as we enter her van. 'So, he hasn't told ye then?' she asks.

'What?'

'He got the sack!'

'No, he hasn't said a word about that. Do you know why Maeve?' I ask.

'He was drunk on the job, so Paid said!'

'No wonder he's been in a raging mood again.'

'So, what have you done to him now Niamh?'

'I've done nothing!'

'As usual, you lazy faggot! You've got to fight Niamh.'

'I did. I fought him last night. He gave up in the end.'

'No. You egit! Fight to keep him! You're going to lose him, that's on the cards!'

'What can I do?' I ask helplessly.

'I told you before. Give him lots of love!'

'I'm expecting again, and I've been sick.'

'How come you're always the one who gets sick?'

'I can't help it!'

'Well, I think it's all in your mind.'

'You're probably right!'

'Try to think of other things, then you'll forget about being sick,' Maeve suggests.

I'm feeling better already. 'I'm going to give it a try.'

'That's better!' Maeve says, happily. 'I'll cut you a big slice of bread and jam Niamh!'

'Thanks Maeve. I'm going to enjoy it too!' I say, accepting Maeve's offer.

A couple of minutes later I'm biting into a neatly cut slice of bread and jam. 'Lovely!'

'Do you want a piece of fresh bread and strawberry jam, James,' Maeve asks James, who's wiggling on my knees.

James' eyes light up as she breaks off a piece of bread and piles jam on top.

'Maeve,' I say hurriedly, 'can you hold on to James, I'm going to be sick.'

I rush outside and throw up all over the grass.

…

Jim has been working at home for the past two months. He's been making copper pots and vases and selling them to the shops. People have been raving over them, calling them pieces of artwork. He's making enough to keep us fed.

One morning, early in April, Maeve comes over, carrying Moiré who's seven months old now. 'The top of the morning to you!'

'Come on in! Too late, you're in!' I say jokingly as she steps inside, holding her latest food contribution, hot cross buns.

'They smell lovely.'

'Put the kettle on and have one. You look like you could do with it because you're so pale. You should do a bit more exercise and get the roses back in your face!'

'I must do that Maeve. I feel grand really. The buns look delicious.'

A few minutes later we sit down to hot tea and sticky hot cross buns. James crawls over and pulls himself up by my knees. He has his hand out. 'Ma, me!'

'Here,' I pull off a small piece and hand it to him.

'Niamh, I was passing by St. Vincent de Paul's shop and I saw this outfit. I thought it would suit James.'

She produces a bright navy and white sailor top with a navy pants from her crocheted bag.

'It's lovely. You are so kind Maeve.'

'And a pair of shoes and socks to go with it,' she says, holding up a red shiny pair of shoes and white socks.

'They're gorgeous. Thank you Maeve. Can I give you something for them?'

'Not at all! I know you've been struggling to make ends meet. I thought he needed something new for the party,' she says.

'What party?'

'Seamus' first birthday party. Mary has invited him.'

'Is he one already?'

'He is. Today.'

'So when is the party?' I ask.

'In a couple of hours.'

'I'd better get him ready, and myself.'

'You're not invited Niamh.'

'I'm not?'

'Only James, and Moiré,' she says. 'She likes James. *He's just like his father*, she says to me the other day.'

'But he's like me.'

'Well, she doesn't know Jim's not his father, so I just went along with it.'

'So, are you going to the party?'

'I am! She is very particular who she invites into her place,' Maeve replies.

'Why do you think she didn't tell me herself?' I quiz Maeve.

'If you must know…and don't repeat this to anyone. I heard a few of the women saying you were stuck up since you came back.'

'I'm not stuck up. I just don't trust this lot any more. If they found out about Niall and me, they might take it out on the Connors, or Kathleen!'

'Sure you're full of wild ideas. If I were you I'd let the grass grow again, so try and be a bit civil, for our family's sake!'

I just stare at Maeve. 'I'll think about it.'

'Don't just think about it. Do something Niamh,' Maeve suggests. 'Well, I'll take James and I'll be off.'

'Come here James.' James creeps over to us, his face sticky and dirty.

'He's filthy. Give his face a wipe and comb his hair Niamh, before you put those nice clothes on. I'll go and change Moiré's shoes. I think these white shoes are a bit small,' Maeve instructs me as she hurries out the door. Fifteen minutes later she returns with Moiré, who's wearing a bright pink ribbon in her hair and a clean pink baby doll dress, matched with pink socks and tiny black patent shoes. Her face is polished to a fine shine.

'She looks so…clean!' I comment.

'Cleanliness is next to Godliness, you should learn that Niamh,' Maeve says, taking James in her arms.

'Maeve, I'll help with James.' I put him into the stroller Jim found.

'Don't use that ugly thing. I'll put them in the double stroller Paid bought me. I think he was hoping we might have another one!' She laughs. 'God willing!'

'So, are you walking all the way to Mary's place?' I ask, wondering how far away it might be.

'A-no. It's too far. Sure she's in a house now. Going up in the world, you might say.'

'So, how are you getting there?'

'Freda is picking us up. She has a car now!' Maeve informs me.

'Who's Freda?' I ask.

'A friend of Mary's! You wouldn't know her. We met through the craft club. Well, she'll be here in any tick of the clock!'

She walks towards the edge of the roadway. I walk with her. 'You go on back Niamh.'

'What's wrong with me?'

'Your hair is dirty and your dress is ripped,' Maeve shudders and shakes her head. 'You look like a tramp.'

'I'll go back then. Bye James. Bye Moiré,' I say, waving as I hurry towards the van, holding the ripped part of my dress, feeling ashamed. I watch from the window as a black car pulls up and Freda helps Maeve with the children. A tear winds its way down my cheek at the same time as the car winds down the road, turning into a small black speck. I take my shawl and put my brogues on. I've decided I'm going on a bit of a walk.

I hurry through the fields, tracing the grassy track to Connor's house. I sit in the long grass behind a blackberry bush and watch the house. Happy memories come flooding back to me, Niall, Finn McCool, Missus Connor, Tom Connor, Toby the dog, Ginger the cat. I sit and bask in the memories of those heavenly days, reliving them. Then my heart gives a big lurch. 'Kathleen!' I stand up to get a better look. I see Missus Connor carrying Kathleen in her arms and chatting to her, then kissing her face. They are so happy together that I feel like crying. They disappear into the rose garden. After a few moments I head off down the track, skipping and humming all the way home. I close the door of the van and lean against it. Thank God Maeve is not back yet! Then I hear someone outside. I quickly pull off my shawl and my brogues, as I don't want her to know what I've been doing. The door opens. I look up from unlacing my shoes. 'Jim?'

'So, what have you been up to?' He closes the door and stares at me.

'Nothing.'

'Ah-so, your face looks flushed. Where were you?'

'I went for a walk.'

'Where's James then?'

'He's gone to a party with Moiré, Seamus' birthday…'

'Why don't you look after your son?'

'Maeve's looking after him. I wasn't invited!'

He throws his head back and laughs sharply. 'Ah! That's a good one!'

'Well it's true. They don't like me!'

'Why don't they like you?'

'I don't know!'

He sits down. 'I know. They're afraid!' he says decisively.

'What are they afraid of?'

'They're probably feared you'll take their men away!'

'Don't be an egit Jim!' I exclaim, genuinely serious.

'Don't call me an egit. You're the stupid one, lying to me.' He takes hold of me by the wrists.

'I'm not lying Jim. And why are you home so early.' I struggle to release myself from his grasp.

He tightens his grip. 'I told you on our wedding day, don't ever question me about my private business.'

'You're hurting me.'

'Sorry.' He lets go.

I rub my wrists. 'Do you want your dinner now?'

'No. I'm off!'

He strides through the door. My heart is thumping so fast I slump into the wooden chair. The room is swaying back and forth. The next thing I know Maeve and James are opening the van door.

'Been sleeping your head off as usual? Well, we had a great time, didn't we James? He needs a nappy change, so I'll leave that with you.' She shoves James into my arms.

'Thanks Maeve.'

That night Jim's voice interrupts my slumber. 'Niamh, I have to talk to you.'

I can smell the stale smell of the drink on his breath.

I can see his frame in the dim light rocking backward and forward above me. 'What's his name?'

He knows I'm awake! My mouth feels dry. 'Whose name?' I whisper.

'You're seeing someone. I know it!' Suddenly his muscular body lands right on top of me. He's too drunk to move. I wriggle from under him, take James in a blanket, still asleep, and head out the door. I'm shaking all over. I bang on Maeve's door. 'It's me,' I call out.

The door opens 'Yerra, what's going on?'

'Can I come in?'

'You're shivering. Come on then,' she says, drawing me inside.

'Thanks Maeve.' I lay James on the sofa and sit next to him.

'I hope you're not stopping long. I've had a bad night with Moiré.'

'Is she sick?' I ask.

'She's just teething. We've had to take her into our bed.' She whispers, 'Try and be quiet, Paid's bunched.' Moiré's whimper rises behind the curtain. Maeve hurries inside and returns a few moments with Moiré in her arms. Moiré is sucking her thumb.

'Don't suck your thumb. Alamax.' Maeve picks up a bottle of milk from a pot of warm water and squeezes a bit on her wrist, then shoves it in Moiré's mouth. Moiré sucks the bottle, staring at me with big blue eyes.

Maeve sits down beside me.' Now, tell me what's wrong?'

'Jim thinks I have another man...' I blurt out.

She pulls her hand away and stares at me. 'And have you?'

'Yerra... no, of course not!'

'Well, you have nothing to worry about then, if you're telling the truth. I just made myself a cup of tea, would you like one?'

'I would Maeve, please. That'd be grand.'

'Here, take her.' She passes Moiré onto my lap, takes a cup from her shelf and pours out the hot black tea. 'There's no alamax left, Moiré's drank the last of it, so you'll have to drink it black.'

'I don't mind!'

'Paid bought me a lovely Madeira cake on his way home from work. Would you like a piece?'

'Yes please.'

'Ma…' Moiré reaches over for cake.

'No. You have your alamax!'

Moiré starts to cry.

'Here, come here. Back to bed then,' she scolds, rocking Moiré and heading inside the curtained doorway. All is quiet. Maeve reappears a few minutes later.

I gaze in admiration at my sister. 'How do you do that?'

'You have to be firm with them at this age!' She looks at James sleeping peacefully on the sofa with his head on my lap. 'You're lucky he's an easy child.'

'I am.'

Maeve proudly cuts a piece of fine Madeira for me and places it on a saucer. My mouth is watering as I watch her.

'Thanks Maeve. I must be hungry.'

'You were always the greedy one!' She smiles wryly.

'Maybe I can have a small piece myself. I don't want to overdo it!' She cuts herself a piece and we enjoy our tea and cake together.

She looks at the clock on the dresser, ticking loudly. 'You realize it's nearly half one?'

'Is it? I'm sorry for disturbing you. I was just afraid…'

'Afraid of what? The boogie man?' She laughs softly.

'Jim!'

'Jim?' she exclaims, shaking her head. 'I'm ashamed to call you my sister. He's your husband, for God's sake. Just talk to him. It works!'

'But he's drunk!'

'When he's sober! Your place is with your husband.'

'You're right Maeve.'

'Well, what are you waiting for? Go on back, kiss and make up!' she urges, yawning.

'Right, I'll go.' I rise, reluctantly.

'I don't know why you had to disturb James too.'

'I don't know why…' I reply.

'I'll bid you goodnight then,' Maeve says, opening the van door as I take James in my arms. 'Hurry up now, before James gets too cold.'

I creep back into into our van and step over Jim, who's lying on the floor. I put James in his little cot and throw a coat over Jim. Then I climb into bed, exhausted. The next thing I know it's about ten in the morning. Jim is standing next to the bed. 'Is James my son?' he asks fiercely.

'Keep your voice down Jim. You'll wake James.'

'So, is he?'

'What do you mean?'

He sits on the side of the bed and leans over me. The fumes from his breath are so toxic, I swear if I lit a match we'd all blow to kingdom come. 'I heard that James is not my son!'

'You heard wrong!'

'Then why are they saying…?' he looks me in the eyes. 'I need you Niamh,' he says, rubbing my shoulders, kissing my face, then my lips.

'Not now Jim. We'll wake James…'

'You're my wife. I want you now!' Jim says vehemently. I hear a tearing sound as he pulls my nightie from my shoulders, scratching my arms. 'Prove you are mine,' he says, crawling under the sheets.

James cries. 'James…' I say.

Jim sits up and hits me in the face. 'James comes before me. Why is that Niamh?'

'I'm his mother. Twas yourself told me to look after my son…' I try to get past Jim. He pulls me back by the arm, throwing me back onto the bed.

'You're a whore, like your mother!'

'Don't bring my mother into this Jim,' I retort quickly. 'Someone's been lying to you Jim…about me and my mother!'

Jim's stands up. He pulls his pants on. His face is white with rage; his black eyes are bulging out of their sockets. 'Kieran wouldn't lie to me. Look at you, lying there, wanting him! You're a whore!' Jim is raising his foot. I roll away from the blow of his foot landing on my stomach. His foot collides with my left side. I double up trying to catch my breath.

'Don't Jim!' I cry out as he raises his hand to hit me again.

'Bitch! Bastard!' he mutters as he stumbles out the door.

After a few minutes I catch my breath. I pull on my cardigan, take James from his cot and stagger to Maeve's place.

'Maeve…' I call through the open door.

'Not you again! What's up?'

'Take James,' I whisper. I can see her reaching out as I collapse in the doorway.

The next voice I hear is Maeve's. 'Get up Niamh!'

She helps me up and I lie on the sofa. 'You're a disgrace! Your nightie is all ripped, and James needs changing,' she says, placing him in Moiré's feeding chair.

'I know. I'll go back in a minute.' I gasp with pain.

I must look bad because Maeve immediately leaves James and turns to me. 'Niamh, what's wrong? You look terrible.'

'The baby…I gasp for breath again.'

'We'd better get Nell,' Maeve suggests.

Ten minutes later Nell comes hurrying through the door. She takes one look at me and says, 'Death. I see death.'

'Death?' Maeve repeats.

'The baby's gone! Slean leat!' Nell says, waddling back out the door.

'She's drunk!' Maeve looks at me, a worried frown crowning her brow. 'I'll get one of the lads to run for the doctor.'

She steps out the door and a few minutes later she returns, with Nora on her heels. 'Diarmud's gone running down the hill.'

Nora looks at me with pity. 'Will I take Moiré and James for a walk?'

'Do that Nora,' Maeve says.

'She's a grand girl, our Nora!' She turns to Nora. 'Use the stroller, it's outside near the window.'

'I will,' she says. 'Come on, let's go for walkies!' She picks Moiré up and takes James by the hand, then lifts him down the step.

Nora turns back from outside the door. 'Will I change James?'

'Do that Nora! You'll make a grand mother, not like some people!' Maeve states, then frowns at me.

'Thanks Nora,' I call out. 'Jim's not there, so just go on inside. There are clean nappies in the room behind the curtain, on the left side…'

An hour later Maeve comes running in. 'It's the young fellow. The good looking one…'

Just then a long thin figure fills the van doorway. 'Hello. You're Niamh?' He holds his hand forward and I touch it. He shakes my hand.

'I'm Doctor Hugh Healy. Let's check baby, shall we?'

I nod my head. He puts his stethoscope on my tummy, 'Mmm. Mmm.' He then gets up. His head is touching the ceiling, so he asks Maeve to go outside with him.

A few minutes later he returns bending over as he moves in the small space. 'I'll have to put you in the hospital immediately. You're a very sick young woman.'

'The baby? Is she all right Doctor?'

'She?' He grins. 'You know more than I do Mam. I'd like to talk to your husband.'

'He's not here,' I say.

'What's wrong Doctor,' Maeve asks.

He lowers his voice. 'There could be a haematoma in the placenta, or incision in the sac.'

Maeve's eyes enlarge. 'Oh. Is that bad?' she asks.

'Very bad I'm afraid.'

He turns to me. 'I want to see your husband as soon as

possible. He needs to pay the fees. In the meantime I'll get you up to the hospital and they can give you a curette.'

'A priest?' I say.

Doctor Healy throws back his head and laughs. 'Not a curate. A curette!'

Maeve digs me in the shoulders. 'Don't show your ignorance!'

'I'll give you something to calm you down.' The doctor opens his bag, extracting a long thin object.

'It's a needle!'

'It is a needle all right. Steady now. You won't feel a thing.' He gives me a jab in the thigh.

'Oh' I cry as I feel a small prick. I'm feeling very drowsy immediately afterwards. I don't remember any more until I wake up to the pungent odour of disinfectant. I realize I'm in a hospital. Maeve is standing next to the bed. She looks like she's got a double.

'You're back?' she says, smiling.

I attempt to sit up but fail. I flop onto the pillow. 'What happened?'

'They got rid of it!'

'Rid of it?'

'It! We nearly lost you as well!'

'You mean the baby is gone?'

'Niamh, that's why you came here. It could have poisoned you.'

'But where is she?'

'The nurse?' Maeve asks.

'No, I don't care about the nurse. Where's my baby!'

'She was dead, like Nell said. She's in Limbo now.'

'What about her wake and funeral?'

'You're too late! They've buried her already.'

'Where?'

She stares angrily at me. 'How in God's name do I know? The best thing you can do is offer up a Mass for her, and say a few "Hail Marys".'

'I want my baby,' I suddenly scream out.

'Whist now! Stop behaving like a baby!' Maeve scolds me. 'Don't disgrace us,' she warns. 'I have to go home now. D'you know Abe McGarry?'

'I've heard of him.'

'He's Paid's boss. He's picking me up in his car in a few minutes. I don't want him to come up here and see you in this state.'

'I'm sorry!' I sniff. 'I just feel upset.'

'Here! Keep this.' Maeve hands me a clean handker-chief.

'Is James all right?' I ask, holding back my tears, wiping my eyes.

'He's grand.'

'What about Jim?'

She moves back a step. 'I've got to run like Billyo now. I'll be back tomorrow, I promise!'

Paid's boss brings the car to pick me up on the Friday. After we get to the campsite, Maeve and Paid insist that I stay with them a while.

'Sit down Niamh. Maeve, can you make her tri a gater?' Paid asks his wife.

'I've just made a pot of tea!'

'Sure that's lovely Maeve. She's a grand wife is Maeve,' Paid says, smiling at her. 'I'll leave you to it then,' Paid says, hurrying out the door to talk with his boss.

I watch as Maeve pours the tea. 'I'm going to take your advice Maeve.'

She glances up from pouring the milk into the tea. 'My advice? What do you mean?'

'I'm going to talk to Jim, tell him everything…'

Maeve shakes her head. 'I think your talking is too late! Now drink your tea,' she orders.

…

It's six months since I came home from hospital and Jim has not been seen around here. I've had to resort to my old trade again, the one my daddy taught me. I've been hammering out flowers, and making spoons from tin, and if I can get it, copper, and trying to sell these in the village.

Sometimes I just sit near a bridge and people drop a coin in my tin pot. Other days I travel around the area, going from door to door, begging. I'm not on me own, there are others begging, so it's getting a bit competitive around here. One evening in the middle of October, I've just come home with James, when Maeve comes over carrying Moiré and a loaf of bread.

'God bless you Maeve,' I say. 'I didn't get a thing all day, so we've got nothing to eat. How did you know?' I ask.

'Begorrah I didn't.' She smiles wryly. 'I always fancied myself as being psychic?' She suddenly laughs. 'Yerra, I'm only joking! Paid was given a whole bag of bread today. I also brought you a few tea bags, and a drop of fresh alamax.'

I take the loaf of bread and milk from her gratefully. 'Maeve, that's very kind of you. Don't stay a-standing, come in.'

'Well, I'll only stay five minutes.' She sits down on the stool.

'It's been six months since Jim drowned Maeve!' I say after a few minutes silence while I break off a piece of bread for James, and pour him a cup of milk.

'Why talk about it now?'

'I just wonder if you've heard anything?'

'I have heard some say he didn't drown at all, but found a boat and went to one of the islands.'

'So, why would he do that?'

'Sure if anyone knows you must!'

'No, I don't haven't a clue why he'd do that!'

'Never mind! Well, whether he's a-dead or alive, I feel he's happier now, far away from all those upsets and things.'

'You mean with myself?'

'You know yourself what went on. But from what I know, I don't blame him.'

'Blame him for what?'

'Running off!'

'He knew I was expecting…'

'If it was his child?' Maeve says curtly.

'It was so!'

'We don't know what goes on behind closed doors, do we?'

'I don't know what you're getting at Maeve?'

'Well, you were always a bit sly!'

'Sly?'

'Is that because I never told him about Niall?'

'Begorrah, it wasn't only your cavorting with Niall that worried us!'

'Cavorting? We were married…'

'If that's what you call it! Did you know that Jim used to come over to our place and ask where you were.'

'I went out for a walks, to catch the air…'

'Catch a man would be more like it!'

'No! I've been going to see Kathleen.'

'Well now, and why are you doing that?'

'I want to see how she is.'

'Niamh, you left her in a better place, you said so yourself. Why go stirring up trouble again?'

'I should never have left her even with Missus Connor I know that now. But I had to see her again.'

'And again…*Laisk my dheel*…!' Frustrated, she stands up.

I look at her angry face. 'Don't say that Maeve…What can I do?'

'Settle down and become a family. Rhonan is still waiting for you, and he gets on well with James.'

'Rhonan?'

'Rhonan is a free spirited man. He never wants to settle down in one place, just like yourself. He'd make a great father for James. Then you'll have someone to talk to, a husband! Someone to wander off with…'

'A- Maeve, I don't even like Rhonan! I'd rather die that marry him!'

'You're too good for him then? Lady Muck! You get on my gall! Just keep your hands off my Paid!'

'Maeve, that's a horrible thing to say,' I shout at her.

'Don't shout in front of children. I'm going home,' she says, picking Moiré up off the floor. 'Look at the state of her now. Her clean frock is filthy. Why don't you wash the floor some time!'

The fresh autumn winds turn into icy rain as Christmas and nineteen seventy-one approach. James and I have been keeping to ourselves. We go out and beg if the weather is not too bad. Every week or so, we walk to the hill and have our dinner, usually sandwiches, while we watch Kathleen playing, or sometimes just looking through the window of the house. James calls her the *pwetty girl.*

The new year speeds by and almost suddenly it's Summer again. Maeve doesn't come over very often, and I rarely go to visit her place, but we are on civil terms with each other.

…

On Wednesday, 4th June, James and I plan to go to our favourite hill to celebrate Kathleen and James' second birthday. First we're going to the shop to buy green and red jellies with the money I've saved up. James is humming a little tune to himself as we walk across the bridge to the local shop. He is such a happy child. I look down at him and I want to pick him up and give him a hug. He stops and looks up at me.

I pick him up and give him a hug.

'I love you James, don't ever forget that.'

'Mammy, lub you,' he says in his tiny voice and then squeezes my neck.

I notice two local country women talking seriously inside the glass door of the shop.

'It's one of those tinkers,' the short woman whispers to the taller, fat woman. The fat woman adjusts her scarf and turns her head to have a look at me. She puts her finger to her nose as if I'm emitting a bad smell. Maybe we wouldn't smell so much if we had all that running water out of a tap and baths and things like that, instead of an old tin bath and a bucket of water from the stream. I walk straight past them into the shop, clutching James' hand.

The short thin woman is talking now. 'The funeral is at three o'clock I hear.'

'God rest her soul,' the tall fat woman says. 'I didn't know Kathleen that well…'

'…Is she having a high Mass then?' The short woman asks.

'Now I wouldn't know about that…'.

'So, what do you want?' Mrs Kelly's voice booms at me from behind the counter.

'Jellies,' James replies. Mrs Kelly turns her attention to the small child pointing to the array of delicious sweets behind the glass.

'Show me your money?' She curls her bottom lip, as though doubting our sincerity.

'Here,' I say sharply, on his behalf. I place a large shiny coin on the counter.

She stares at the money. 'Are we going to spend all that? That's *twenty* sweeties,' she says sweetly to James. She is all smiles now, and very glad to take my coin off me.

'Wenty weeties,' James repeats.

'No,' I say. James looks at me, his face the epitome of disappointment. 'All right then, count out twenty. Can we have red and green please.' That'll give me another few minutes to hear the rest of the conversation of the two women nearby.

'You can, to be sure,' Mrs Kelly says, delighted to have our custom. This is her lucky day I think, getting all of that money!

'Is there a funeral…?' I ask Missus Kelly as she rolls a piece of newspaper into a cone shape and counts the jellies as they fall in.

'Don't interrupt me now…twenty. There.' She looks into my face. 'Three o'clock I believe. Did you know Missus Connor?'

'Missus Connor!' I almost faint. 'I met her…' I reply.

'I suppose you did. You folk get around.' She looks out the window as though she can see into Missus Connor's. 'Kept to herself a bit… God rest her soul,' Missus Kelly laments.

'Yes, God rest her soul. Thanks very much. I'm off now,' I say, taking James' other hand. The doorbell chimes as we leave.

'Come on James, we're going to see the pretty girl.'

'Pwetty gel,' James says, trudging alongside me. 'Weets,' he cries, holding up the little cone shaped package.

'Don't open it! Not yet James. We have to go up the hill. We'll sing our special song about Missus Kelly?'

We sing together, 'Missus Kelly broke her belly sliding down a lump of jelly!' We both laugh, and repeat the ditty until we reach our special spot on the hill.

'We sit down on a rock. 'Good boy? I undo the paper cone. 'Here's a sweetie.' I hand him a green jelly. He chews on it. I'm chewing on a red one. 'I wish I had a drink James, a nice tri a gater!'

James nods his head.

I watch the Connor's house. Half an hour later I see a big black hearse coming up the driveway. Two men in black get out of the front seat. A black car is pulling up behind the hearse. Two men and a woman get out of that and go into the house.

'Oh, God,' I say aloud.

A tall blonde haired woman comes out the door of the house carrying a small child. 'It's Kathleen,' I whisper.

'Tatlen,' James whispers back. I smile. One day I'll tell him about his sister.

Kathleen is dressed in a dark coloured dress with white frills. I can see her frilly underskirt. She has black shiny shoes and white stockings. She has a little bonnet with a white ribbon tied over her dark soft curled hair. Mister Connor comes out through the front door, and turns around. He stands beside the blonde women holding Kathleen. The child is lurching towards Mister Connor, but the woman pulls her back, gives her a shake and slaps her on the wrist.

Mister Connor ignores the activities around him. The dark shapes of men moving slowly fills the front door, two, four, six...! They are carrying the coffin!

Tears fall down my cheeks.

'Mammy, Mammy, not cwy,' James is calling softly to me.

'Missus Connor is dead!' I hug James.

A lonely butterfly flutters by. James reaches up to try to catch it. 'Buttafi, buttafi,' he says, pushing away from me and romping through the grass.

I watch as the funeral procession moves slowly along the narrow road, like a tired slug. Tears run freely down my face and along my neck. After a time I feel the cold air blowing on my neck, cooling me. I realize the night is closing in on us. I look around and realise that James is gone.

'James, James,' I'm calling out. I can see the sun sliding away behind the hills. 'Where are you James,' I call as I plod through the high grass. He's gone! 'Oh God help!' I wail. Then, I relax as I see a little brogue clad foot behind a grassy rock.

There's James, fast asleep. In his tightly closed hand there's a brown and white butterfly. I pick James up and carry him home.

The next day I meet Maeve in the yard around the van. I relate the news to her. 'Missus Connor funeral was yesterday!'

'How do you know that?'

'I saw the coffin.'

'So, you were snooping again. Idle minds are the devil's work Niamh. You should try to keep yourself busy.'

I ignore her remark. 'They might send Kathleen away now,' I remark, exposing my thoughts.

'Niamh, it's none of your business. The whole world doesn't rotate around you.'

'You're right Maeve.' I pause before I ask her a favour. 'I was wondering if I could ask you to look after James? He's a bit weary from walking yesterday.'

'You want to see her *ala*?' Maeve says, her hands on her hips.

'Just this once.'

'I've got me own child to take care of, and a husband, and a home.'

'I know that. I just need to…'

'Go on; get it out of your system. Swear it will be the last time? Go on!'

'I swear. This will be the last time.'

Twenty minutes later I'm sitting on the hill, watching the Connors' house. After a long wait I don't see any one, so decide to leave. My bum's stiff! I rise to go, and then I see Tom Connor walking towards the back of the house. I see the woman with the blonde hair coming from the rose garden to greet him. I watch them, shocked by what I see…

I call in to Maeve's. 'I thought I'd give them a bit of food,' she says, mashing up potatoes and carrots for James and Moiré.

'That looks delicious,' I say, my mouth watering.

'Well, there's only enough for these pair. You'll have to cook your own vegetables.'

'I will. Thanks for feeding James.'

'It's what sisters are for! It's a pity you can't do the same for me some time. So, you got to get that girleen out of your system then?' Maeve asks, placing a bib around Moiré's neck. She places a bowl and spoon in front of each of them at the small table.

'No, not exactly. I did see Mister Connor. Maeve, you wouldn't believe it!'

Maeve sits down next to me on the sofa. 'What wouldn't I believe?'

'I saw him and his girlfriend cavorting…'

'Niamh, how can you use such vulgar language in front of the children?' She leans closer and whispers. 'Well, maybe he needs *a*la woman.'

'Maeve, he buried his wife yesterday!'

'It's not our business. We shouldn't judge the man. I heard she has been sick for months! You didn't know that did you?'

'No, I didn't.'

'There y'are now. Put the whole thing out of your head now and get back to work.'

'I will, but first I'm going back. Tomorrow.'

'You swore today would be the last time!'

'I didn't see Kathleen!'

'*Awast!* with your romancing,' Maeve says, rising up and pouring a cup of milk for the two children. 'I can't bear the sight of you! Go on home. I'll bring James over when he's finished his dinner.'

The next day I take James with me.' Look for butter-flies,' I'm telling James. 'Off he goes.' After a short while I spot Kathleen. The blonde haired woman plonks her into a playpen in the front yard and disappears inside, leaving Kathleen walking around the playpen. Drops of rain tickle my nose. 'Sit under the rock,' I tell James as the rain falls harder. I quickly do what I came to do, and then return home. I'm just inside when Maeve turns up at the door.

'I wanted to ask you for something…'

'Come in. Close the door!' I literally pull her inside.

Her mouth drops open. 'What in God's name…?'

She stands with her arms on her hips.

'Kathleen, this is your aunty Maeve.'

'Niamh, what is she doing here?'.

'It's her second birthday! I took her back,' I exclaim.

'Niamh, she doesn't belong here.'

'She does. I love her! Missus Connor's dead. Nobody loves her there.'

'How did you get away with it?' Maeve asks in a nasty voice.

'She was stuck in a playpen, out in the rain. I just lifted her in my arms and took her with me,' I explain.

'Niamh, you've kidnapped her. That's a crime! We'll all end up behind bars! Take her back up there! Go on, before they find out what happened.'

'I will not.' I pick Kathleen up and step away from Maeve.

'The garda will be here any minute.'

'Don't be daft, Maeve. They'll think she ran off.'

'Niamh, she's two years old, how can she run away!' She leans over towards me and her face is close to mine.' If you bring more trouble on our family you're finished. I'll never forgive you.'

'What else can I do?'

'Get out of here. Leave us alone.'

'Maeve, I thought you wanted me here?'

'Well, I don't any more! You may as well know what's going on. Paid and I are on a list for a house. We're very close to getting one. We don't need any criminal charges… You have two choices, bring her back to the Connors, or leave!'

She is suddenly quiet.

'Maeve, I should never have given her away. I know that I made a mistake.'

'Look, I'm sick of you! You run away, you come back, telling us you were married to some great fellow. All la de da! Then you stupidly give your child away. Then you force your husband to drown himself! After all that you finally decide you made a mistake, and make another one by kidnapping a child! I've had enough of your crazy schemes. Just go, while you can.'

'But now I want to stay.'

'You always want the opposite of what's good for our family. If you don't go I'll tell the garda that you kidnapped the Connors' child.'

'But where can I go?'

'Somewhere! By bus.'

'I never go on the bus. I don't have money.'

'I'll tell you where it goes, and when, and I'll give you money. There's one going this evening, up at the crossroads.'

'So, are you going to look after the children?'

'Not on your nanny! Egit! Take them with you. They're yours now!'

'All right. If you don't want me here, I'll go. I'll get James' things,' I stammer.

'Put some of James' clothes on Kathleen. Say she's a boy.'

'She's too pretty to be a boy.'

'She has to be a boy.'

'Why?'

'Because they'll be looking for a girl.'

'If she's a boy why can't we just stay here until it all blows over?'

'It won't blow over in a hurry. I just know that. You'll bring trouble on your whole family if you stay. If you're not here they'll probably not worry us.'

'It took me ages to find out where the Connors' farm is. I don't know anywhere but walking around these parts.'

'We've got some relations near Moycullen. Ballycuirke, I think they said.'

'What relations are they?'

'My aunty Biddy and uncle Bill McCann. They were at the wedding. They have two caravans and three or four horses. Very well to do! They've probably got a house by now! Just say you're my sister and they'll welcome you with open arms.'

'What if they chase me off?'

'They won't. They're your own flesh and blood, on my mother's side. Now, what you have to do is stay with them for a while, then come back.'

I haul out a little pair of trousers and a hat from a cardboard box. 'Will these do for Kathleen?' I ask Maeve.

'They'll do. Hurry, and don't call her Kathleen! Call her…Larry!'

'Larry? She doesn't look like a Larry!'

'Larry is a great name. She looks like a Larry to me! Put those things on and you'll see!'

'There!' I say, pulling the trousers up and lifting Kathleen off her little feet with the jerk.

'There, she looks like a Larry now. A real little larrikin!'

'I don't want her to have that name…'

'Bring a bit of food for the night. Don't wear your shawl; otherwise you'll look like a Tinceard!

'But I am…'

'I'm telling you now. Comb your hair, put your best clothes on. Go on. Quick! I've got to get back to Moiré. Paid's looking after her. He'll be worried. I only came to borrow a cup of sugar to make pancakes…never mind that now.' Maeve leaves and comes back ten minutes later. I have a large canvas bag packed as she instructed, and I'm wearing my best clothes, a light green silk blouse that Maeve gave me on my seventeenth birthday, with a silk ribbon in a band around my hair, and an A-line green and brown coloured tartan skirt that has big pockets on the inside. I make sure I have my savings and rings as well as some bread and milk, and a few other bits and pieces.

'I told him you need company for half an hour, that you're depressed *arirt.*'

'I'm not depressed.'

'We'll all be depressed if you don't hurry up!' she says, handing me her old crocheted bag.

'Here's some things to keep you going. Come on now and shift yourself. I'll carry James.'

'We're on your heels, aren't we Kathleen?'

Maeve turns back with a sour look. 'Call her Larry! Let's use the short cut.'

The four of us head off through the fields to where the bus stops.

'All right. You wait here. Now if Aunty Biddy and Uncle Bill aren't there, go on to Cork.'

'I thought you said they'd welcome me with open arms?'

'Oh, they will, if they're still at Ballykuirke. You know how it is; we can't stop in the same place too long. They might have had to move. I'm just giving you a fair warning, that's all. At the wedding they said they were thinking of travelling to Cork. Bill knew someone who had a business there.'

'Cork is such a long way off.'

'They won't find you there!'

'Who?'

'The garda! Stupid!'

'Maeve, you and the garda! I don't know anything about Cork. I'll be lost there. It's supposed to be a really big place…'

'Niamh, the bigger the place the harder it will be to find you. You always talk about going to America. Now you won't even go to Cork.'

'But what if I can't find Uncle Bill and Aunty Biddy?'

'God you're a moron! Just go to the priest if you can't find them. Someone will help you. Here's ten quid.' She hands me two five-pound notes.

'Thanks Maeve.' I take the notes and stuff them in the bottom of my pocket.

'What'll I do then?'

'Stay in Cork until for a few months, until all this blows over. You can come back and visit us when we're settled in our new house. We're thinking of getting a television as well!'

'Oh Maeve…'

'I've been longing for a television! I don't want anything to go wrong now. Do you understand?'

'No, I've never wanted a television.'

'That's not what I mean! Yerra, I think I hear the bus… Slean leat! ' Till we meet again.' Maeve gives me a quick hug and runs to hide behind the bushes and high grass.

'Slean,' I say. 'There's sugar in the old brown tea tin on the shelf…' I call out, but I can't see her now.

I climb on the bus with my two toddlers, wondering if it's all a bad dream. I pay the fare with one of Maeve's notes and get my change. I catch a glimpse of Maeve as she heads off home, stopping to watch the bus move on. I wonder if she heard me telling her about the sugar.

Chapter seven

The bus driver is a withered looking man with a clean shaved look. A few strands of brownish hair are flattened against his polished head. His driver's cap is on the seat next to him. His eyes are alert and bright blue. 'So are them children under four?'

'They surely are. Sean is two and K...Larry is three' I reply sharply.

'They can't sit on the seats. You have to hold them on your lap!' His eyes go even a brighter blue when he says this. 'Them's the rules!' He smiles, showing the gaps in his brown teeth.

I notice there are only about half a dozen passengers with plenty of spare seats.

'Right.' I nod and sit down balancing my two children on my lap. My two bags are on the floor near my feet.

Nobody wants to sit next to me, so after a short time, when my knee is nearly numb I'm sliding James into the empty part of the seat. He is too small to be seen by the driver anyway. I'm watching the world passing by. I've wanted to leave home but gave up a long time ago. Anyway, I didn't mean like this. Not with two toddlers!

By the time we reach Moycullen there's nobody left on the bus but myself and the driver.

'This is it then. Off you get now. Slean. Dei's Muire dhuit! This is where we stop for the night!' The driver pulls on the brake hard and starts packing up his paperwork.'

'How do I get to Ballykuirke?'

'There's nothing there.'

'My friend's meeting me…' I reply, trying to sound like I know what I'm doing.

'Follow the wiggly woggly road and then you'll come to a lake, if you could call it that.'

'Right'

'When's the bus to Cork?'

'Where do you think y'are? Dublin? They have buses every five minutes there, or so they tell me.' He nods his head and smiles longingly. 'They must make an awful lot of money?'

'They must. So what about the bus to Cork?'

'You've got to go to Galway first! Tomorrow. Around ten o'clock.'

'Dei's Muiré dhuit, agus Padraig,' I mumble.

He leans forward. 'The Banshee lives around these parts. If you hear her, cover their ears!'

I shiver. 'Gora mait dhuit. I'll remember!' I mumble as I head off down the wiggly-woggly road, with the bus driver watching me as I go. I'm chatting to the children, and glancing back from the corner of my eye. He finally walks off. I'm really wondering what's to become of us. I thought we would be happy together for ever in our little caravan. Now I don't know what's going to happen in one night. What can I tell our relatives at Ballycuirke? First I have to find them. After half an hour of a long walk with two little ones, I still can't see any sign of any living creature, just an odd cow, sheep or horse. We cross over a small stone bridge with a stream going under. I notice a stone wall and a crumbled remains of a shed.

'There's our house!' I exclaimed to James and Kathleen. I try to sound excited.

The three of us run towards the fallen down building. We sit inside the wall on the grass and I open my bag. I have a bottle of milk and two little copper cups that Jim made, and some biscuits.

'Goodies for good children,' I said.

'Dood chlen. Me dood!' James said, clapping his little hands.

Kathleen just stares at the food, then reaches out to take a biscuit.

'No', I say crossly.

'Wa…wa…' she screams.

'Shush! Here, have one then!' I shove a biscuit in her hand.

She stops crying. 'Thank God!'

'Gank Dod!' James repeats.

I am dying for a cup of tea, but I don't dare light a fire and boil my small copper pot, which Jim made for me. I decide to let the children eat and just think about a cup of tea. I cover the children with my tartan shawl-blanket and we sleep very well indeed, sheltered by the firm rocks around us. 'Sure it's just like home,' I whisper into James' ear.

'Mammy…' he mumbles.

…

The next morning the sun is up just before us, hiding its face behind a thick black cloud, which quickly scurries away, leaving the rays of the sun sparkling on my copper pot. I give the children some more biscuits and the rest of the milk. It's a chilly day, so I've decided to light a small fire and make a cup of tea for myself before anyone comes by. While the children are eating their biscuits and milk I head off to an old pump I noticed on the way here last night. It looks like people don't use it much as the pump is stiff as a poker. After a few tries, a trickle of lovely cold water comes out. I'm filling up my little copper pot. I can use some of it to clean the children's faces. Back I go to the pile of rocks and start a small fire with some dry sticks and hay. I have a box of matches in the bottom of my bag.

In half an hour or a bit longer, I'm enjoying the best cup of tea I've ever had.

After breakfast we clean up the mess. I get the two children to squat down and go to the toilet near a bush. Kathleen is not properly toilet trained, as she was wearing a nappy when I found her. I put a fresh nappy back on her. Maeve put about six in the bag she gave me, and some baby powder. James has been out of nappies for half a year or more, so that's good news. We head back to where the bus stopped the night before. It takes us nearly an hour to get to the bus stop. I can judge the time from the sun's rising. Well, we wait and not long after, the little green and yellow bus screeches to a halt.

'The top of the morning to ye!' the bus driver yells out in a loud voice.

'Dei is Moiré dhuit!' I reply, lifting the two children up the steps of the bus.

'Did you find your friend?'

'Friend?'

'The one you were meeting?'

'I did.' I reply, not daring to look at the bus driver's face.

'That's a miracle. I never saw a soul over that way for a long time. 'T wasn't a ghost now, was it?'

'It might have been!'

I sit in the nearest seat and stare out the window as we fly by the rolling countryside.

'Dwink Mammy,' James says.

'Here's a sweetie,' I reply.

'Weet, weet!' Kathleen shouts.

'Here,' I hand her a red jelly.

A woman in the seat opposite glances over the top of a book she's got her nose into.

I look out the window.

'They're grand looking children. God bless them!'

'Thanks very much!' I reply, and I stare out the window again.

The woman buries her head in her book. The children are sucking their sweets.

We finally arrive in Galway and I help the children off the bus.

'They're lovely children, God bless them,' the woman with the nose in the book says as we climb off the bus.

'Gora mait dhuit' I reply.

'Here' she says, handing me a pound note. 'You're very young having such a big responsibility. I wish you all the best now with your little boy and girl.'

'Two boys!'

'God, who would believe he's a boy! Such a smashing looking child.'

'Everyone says that!' I say, hurrying down the street.

'Well, thank you very much. I think they need to go to the lav,' I add, hurrying towards a public convenience I notice out of the corner of my eye. 'Slean leat!'

'Slean.' She stands staring at us as we enter the toilet building. I give her a friendly wave and off she goes. 'Would you look at this James,' I say, noting the toilet door is shut. 'I need a penny to get this open. I don't have one!' Just then a woman comes out of the last toilet. 'Here, I'll hold the door for you.'

'Gora mait dhuit!' I say, breathing a sigh of relief.

As we come out of the toilets I notice a bus standing at the kerb nearby.

'Is this bus going to Cork?' I ask a bus driver who's boarding it.

'No, we're off to Limerick. In five minutes!'

'All right then. Come on you two, jump up,' I say to James and Kathleen, giving them a whoosh up.

'Here,' I hand him the five pound note Maeve gave me.

He gives me the change.

Kathleen falls asleep after a short time. James is still as bright as a button, pointing out cows and sheep as he sees them.

Then my heart sinks as Kathleen starts sweating and making gurgling noises. The next thing I know she's vomited all over my lap.

'There's a bad smell around here,' a woman in a black coat says from behind me. The woman puckers her face into an ugly contortion.

'S…He's just sicked up, that's all!' I say in reply to her snide remark.

'Childers shouldn't be allowed on public buses, especially when they don't even pay. They should be kept at home with their mothers. That's what I say.'

'I am their mother!' Kathleen's head lurches again and she makes more horrible sounds.

'I need to get off here,' I call to the driver who's only a few seats down the front from me. 'My child is sick.'

'Next stop then!' he calls back.

The woman in the black coat nods her head. 'That's a grand idea altogether.'

The bus pulls up and we all lurch forward. 'Gort,' he calls out.

I stand up, holding Kathleen with one arm, and my bags over my shoulder.

'Come on James. We have to get off here,' I say, holding James by the hand as we wobble down the aisle of the bus.

'When's the next bus to Limerick?' I ask the driver as we embark.

'At half-two.'

'Right!' I'm wondering if I should ask for some of my money back.

'Step down please. You're holding me up.'

I don't think I'm getting my fare back. 'Gora mait dhuit.' I step off with my children.

'Slean leat!'

'Slean.'

Six hours later, after another fare and bus trip, we finally get to Limerick. 'Limerick! All off,' the driver calls out as we pull up with a jerk. I'm holding a sleepy Kathleen and take James by the hand.

'I'll give you a hand with your bag.' A smiling young man with dark hair and blue eyes says in a lilting Cork accent. I stand up with my burdens.

'I'm all right. Gora mait dhuit, thanks.'

'Here, I'll take the lad,' he says, picking James up and carrying him off the bus.

'Gora mait dhuit,' I repeat, as he places James on the footpath.

'Are you all right then?' he asks. 'Can I buy you a drink?'

'No thanks. I'm just passing through on my way to Cork, to meet my husband!' I lie.

'I see. It's been grand meeting you anyhow!' He salutes me as he heads down the footpath, glancing back once or twice.

'I'm finished with men! I've had enough of them. They only bring trouble, that's all,' I mutter to James as we head off. 'Daddy' he says as he waves to the man.

'No Daddy,' I say, yanking him closer to my leg.

'No Daddy!' he repeats.

'That's right James. Good boy.'

'Dood boy.'

I wondered if we had any relatives in Limerick, so I find the post office and lean over the counter.

A thin, grey haired man looks up at me from his work at a small desk. He's wearing very thick glasses. He glares. 'What?'

'I was wondering if you know of any Murphys, or O'Briens, or McCann's living in Limerick.

He turns back to his work. 'Gerroff with you now. You're pulling me leg.'

'How do you mean?' I ask seriously.

'How many fish are in the sea?'

'How should I know?' I reply, still puzzled by his remark.

'How should I know how many Murphys O'Briens or McCann's there are in Limerick?'

…

I find a quiet dry spot near a bridge and camp overnight

in Limerick. I decide to head for Cork as Maeve suggested; maybe I can find our relations there?

Late the following evening we arrive in Cork. Kathleen doesn't get sick this time, thank God. This is because I've learned the trick of feeding her dry bread while we travel. Well, you never saw such a busy place as Cork. There are shops and buildings everywhere, and well dressed folk rushing about. I feel the excitement of being in a big city. It's like a dream come true. We walk across a bridge to Cobh and sit on a stone wall with the two children beside me. It's a beautiful soft summers evening. I give them milk and biscuits. I find a nice cosy spot near some trees on the side of the bridge and settle the children for the night.

We're not far from the dock, so I go for a stroll in the cool evening air. I walk along the dockside, staring out into the shimmering dark water, which relentlessly surges backwards and forwards, gurgling loudly and then softly. A shiver runs down my spine as I remember the day I almost drowned… But before I can become remorseful the figure of a man pulls up alongside the nearby pylon in a small fishing boat 'Do you need a boat Miss?'

'Do you go to the islands?'

'I do, every day.'

'What about tomorrow?'

'No. Not tomorrow, there's one ship leaving tomorrow. It's her!'

'That big ship over there?'

'Queenstown II. It was made right here in Cork. It's off to America. Cargo, and passengers. Now I'd give my right arm to be going on that girl.'

'Me too! I hear the streets are paved with gold in America. It's even bigger than Cork!'

'Aye, and all that.'

'You wouldn't happen to know how much it costs to go on that big ship?'

'It's very dear. Hundreds of pounds I think! I know someone who's going on her tomorrow. He'll know more about it.'

'Who's that?'

'Mick Brady. Grand lad. Off to make his fortune. Great pal of mine for years. Said I'd have a drink with him before he leaves tomorrow. Did you want to meet him yourself?'

'I'll check on the children first,' I point to the hotel across the road.

'So, you're staying at the Commodore?'

I give him a nod as though he's right!

'I'll wait here for ye!' he says politely as I rush off.

A few minutes later I join him. 'They're fine.'

I see his head nod in the darkness. 'Mick lives over there, next to Flannnery's butcher shop.'

'The name's Maguire, Ted Maguire, fishing entrepreneur,' he says. The lone street light displays his smiling, twinkling eyes.

'Niamh. Niamh Farrell,' I reply, holding my ringed finger for him to see.

'Niamh, Queen of the land.' His lips touch the back of my hand as it collides with his stiff stubble.

'My mother's name was Niamh, and she was queen of Cork, I can tell you that! She never put the cork in the bottle! Too fond of the drink!' He laughs, and then shakes his head.

Five minutes later Ted is banging on a stout green door.

A thin man with fair hair cut in a fringe across his eyes opens the door. 'Come on in, Ted, who's the young lady?'

'This is Queen Niamh. Niamh, this is Mick Brady.' He looks at Mick. 'She wants to meet a man going to America! I'm out of luck again.'

'She's come to the right place then.' He stares at me. 'Come on in. I've been saying my goodbyes to the lads.'

We walk through a hallway and into a room, which is crowded with men of all ages and two older women sitting near a table, drinking shandies, absorbed in their urgent conversation.

'This is Niamh and you all know Ted. They've come to say goodbye.'

Several hands reach forward to shake mine. Mick turns towards me, leaning cautiously on a kitchen cupboard. 'So, are you off to America too?' Mick asks me.

'No!'

'She wanted to know how much the fare was?' Ted pipes in from around a corner of the room.

'You couldn't afford it.'

'How do you know that?'

'No offence meant. Nobody could afford it, not the ordinary Irish man…or woman. My uncle Brendan is over there. He's bringing me. Sure if I lived to be a hundred I couldn't save enough to get to Dublin, let alone America.'

'Don't believe him Niamh. He's got the first penny he ever earned.'

'You'd need more than a houseful of pennies to get to America.'

'Sure go on with ye!' Ted mocks. 'He never spends a penny without thinking about it for a month or more!'

'Ted is just jealous of my good luck. Would you like a shandy Niamh?'

'That sounds lovely. Yes please.'

Twenty minutes later Mick returns with a large glass of shandy.

'Fit for a queen.' He says handing me the cool glass.

I sip. It tastes bitter sweet. 'I've never tasted anything like this before.'

'It's my special brew,' Mick says.

'What time are you off then?'

'To bed?'

'No, to America?'

'Of course, that's where I'm going all right! America the home of the free! Early. Seven sharp.'

'Is Ted seeing you off?'

Ted's eyes fill with liquid as he turns towards us. 'I'm seeing Mick off if it's the last thing I do on this earth. I'll be right there on the ship until it sails away!'

'Will they let you on the ship then?'

'Oh, God yes! They usually always do so. However, because of several incidents they may not …'

'Why not,' I venture to ask.

'Because, my dear Queen Niamh,' Ted says in his most eloquent voice, 'they found that some young lads and even lassies were not getting off at all, before the ship set sail, when they hadn't paid their fare.'

'How could they do that?'

'They jump in those little boats on the sides and stay there until she's out at sea, then it's too late to come back. They eventually do, so what's the point.'

'Do what?'

'Come back. But they boast about being to America. They say it's worth it!'

'What's worth it?'

'Yerra girl, gaol! That's where they end up. Mind you,' he suddenly places his hand near his face as if divulging a secret, 'a few have made it!'

'To America?'

'That's correct. Would you like another drop?'

'No…God, what time is it?'

'Nearly ten,' Ted replies, pulling a watch from his breast pocket.

'It's getting late! Ted, Mick, I've had a great evening. Now I've really got to go. Thanks very much for introducing me to Mick. It's been a pleasure!'

'So, you're not staying the night then?' Ted says, jokingly.

'No, not tonight!' I try to sound real casual like.

'Not tonight Josephine!' Ted squeals.

'Stop it Ted,' Mick chides, grinning delightedly at me.

'My husband might be here now,' I lie. 'He's over six feet tall. He's Australian!'

'He's a very lucky man!' Ted's eyebrows rise as he steps back.

'Well, slean leat now,' Mick says, holding his glass of black liquid steady in his hand.

I run towards the spot where the children are still sleeping soundly. I sit up all night in case I might be asleep when the boat leaves. I have the privilege of seeing the sun glimmer through the misty morning. It rises slowly, carefully, twinkling all the time. I've brought my old scissors with me, one that Jim made. After breakfast, I take a deep breath and cut Kathleen's curls off, one by one. After that ordeal I've put the children's warm things on them, as it's a cold morning for summertime.

…

We're soon on the dock and the Queenstown II is anchored near the dockside, proudly waiting to set sail. It's an amazing sight. I'm sitting near the dock and watching what's going on. James is still half-asleep and Kathleen won't stop eating or drinking. There's hardly any milk left. I'm waiting to see Mick Brady. I'm here a bit too early it seems. Just then he makes his dramatic appearance. His eyes struggle to see from under the long fringe. He's wearing a pink shirt and a pale green suit with fashionable flared trouser legs. He's wearing cream coloured suede shoes and he's carrying two large brown suitcases. 'Mick Brady,' I say excitedly to James. 'He's going on the ship. We're going to talk to him.'

Just at that moment he spots us and comes over. 'There y'are. Is the big fella still sleeping?'

'The big fella?'

'Your husband, the Australian.'

'He is…begorrah.' I can feel the lie making my face red

'It's nice of you to see me off anyhow.'

'It's not often I know someone going to America!'

His chin lifts in mock pride. 'You're privileged then!'

We continue up the ramp to the ship. James is walking and I'm carrying Kathleen.

'So, what part are you going to?'

'Just above the water! C deck.'

'That's nice. But what I mean is, whereabouts in America.'

'Oh that! The Big Apple! That's what my Uncle Brendan calls it. New York, Manhattan, is the place where he lives.

He's getting on a bit now, but I can stay a while with him until I get settled.'

'So, do they grow apples there?'

'Well now, I suppose they must with a name like that! They make big money there, for Uncle Brendan paid my fare and all, and I've never met him...'

'So, he doesn't even know who he's paying for! He must have money to burn.'

'He must! He even sent me some American dollars and all. That's how I bought these new clothes.'

'Sure you're looking grand, a real toff.'

We move together for a few moments. 'Are there many seeing you off then?'

'Ted and maybe some others. They'll come aboard for a while. We've got nearly an hour yet.'

We approach the man checking the tickets.

'They're with me. Just saying our last goodbyes.'

He hardly glances at us. 'That's fine. Just make sure they're disembarked before takeoff. If anyone unauthorised is found on board there are stiff penalties.'

'Well, she won't be staying. Her owld fella is probably coming to get her now,' Mick assures the man.

The man grunts and looks at the next couple coming through.

'Begorrah, there's Ted! He's brought Mark and Liam with him too.'

'We'll have to go,' I say to Mick. 'The children need to go to the lav.'

'When nature calls you must attend...' he replies eloquently.

'I must. Well, have a pleasant journey. May the seas rise up to meet you and the wind be always at your back,' I say as eloquently as possible.

'If ever you, and your husband come to America, look me up, now.'

'We will! God, I have to go! James is wandering over there.' I point to where he's heading. 'Before we get into trouble.'

'Slean!'

I rush off to get James who has run along the deck. I carry Kathleen with one arm, and two bags in my other. I find James hiding behind some small boats about ten feet away. 'There you are James, I call as I bend down to tie his shoelaces. 'These are the ones people hide in James,' I whisper. 'Good boy James.' I kiss his cheek. He smiles cheekily. 'In this game, everyone has to be really, really quiet,' I whisper. Kathleen stares at me with her big brown eyes, chewing away on a crust. James is listening intently. 'See that little boat, we're going to go inside it and stay there for a long time! This is our secret adventure.'

James nods his head enthusiastically. Cautiously, I'm undoing a stiff rope and placing my foot inside the boat.

'Get your foot off me!' A voice calls out from the darkness.

God Almighty! 'Sorry. I didn't know you were here.'

'Find your own!' the voice says.

I lift my leg back over the side. We move along to the next boat, and ever so carefully I lift the cover. Again, I hear voices. I can see nothing. 'Shush. Get away with you…'

'I'm sorry.' I reply to some unknown person. And I thought I had a bright idea!

'Hello, anyone in there?' I ask as I move on to the fourth boat in the row. No answer. 'This is it!'

We climb in and sit still. I give the children sweets, one in each tiny hand. They chew happily.

I hear voices outside, and shouting, then footsteps running. My heart is in my mouth wondering if the cover is going to be lifted any minute. Nothing happens. I can hear the engines purring and feel the ship slithering away. I long to scream and shout, 'We're off. Hurray!' but I just swallow and hold my breath for a moment, suddenly feeling sick inside. 'Let's have a little sleep,' I suggest. Kathleen puts her head down on my knee and James leans against my arm. 'Hush little baby, don't say a word…' I sing quietly. It's rather cosy in here. At least we're together, the three of us. I haven't felt this happy since I fell in love with Niall. James and Kathleen are falling asleep and I feel so tired I'm falling asleep myself, even though my stomach is twisting and turning.

…

I don't know how long we've been sleeping, but all of a sudden I'm wide-awake. I'm peeping out from under the covers. There's sea around us! What a sight. We must be miles away from Cork now. I'm feeling very hungry and my tummy is still squeamish. I know the children will be hungry when they wake up. I'm crawling out of the little boat and I feel as stiff as a board. The pins and needles are running through my feet and legs. I'm creeping along the back of the boats next to the rail, breathing in the fresh salty air. Suddenly, two heads pop from another little boat, giving me a terrible fright. At the same moment the boat lurches and my stomach throws its contents upwards. I lean over the rail.

'Don't do that…' the young man says, leaning over nearby and throwing up, making an awful noise. A moment later the girl is doing the same. After a few minutes, I wipe my mouth. 'I feel better now.'

'Me too,' the lad says, 'it's great to spew!'

'Don't say that word,' the girl says, leaning over the rail again.

A few minutes later she joins us.

'I thought you must've got caught?'

'No. They didn't even look for us. That was our friend Andrew in the other boat. Poor sod,' the girl says.

'We should introduce ourselves!' I suggest.

'Should we?' the girl replies, looking at me under her eyelids.

'I'm not the garda! I'm Niamh Farrell, and my two children; James and …Larry are in the boat up the back! What's your names?'

'I'm Teresa Lennon and this geyser is my brother Noel.'

'I'm not a geyser,' Noel protests. 'And I know my own name!' He pushes Teresa.

'Don't you dare push me.' She retaliates, making a fist.

'Stop your fighting or we'll all be caught. Neither of you look old enough to be here on your own anyway!'

'I'm fourteen and he's nearly twelve.'

'Well, act your age why don't you?' I chide.

'Yeah, why don't you,' Teresa says to Noel.

'Na,' he replies, sticking out his tongue.

'That's enough, the pair of you.' I reprimand them, feeling like I'm their big sister already.

Teresa is a slim girl nearly as tall as myself. She has dark brown hair, long and straight, parted in the middle, hanging down listlessly around her elfin shaped face. She has the fairest skin I've ever seen. Her eyes are deep grey with a sad look. Noel is shorter, scrawny, with sandy coloured hair, that desperately needs cutting. His freckles cover his cheeks in a mosaic type pattern.

'Where do we get grub?' I ask.

'I'll go,' Noel says. 'My Daddy says I'm a thief at heart.'

'Yes, he could steal your eye and come back for the eyelashes and you wouldn't know,' Teresa agrees, giggling happily, then covering her mouth. 'But what's the point of eating if we get sick again?'

'If the children don't eat they'll start to cry,' I say wisely, having learned that much in life.

'You'd better get food then Noel,' Teresa suggests.

'Righto!' Noel scurries off into the shadows.

'I'll go and find where the lav is,' Teresa says, ducking down and waddling along awkwardly in her mini, tight skirt, close to the rail behind the small boats. 'You stay here. I'll be back.'

Ten minutes later she comes crawling back. 'Come on, I found a really great lav. Nobody's there!'

'I wonder if anybody ever comes up here,' I remark as we move in a train, carrying Kathleen and James. We follow Teresa along a narrow corridor. 'Here.' She points to a door with a picture of a woman's head with a high hairdo and a cigarette in her mouth. It's a beautiful little lavatory, so clean and sparkling. I place James on the seat and then Kathleen. After that I lift Kathleen on the small bench at the sink.

'I thought she was a boy?' Teresa says watching me put powder and a nappy on Kathleen.

'Did you now?' I reply.

She keeps staring at Kathleen. 'I'd keep an eye on her.'

'She's a good child,' I respond.

'People steal children now. They might want money,' she says knowingly.

'Well, we don't have any, so why would anybody steal her?' I ask casually.

'I heard that a baby got stolen in the West of Ireland.'

'Oh, who told you that?'

'Nobody told me. Noel's got a portable radio and we listened to the news this morning. They said the baby got taken a few days ago. Now what was her name? I forget that bit! But they said she was about two, with dark curly hair!'

'Well L..oretta doesn't have curly hair.'

'You're right there. It looks like someone's hacked it to pieces.'

'It grows like that!' I reply, red faced now. 'Don't hurt her feelings Teresa.'

'Sorry Loretta, that's a lovely name!' Teresa says to Kathleen, tickling her bare tummy.

Kathleen giggles.

'Can you look after her and James while I go.'

'Of course I will.'

I sit on the toilet and enjoy the peace for a minute, wishing Teresa and Noel had stayed in Cork. But then, they're just like me, needing a place to run to. We sneak back to the small tied up boats and can smell the food ten yards away.

'Over here,' a voice whispers. We hurry along and there before us is a feast.

'Noel, you're a wonder!'

'Hot food for all,' he says, his mouth full of chicken.

'I got bread, chicken, chips, cakes and a bottle of drink.'

That was the most wonderful meal. We are all so hungry we forget where we are for a few minutes.

'So, do you have more children?' Teresa asks me through eating a plump breast of chicken and passing the bottle of drink.

'I lost a child.'

'So, are you married?'

'I was. My last husband drowned.'

'God that's bloody awful,' Teresa exclaims.

'Shh, don't say that word in front of Kathleen and James!' I admonish her sharply.

'Bloody hell, who's Kathleen?'

'I meant Loretta! Sorry, I get mixed up with names.'

'You can say that again. She's your own child, for God's sake!' Teresa says, her eyes growing large.

'I'm a bit off colour today. What about your family? Any more sisters and brothers?' I ask, quickly moving the topic.

'Mammy lost a few children. I think she lost twins two years ago.'

'Did she?' Noel asks.

'You wouldn't understand these things. You're a boy!'

'I would so. I brought the grub.'

'You did too. But you don't know about babies and s…e…x (she spells the word) and things.'

'I can spell! I know more than you think. I saw Aunty Joan with her big stomach.'

'She was just fat.'

'She had a baby.'

'No she didn't. She doesn't have any babies.'

'Well, she shouldn't be so fat then!'

'You're rude!'

'Shh, you two.' I whisper. We can hear someone walking

towards us. We all keep quiet as a sailor walks by, with binoculars in hand. He peers over the rail and stands there staring out into the ocean.

James starts choking on a piece of chicken. I place my hand over his mouth. Noel hops away like a frightened rabbit. Teresa takes hold of Kathleen and puts her hand over her mouth. We stare at each other. Our hearts are stopping. We hear someone coughing a few yards away. 'It's Noel!'

'Hey, who goes there?' the sailor asks, heading towards Noel, who is now racing away on the deck. The sailor chases after him.

'Noel!' Teresa cries softly.

The last sound we hear is, 'Let me go, you b…b…'

'He's a goner!' Teresa says solemnly, her eyes darting left and right. 'Let's get back in the boats and lie low. He won't snitch on us. I told him I'd kill him if he did!'

The four of us climb back into boat number four and stay still. We remain there for several hours. Kathleen and James fall asleep again, out of sheer boredom.

'We might be in America soon!' Teresa whispers.

'What are you going to do when you get there?' I ask.

'I'll probably find a job, get some money, and buy lots of nice clothes and shoes, and makeup,' she states categorically.

'What about getting married?'

'Maybe, when I'm old. Maybe I'll be a famous film star by then. Actually, you'd make a great film star. You're really gorgeous you know.'

'I was thinking the same thing about you!'

'Go on!'

We both laugh. Suddenly, the covers are pulled back. Two faces peer into ours. 'Who goes there?' A solidly built young male who sports dark hair, rugged features and the whitest teeth I had ever seen accompanies an American accent. He takes Teresa out by the arm. 'Get out!'

'You too girl!' The other face, belonging to a more softly spoken American with curly fair hair, says to me. The two are wearing sparkling white uniforms.

'Albert, I think half of Ireland stowed away on this ship.'

'Well, I found myself a little doll.' Albert is holding tightly on to Teresa, who is squirming in his arms. 'Let me go. Please. I'll do anything you want?'

'Oh yeah!' says Albert.

'I mean it. Anything. Just let me get to America, that's all. Please don't send me back to Ireland. My father beats me with a strap...'

'Maybe we can help these little darlings? Hey Sam?'

'We have to report them!' Sam replies. He turns his attention to me. 'Your name?'

'Niamh...Farrell'

'Niamh. What a quaint name. What else have we got in here?' He stares at Kathleen and James who stare back. Kathleen cries, then James sniffs.

'Hush now. Don't worry.' I try to comfort them. 'They're my childers.'

'So, come on now. It's fine. We won't hurt you! What's your name little man?' Sam asks James as he lifts him over the side.

'Jaes,' James says.

'James?'

'That's right Sir,' I confirm.

'Why, hello there James!' Sam salutes James. James stares at Sam.

'Come on you pretty little thing. What's your name?'

'Loretta!' I say quickly before Teresa buts in.

'Loretta! Come on. Time to go.'

Albert is whispering in Teresa's ear, then calls Sam over. Sam's face is suddenly a mask of worry.

'Get back in the boat. I'll see y'all later,' Sam whispers to me as they leave.

'What's going on?' I ask, watching them leave, and lifting the two children back into their hiding place.

'I said we'd stay until they give us the word,' Teresa explains, getting into the boat next to ours.

'Why don't we hide somewhere else?' I suggest.

'No!' she seems suddenly angry. 'I promised,' she states more quietly. 'They'd find us anyway.'

'Probably right,' I remark.

We settle down in our small space, and we're all inclined to doze off in the darkness. Some time later, Teresa shakes me.

'It's time. Come on. I'll lead the way.'

'Shh. The children are sleeping again.'

'We can go without them!' she says.

'Not on your nanny! Come on James, time for walkies. Kathleen, come on Alanna…' I whisper so that Teresa can't hear me saying Kathleen's name. I shake them ever so gently.

'Have it your way. I'll take Loretta…' Teresa snaps, reaching down and picking up the sleepy child.

I take James and follow Teresa down some awkward spiral steps.

After four rounds of steps I'm feeling dizzy and nauseous again. The children look white in the face.

'This is it!' Teresa declares, walking through a narrow corridor with slim doors on one side. I'm following close behind. 'What are we doing here?'

'We made a deal!'

'What do you mean?' I ask.

Before Teresa can answer, Albert appears in the doorway. 'Hey, come in y'all. Sam, your broad's here.'

'Hi. Please excuse his bad language!' Sam comes through the door at the far end of the room.

'You're with Sam. I'm with Albert!' Teresa whispers.

'Come on, I'm in here.' Sam leads James and me through the door into another tiny room with two bunk beds on one side.

'Here, take her…' Teresa says, passing Kathleen into Sam's arms.

'Hey there Loretta…' he whispers. Kathleen jerks backwards. 'Hey there, it's me, Uncle Sam!'

Teresa closes the door behind her, leaving me with Sam and the two children in the small space.

'What's going on?' I ask Sam.

'Teresa offered her services to Albert, in exchange for protection.'

'Services?'

He looks at me with furled brows. 'You know…?'

I gasp. 'Do you mean …s…e…x?' (I spell out the letters).

'Look, it's ok. I owe Albert a favour…we could hand you over…'

'We'd be sent back to Ireland, wouldn't we?'

He nods his head.

'What happens if we get to America?' I ask.

'You will probably be exported back to Ireland.'

'It's hopeless then,' I remark. 'I'm an egit…'

'Niamh, you can take your case to the court. You might have the luck of the Irish and be allowed asylum in America…'

'What if I've done something…bad?'

'Well, there is still some justice in America. Your voice will be heard. It's a democratic country you know?'

'So, there's hope for me?'

'There sure as hell is!'

'I'm probably going there anyway!'

'What do you mean gal?'

'Hell!'

'Sure!' He grins, thinking I'm joking.

Sam looks at James. 'James how would you like to go up in here?' he bounces James off his feet and swings him into the top bunk. James giggles.

'And you Loretta? Up you go.' Kathleen giggles as she is scooped into the air. 'I have some chocolate for you.' He unwraps the foil from a large bar of milk chocolate. He gives them each a piece.

'Mind your manners. Say thanks!' I instruct the two happily feeding faces.

'Ganks!' they reply in unison.

'Would you like some?' he asks.

'I would, thanks very much!' I say, 'mm', enjoying the creamy taste, forgetting how ill I've been feeling.

'Sit down, Niamh, relax.'

I sit on the bottom bunk next to him. 'Could you get into trouble for this?' I ask.

Sam makes a face. 'A lot of trouble, unfortunately. Albert thinks it's worth it…'

'Did you know Teresa is only fourteen?'

'No.' He pauses. 'And you didn't tell me, ok?'

'You should tell your friend!' I suggest.

'Niamh, don't worry about Teresa…she's not your problem?'

'She's a child…'

'Niamh, let's not talk about them. I want to know more about you…'

'Why?' I ask. 'What if I don't want to tell you anything?'

He lies on the bed. 'Come on, just lie next to me.'

'No. I'm tired of lying.'

He closes his eyes. 'I'm just exhausted. I've been up for twenty-four hours,' he says sleepily.

I lie down next to him. 'All right, but just don't touch me…' I say. The sound of low snoring tells me he's sleeping! After lying there, thinking for some time, I doze off too.

I wake up to strange noises. I sit up, just in time to see Sam coming out of the small bath room with a towel around him. I gasp in fright.

'Sorry. I didn't mean to frighten you. I'm going on duty,' he explains. 'I have to get dressed!' he adds.

'I won't look,' I reply, turning away.

A few minutes later he calls out. 'You can turn around now!'

I turn around. 'How do you keep yourself clean,' I ask, noting his smart white uniform.

'White makes it easy to spot the stains.'

'You're very handsome,' I comment.

'Thank you very much.' His white teeth shine as he smiles spontaneously. 'If you want to use the shower please be discrete. It's a communal facility.'

'Others? They'll find us...'

'They already know about you. I just didn't want you to be unduly surprised, that's all.'

'They know about us, and they won't snitch?'

'It's just those who live here, me, Albert, and Charlie, who's on duty now.'

'They won't report us?'

'We've made a deal. But there's one snag.'

'Snag?'

'Inspection! We had one before we set sail, so the coast should remain clear for a day or so. They do come unannounced.'

'What'll we do then?'

'I don't know. We can just keep our fingers crossed, maybe we'll reach shore by then. God knows. Well, y'all, I have to leave. I'll bring something home.'

...

I sit and stare at the clock on the wall, watching the hours go by. The porthole is in the room with the shower, so occasionally I get up and stare into the black water behind that. Nothing happens for several hours. I take the children to the toilet and give them a drink of water, and put them back in bed. I lie back on the bed, feeling really sick inside my body. I find that the humming noises of the ship's engines are making me feel drowsy.

'They're coming to get me...gerroff...' I hear myself mumbling as I push the monsters away. 'They're back!' I burst out into a cold sweat.

'What's wrong...?' I feel an arm around my shoulders. I open my eyes,

'Sam, Oh Sam!'

'What happened? You all right? Hey, you're trembling.'

'The monsters… Ugly monsters, with pitch forks!'

'It's ok now!' he soothes me.

I take a deep breath and begin to feel better. I stare into Sam's eyes. 'We're going to be caught, I just know it!'

'Hey, you're with me now. Everything's fine.'

I jump up and check the top bunk. 'The children…are they all right?'

'They're fine. I gave them a drink of pop at around two when I came off shift.'

'They'll wet the bed!'

'I took them to the toilet. I changed Kathleen's diaper.'

'Her what? What have you changed on her?'

'She was wet! I just put a fresh diaper on. I found them in one of your bags.'

'Oh, you mean nappy?'

'Yes, nappy!' He's chuckling with mirth now.

I almost fall over with shock. 'But you're a man!'

'I know I'm a man. So what does that imply?'

'Men don't change nappies…diapers!'

'It's just another job!'

'Well, I never heard the like of it before! You're a marvel, that's what!'

'I have never had that title before! Now, you go back to sleep. It's still early.'

I notice a blanket and a pillow on the floor. 'Have you been sleeping on the floor?'

'I was afraid I'd upset you.'

'You won't! It is your bed. I can share it!' I suggest surprisingly, even to myself.

'What about your honour?' he asks.

'Well, if you keep your hands to yourself, I'll keep my honour,' I reply.

He sits on the side of the bed and his mouth breaks into a great American smile. 'I hope you don't mind, but I brought you something,' he says, pulling open a bag.

'What?' I ask.

He hands me a fresh sandwich.

'I'm not hungry,' I tell him.

'Still feeling nauseous?'

I nod my head. I feel worse by the minute.

'By the way, the children have eaten. I also gave them one of these.' He hands me something in a foil packing.

'What is that?' I shy away from the object.

'It's only a seasickness tablet! I thought you could use one.'

'Do you think a little white pill can make me better?' I take the tablet from his fingers.

He hands me a bottle. 'Here, have a drink.'

'What sort of drink is that?' I ask as I down a mouthful. 'It's great!'

'Fizzor!'

'That's a strange name for a lovely drink.'

'Glad you approve. I brought you something else.' He takes a garment from the bag. 'Something to wear.' He holds up a pale blue silk nightdress.

'It's gorgeous.' I resist the urge to ask him where he got it, as Jim's angry face comes to mind. 'It's silk!'

'Glad you approve. Now, I must be off, so I'll see y'all soon.'

Sam is suddenly gone.

About an hour later the twins wake up.

'Come on, we'll all go to the lav, then you can have a drink and breakfast!'

'Lav,' James repeats, holding his willie.

After that I feel so good I decide we all need a bath! We all take our clothes off and step into the little shower room. 'God this is wonderful, like warm rain!' I laugh. The children sense my excitement and forget their fear. 'Ah, don't touch these taps now!'

The children shake their heads.

'Good!'

I'm washing Kathleen's hair with some lovely shampoo in a plastic bottle. Next thing I know, she's crying. 'Mammy...Mammy!' She rubs her eyes.

'What's wrong mo chaileen ban?'

I realize it's the shampoo. 'It's all right Alanna! Mammy will wash it all away.'

The shower curtain suddenly flaps against my legs. My skin feels prickly and cool. I peer out from behind the shower curtain and emit a gasp. There's a man! He's wearing a moustache and a towel around his waist. It's not Albert and it's not Sam! It must be Charlie. I crouch down and hold on tightly to Kathleen and James. 'I'm sorry; we won't be a tick,' I call from behind the curtain. 'Please go,' I plead.

Suddenly the shower curtain is pulled over and a hand turns the taps off. The man stands in the doorway in a most intimidating manner. I take a deep breath. 'I need the towel.' I point to the three fluffy towels Sam left hanging near the door.

He folds his arms and grins. 'Git it yerself Gal!'

I reach out between him and the towel. As my fingers grasp the towel, he gets hold of my arm and clenches me tightly.

'You do as I say, or else!' He flexes his muscles, and pulls my face to his. 'What a mighty sight y'all are!'

'Please don't …the children,' I whisper, moving in front of the two.

'Kiss?' He puckers his lips.

Behind me Kathleen and James start to whimper.

'You're Charlie, aren't you?'

'Well, I'll be…' He pulls my face towards his pursed lips. 'We're old friends now darling!'

'Stop it…the children…' I pull my head away from him.

He pushes me away, and throws the two other towels at me. 'Here!' he says in a gravel-rich tone.

I pin the first towel around myself and quickly wrap the second two towels around the children.

My hands are trembling as I try to dry the children off.

'Hurry it up will ya!' he growls at me. 'Let me assist you there Gal,' he says, taking Katheen in her towel and throwing her on the top bunk. He does the same with James. The children screw up their faces and stare at me, shocked. 'Don't ya dare cry!' he says, pointing his finger at them.

'Look at the lovely toys,' I say, handing each one a squeaky animal. They reach out and take their toys. 'Mammy,' Kathleen cries. 'Take your toy under the blanket. They'll get cold,' I say quietly, lifting the blanket up for them. They both snuggle under the warm blanket. I grab my nightie, which is lying on the bottom bunk. I still have the towel around me, which I'm holding onto with one hand, and I'm attempting to pull my nightie over my head with the other hand. Charlie steps close to me. I feel cornered.

'Are you free Sweetheart?' He takes hold of my nightie and yanks it back off my head. I grasp hold of it until I hear a tearing sound, then I let go. He grabs me around the neck and places his large hand over my mouth. I respond to his move by biting his finger!

'Bitch!' he yelps as he pushes me away. I fall backwards onto Sam's bunk. Charlie's shadow immediately fills the space in front of me. He's sucking his damaged finger and I can feel his anger looming above me. All I can think of is the children. 'Don't …the children!' I whisper.

He takes a tight grip of my arms and pulls them outwards. His muscles bulge with strength. 'Ouch,' I say, suppressing a scream. Holding my arms, he tries to press his mouth against mine. I twist my head and spit at him.

'Co-operate or…I'll turn you in, Bitch,' he says in his low gravel tone. He tosses me with full force onto the bed. I hear a cracking sound as I fall backwards.

'Me back…it's broken…' I whisper as pain sears through my bones and his body lands on top of me.

'Get off her, Charlie, you Son of a Bitch,' Sam's voice rings into my ears and Charlie is pulled off me. I lie still as a fight ensues. I cover my face for a moment, and when I look Sam is pushing Charlie out the door.

'Don't forget your towel!' Sam's angry words give me a strange satisfaction. The door closes. Sam turns the key.

'I'll get you for this,' I can hear as the door is pounded from without.

Sam ignores the noises. 'Are you ok? Did he…?'

'My back…something cracked,' I whisper, clutching the towel, hardly daring to move.

Sam places his arm around me. 'Try to sit.' Slowly I move forward into a sitting position.

'I think I'm all right…'

Sam's voice is full of emotion, huskily he asks, 'If he hurt you, I swear I'll kill him!' He's holding me close.

'He was trying to kiss me…he shoved me backwards and I heard a terrible cracking sound…'

The cracking sound returns right then, throwing us both into the air. The bed has collapsed. Our heads are on floor level, sandwiched to each other; our feet are sticking up in the air on the end of the bed that hasn't fallen down. We're suddenly both laughing. 'Did I mention the cracking noise?' I say, bursting into laughter. Kathleen and James peer over the side of their bunk bed and giggle.

'Get back under the blanket. Now!' I call out. Their faces disappear from view. I'm staring into Sam's face and he's smiling from ear to ear. 'I'm so sorry! I'm so sorry,' I repeat myself.

Sam hugs me. 'It's not your fault. I'm sure you didn't entice him.'

I smile into his very close face. 'No, I'm sorry about the bed.'

We both laugh.

Sam kisses my cheek. 'I glad you're ok! You are ok?'

When we wriggle to get out, suddenly I'm aware of pain. 'My back. It does hurt. I can't stand up…' I say, bending forward.

Sam holds me close in his arms. I think he's hugging me again. I gasp as he quickly and strongly jerks my body towards him. He releases me. I'm standing straight. 'The pain's gone!' I say, 'It's a miracle. How did you do that?' I ask, amazed.

'It's an old chiropractic trick of mine…' he laughs.

'Here, I've been shopping again,' he says, picking up a brown paper bag off the floor.

I look inside. There's a green skirt and an apricot coloured finely knitted jumper, plus a really wide belt with a fancy golden buckle on the front. 'They're beautiful. You must know a good shop,' I say. 'Can I try them on?'

'Sure.'

'Turn around!' I instruct him. 'They're on. What do you think?' I ask, swinging my hips.

'Wowee! You look terrific Niamh.'

'They're exactly my size. It's amazing,' I say smiling happily. I shove my hands into the side pockets of the skirt. 'Lovely deep pockets too, like my other skirt.'

'I'm am glad you approve. And I brought you this.' He hands me a lovely hairbrush.

'Oh, I really need one of these?' I say, immediately brushing my hair. I'm still wondering from where he's getting these but I daren't ask.

As if he's reading my mind, he says, 'Aren't you going to ask where I got these from?'

I shake my head.

'Would you like to know?'

'I would love to know, but I don't want to make you mad,' I explain.

'I could never be angry with such an angel as you are.'

'I warn you, I'm no angel.'

'You're very close…'

I smile at Sam, flattered. 'You remind me of Brian Boru,' I exclaim.

'An old boyfriend of yours?' he asks.

'No, he was the first king of Ireland.'

'A king? I like that.' His eyes are suddenly teary.

'What's up? I ask.

'You! You're such an amazing person. You've risked so much for your children. You're the bravest woman I ever met. Braver than my Grand-aunt Elizabeth…'

He's not joking? I wonder, staring into his face.

'No one has ever called me brave before.' I reply. Then

I think of Maeve. 'My sister would call me a right egit if she could see me.'

'My great Aunt Elizabeth would call you honourable, brave and a beautiful angel.'

'Your Aunt…? '

'Niamh, sit down.' We sit on the edge of the broken bed. 'She was a fine woman. The Sioux Indians captured her, along with her small sister. She grew up with Indians, and twenty years later she persuaded them to let her go back to her white community with her two small children, after her husband, Big Horn, was killed in a battle. She rode into an American camp, and met my great Uncle Theodore…,'

'Did they fall in love?' I ask as he pauses.

'They sure did. They got married and lived happily ever after.'

'Ah, sure you're having me on!' I say shaking my head, smiling. 'I know that's definitely not how my life works.'

He opens his top buttons and reveals a leather cord with a gold ring hanging on it. He takes it over his head and holds the glimmering ring. 'Niamh, what I say is the Gospel truth. See this?'

'I do, it's a ring!'

'That's correct. Can you see the tiny engraving on the inside?'

'Sure I can't read an ordinary newspaper, let alone a tiny engraving. Can you read it?'

'It says, Elizabeth, love Theo.'

'Sure that's very romantic, but it doesn't prove anything.'

'I know their story is true, and true love can happen.'

'I think that's a very true statement,' I say agreeably, remembering Niall, smiling at my thoughts.

'That's an encouraging statement! Every woman deserves such love.'

'And every man too!' I say, agreeing, remembering Niall's happiness and mine.

'My Queen Niamh…' His mouth is suddenly on mine. For an instant I respond, with thoughts of Niall flooding my mind. His kiss tastes like chocolate. Oh God, I wish this was Niall, I pray as our lips and mouths become a sweet delight to each other for a single moment.

'No, I can't...,' I whisper, faintly resisting him.

He hugs me tenderly. I yield myself to his sweet embrace.

We do not see the door being unlocked.

Chapter eight

'A rrest him.' A booming voice thunders through the
opening, severing us apart as though it was a guillo-
tine. The booming voice is that of Captain Perceval
Simms, in decorative array, his shoulders and chest brightly
adorned by medals and striped ribbons. A man of distinction, honour and unfortunately for us, power! Charlie, with
a sharp expression, steel eyes and trimmed moustache, in
full-decorated gleaming white uniform, follows his master,
panting like a hound. I get such a fright I slip off the bed
onto the floor. Sam bends down to help me up. We stand
up together, holding each other.

'Oh my God…Charlie…why?' Sam exclaims, his face
showing amazement.

Charlie stares back. His mouth twitches underneath the
burnished bronze moustache, which flicks silently up and
down in its own intense rhythm. Two more men in uniforms
with weapons in their hands fill the tiny room..

'Don't touch her, or the children,' Sam says, shielding
me with his outstretched arm.

Roughly they rotate him, pull his hands together and
clip handcuffs on.

'I hereby arrest you for concealing an unauthorized

person. Anything you say can be used against you…' They shove him outside the door and they march him off.

At that moment I notice something shiny on the floor. I bend down and pick it up. It's Sam's chain and ring. 'Sam,' I call out.

Immediately Charlie stands in front of me. 'He's out of bounds woman!'

'Arrest this woman,' Charlie shouts, 'she's a criminal, a kidnapper!'

'I am not!' I deny his accusation.

'She kidnapped the children,' Charlie advised Captain Simms, who comes through the door immediately.

'God strike me dead! They're mine!' I cry.

'I'm sorry,' Captain Simms says, 'I am Captain of this ship, and it is my duty to arrest all vagrants aboard. Anything you say can be used as evidence against you. You may choose to remain silent. You are hereby arrested for vagrancy and for unlawfully occupying ship's quarters without official consent.'

'Put your hands behind your back,' he says.

'I've got something belonging to Sam,' I reply. 'I need to see him.'

'I bet you do! But you are not going to see that Son of a Bitch!' Charlie says, his moustache twitching horribly.

'Put your hands behind your back. That's an order,' Captain Simms repeats sternly.

The second man holds a pair of handcuffs in his hands, and politely waits for me to turn around.

I quickly slip the smooth gold bundle into my skirt pocket and then turn with my back to him. My arms are pulled back, and I feel the cold metal handcuffs snapping my wrists together.

'My children…' I cry, beckoning towards the bunk beds.

'We'll take care of them, Sir!' the man who cuffed me says. He swiftly takes Kathleen and James from the bunk bed, wraps them in their towels, and carries them in his arms.

I follow the captain, with Charlie at my rear and the children in the arms of the other man. We travel in a line up two winding stairways. We come to a door and halt. I'm pushed inside and the door is closed. I can hear Kathleen's muffled screams as they move past the doorway. The lock goes 'click'. 'Let me out!' I wail as I bang on the door with my feet. I look around. It's a bigger room than Sam's room. There's a small room on the left side of a single porthole, which is being pounded by waves. There's a long cupboard on its right. Two bunk beds are arranged on either side of these two structures. The room is dark, but after a minute, I notice two figures huddled on the floor. 'Teresa and Noel? What are you doing here?' I ask as they glare at me.

'You snitched on us,' Teresa says cattily.

'How come I've got these on,' I say, showing my hand-cuffs at my back.

'Oh well, we're all in the same boat!' Teresa retorts, then laughs. We all laugh at the joke.

'It's not funny though,' Teresa comments after a minute. We both look at Noel.

'Me? No, I swear I didn't snitch!'

'You said it was Niamh,' Teresa shouts at Noel. 'You're always boasting about lying. It was you! There's nobody else?' she screams.

'All right. I did!' he snarls.

'I knew it!' Teresa suggests emphatically. 'Tinker!'

Noel shrugs his shoulders. 'Don't call me names. Well now they'll probably throw you girls into the freezing water. Boys are more valuable than girls. They can think!'

'Shut your gob.' She looks at me. 'I think they might bring us to America, because we're too far from Ireland now. When I get there I'm going to run off with Albert! He's my boyfriend now!'

'Half your luck,' I say sliding down the wall into a sitting position on the cold floor. There's silence for a few moments. I can feel the fear all around us, like a heavy Irish mist.

'Did you say anything about my childers?' I put the question to Teresa.

'No! Nothing. I said nothing.'

'Yes you did.' Noel reminds Teresa. 'She snitched on you. Teresa said the children were kidnapped!'

Fear strangles my throat. 'Why did you say that? I never told you that.'

'I heard you call her Kathleen. Then I remembered what they said on the radio. Her name was Kathleen. I think you hacked her curls off and changed her name.'

'You are so smart Teresa! So why did you do that?'

'I thought they'd let me off if I told them.' She shrugs her shoulders. 'I had to look after meself.'

…

'Time to go!' A voice rings in the unlocked door. Three officers march into the room and each one takes hold of one of us.

'Are you throwing us overboard?' I ask as we're pulled to our feet.

'Sure are,' the officer replies. 'Come on, single file, up the stairs,' one officer says, pushing me from behind.

Teresa screams, so they tie a cloth around her face. Noel and I keep quiet then.

All my dreams are vanishing like the stars at daybreak as I trudge down the narrow corridor. We reach an opening and stop. 'Turn around,' one officer with a white hat says to us. We turn around. For a second a cloud of fear falls over me. 'They're going to push us over,' Noel whispers in my ear.

Even the thought of the cold sea makes me shiver. 'My childers…'

Then I feel someone unlocking my cufflinks. 'Regulation,' he says, strapping a bright yellow lifejacket on each of us. 'Over you go, Mam,' he says to me. I look down and there's a boat alongside the big ship. 'What about my childers?' I ask, trembling.

'Mam, just follow orders and step over. Get your legs around the rope, and hold on tight.' I hang onto a rope and I'm lowered into the boat. Teresa is followed by Noel. We land in the smaller boat and are greeted by a round, red faced man in a black peaked hat. He smiles, showing a thousand wrinkles on his old weather beaten face. 'Where are we going?' I ask him.

'The smallest town on earth, Cork!'

We're told to descend a short stair and find ourselves in a small room with seats in a half-circle.

'James, Kathleen,' I say loudly as I see my two little darlings sitting next to a female officer in two little seats at the end of the room.

'Can I sit with my children?' I ask the woman.

Her face buckles into a thin smile. 'Sorry, I have strict orders to care for these children.'

A hand is placed on my shoulder. I turn around to see a male officer. 'Mam, please sit down back here.'

'But these are my children. They need their mother,' I protest.

'I am sorry Mam. Please put your hands forward.'

I automatically put my hands out and he clasps handcuffs on again.

I stumble back to where Teresa and Noel are seated. They are both handcuffed again and Teresa's gob stopper has been removed.

'You'd think we were criminals,' I comment to Teresa.

A Negro guard sitting next to Noel must have heard me. 'You are!' he remarks laughing.

…

The remainder of the journey seems long and miserable. Being a smaller boat it lurches much more than the big ship. The engine seems very noisy too, and we have to shout if we want to speak, so we just try to sleep and be quiet for most of the journey. We have been offered food several times, but the three of us feel too sick to eat. I can just see Kathleen and James, who have been lying still most of the way. The conversation is sparse and we're all freezing cold as we return from whence we came.

Cork Harbour is shrouded in a fine mist when we arrive like ghosts on the water. A lone man's voice echoes across the waves as our boat is tied to the dock. A figure stoops to fix the gangplank in the dim night-light.

'Come on out you lot. Get up and be quick about it,' a guard says as we climb up the stairs to the main deck. It's the middle of the night, and all we can see are shadows. The place is so quiet we can hear the lapping of the waves against the shore. The three of us are paraded down a short ramp and we climb in the back of a black van and are taken to the local gaol, where Noel is subsequently ushered somewhere, flanked by two guards. Teresa tries to say goodbye, but he disappears into the misty night in a flash. We are put into a room with bars. It has two hard beds and a sink and a toilet. 'I'll take these off ye,' the warder, says as we enter the cell. 'Give your wrists a good rub to get the circulation right,' she advises us kindly.

'We both rub our sore wrists. 'At lease we've stopped moving,' I comment as the door of bars is locked.

'My wrists are all red,' Teresa says, staring at herself.

'Maybe you're rubbing them too hard?' I suggest. 'Mine are all right.' I remark, 'Which bed do you want?'

'This one,' Teresa says, flopping onto the one next to the wall.

'Why not?' I mutter as I fall onto the other bed facing the barred door. 'They're all the same,' I say. We must have fallen asleep after that. A loud bell wakes us up.

'Come on you two chaileen, off to the wash house.'

'But I had a one this week!' Teresa complains.

'Time for another one then. Wash all that muck off you,' the female warden says. 'We couldn't wash the muck off your souls, you pair of whores.'

'I'm not one of those, I'm a mother.' I protest.

'And I'm Officer Sheila O'Donaghue. I'm in charge here, so shut up and follow me.' She marches to a room with a bath half full of water. 'Get your clothes off and get in there. Use the soap.'

'I'm not taking my clothes off in front of her,' I protest.

'If you strip for men, you can strip for women,' she says
sarcastically.

'I won't look,' Teresa whispers, turning around.

'No yabbering you two. Put these on when you come
out!'

'O'Donaghue throws two baggy frocks and two large
knickers on the lone chair.

'I'll take these and have them burned. I'm taking your
shoes as well.'

'You can take my shoes, but please don't take my new
skirt and top. No! They were a present!' I utter, attempting
to get out of the bath.

'Rubbish!' The female guard says as she pushes me back
in the water. 'You're afraid of water are you?'

'No!' I reply

'You're very brazen. You need to wash your mouth out
with soap! These are rubbish and they're getting burned.
Have you anything else to say?' She scowls at me.

'My rings. Can I have them?'

'Not on your life! We don't want you doing harm to
yourself,' she snarls back.

'How could a ring do me harm? I just wear it on my
finger,' I say pleadingly.

'You could use it as a weapon to buy illegal drugs! Don't
argue with me. Get in there now!'

I sink into the bathtub of cold water, take the soap and
I'm washing myself. I get out and Teresa gets in.

'It's freezing in here. We may as well have drowned in
the cold sea.' Teresa whispers.

The next day Teresa's father arrives to see her.

'Out here, now!' another female warder, Molly O'Toole
says, opening the door with her huge key.

She's lucky, I'm thinking, as Teresa is marched off.

She comes back an hour later. After O'Toole locks her
in with me, I ask what went on.

Teresa says, 'I've got to go to court tomorrow. Me da's going to take me back home.'

'I'm very pleased for you then,' I say.

'I don't want to go back to me da. Ever!' She flops on the bed and stares at the ceiling.

I sit on the edge of her bed. 'You're lucky your da cares about you.'

'I hate him!' Teresa says ferociously.

'Hey, you're getting out of this dump, so don't get your knickers in a knot!' I reply.

'Shut your gob!' she retorts bitterly.

The next morning I wake up to a weird moaning noise.

'Teresa?' I can barely whisper the words. She is lying half on the bed and on the floor and there's blood everywhere. Her skin has turned as grey as an Irish sky.

'Help, someone help!' I yell, rattling the door as much as I can. I'm screaming as loud as I can. Keys rattle. A male guard follows Margaret O'Halloran, another female warder. They enter the cell.

'What's up?' she bursts out.

My shaking finger is pointing towards Teresa. 'She's dead, I think she's dead!'

'Call the ambulance Byrne!' she orders.

'Right!' Byrne says, swivelling on his heels and racing back down the corridor.

O'Halloran bends down beside Teresa. 'What have you done?' she asks as I shuffle closer.

'Me?'

'Misha, Me, is right! Tell me now, who else could have done this?'

Words escape me. I shake my head.

'It could be attempted murder,' O'Halloran says dramatically. She turns towards me. 'If you know anything you may as well spit it out now,' O'Halloran insists.

I feel myself going weak in the stomach and at the knees, so I quickly flop onto the bed.

Two men in uniforms carrying a pole stretcher come into the small room and take Teresa away on the stretcher.

'Come on, out,' O'Halloran says to me. She grasps my wrists and roughly places handcuffs on me. I trail after her.

'In here,' she says, opening a small cell, which has a door with a window of bars. There's one bed and a toilet. She goes to leave, when I call out. 'Are you taking these off?' I raise my handcuffed hands.

Her eyes narrow as she stares into mine. She sighs, and whispers as she turns the key, 'We'll find out who did it you know!'

Two days later a young handsome man, tall, fair, wearing a black full-length surplus and a purple silk scapular, suddenly appears in the doorway.

'The top of the morning to you now. I'm Father Martin O'Reardon, I'm here to help you…may I?' he asks politely.

I nod my head. He sits on the bed next to me. I stare at my wrists.

'Is Teresa all right?' I ask.

'Now who's that?' he replies, leaning forward like he's going to hear my confessions.

'They think I killed her,' I say.

'Do you think you did? You can tell me you know,' he says, leaning over so closely a loose strand of his hair is touching my forehead. His voice is soft as melted butter.

I move away. 'No!'

'I understand. You're in denial! It's all in your mentality.'

'So, I'm mental now?'

'No. You're just refusing to face your demons, that's all.' He leans close again and whispers. 'Just confide in me. Everything will work itself out. You'll see.'

'I swear I didn't do anything to Teresa,' I protest.

'You did kidnap her?'

'No! That was Kathleen!'

'So, who's Loretta?' he asks cunningly.

'Nobody. That's really Kathleen.'

He pats my hand. 'I see! So, Teresa is your third victim?'

'No. She killed herself!'

'Is that right? Was that when you kidnapped her?'

'No! I didn't even know her…She ran away…'

He sighs and smiles. 'You're just confused now. I'll leave you these rosaries, and you can enjoy a time of prayer and penance.' He places a pair of smooth black rosary beads on the bed next to me.

'I'll return tomorrow,' he says, then whispers again, 'Remember, I'm on your side!' He calls the guard to open the door.

I put the rosary beads over my head, and tuck them behind my shift. I am definitely getting confused in my thoughts, I concur. He comes back as promised, and returns every day for two weeks. Each time he encourages me to share something from my past with him. He seems genuinely interested in me. In the last day or two he's been sitting so close to me, holding me, and once he accidentally touched my breasts outside my shift. Around the fifteenth visit he comes in with an extra bounce in his step. He smiles.

'I have good news for you.'

I look up. Can there be such a thing? 'What?' I mutter.

'Teresa is …alive. She's going to be fine.'

'Did she blame me?' I ask nervously.

He looks at me with his kind eyes. 'No, she admitted that she tried to harm herself.' He pauses. 'That leaves you in the clear.'

'Will she be sent back to her da?'

'Most likely, but that's not your business, Missus Farrell.' He suddenly stops and stares at me. 'It's enough that your dear husband was drowned.' He suddenly sits down very close to me. 'I am sorry.' He reaches for my hand and holds it a moment. 'May I call you Niamh?'

I nod my head. I slip my hand from under his.

He holds his own hands together, like he's praying. 'Now is there anything you want to tell me today?'

'About what?'

'What's troubling you?' he says quietly.

'My children.'

'Why are they troubling you today?'

'I don't know where they are,' I reply. 'I've told you that already.'

'I know that.' He suddenly puts his arm around me and holds me tightly. His hand is resting on my right breast again! He whispers in my ear as thought he's telling a secret. 'If I tell you they're safe, would you believe me?'

I wiggle to move a little away from him. 'I want to see them!'

'Of course you do.' He hugs me again, drawing me right up to his chest, holding me in a unyielding grip.

'You believe they're mine then?'

He stares into my face and brushes a hair away from my eyes, very gently. 'I believe I do.'

'So, can I see them?' I ask, ignoring his bodily contact, concentrating on thoughts of my children.

'Your case has to come to trial first.' He releases his hold on me.

I shuffle away six inches. I know priests have unnatural power. 'Can't you do something?'

He leans over and places his hand on my shoulder. 'I have connections in high places, you might say.'

'I know! So, you'll help me?' I ask, daring to look into his grey misty eyes.

'I will do everything in my power to help you,' he says in a low croaky voice. He's probably coming down with a cold, I'm thinking.

'So, I can see my childers?'

He looks at me with such compassion that I believe him absolutely. 'I pray to God you will,' he states passionately. There are tears in his eyes and his mouth is set in determination.

...

The next day he returns around the same time. He seems like an old friend already. I'm waiting for him. He sits on the bed and then bends forward with his hands locked together. I think he's praying.

He looks up. 'You need evidence,' he says at last.

'Evidence?' I repeat.

'Someone who knows what you say is true.'

'My sister. She knows.'

'How can I find your sister?'

'Her name is Maeve Flynn. She lives near Scriob.'

He leans over and takes my hand. He squeezes it, then kisses the back of my hand. 'Such rough hands, you need much care! I'll see what I can do.'

Just as he goes to rise, he stares at my neckline. He gently moves the neck of my shift and smiles. 'I'm very pleased to see that you're wearing the rosary beads I gave you!'

'They make me feel safer.'

He smiles, releasing his hands from my neckline. 'I'm here to help in any way I can.' He leaves.

Five days go by before Father Martin reappears in the doorway accompanied by the rattling of keys. He looks very powerful in his black priestly garb.

I jump up to greet him.

'How are you Niamh?'

'Fine. What did Maeve say?' I ask excitedly, then stop because of the seriousness of his expression.

'Niamh. Sit down. I'm afraid I have bad news.'

I sit next to him. 'What?' I ask, trembling.

'She wasn't there!'

'But she's lived there for the last five years. Near McCarthy's Barn...' I pause to swallow the lump in my throat. 'Me da....Did you see anyone?'

'The place is deserted. Nobody has lived there for ages, I was told.'

I shake my head, dismayed. 'But I've only been gone...a month!'

He places his arm around my shoulders. 'I'm very sorry Niamh.'

'What am I to do?' I ask sadly.

'Come here, my child,' he says, as he gently leans my head on his shoulder. He kisses my forehead. I suddenly find tears tumbling over my eyelashes. 'Hush,' he croons, tilting my head upwards, toward his. I think he's going to kiss me on the lips when he suddenly gets up and leaves, turning at the door. He has a strange look in his eyes. 'I'll be back soon.'

He comes back every day that week, teaching me how to behave in court. On the following Monday he turns up before eight o'clock in the morning.

'Niamh, today is your big day at court! I'm coming with you.'

The guards come around a few minutes later and I'm handcuffed and taken along a corridor, out of the building, across the yard and into another building, through a wide corridor and into a dark room.

There's a series of seats with desks at the front; up one end there's a huge desk and a big plaque on the wall above that.

'This is the court room for the prisoners.' Father Martin whispers. 'This is Mister Gabriel Curry, your legal representative.' He introduces me to a round looking man in a suit. It's obvious to me he's wearing a wig. He must be bald, I'm thinking.

'Don't worry! Just do as Mister Curry directs you.' He smiles with his compassionate eyes. '...And stand when Judge Declan Moran comes in, remember?'

'I will.'

I sit down next to Father Martin. I notice a couple of men wearing wigs like Mister Curry. A man in a suit, also wearing a wig, comes over to me. He shakes hands with Mister Curry and Father Martin, introducing himself.

'I'm Padraig O'Faoline, legal representative for the Connors.' They shake hands. He tips his head in my direction. 'Missus Farrell,' is all he says.

Judge Moran comes in. We all stand up. He's wearing a longer wig. I'm thinking they must all be bald, or cold. I wait while other convicts' cases are dealt with. My name is eventually called, and I'm told to stand on a small platform. I do that. After I swear to tell the truth with my hand on a fat bible, O'Faoline steps across and catches my eyes with his. 'Did you or did you not take a child from the home of the Connors on the sixth day of June, nineteen hundred and seventy-one?'

'I think so,' I answer. 'I'm not sure what date…'

'Answer yes or no,' he says coldly.

'Yes…' I begin.

'Exhibit one.' He holds my shoes in a plastic bag.

'Are these your shoes?'

'They are…'

'And you were wearing them on the day of the crime aforesaid?'

'They're my only pair, except for these new prison ones…'

'Your honour, the footprints found at the Connors match these shoes exactly.' He takes the shoes and places them on the Judge's bench.

'That is all! You may step down,' he says to me.

Mister Curry comes over. 'Sit down now,' he whispers. I sit down.

'All rise,' a man says. We all get up. The judge goes out. Then he comes back in again. We all stand up to greet him. We all sit down again. It reminds me of what we do at Mass.

'Will the defendant please rise,' he instructs.

Mister Curry and Father Martin rise up. They tell me to stand. I stand up.

The judge reads: 'Missus Niamh Farrell, you are hereby charged with one count of kidnapping a baby, which you subsequently smuggled on board a ship, in an attempt to abscond to America with the said child.' He pauses and turns to look at me above his spectacles. 'How do you plead?' he asks.

'What do you mean your Highness?'

'Your Honour!'

'Sam didn't take away my honour, your Highness, that's the honest truth…'

Everyone laughs. The judge purses his lips and scowls at me. I gasp in horror.

'You're to say 'guilty, your Honour!',' Mister Curry whispers so loudly others hear. There's a tittering among the small crowd.

'You're guilty, Your Honour!' I repeat.

They laugh again.

The judge coughs and his brows are knitting together. 'I will ask you again. How do you plead?'

Mister Curry is going red and nodding his head, mouthing 'guilty' to me.

I take a deep breath. 'Kathleen is my child. I gave her to the Connors, then I took her back, that's all. I did get on a ship to America, but that was because I had no money…'

'You are then pleading guilty?' Judge Moran asserts.

'Guilty…?' I stutter. 'I…'

Then he says, 'I sentence you to a period of five years incarceration.'

'In… where?' I ask.

Some laugh.

'Gaol,' Father Martin whispers.

'Court is adjourned.' *Bang.* Judge Moran hits the bench.

I jump.

'I'm going to appeal your sentence on the grounds of insanity.' Father Martin says as we leave the courtroom.

'Insanity?' I repeat his words.

Father Martin holds my shoulders in his firm grasp. 'That means instability of mind…'

I interrupt him. 'I know what it means…'

'Ok. So, I'm going to say that you were deeply disturbed and that is why you kidnapped Kathleen.'

I just look at him. 'How will that help?' I ask.

'It might get your sentence deferred. You could have James returned to you.'

'I don't understand,' I say. 'If I'm mad, they'll put me in a madhouse, then I'll really go mad!'

'Niamh, we can only take one step at a time. Trust me.' He looks at me with his kind eyes.

Two guards come over and take me back to my little cell.

Father Martin visits me every day that week, comforting me, assuring me of his help.

A week later when Father Martin comes by I notice that he has his own key to my cell now, so he unlocks the door himself and comes in. 'How are you?' he asks.

'Fine, thanks Father Martin. Sit down.' I indicate the new chair I've just been given.

'Going up in the world!' he smiles. 'Thanks.' He sits.

I sit on the bed.

'Niamh,' he says, taking my hand.

'What Father?'

'I have good news for you. They are going to review your case. I'm going to get you out of this Hell-hole.'

'What about Kathleen?'

'I'm afraid that's out of my league now.'

My face drops with dismay.

He raises his smooth eyebrows. 'I might be able to get you a visit to see James.'

'Could I?' I stare into his soft grey eyes.

'You certainly shall. I delight in your fresh smile.' He pauses and looks into my eyes.

He's my saviour. I adore him. I'm going to see my child, thanks to this saint.

He leans forward and with a kiss like a whisper, gently touches my forehead with his lips. Then he gets up, abruptly. 'Leave it to me.'

He visits me every other day for a week, assuring me of progress in the arrangements to see the children.

A week later he says, 'Niamh, you're going to see James.'

I almost burst into tears. 'Oh thank you! Where is he? When.'

He holds my hands in his. 'You are impetuous!' His smile is like a fascinating painting.

I laugh.

'We have to go to Fermoy.'

'Fermoy?'

'It's not far!'

'How will I get there?'

'I'll take you.'

I must look surprised. 'I'll have to leave here…'

'I know people in high places, remember,' he says happily.

'When?'

'Wednesday.'

'That's still two days away.'

Father Martin places his arm around my shoulders. 'It will go quickly,' he assures me.

On Wednesday I am up, bathed and ready for anything before breakfast.

'You're bright and early today,' the friendly female guard, Patricia Monaghan says as she unlocks my door. 'Got a date?'

'James!'

'Is he handsome?' she asks with a twinkle in her eye.

'Very. He's my son. He's two.'

She suddenly hugs me. 'That's great. I've got something for you.' She hands me a paper bag containing my jumper and skirt.

'They didn't burn them?'

She whispers, 'I told them they looked too good to burn, so they agreed to keep them,' she confides in me. 'They wouldn't give me your three rings,' she says. 'They're safe anyway.'

'Thank you.' I give her a friendly smile. 'Sorry, you probably want to put handcuffs on…' I hold out my wrists for her convenience.

'Not today! You're as free as a bird,' she says kindly, not even looking at my wrists.

I sigh with delight. Suddenly the world seems bright and cheerful, despite the fact that it's raining outside.

Father Martin comes by at ten. He stops when he sees me. 'You look like a picture Niamh!'

I just smile. I'm going to see James. Why wouldn't I be happy!

'Come on. All the paperwork's done.' He walks in front of me and I follow, smiling as I go. I enjoy the cool misty air. I breathe deeply. Father Martin opens the door of a cream coloured sedan.

'Thank you,' I say as I slip into the passenger side seat.

An hour later we approach Fermoy. 'We're to meet in a hotel on the main street.'

We stop at a public toilet. 'I won't be a minute. Wait here', he says, hurrying off, and heading for the 'Buccal' side. Five minutes later he comes out. He's changed from his official black uniform to a lime green shirt and cream coloured flared leg pants, co-ordinated with bone coloured shoes.

'You look...great...normal!'

'I am normal. Very normal!'

'I thought you had to wear those funny clothes all the time?'

'We're at liberty to wear casual clothing when we're not on strictly priestly duties,' he says, smiling.

'Oh!' I say.

Father Martin whispers. 'People don't know me here, so I'll just say we're together, to save embarrasing questions.'

'I thought it was all...official Father?'

'It is. But tongues wag in these country areas! I don't want any problems, you know, me being a priest and you being a beautiful young lady.'

'Ah, go on Father!' I laugh.

He pulls the car over, stops the engine and turns to face me. 'Niamh, please call me Martin.'

'Right, Martin!' I reply readily.

He suddenly leans over and kisses my cheek. 'You're a wonderful, beautiful lady.'

'You're the wonderful one,' I reply. 'What can I do to

express my gratitude for getting me out of the Hell hole and seeing my son?'

'You can do something for me.'

'Anything!' I reply sincerely.

'Will you play a little game?'

'I'm not very good at ball games, but I'm a good runner…'

'A pretend game, just to humour me?' he asks with a twinkle in his eye.

'I can do that,' I reply.

'Will you pretend that you're my …wife, just for these few hours?'

'Your wife?' I say. 'No. I can't…'

He places his arm around my shoulders. 'Just look at us. Could we be a husband and wife?'

I look at him. 'You're too good for me Father,' I say.

'No! And please don't call me Father while we're here. It would give me such a thrill to feel I belonged to a beautiful woman, even for a few hours.'

I'm starting to feel nervous about this game. 'I can't…They didn't give me my rings. A wife needs a ring,' I say jokingly.

'You're a smart girl,' he says. 'Of course we need a ring. Why didn't I think of that?'

He thinks I'm smart, I reflect smugly! I relax.

'What about this?' he says, holding up his little finger.

'It's got a ring on it!' I exclaim. 'What are you doing?'

He's screwing up his face and his finger is turning red as he tries to remove it.' It's too tight,' he says. He sucks his finger. Suddenly there's a ring in his other hand. 'There y'are! It's off!'

He looks at me. 'You wanted a ring. Show me your finger,' he says.

He places it on my finger. 'With this ring I thee wed. Off with your…'

'…clothes and jump into bed!' I finish the sentence for him. We both laugh heartily at this.

'It nearly fits!' I announce, surprised.

'And I nearly had a fit!' he replies. We laugh again.

'It looks like it was meant for you, not me.'

'It looks like a wedding ring!'

'My father gave it to me when I was ordained. 'Married to God,' were his very words. It fitted my ring finger then. I was a skinny lad.' He turns to me and with his misty grey eyes, and stares into mine.

'Niamh, you're great company. I'm really enjoying myself. Let's pretend we're on our honeymoon, just for fun.'

'Go on! I'm only coming to see James. Shouldn't he be here now?'

'He should. This is the hotel.'

The place is deserted.

We sit in the lounge. 'I'll see if I can get you a drink.'

'That'll be nice.'

A few minutes later he returns from the bar. 'Irish coffee! I recommend it.'

He sits down in the armchair next to mine. I'm beginning to feel anxious about James' arrival. 'What's going on. Where's James?'

'I have a bit of bad news.'

'Jesus, Mary and Joseph, what's happened to James?' I say, jumping up.

'Sit down Niamh; it's nothing like that. The river burst its banks and they can't get through right away. We'll just have to wait a bit. At least you're out of that hell hole!'

'But what about James? I'm so longing to see his little face again,' I whisper.

He leans over and puts his arm around me. 'I know. I feel the same. Such a lovely child,' he says.

'So, you've met him?' I ask.

'I have met him, and Kathleen, and their guardians.'

'They should be with me…not some guardians. I'm their mother…' I say lamely.

'I know you are. Niamh, I don't want you to get upset just waiting here. Let's kill a bit of time and have a walk around the town?'

'You're right. I just wish…' I finish drinking my Irish coffee.

We sit under a shady oak tree near a pond and enjoy fish, chips and lemonade for lunch.

'Let's feed the ducks,' Martin suggests as two little greenish ducks come quacking along and we throw bits of our food towards them. I slip on the edge of the bank, 'Mammy…' I cry.

Martin quickly hooks his arm around my waist and retrieves me. For a moment I think he's going to plant a kiss on my lips, but then he lets go. At four o'clock we return to the hotel and he goes off to make a telephone call. I'm waiting in the lounge, anxiously sipping an orange juice.

Martin looks worried when he returns. 'Niamh, they're not going to get here today. The roads are blocked. They're going back to Dungarvan and they'll try again tomorrow.'

'Oh no! We'll have to go back to Cork then.'

'I've rung the *Gates of Hell* and told them what's happened. They understand, surprisingly.' He laughs at this. 'We'll have to stay the night.'

'Where?'

'I'll book two rooms.'

'All right.'

'Wait here.' Ten minutes later he returns. 'Niamh, they only had one double room available tonight. I said we'd take it!'

'You didn't say we're married!'

'It's none of their business! Don't worry, I won't touch you.'

'Maybe there's a tinceard's camp around here?' I say my thoughts aloud. 'We could stay with them.'

'I won't let you go back to that way of life! Anyway, I'm obliged to take care of you myself. That's the agreement I have with the warders.'

'I think we should go back to Cork…' I suggest.

Martin seems slightly perturbed by that suggestion, pauses and says, 'It's too late. I've paid for it now.'

I don't want to upset him after all he's done for me. I try to smile and say, 'All right.'

'Don't look so downcast fair maiden. I shall sleep on the floor and you shall sleep on the feather bed. What I propose is this. I dine you and wine you and then we return here for the night!'

Martin looks so happy. It's only a game I suppose. It's only one night! 'At least I'll see James tomorrow.'

'That's the spirit.' He offers me the crook of his arm. 'Come, I shall show you to your boudoir.'

I still feel worried, even as I tuck my arm in his and we stroll through the corridor, walking on soft carpet, ending up at a door with a shining brass number eleven. We go in. The room is lovely, with a double bed and bathroom next to it.

It's now I realize something. 'Martin, I've got nothing to wear…in bed!'

'That's not a problem for me,' he says grinning.

I feel pink in the face. 'It is for me Martin, seriously!'

He sits on the bed staring at me with a sheepish look of repentance. 'I don't want you to have any problems Niamh. I'll get you something suitable to wear.'

'Where?' I ask, looking around.

'In the shops!' he replies whimsically.

I shrug my shoulders. I never thought of that! Off we go down the streets, gazing into a women's dress shop. There's two, one either end of the town. We traipse to the second one.

'Do you like these, darling?' he asks me as he picks out this lovely light blue coloured satin nightdress and a robe to match, and underpants in blue satin. I just let my eyeballs fall out. I nod.

'My wife would love these, please!'

Liar, liar, I'm saying inside. 'They're lovely,' I say politely but meaning it. They're glorious!

The shop assistant, a woman with slicked-back dark hair, deepset eyes, a long bony nose, high cheekbones and bright red cupid lips, smiles by pursing up her lips! 'Will I gift wrap them for you Sir?'

Martin winks at me and replies, 'Yes please. We're on our honeymoon.'

'That's lovely! You won't need these for long then!' She takes a piece of floral wrapping paper from under the counter and begins the wrapping process, glancing at us in between moves, smiling cupidly. 'This is your lucky day!' she says warmly.

'How's that?' Martin asks.

'It's ten past five! We should have closed ten minutes ago.'

'Is that right?' Martin replies. 'This is our lucky day then.' He hands over his cash. 'Thank you kindly, Mam,' he says. She watches us with amusement as we leave.

I shake my head as the doorbell of the shop rings to signal our exit.

He glances back into the shop. The woman is watching attentively. Martin suddenly spins me around to face him. 'Kiss me!' he commands. 'She's watching!' Somehow our lips meet, and we kiss. Martin holds me under the armpit and smoothly moves me few steps away from the shop as he's kissing me, almost roughly. He looks into my eyes and then he releases me from the suction power of his lips.

'You shouldn't have done that!' My lips are tingling. I give them a rub.

'Why not? We're on our honeymoon!'

I recollect my wits. 'Martin! It's a big fat lie.'

He sighs. 'I wish it was true Niamh. That kiss was tremendous!' He nods his head agreeably.

The kiss was more of a shock than a nice surprise. I wouldn't want to say that. I just smile.

After finishing a bottle of wine with our dinner we make our way up the stairs to the bedroom. I collapse on the bed. My mind feels fuzzy.

'Shall I run Madame's bath?'

'Mm,' I reply hazily.

After having a bath my head feels clearer.

'How about giving me a fashion show,' Martin says, lying on the bed in a very relaxed pose as I emerge from the bathroom. I twirl around in the blue robe.

'That's lovely. What about the other gear I bought you?' he asks.

I remove the robe and flaunt the nightie.

'You're like a queen,' he says. 'What about the knickers?' He comes over and puts his arms around me now.

'You saw it in the shop!' I say, removing his arms and climbing between the sheets. I sigh. 'This is like Heaven.'

'It is,' Martin agrees with me. He grins from ear to ear as he heads for the bathroom. 'I'll get some of the muck off me.'

I close my eyes and drift into sleep.

'I shall camp here, like a Tinceard!' Martin says, coming from the bathroom with nothing but a towel on. He flops down on the floor, pummelling his trousers into a pillow, using the towel as a blanket.

I feel myself being pulled from my sleepiness by his voice. 'You're in the nip!' I say, alarmed, blinking as I stare at his silhouette through the towel. He forgot to get himself a pyjamas, I'm thinking. Maybe all his money was gone on my expensive nightwear? I stare at the wall.

'I always sleep like this,' is his response, 'God this floor is as hard as a rock,' he grumbles momentarily. 'The towel is damp too…'

I feel bad about his discomfort. I close my eyes tightly. 'Goodnight Martin!'

'Niamh,' Martin whispers after he puts the light out.

'What?' I say, responding to his voice.

'The floor must be concrete. It's terribly cold. Can I sleep with you. I promise I won't touch you, not even with my breath.'

'Ask for another blanket,' I suggest.

'I did that. They said some of the blankets are at the dry cleaners. They suggested we keep each other warm.' His reply shocks me.

'They're rude,' I say.

He sighs and lies back down. I can hear him groaning pitifully, rolling around.

He'll never get to sleep on that hard floor, without a blanket. 'All right. You can sleep under the blanket, just to keep warm. Remember, no touching.'

He creeps under the blankets.

I fall into a deep sleep until I hear this terrible noise.

I wake up, alarmed. 'You're snoring.' I give Martin a dig in the ribs.

'I am still freezing,' Martin says, curling up.

I can feel him shaking with the cold. I hate that feeling myself. 'Snuggle up to me then, and stop snoring,' I suggest, sighing.

'Thanks Niamh. You are a real angel of the night!' He puts his arm around me and I can feel his body warming up next to me. The only barrier between us now is the silk nightwear!

We both wake up early, before six. His face is next to mine. He's got a scapula around his neck.

'What's that for?' I ask.

He smiles. 'I'm going to confess something.'

'I thought you wore that to hear confessions, not to confess,' I say.

'You are so smart. Here I'll put it around your neck.' He takes the purple scarf with fringes and places it around my neck, holding each end close to my breast. 'There! I confess this a dream come true for me Niamh. Waking up next to a beautiful wife.'

I stare into his misty eyes, replying sleepily, 'And hearing your confessions.'

'What's my penance?' he says, grinning his beautiful smile.

I shake my head. He's mad!

'How about I have to kiss you a hundred times?' he says, laughing.

'You've been kissing the Blarney stone…' I say, sighing. I move my face close to his.

'You're my blarney stone.' He kisses me on the lips. 'Definitely softer.'

We kiss for a few moments. He suddenly sits up. 'Sorry Niamh, I forgot myself. I'd better go and ring this chaperone and see what's happening?'

'It's quarter to six. It might be a bit early.'

'You're right Niamh. I am still jaded,' he says, snuggling under the blankets.

'It's too cold out here,' I say pulling the warm blanket over my shoulder and closing my eyes.

'You look like an angel now,' Martin says, running his finger down my cheek. I turn around.

His eyes are full of love. He kisses me all over my face, then on the mouth…

'Twenty, twenty one…' he says, between kisses. I close my eyes and think of Niall. I find myself responding to Martin. Before I know it we are going 'all the way'. Afterwards, we're lying together, quiet.

'I'm sorry Niamh. I didn't mean for that to happen, please forgive me?'

'I forgive you!' I reply.

He props himself up on his elbow and looks at me lovingly. 'But it was wonderful! Niamh. I've been thinking.'

'Thinking of what?' I ask.

'About you and James and Kathleen.'

The faces of my children leap into my mind. 'What about us?'

'I'm thinking of leaving the priesthood.'

I sit up at that remark and look into his disturbed face. 'Why?'

'I don't think I can live as a priest any longer. I think… I'm in love. With yourself James and Kathleen!'

'You can't be in love with three people!'

'All three!'

'You must be joking!'

He shakes his head. 'I'm deadly serious.'

He looks at me so seriously I laugh. 'Sorry, I shouldn't laugh! You can't do that. You made a vow!'

'Nobody can tell the future Niamh. My dream now is to vow to marry you and go to Australia with you James and Kathleen.'

'We can't do that. Remember, I'm a …convict. I still

have nearly five years to do. I probably shouldn't even be here…'

'I nearly forgot about that. You are so beautiful any man would forget himself with you.' He kisses me passionately again, then stops suddenly. 'I'm sure I can get you out of that prison. I'm bloody well going to try, if it's the last thing I do on this earth.'

Finally, that afternoon, a woman who's wearing a navy business suit and white tailored shirt arrives on the bus with James. Just before we greet them, Martin whispers, 'They think we went back to Cork, so don't say anything about staying here overnight, will you? And they were not told I'm a priest, for political purposes, so mum's the word!'

James is here, that's what matters to me right now. 'All right,' I reply lightly.

'Mammy, Mammy,' he yells when he sees me coming towards him.

I hug him and give him a big swing. 'James! Mammy loves you.'

'Lub you,' he whispers back.

'Martin O'Reardon - Niamh's chaperone.' He extends his manly hand to Jane.

'Jane Priest.' She holds her slim hand out, looking down her large nose at Martin. The largeness of her nose contrasts with her pale elfin shaped face. Her brown hair is tied in a bun at the back of her head. Her eyes are hazel and sharp. Her lips are pale and uncoloured.

'That's an interesting name!' he states, his face remaining blank.

'Thank you Mister O'Reardon,' Jane states politely, lamely dropping her hand into his.

'Call me Martin, please!'

'If you wish.' Her French manicured fingers move to her face decorously. Her index finger rests for a moment under her jaw line. He returns her smile, catching her eyes in his for a moment. Under her watchful eyes we play games, feed the ducks and have lots of hugs for around an hour and a half. We're sitting on a bench seat watching James running back and forth in a lush grassy patch.

'The bus is due to arrive at half four,' Miss Priest announces, glancing at her watch.

James falls over at that moment, so I rise up and rush towards him. Martin follows me.

I pick James up and examine his knee. 'Mammy will kiss it better.' I kiss his knee and brush a piece of grass away. James giggles. A feeling of anxiety suddenly grasps my heart. 'Martin, how can I say goodbye. He's going to be so upset… I haven't prepared for this.'

Martin kneels down next to me and speaks quietly. 'I'll handle it. Watch me.'

He turns to James who's just about to run off again. 'James, why don't we get you an ice cream, then you can get on the bus for a drive.'

James stops and revolves himself. 'Ice keam!'

'You wait here with Mammy.' Martin says, going to nearby shop with an ice cream sign hanging outside. A few minutes later he comes back with four soft ice cream cones, two in each hand.

'Very good value, much better than Cork!' he exclaims as he gives Jane Priest and me an ice cream.

'Serviette!' he adds, pulling some paper napkins from his back trouser pocket.

'Thank you kindly,' Jane Priest says demurely, and then notices the bus coming around the corner.

'… the bus, it's early!'

My heart drops at her words. I try to lick my ice cream cone. The bus pulls up. James is sitting in the grass, hand outstretched for his ice cream.

'Now before you get this you have to go on the bus,' Martin says.

'Bus.' He pushes himself off the ground and immediately marches towards Martin. Martin lifts him as though he's a feather and puts him on the bus. Miss Priest sits next to him. I stand near the doorway of the bus.

'Here's your ice cream,' Martin says, placing a serviette under the neck of his shirt and putting the cone in his hand.

'Wave to Mammy,' Martin states authoritatively.

James waves momentarily. His eyes are on his ice cream. He licks it greedily.

'Quick, let's get out of sight,' Martin says, leaping off the bus and hurrying me along the footpath in the opposite direction.

'I can't…' I whisper, stopping in my tracks.

Martin puts his arm around me. 'You can… 'Don't look back. You've had a good time. Remember that!'

'I will.' The tears drop onto my ice cream. 'You're always right!'

The bus disappears out of sight. My last picture of James is him with a blob of ice cream on his sweet nose.

Shortly after that we head back to Cork. On our way out of town we stop at the public toilets. I go to the *Chaileen* side. Martin goes in with a bag and comes out dressed in black.

'Right. I'm a priest again. Remember Niamh, if you want someone to marry you, always call a priest.'

I laugh. Martin has been good to me, I reflect, even if we did do the wrong thing last night, and I wonder if God will forgive us! I know now that he's just another human being trying to help others.

'You're funny! Thanks for a special day Martin.'

'My pleasure, all my pleasure,' he says, pressing his foot down hard on the accelerator. In less than two hours we're back in Cork.

'So, you look refreshed. Had a good time in Dublin then?'

'Dublin? We didn't go to Dublin, just Fermoy,' I reply to Patricia Monaghan, as I check in; while Martin is talking to the supervisor. She runs her hands over my body. It makes me think of someone creeping over my grave.

'I won't ask you to take off all your clothes. It's too cold.'

'Thanks!' I suddenly notice I'm still wearing Martin's

ring. I slip it into my mouth while she's writing something in a book.

'So what did you do there, in Fermoy?'

I can feel the blood rushing up my neck. It's hard to talk with a ring next to my teeth. 'We had to wait for James because of the river bursting its banks.'

'What river?'

'Blackwater…' I mumble.

'That's the first I've heard of it! God we hear nothing in this place! You'd think we were in prison!' she exclaims. 'Here, put this on.' She hands me a clean prison dress. 'Put your things back in the bag. I'll make sure they're safe. Oh, and spit that thing out,' she says coolly.

I nearly swallow the ring with fright. I spit the ring into my hand, wipe it in my prison shift, and hand it over. 'How did you know?'

She looks at me with amusement. 'I didn't come down with the last shower!' She looks at me. 'You didn't nick it by any chance?'

'No…somebody gave it to me…' My face feels red even as I speak.

'I have a mind to report O'Halloran.'

'Why, what did she do?' I ask, mystified.

'It's what she didn't do. She should have seen that ring when you first came here.'

'Please…don't say anything. I don't want trouble,' I beg.

She folds her arms and stares at me, then unfolds them. 'All right, I'll do that this one time! At least it'll be safe if I put it away.'

'You're very kind.'

'On this occasion.'

'Thanks Miss Monaghan,' I say as she hurries me into my cell.

'Call me Patricia,' she says quietly.

As the days drag on I am beginning to doubt I will see Martin again. It's the fifteenth of August, thirty five days since we were together. The next day he marches into my cell and sits on the edge of the bed as though it was yesterday we were together. 'How are you Niamh?' he asks casually. He's got his hands together, praying, I suppose.

'Fine! I thought you might not come back!'

'I had things to sort out…'

'They took your ring. I'm sorry,' I say.

'I could say you stole it?' He laughs heartily immediately. 'Sure no, I'm only joking!' He sits beside me on the bed. 'Keep it for now. It's only rolled gold, so it's not worth much! The important question is us! I need you Niamh, like a duck needs water.'

He puts his arm around my shoulders and hugs me tightly. 'And I've got great news for you.'

'I can see Kathleen?'

'Sorry! No! She's gone back to be with her parents, the Connors. Guess again…?'

'Something about James?'

He pats my hand. 'You're dead right! You can pay him a visit once a month.'

'How did you manage that?'

'I pulled a few strings in high places.'

'Next Wednesday, be ready. We can have a grand time together again.' His hand grasps my breast through my coarse cotton frock.

I ignore his hand and stare into his face. 'I've been sick!'

He removes his hand. 'Oh my poor darling. The warder didn't say anything…'

'I'm expecting!'

'You're joking!'

'No, I'm not. Honest to God. I always get sick in the mornings when I'm expecting, or when I'm on a ship…'

He comes so close I see tiny lines under his misty eyes. 'Niamh, that's terrible! You need to see a doctor, quick!'

'You mean to check and see if I am?'

'If you are he'll get rid of it.'

I feel startled at his reply. 'Get rid of it?'

'It's best to do it quickly, while it's still an embryo.'

'What are you talking about Martin?'

'It's not really a human at this stage! It's just cells joined together, like a bag of marbles.'

'Marbles?'

'I've seen pictures.' He sits a bit closer again. 'I'll explain... You see it doesn't become a real human until around twenty weeks! We can go to Dublin and visit a doctor, discretely. I'd work that out, and pay the cost. If you're quick you can get it done there, otherwise you'll have to go to England.' He stops and reflects for a moment. 'That might be a problem ...'

'What about God? What about your religion?'

'Niamh, we're not in the dark ages now, we've...well some people have ...advanced. These things have been going on for millions of years.'

'This has only been going on for five weeks! It's my child, and I'm keeping It!'

'Niamh, you're too ignorant. Don't be an egit.' He's grinning at me.

I can feel the colour fading from my face. I shiver.

He sees how upset I am, so calms down. 'I'm sorry, I shouldn't have said that. Listen now. I have taken care of you up to now, haven't I?' I'll continue to do so!'

'Please, don't murder the baby!'

He looks at me with utter contempt 'How dare you accuse me of murder, Niamh, when all I'm trying to do is help you. I have compromised myself for you!'

I take a deep breath. 'What about what you said about us being a family, going to Australia. Now we can have our own child as well?'

'Keep your voice down.' He's holding both my wrists tightly. 'I thought I loved you, but you might have planned this pregnancy, even seduced me!'

I begin to cry. Tears cascade down my cheeks.

His demeanour softens. 'Don't cry. I really want to help you Niamh. Please say 'yes' to my generous offer?'

'Offer?' I reply, 'to have an abortion? No thanks!'

'If it's gone we can continue to have good times together.'

'And what if it's not…gone?'

'Niamh. My reputation is at stake! I just can't have this happen! It's your choice. I won't force you to do anything!'

I just shake my head. I don't trust myself to speak.

He turns away. 'All right…Have it your way!' he says gruffly. He turns on his heels and storms out the door.

The next day Patricia Monaghan makes a comment as we head down the corridor to the bathroom.

'What was that all about yesterday?' she asks.

'What?'

'Your man.'

'What do you mean, 'your man'?'

'You know very well. Father O'Reardon! Walls have ears.'

'What did you hear then?'

'Just urgent murmuring! We were close to barging in! He's not done you harm has he?'

'No!' I assure her. 'It's James,' I say, licking my lying lips. 'Patricia, I don't think I'm ever going to see him again. He'll be nearly eight before I get out of here.' We stop at the door of the bathroom.

'I'll tell you a little secret Missus Farrell - Niamh.' She leans towards me and whispers, 'If you're a good girl you can be out of here in less than two years!'

'Two years? '

'That's right. I've seen it with my own eyes.'

'But even in two years James might have forgotten me altogether.'

'Children don't forget a good mother, remember that!' she says as she holds the door of the bathroom open and I enter. 'I think you're probably a good mother!' she concludes as she sits on the chair near the doorway. I turn on the tap. A gentle trickle pours over my hands. I cup my hands and bring the cold water to my face. My tears are mingling with the water.

…

A forthnight later a different priest visits me.

'Father John Hurley wants to talk to you,' Patricia Monaghan announces as I sit in my cell staring at the wall.

A tall, grey haired man in a black suit and white back the front shirt collar calls out, 'Hello, you're Niamh Farrell?'

'I am.' I look up at him.

'May I come in?' He smiles at me. His face crinkles and his eyes twinkle.

'Come in.' He sits on the bed and leans over to me.

'Niamh, you're to be reunited with your son James.'

'When?'

'In a few days time. I have received this from the Minister.' He hands me a piece of crisp paper.

I stare at the black words on the cream coloured parchment, then hand it back. 'I don't...I can't read...'

'I understand. It's an emotional moment for yourself. I'll read it aloud if you like?'

I simply nod my head.

Father Hurley reads, '*In response to a request by Father Martin O'Reardon, Missus Niamh Farrell is hereby deemed to have been mentally unstable during her previous misadventures due to an emotional occurrence, from which she has since recovered. This has prompted the Judge and the Minster to accept the appeal against Missus Farrell's incarceration. Forthwith Missus Farrell is be exonerated and is placed on a good behaviour bond for a period of five years, commencing from the first day of September, nineteen hundred and seventy one...*' He puts the paper down and stares at me.

I'm not sure whether to shout or laugh. 'What does all that mean?'

'You are free!'

'I am?' I say in astonishment. 'I can go to Scriob...?'

'No! To Australia!'

'I don't know anyone in Australia,' I say, blankly.

'I will escort you.'

'But I don't know you...'

'We shall become acquainted on the voyage.'

He is pretty ancient, so he can't do me much harm. I find myself smiling at my thoughts. 'Why you?'

'I will answer your question, although I am not bound to! I am retired, and I have a brother in Australia. I was going to travel there shortly anyway.'

'What about…Martin…Father O'Reardon?'

'Father O'Reardon has been transferred to a parish in northern Spain.'

'Oh'. There's a pause. 'Spain?' I exclaim.

'Yes. Permanently. God has called him.' He looks at the floor, then looks up at me. 'Well, I'll return in a few days with some official papers. You can start packing.'

'And James?'

'James? All in good time.'

'I'll see him soon?'

'You will. Just one other thing.' He stops on his way out.

'What?'

'You need a full medical examination.'

'With a doctor?' I ask.

'Yes, of course. That will be arranged immediately.' He pauses and stares at me with compassion in his eyes. His mouth opens again. 'It was grand meeting you. I'll say good day to you now.'

A week later, he returns. 'I have a message for you, from Father O'Reardon.'

'What message?'

'He gave….sent you this.' He hands me a sealed envelope.

I open it. The sea of words mean nothing to me as I still can't read properly. 'Thank you,' I say, folding it and replacing it in the envelope.

'He also sent you these.' The priest hands me a brown paper bag, sealed with tape. 'He said they were personal.'

I accept the bag. 'Thanks.'

'You just need to sign these papers.'

'What are they?'

He places them on the seat of the chair, 'Emigration papers, saying you're willing to travel to Australia.'

'What about the doctor's examination?' I ask.

'He stated you are in good health.' He pauses and looks up at me. 'Here's his report. His eye scans the document. 'Doctors are terrible writers, and me eyes aren't that good either! Now let's see, Heart… good…Blood Pressure…good.' He looks at me. 'You've had all your vaccinations, I see.'

'What would happen if I was expecting?' I ask.

Father Hurley coughs and looks at me. 'That would be a rather serious matter, which would jeopardize your future.'

'Why would that be?'

'That's the law. If you became pregnant whilst under the jurisdiction of the crown, the child would become a ward of the state.'

'So I'd have to stay here?'

'Probably. You certainly could not travel to Australia.'

'Could I still see James?'

He leans closer to me. 'Probably not. So, I hope you aren't considering having a child?'

'No, I wasn't!'

'Well, there's no problem then.' He takes off his glasses and rubs them with a large white handkerchief.

'Missus Farrell, this is a great opportunity for you and James. I trust you can see that?'

'I can Father. At least I can be with my son.'

'That's the spirit! I shall make a final report that you are stable both in mind and body. If you desire confessions, I shall oblige on another occasion.'

'No. I received confessions a few weeks ago…' A distracting picture of Martin, in the nip, with the scapular on in bed flashes through my mind.

'Where do I sign?'

He points to a dotted line and hands me his ballpoint pen. I sit on the edge of the bed and begin to write. 'Here.' Slowly

I write Niamh Far…and stop. 'Sorry, I forget how to do the rest…' He looks down at it. 'That'll do. I'll witness it.'

I move over along the edge of the bed. He sits awkwardly beside me and takes the pen. After a quick scribble he turns his face towards me. His eyes sparkle as he smiles at me. He suddenly looks familiar.

'Start packing your bags. God willing I shall return in a few days.'

Ten days later I'm saying goodbye to Patricia Monaghan. She hands me my two bags, with everything still inside, including Kathleen's nappies. 'I think you'll find everything there, including four rings!' she remarks, making her eyebrows rise and fall. 'I hope you get to meet your son. I'll miss you Niamh.' She puts her hand out and I hold it for a moment. Her eyes look like an Irish mist.

'Thanks very much for the rings and …everything Patricia.'

With Father John Hurley by my side I'm having my first aeroplane flight from Cork to Southampton in England. I'm enjoying the experience and the strange shapes of the clouds beneath us when I suddenly get this retching feeling in the pit of my stomach.

'Niamh, you're turned as white as a ghost. Here,' Father John points to a paper bag. For the remainder of the journey, my view is focussed on the serrated edges of its rustic perimeters.

…

Two days later we board the *Australis* and leave for Australia's shores. As we head down several flights of steps towards our cabins, a peculiar fear comes over me. I haven't seen my son yet. 'What about James, Father John?' I ask, as he sits with me in a small cabin on 'D' deck. I look around the room. The porthole is covered by a view of a deep green sea, which means we're right under the water. I quickly pull a small blind across the round window. There are two bunk beds along one wall and a small bathroom and a cupboard

along the other side. I'm looking around as though his little face might suddenly appear from under the furniture.
'Where is he?'

'You'll meet each other in good time. Patience is a virtue,
remember that. Now do stop biting your nails Niamh. It
won't help. If you need to leave the cabin, knock on this
wall,' he informs me. 'I'll be right next door.' He turns to
leave, smiling apologetically. 'Sorry, but I'm obliged to lock
this, for your own good.'

A whole week goes by. I'm lying on the little bed in the
tiny room, which is around the same size as my cell in prison.
There's a knock on the door.

'Come on in,' I call out.

'How are you feeling now Niamh?' Father John asks, still
standing in the doorway.

'Still sick,' I reply feebly, trying to sit up.

'You are very pale. But, if it's any comfort, there are several cases of sickness on board. It's quite normal. 'Are you
quite sure you don't want to take something for it?'

'No. Sure I'll be all right.'

'Whatever you want.' He sits on the bed beside me. 'I
know how anxious you have been about your son, so I have
arranged a meeting with James at noon today. Do you think
you will be up to it?'

I sit up when he says that. 'That's the best medicine I've
had today.'

'That's the spirit!' he says, patting my hand. 'I'll escort
you.'

At twelve noon exactly I enter the port side lounge with
Father John. Everything is decorated with a pink textile
fabric. The tables are veneered in a dappled pink colour.
The walls of the counter, which is also a bar, are in pink.
I immediately spot James, seated with a female a bit older
than me. They're in a corner seat at the window, looking
out into the ocean.

As I come closer, James' cry echoes through the room,
'Mammy…Mammy!'

'James.' I thank God he hasn't forgotten me! I hold him for a long time. Then I realize the woman is waiting.

Father John introduces me. 'This is Naimh Farrell, James' mother.'

The sandy haired heavy-set young woman, with round eyes and a round face to match, smiles to display straight white dentures. She tosses her petit nose in the air as she lunges forward. 'Pleased to meet you. I'm Colette Dunn. I'll be taking care of James as far as Melbourne.'

We enjoy our time together.

…

As we leave I ask Father John: 'Are we staying in Melbourne?'

'No, we're travelling to Sydney, then to Queensland.'

'That's interesting,' I comment.

'Why Niamh?' Father John asks, peering at me inquisitively.

'My name means Queen of the land?'

His eyes veer upwards. 'It's providence!'

Every few days I have half an hour with James. It seems to take weeks before we reach Melbourne.

One morning, bright and early, Father John knocks on the cabin door. 'Come in,' I call from underneath the blanket. He unlocks the door and enters.

'Are you all right?' he asks anxiously.

'I do feel a lot better today. I wonder why?' I say, relieved.

'Perhaps it's because we've stopped! We're in Melbourne!' he informs me.

'Are we now? Can we get off?'

He shakes his head. 'I'm very sorry! No, not until we reach Sydney…' Father John explains to me. 'Are you well enough to say farewell to Miss Dunn?'

'I'm well enough! I'll get dressed,' I reply.

'I'll wait outside.' Father John steps outside and pulls the door shut. 'Don't be too long,' he calls out after five minutes.

I wave goodbye to Colette Dunn. There she goes, walking

off down the street with a couple of people, stepping jauntily. She glances back, and gives me such a wave you'd think we'd been friends forever!

I move away from the rail to where Father John is standing, holding James' hand.

'He's your responsibility now Niamh,' Father John says, as he nudges James towards me. James suddenly tears across the space into my outstretched arms. I grasp him tightly and swing him around for joy.

'That's enough of that!' I hear Father John's voice as it intrudes on our delightful play. 'Let me buy you both a nice cool drink.' We walk happily along the deck, down the steps to the starboard side of the ship and through the door marked 'Blue Lounge'.

James and I just sit and smile at each other, like two children discovering friendship for the first time.

'Lemonade,' Father John's voice penetrates our happiness. The sparkling drinks in shiny glasses reflect our mood.

'Say yes please!' I remind James.

Father John sits down next to James, facing me. 'Now that I've got my wits about me, can you tell me whereabouts we'll be stopping in Queensland?' I ask.

'You're bound to find out anyway. Sure they're cane farmers.'

'I don't know anything about cane farming.'

'Don't worry your head about that. They need someone to help with the children.'

I help James hold his drink with two hands, then turn towards Father John. 'Will I be a governess Father John?'

'You will, and more! I believe they have twins. They'll need help in the kitchen too!'

'What in God's name are children doing working in the kitchen?'

'No Niamh, you will be working in the kitchen, not the children,' he explains.

'Right! I can do that. So, what are these twins like? Maybe I won't be able to handle them!'

Five Golden Rings and a Diamond

'I hear they are a wild pair, but I have a hunch you'll be on top of it all in no time…'

'I'm very glad someone has confidence in me Father,' I say wryly.

We wait for James to finish his drink, then Father announces, 'If you're feeling up to it, James can stop with you for the remainder of the journey!'

'I am. I do…I never felt better in my life,' I laugh happily, hugging James.

Somehow my sickness has almost gone completely since Melbourne. During the last couple of days, Father John takes me to see a film about Australia, its climate, schools and some amazing creatures, such as the kangaroo, koala, funnel web and redback spiders, and a variety of slithering snakes. They show enlarged pictures of mosquitoes, which seem prolific in the area we're going to. That night I wake up covered in perspiration, from a nightmare in which I'm surrounded by giant mosquitoes!

A few days later we sail into Sydney Harbour. The opera house looks like a big white sailing ship surrounded by a rainbow made of intrigued steel, which flashes hues of colour from the slowly rising sun. 'I've never seen the like in my life. It's spectacular!' I exclaim as we sail into her inviting arms.

'It is indeed,' Father John states agreeably. 'Time to disembark!' he announces brightly. He seems as relieved as I am to be going on shore.

'James, we're here!' I hug James and we both laugh.

Father John looks on with a reserved smile on his face. 'We'll be staying in a hostel for a few nights, then we fly up to Queensland.'

Chapter nine

Three days later we're boarding a 'plane that flies to Brisbane. After a short stopover at the sun-drenched airport we board a smaller 'plane and head for a place called Maryborough.

'It sounds like a very Christian town,' Father John notes in a pleased tone. He glances at me as we lurch to a stop. 'You look white Niamh!'

'I feel white!' I reply.

His face collapses into a frowning facade.

I quickly add that '…but I'll be fine after I find my sea legs.'

He relaxes, which helps me to relax as well.

'Welcome to Meraboro,' the flight attendant says, announcing our arrival.

'My God, it sounds like a foreign language,' Father John whispers, emphasising the vowels in the name.

I pick James up and follow Father to the exit. 'There's nobody here,' I say, looking around at the deserted land as we walk down a small ramp.

Father John looks around. 'Paddy said that someone was coming to pick us up and taking us to the cane farm property.'

A voice startles us. 'Your suitcases Fadda!' The lone airport worker says, handing us our luggage. His faded navy blue overall is opened from the neck to the waist, revealing a white vest. His sleeves are rolled up to his elbows. His face, and other exposed body parts are tanned and covered with tiny beads of perspiration.

'Thank you Sir,' Father John replies, staring at the heavy cases on the grass in front of us. 'Did you hear what he called me?' he says as an offside, his eyebrows rising high into his balding head.

I nod my head. 'Fadda!' I can't help smiling at his disgusted expression.

'Well, we've got to soldier on!' Father John says, heaving the cases and trudging towards what looks like a roadway in the distance. 'I hope we don't have to walk too far.'

I place James on the ground. 'It's so hot,' I say. I'm feeling quite faint.

'I knew someone would come!' Father points to a person with a truck waiting under the scanty shade of trees in the distance. At that instant the parked truck moves towards us. 'Thank God,' he exclaims, dropping the cases on the spot.

'G'day! Welcome to Meraboro. Luigi's the name...'

The men shake hands. I smile. He nods at me. 'Mam,' he says, picking up the cases effortlessly. We happily follow him as if he was a king. A king who's wardrobe needs replenishing! He's wearing only a white vest and a pair of pale greenish blue shorts, and plastic thongs on his feet. A brown hat with a brim crowns his head, covering his unruly dark mop of hair. Black sunglasses shield his eyes.

'He looks like a real Ned Kelly,' Father whispers to me as we trudge after him.

I shiver, despite the oppressive heat. He gives me a creepy feeling! Twenty minutes later we arrive at the home of Aaron and Olga Schmidt. It's a high-set 'Queenslander', with built-in rooms underneath. The steps and ornate frontage make it appear inviting. We file up the steps to an open front door. Olga and Aaron come to greet us.

'G'day,' they say, offering a handshake, inviting us into the wide hallway.

'These are our two terrors,' Aaron says, directing our attention to two small blonde haired, bronze skinned boys, who come running through from the back of the house. Their only item of clothing is a pair of shorts. I can see Father John's eyes popping at the sight.

'This is Ben and Adam,' Aaron says, catching the two by an arm and holding on to them while they calm down momentarily.

My worst fear surfaces as four round hazel coloured eyes stare into mine. 'I'll never be able to tell them apart,' I exclaim.

'I'll show you how....' Olga says. 'Come here Ben.' Ben steps forward. 'Ben has a mole on his right ear, and... Adam!' Adam comes reluctantly. 'Adam is the shy one. He has a mole on his left ear.'

'All you need to know is your left from your right,' Father John declares jovially.

We all laugh to be polite, except the three boys.

'This is James,' I say, manoeuvring him from behind my skirt.

'How old are you James?' Olga asks.

James ducks behind my skirt again. 'He's nearly two and a half,' I reply on his behalf. James looks like a small white ghost in comparison to the twins, I'm thinking.

'Ben and Adam will turn three in the New Year.... Wanna see the room?' Olga asks, marching towards the back of the house. 'Aaron, can you look after Fadda?'

'Struth yes! Come on Fadda, how's about we have a cold one on the verandah,' Aaron suggests, heading in the opposite direction, followed by Father John.

James and I follow Olga through an open door. 'This was a verandah, but we had it built in. I think you and James will have 'nuf room. You can open the louvres to catch the breeze. Give the lever a good yank...' she instructs, yanking the lever. Immediately a soft breeze stirs the air.

I'm listening and looking around the room at the same time, trying to absorb everything. The room is long and narrow. The roofline seems lower on the window side, which are mostly opaque glass, so they're private. There are blue floral curtains on the two short sides of the room where the two single beds are positioned. They both have a long white tulle curtain hanging from the ceiling, making them appear bridal. On the side opposite the windows there's a long low wooden cupboard with a row of drawers and two doors, a bookcase, a desk, a tall darkly stained wardrobe with a mirror, a dressing table with a small mirror and a varnished wooden chair. The door is in the centre of this wall. 'It's grand. May I ask what the wedding veils are for?'

'They're mozzie nets. Olga looks at me with disbelieving expression. 'You haven't heard of our mosquitoes?'

'Those! Yes, I have.'

'You can't go to bed without a net. There's a can of mozzie spray as well,' she explains, picking up a blue can from the wooden bookshelf. 'One whiff and they're off!' she exclaims triumphantly, spraying a passing fly, which immediately succumbs to its pungent fragrance and drops on the floor.

I stare in amazement. I love that can already!

'Come and meet Barbara.' We follow Olga through a corridor through a double door into the kitchen area. Olga addresses an aboriginal woman about my age. 'Barbie, this is Niamh.'

Barbara is at a bench near a sink, busy cutting slabs of cake that have thick pink icing.

'G'day,' Barbara greets Olga and me with an explosive smile. She's holding a large carving knife, whose edges are covered in pink icing. 'Pleased to meet ya!' she exclaims, placing the knife on a chopping board, rubbing her hands in the sides of the apron around her waist, and throwing her arms around me. 'Gees, it's great to see ya! I feel as I know you already!'

I stare at her sparkling deep brown eyes and flashing

white toothy smile, and feel overwhelmed by her words and actions. 'You know about me?'

'Paddy told us you were coming. He's such a comedian. Said you were true Irish, not just a descendant. An aboriginal, like me!'

'I...never thought of it like that...' I say flatly.

'Tea?' Barbara addresses Olga now.

'Thanks Babs. On the patio. It's such a hot day!'

'No worries Mate!'

'Is it always this warm?' I ask, wiping the perspiration from my brow with the back of my hand.

'It's usually hotter, especially in summer,' Olga replies, pushing back a strand of hair from her forehead.

'When's that?'

'December. It's still a month away!'

'Oh God!' I exclaim quietly.

Olga must have heard me. 'Don't worry darl, you'll get used to it. You'll have to get your gear off.'

I must look shocked for she smiles.

'It's too hot for jumpers! You'll need some lighter clothes for starters! Here, take this plate to the patio. It's cooler there!'

Gingerly I pick up two plates piled high with pink iced pieces of cake and stand, waiting for instructions.

Olga reaches for two large jugs of water, with bits of lemon and ice floating harmoniously together. She moves swiftly towards the patio at the side of the house. I follow close on her heels.

'It's hard to believe but it's cold here in the mornings!' she says, placing the jugs on the table where Aaron and Father John are seated. I notice Father has removed his black jacket.

'Where do you want...this?'

'Here.' She indicates the table. 'Sit down and relax. I'll go and get the others...' Olga gracefully moves around the table and back through the doorway. I subtly remove my cardigan and sit down on a bench seat. I place James next to me.

Barbie's presence fills the doorway as she enters with a tray full of cups, glasses and a pot of tea. 'Here we are!' She places the tray down. She separates the glasses and pours me a drink. 'Cool drink?' she asks, holding the glass out to me. I take it gratefully. 'Thanks very much!'

'What about you guys?' she asks Aaron and Father John.

'We're right! 'Aving a beeah…' Aaron says, holding up a fat brown glass bottle of beer with a yellow and red label.

Father John nods his head happily. 'Slainte! The first today!' He raises his brown bottle.

Luigi stomps up the steps with Olga and the twins.

'Come on you little guys, you can have this one all to yourselves.' Barbie indicates a small table in the corner of the patio. She pulls up a third plastic chair. Ben and Adam climb onto their chair. James leans closer to me.

'Come on James! Join the big boys,' Barbie says. James immediately slips off the bench chair and runs over to Barbie. She lifts him onto the chair and puts a plastic plate next to his face. He looks at me and grins from ear to ear, happily filling his mouth with cake.

That night I lie in my new bed and try to ignore the heat. I'm just wearing a thin cotton nightie, but the sweat is beading on my forehead. A free-standing fan, kindly donated by Barbara, is whirring in my ear. James is lying on the other small bed with thin pyjamas on him, compliments of the Schmidts. Olga also gave him a few light pieces of clothing to keep him going.

'Well, we've arrived in Australia, James,' I say, mopping my forehead with the edge of the thin sheet over me. 'James?' He doesn't reply. I look across the room and all I can see is a still small form. He's fast asleep. Then I realize someone else is still awake! I feel a small flutter inside my stomach! I can't help smiling.

'Hello!' I say, patting my stomach. 'How on earth am I going to tell anyone about you?'

It seems like only a few minutes later a voice barges into my world of dreams.

'Niamh, the alarm's gone off.'

'What?' I open my eyes to see a dark face with white eyes and shining teeth, 'Barbie?'

'Come on. Here y'are, I'll leave these here. The showa's free.'

Showa? I muse. What is she talking about? Barbie has left some clean clothes on a wooden chair near the door.

After a quick cold shower, Barbie's voice rings out again. 'Come on Niamh, we've got to get brekkie!'

'I'm on your heels,' I reply, brushing my hair and putting some of the special face cream on my face, which Olga left for me on the dressing table.

'Come on James, off to work!' The pair of us head towards the kitchen.

I sniff, 'Where's the sausages?' I ask Barbie, who's busy cutting up beautiful coloured fruit.

'Naw…no sausages. They're for the Ba'bie.' She continues cutting fruit.

'So, d'ya have sausages for brekkie in I'eland?'

'We do… So what's for breakfast then?'

'We make coffee, tea, fruit juice, fruit, cereal and milk.' All the stuff is in the pantry or fridge. And, we need to make some toast. The toaster's on the bench. C'n you do that?' Barbie asks.

'No worries Mate,' I reply, smiling, beginning my journey through the pantry and fridge to locate the 'bread.'

Half an hour later, Olga, Aaron, Ben, Adam, James, Luigi and another older man called Bob saunter inside and sit down at the huge kitchen table. I sit down next to Barbie and the three boys.

'This is the lucky country! So much food,' I exclaim.

'We love our tucka! But wait, there's always the washing up!' Barbie says, helping herself to a second piece of toast. She dribbles honey on it. I do the same.

'Once we've cleared the tables we let the kids watch the TV,' she explains as we place all the dishes in a dishwasher and press the button.

'Good God, who would have thought of having such a machine!' I exclaim, surprised at how quickly we cleaned up.

'The biggest job is clearing it...' Barbie reminds me, grinning broadly.

Barbie, the kids and I sit in the family room and Barbie puts the TV on. There's a children's show just starting.

'You have television!' I exclaim.

'We've had it for yonks!'

'Yonks?'

'Years. Everyone's got one now. Some have one in every room. It's our culture, that's what I think. I don't like the kids watching some of the rubbish on it though!' she exclaims forcefully.

James is fascinated, and the other pair, I must say, are just as fascinated by the small black, white and grey characters in 'Play School.'

I'm fascinated! I can't keep my eyes off the person saying the Alphabet and then the letter pops up in front of her.

'Repeat with me...A, B, C, D...' The boys and me repeat what she is saying. After the television show is finished, Barbie flicks off the bright screen. 'Morning tea...' she announces, getting up and heading towards the kitchen. I follow after her.

'That show was great, wasn't it? I nearly know the alphabet now!'

Barbie stares at me with a quizzical look. 'What' d'ya mean?'

'Oh! ' I can feel my face going hot and it's not just the weather. 'I...only went to school for around three months, before I made my first communion.'

'Struth! That's terrible. Some people are like that. They hate school. Wag it all the time!'

'Are they? I mean do they?'

'Too right mate! Did you hate school?' She's chopping up bananas and apples as we talk.

'No, I had to beg instead.'

'Beg? In I'eland? Naw!'

'It's the God's honest truth.'

'So, you never learned the alphabet.'

'No.'

'So, can you read?'

'A few words. Niall taught me…'

'She'll be apples mate! Niamh, I'll teach you real good!'

'Would you?'

'I will. When the children are having their afternoon nap! Before we have ours. Education is very important darl'. Otherwise you'll get left behind, that's what I think! No! That's what I know!'

'I'd love that. I want to learn to read and write.'

'That settles it then. I'll teach you. I Promise!'

We can hear the boys having a bit of a friendly fight just then, so Barbie announces, 'Food, come and get it guys.'

The three run towards Barbie and take a couple of pieces of fruit in their hands.

Barbie and I sit down. 'Would you like a cuppa with your fruit?'

'A cuppa?'

'Coffee, tea?'

'That'd be grand.' We sit on the patio and enjoy a light easterly breeze.

'How hot does it get in summer?'

'Very hot, and wet,' Barbie says, grinning.

'Oh God! I'm sweating now!'

'Naw, you're not!'

'I'm not!'

'Naw, men sweat, women perspire!' She laughs.

I laugh.

'You'll get used to it mate. You'll love it.' She flashes her white teeth.

I almost believe her.

'How are you settling in?' Olga comes marching onto the back verandah.

'Fine Missus Schmidt, really fine.'

'Call me Olga.' She smiles warmly. 'We've got to see the bank manager, so I'll pick up a few things along the way. Do you need anything girls?'

'Sure do! There's a list on the fridge,' Barbie says, finishing her coffee and jumping up. 'I'll get it.' She heads off to the kitchen.

'Niamh, you 'aven't been told about your employment conditions, 'ave you?'

'No Mam, I mean Olga.'

'Well, we've agreed to give you a small retainer, plus your boa'd and lodging's. You should be able to get some allowance for James. We'll have to fill in some papers.'

'I think Father John did that already Mam...Olga.'

'You right with that?'

'Yes, right!'

Barbie returns with her list, 'Here. And c'n you post these for me?'

'Sure. Barbie, if I'm not back can you give the guys a bit of lunch?'

'No worries!' Barbie replies, picking up our dirty cups and heading for the kitchen again. I follow her with the children's empty glasses.

'We're 'aving sandwiches for lunch. We're having a Ba'bie for tea.'

'You're Barbie,' I say, puzzled.

'Bar-beque. They're not bab-bequing me! Steak and sausages!'

'Oh!' I reply. Martin would call me an egit if he was here. 'I'm never going to understand...' I moan.

'No worries mate. You'll get the hang of it. Honest, you're doin' great!'

That evening I sniff the most wonderful aroma of an Australian barbeque. Just thinking of it makes my nose twitch and my mouth water.

Early on Sunday morning, Father John arrives with his brother Paddy in a his car, a sedan, they call it.

'It's yellow, the safe colour,' Paddy says. 'It's grand to

meet you Niamh.' He shakes my hand. 'And this must be James?' He extends his hand to James.

James stares and puts his fingers in his mouth. 'Call me Uncle Paddy, if you like!'

I shake James' arm. 'Say hello *Uncle Paddy*,'

'Ello, Uncle Paddee,' James repeats.

'Well, that settles that!' Paddy's eyes light up with delight. 'Uncle Paddy, that's me! Ha'vey Bay, here we come!'

'What does he mean by have a bay?' I whisper to Father John.

'He means just that,' he replies.

Well, I'll soon find out what 'have a bay' is!

A few minutes later I'm sitting in the back seat of the car with James, going to Mass at a place called Hervey Bay, I find out later.

'So, are you settled in all right?' Paddy asks as he turns the key in the ignition.

'I am. I never saw so much food in my life.'

'The tucka's great all right. It's a great country altogether,' Paddy acknowledges, wiggling his head.

'Did Missus Schmidt give you some new clothes?' Father John asks.

'Yes, Olga gave me quite a few things to wear. She's so kind,' I reply. I'm wearing a pale blue cotton baby-doll dress that is very short. I place my hands over my knees where the hem stops.

'You call your boss Olga?'

'She told me to…'

He's quiet for a moment, then his neck twists to look in disgust at my bony knees. 'It's a bit short don't you think?'

'The mini skirts are very fashionable 'round here,' I reply, turning my knees slightly to the side and pulling the flowing skirt over my knees as much as possible.

'What is the world coming to at all, at all,' he moans, turning back and staring out the front window.

Thank God I didn't wear some of the other dresses she

gave me with the halter necks! They're low at the top and bottom! We sit in silence for a few minutes after that. We're enjoying the fleeting scenery of bright yellow cane, rising high and blowing in the soft breeze.

'They grow a lot of cane here. I've never seen the like of it in my life. There must be a lot of sweet tooths in Australia, I should think,' Father John says as we speed past fields of cane.

'There's more than sugar in that lot!'

'How's that Paddy?' Father John asks thoughtfully.

'There's snakes and toad frogs in there,' Paddy assures us.

'Have you ever seen them Paddy?' I ask anxiously.

'I've seen a few snakes around these parts. They sunbake on the roads and the toad frogs are everywhere!'

'There's no snakes in Ireland, you know that?' Father John informs us loudly, then adds, 'only the two legged kinds!' He laughs at the old joke.

'You're probably right there,' Paddy comments, grinning.

'And of course it was Saint Patrick who banished them from Ireland,' Father John tells us.

'Do you think they emigrated to Australia John?' Paddy asks sarcastically.

'They might have swum across the sea…' Father John says musingly.

I feel a shiver run up my spine as the conversation turns to spiders and frogs. I am stiff with fright by the time we reach Hervey Bay.

…

Mass is the same as in Ireland, thank God for something familiar! It's in English too, so that's another similarity. The only difference is in the fashions around here. People are wearing much lighter coloured clothes here, less clothes, thinner fabrics. There are a few hats, mostly sun hats with wide brims, and a few people are wearing the old fashioned scarf and some are wearing mantillas. Father John goes out the back to the vestry to help with something, so I have a grand time looking around at all the latest styles in Hervey Bay, pronounced *Have a Bay!* After Mass we go to Paddy's home. It's a small lowset fibro home with a tiny garden at the front, surrounded by a wire fence and a white metal gate. There's only a road separating it from the beach.

'You can see the waves splashing on the shore from here,' I exclaim as I lift the latch of the gate.

'It was wonderful twenty years ago. So peaceful you'd hear every wave hitting the shore like a roar!'

'You're a poet and you didn't know it,' Father John says laughing.

We all laugh at the joke.

'How about we have a picnic,' Paddy announces. 'We don't have far to go, just cross the street. It used to be a very quiet place…'

A car roars by.

'Now the roar is not the tide, it's the tyres!' Father John says, laughing heartily at his joke.

We are all relaxed and laughing by the time we go to sit down in the family room. Paddy disappears into the small kitchen, emerging with two drinks in his hands. 'One for James, and one for Niamh. I'll get yours in a minute John, when you stop laughing.'

'I'll try.' Father John mops his brow, then blows his nose loudly.

'I think James will enjoy having lunch on the beach,' Paddy say loudly, above the noise. He hands a glass to James.

'Put your two hands on the glass, otherwise you might spill it, and upset Uncle Paddy,' I instruct.

'You won't upset me in a hurry mate. The carpet needs a clean anyway.'

Father John seems calmer now. 'Paddy has done very well for himself, getting such a great place!'

'What's that?' Paddy asks from the kitchen.

'You've done well Paddy,' Father John says.

'I have! I'm a lucky man. The luck of the Irish!' Paddy

returns with two more glasses. He hands a drink to his brother and sits in an armchair. He raises his glass, 'Slainte! Niamh, you're welcome to visit us any time, and James, of course!'

'Thanks very much,' I reply.

'I'll just go down the road and pick up a chook and bring a loaf of bread and a few cold ones,' Paddy announces, collecting our glasses and placing them on the kitchen sink drainer. 'I'll only be a few minutes,' he says, skipping out the front door.

'So, Niamh, how are you getting along with the Schmidts?' Father John asks after Paddy leaves.

'Great. Really great. It's more like being on holidays. Barbara reads the Bible to us every day,' I say, trying to impress him!

'I'd be careful if I were you. You don't want to become a fanatic!'

'I won't…'

'As long as you don't neglect your duties!'

'No, I'd never do that Father.'

He leans over as he gives me a piece of advice. 'You're not there to study, you're there to learn!'

'Yes, Father,' I reply.

'Good girl. There's a place for everything and everything has its place! Too much study can be a dangerous thing, a very dangerous thing.' He looks so serious I almost laugh.

'We've been doing a bit of painting as well,' I add.

'Outside or inside?' he asks.

A picture of Barbie, the three boys and me painting in the play room inside when it's windy, and sitting on a rug in the shade of the house on a fine day whiz through my mind. 'Both. Barbie and I love it. We've been teaching the children as well.'

'They're a bit young for strenuous manual work, I would have thought!' Father John says, thoughtfully.

'I don't think so! Children in Australia are very advanced for their age.'

'Is that right? Well, as long as your employer is satisfied. A woman's place is in the kitchen. That's where she should be!'

'But, Barbie has a lot of talent. She's been painting for years. Lovely colours, real Australian.'

'I thought she was a school teacher.'

'She is. She teaches art as well.'

'Art? Does she? Perhaps you should teach the children art instead of painting?' he suggests seriously.

'Yes Father…' I reply, trying not to smile too obviously.

'And how is James getting along with A and B?'

'A and B?' I repeat. 'Oh, you mean Adam and Ben! I never thought of them that way. You're brilliant Father,' I say admiringly.

'I'm probably advanced for my age!' he says proudly. 'Did you know that Ireland was once called the Island of Saints and scholars?'

'I heard that…'

'And I suppose you heard the rest?'

'The rogues and robbers?' I reply.

'Sadly, that's true now.' He places his glass on a small table next to a vase of artificial flowers. 'And what about yourself then?'

'I'm fine thanks,' I reply.

'No. what I mean is, have you met any young people?'

'Just Barbie. I have James to take care of, and with looking after the twins I don't get out to meet anybody else…except yourself and Uncle Paddy.'

'You should be on the lookout for a nice young man.'

'Yes Father…'

'A catholic boy, of course. James needs a father to support him, not some social system!'

'Yes Father.'

'I'm sure we can find someone to suit…' There's silence. We can hear the waves splashing on the shore, mixed with sounds of laughter and car engines revving.

'Father John, do you know what a chuck is?' I ask.

'It's a kind of bolt for holding a piece of machinery. Or my mother throwing a plate at me!'

'That's what I thought! Uncle Paddy said he's getting a chuck.'

'Did he say that?'

'He did.'

'Perhaps his car is in need of repair? Or perhaps he wants to throw something away…'

As if he heard us, just then we hear the gate clang shut and Paddy's form fills the doorway.

'Got a family size chook!' he announces as he enters the living room.

'The mystery is solved Niamh. It's a chicken. Bac, bac!' Father John says, roaring with laughter, flapping his elbows.

'Oh.' Maeve would have called me an egit now. My face glows. I can feel it.

'Don't you like chook?' Paddy asks me, placing his parcels on the kitchen table.

'No, it's not that…I didn't realize what a chuck was!' I stammer.

'Chook, not chuck!' Paddy corrects me.

We head across the road to the beach and sit on a rug in the sand.

'Here James, have a piece of chuck!' I instruct, smiling at Uncle Paddy.

'Close! You're a true Aussie already!' he exclaims.

I beam.

''Ave a cold one!' he opens a bottle and passes the cold lemonade.

'It's a wonderful place altogether,' Father John says pensively, gazing out towards the horizon. 'If we only had old Ireland over here…'

'It's like being in heaven,' I agree, munching and drinking.

'How about an ice cream?' Paddy asks, getting up on his feet, brushing sand and crumbs off.

'Icekeem.' James claps his hands.

The hot spring days turn into hotter, more humid summer days. My ever-growing baby is becoming more difficult to hide, even with a large apron I borrowed from Barbie.

'How's about we go to the Mera'bora' pool today,' Barbie says one extremely hot and humid day just before Christmas.

'I haven't got a swimming costume,' I protest, 'or James!'

'No worries mate. You can 'ave one of mine. I've got heaps! James can wear one of the boys' old ones. They've got heaps.'

'But...'

'No buts. I think we need time off in a cool pool! I'll check with Olga if you like?'

'Yes, do that!' I say. Hopefully, I'm thinking, she'll say 'no'!

Barbie goes off to find Olga. She returns elated, holding two swimming costumes.

'I can't swim!' I say emphatically.

'I taught you readin' and writing. I can teach you to swim.' Barbie says undaunted at my protesting. 'Cossie for you!'

'Cossie?' I take the scant item of clothing while Barbie helps the boys get dressed for the pool.

'Oh God. It's too small,' I say as I stare at my round bulge in the mirror.

'You ok?' Barbie pops her head in the door, looks around, comes into the room and sits on the bed.

'The boys! They're waiting.' I whisper.

'They're right! Struth, why didn't you say somethin,' Barbie says calmly.

'Please don't say anything!' I beg.

'You can't hide that forever.' She shakes her head. 'Your sin will find you out!'

'Don't preach...!'

'Mammy, Mammy, I've got a cossie,' James says, running into the room.

'Put a tee shirt over the top,' Barbie instructs, opening my drawers and bringing out a large blue shirt with a cartoon character on the front. 'Here.'

'Thanks,' I say, gratefully pulling the shirt over my head.

'She'll be apples, matey,' she replies.

We head for the cool pool.

…

That year I had the strangest Christmas of my life. The Schmidts invite Paddy and Father John, along with Luigi, and Bob, and two new workers. One is a young man from Canberra called Nigel, who complains about the heat all the time. The other is an aboriginal young man called Barney whose teeth look like snowdrops in his black face.

In the week before Christmas Barbie shows me how to make White Christmas and frozen Christmas puddings. Olga buys some Lyons Christmas cakes and puddings and custard in cartons.

'At the Connors' we made our own custard,' I exclaim as Barbie and I stack the puddings in the cupboard.

Barbie smiles, 'We still have to get them out of the tuck-a-box freeza!' she says, laughing. 'That's my favourite part.'

'I like this kind of cooking too,' I say, handing her a box with an iced cake on the front.

'Aaron's bought half a cow for the barbie. They'll also get prawns and muddies!' she adds triumphantly.

I wonder what muddies are?

'I told Olga we'd make the salads, that's 'nuf.'

'That's nuf' I agree, smiling.

'We gotta go shopping too, we must remember that.'

'Shopping?'

'The pressies!'

'Pressies?'

'Chrissie pressies,' she says happily. 'I asked Bob if he'll look after the kids while they're having their nap. Let's go shopping Niamh!'

'What'll I bring?'

'A purse!'

Early on Christmas morning, I wake up suddenly. I slip across the hallway into the lavatory. After a quick visit I wash my hands and on the way back to my room. I stare in awe at the sun rising. My baby gives me a kick just then. 'Hey, in there, can you believe it! There's probably snow in Ireland, and here we're sweltering,' I say softly, patting what I think is baby's head, but it might be its bottom.

I notice someone in the corner of my eye and turn to see Olga creeping past in her flapping pale pink dressing gown and bare feet. Her arms are full of wrapped gifts she's taken from the hall cupboard.

'Olga!' I say, almost jumping in fright.

'Sorry…Shh,' she whispers back. 'I'm just placing these under the tree…' She stops abruptly in her tracks and stares at my bulge.

'Merry Christmas,' I say sucking in my tummy.

'Merry Christmas…' she says, turning and heading into the family room.

I hurry to my room and a few moments later I'm sitting on the bed. I'm trembling from head to toe.

An hour later Paddy and Father John pick up James and me for early Mass. I hardly remember the trip to Hervey Bay. The priest gets through the whole thing in twenty minutes, much to everyone's delight. The small congregation rush away, leaving the carpark almost bare in about fifteen minutes. Father John is busy talking to another priest, so we're the last to leave. We arrive back at the Schmidts by eight o'clock. I head into the kitchen to help Barbara with breakfast.

'Happy Christmas!' we both say. We hug. 'Everything ok?' she asks, her eyes filled with concern.

'Fine,' I lie.

'Brekkie is on the patio,' Barbie says. 'Give us a hand with these.' She points to four large plastic jugs of orange juice. 'You shouldn't be carrying stuff. Only take two,' she directs.

We take the drinks to the patio where the two tables have been set for a casual breakfast. There's a long table at the side of the patio decorated with a red tablecloth and an arrangement of different cereals, fresh bread for toasting, sliced mangoes, cut watermelon, coffee and tea. 'You did a great job Barbie,' I comment, delighted with the whole arrangement.

'Olga helped…' she smiles and places the tray of glasses and jugs on the side table.

Olga comes in with a couple of boxes of cereal. 'Just in case…Ba'bie,' she says. She stares at me and turns away. 'I'll get the boys,' she says, hurrying back down the hallway.

I stare at her. She knows. I know she knows. I sigh.

'Let's enjoy brekkie?' Barbara says.

I can hear Olga's voice as she returns through the hallway. 'Brekkie first,' she states, holding two boys by the hands.

The faces of the boys speak for themselves. 'I'm not hungry,' Ben says, pouting.

'Me either,' Adam says.

'Santa told me that you had to eat your brekkie before you opened your pressies,' Olga says sternly. She holds their hands tightly until they appear to concede. Suddenly she releases her firm grip.

'Come on,' Adam says, hurrying towards the table. 'Let's eat.'

'Hey, wait for everyone else,' Olga quickly reminds them.

'Did Santa say that?' Ben asks, inquisitively, turning back from following Adam's footsteps.

'He didn't but he should've,' Olga replies.

'Oh,' he responds, climbing up on a chair next to his brother.

Just then Father John and Uncle Paddy emerge from the garden and traverse onto the Patio with Aaron, Luigi, Nigel, Barney, and finally Bob, following.

'Happy Christmas,' Father John says.

After breakfast Barbie and I clean up. The men help

remove the tables, except the one at the side with the drinks and plastic glasses. They ceremonially transport the fake Christmas tree from the family room onto the patio. Father John gives directions as they manoeuvre through the doorway. The children help by carrying presents.

'Just throw these in the bin,' Barbie directs, indicating the paper bowls and plates we've just used.

'This is the kind of washing up I like,' I say triumphantly plopping a pile of used paper plates into the plastic-lined bin.

Fifteen minutes or so later we're all assembled around the tree.

'James, Ben and Adam, you go first,' Olga says.

Ben and Adam rush to open their toy sacks. Each sack has the boys' names, Ben, Adam and James.

James is so excited he stands looking at me before he moves.

'Go on James, there's yours.' I point to a buff coloured sack with James written on it in red. James looks white and he's trembling. He's hardly able to tear the paper off.

The boys are ecstatic with their array of cars, play doh, tee shirts, a teddy bear, each with a different coloured jacket and hat, shorts and bags of sweets, which they call lollies.

As the adults watch the boys impatiently rip each wrapped gift, we enjoy a cool drink.

'I must confess, it's a lot cooler at Hervey Bay,' Father John says, mopping his sweaty brow.

'Why don't you wear shorts like Paddy?' I ask Father John.

'I'm a priest Niamh. I don't want to look like a…boyo!' he replies, rubbing his red, hot neck under his black shirt and white collar.

'So, I look like a boyo do I?' Paddy asks, gritting his teeth.

'You look fine Uncle Paddy,' I say quickly evading a hot discussion. Paddy calms down quickly in his cream shorts and a short-sleeved shirt with an open neck, with cool 'thongs' on his feet.

'Open your present, Father John,' I insist.

Immediately he reaches for a green-wrapped parcel. 'All right. I noticed this one earlier,' he says, suddenly forgetting the altercation, absorbing himself in ripping the paper carefully.

'Come on Niamh, open yours!' Barbie encourages me.

I find three gifts wrapped with my name on them. The first is a blouse from Barbie.

'It's lovely Barbs, my favourite colour, pale green.' It's the latest peasant style, with elasticised neck and short sleeves. I hold it in front of me. 'What do you think?'

'Struth it's your colour. Looks great!' Barbie says happily. 'I got a slightly bigger size...' she whispers. 'It's gorgeous. Thanks very much,' I say, smiling.

The next gift I open is very large, wrapped in red Christmas paper with green silky ribbon. 'From ...Olga and Aaron. Happy Christmas,' I read slowly. 'Wow,' I exclaim, almost breathless with amazement! 'Look at this Barbie!'

'It's the same as mine!'

'Amazing!' I exclaim, examining each piece as I unfold the paper, astounded.

'Must've cost a bomb!' Barbie exclaims, unwrapping hers.

'Thank you...' I whisper to Olga and Aaron. 'I can't believe it!'

'We made the right choice then!' Olga remarks, smiling.

'We can really paint now!' Barbie says, placing four brushes side by side. 'I've been askin' the Lord about new brushes, and paints! They were too expensive... thank you so much,' she says gratefully to Olga and Aaron.

I open my gift from Bob. 'It's small,' I say, noting the tiny little box. 'Good things come in small packaging, me da says,' I say, smiling at Bob.

'The others chipped in as well, Luigi, Nigel and Barney.'

'It's beautiful Bob, thanks,' I say, genuinely grateful.

'We didn't know what else to get you sheilas,' he says, and I am sure his face was going pink as Barbie gives him a hug, then hugs the three lads sitting in the background. They all enjoyed it by the looks on their faces, especially Barney, whose grin fills his face from ear to ear.

'Opals,' Barbie says, holding her jewel up for all to see. 'My favourite stone. It's beaut!'

'So that's what an opal is!' I remark.

'Bob's got claims on an Opal mine, at Grawin. That right Bob?'

'That's right Barbie. Haven't had a big strike yet though...'

'One day Bob!' Barbie says, draping the gold chain with its jewel on her neck.

Bob just smiles. 'One day! Here's hoping,' He raises his can of beer.

'So what have we got here? I ask, staring at Father John and Uncle Paddy.

'You'll never guess! Will we give you a clue?' Father John asks.

'Our own dear mother used it!' Father John says, delighted with his idea.

'Did she?' Uncle Paddy asks, genuinely surprised.

'Don't you remember now? She always had one on the little dresser in her room?'

'I can't say that I do.'

I remove the firmly sellotaped gift and reveal a brush, comb and hand mirror, with silver plated backing. 'They're gorgeous,' I say, beaming at them.

The two brothers look at each other. 'I told you she'd love it,' Father John comments.

'I said that...' Paddy argues.

I interrupt their avid conversation. 'Paddy, this is from Barbie and me,' I say, handing him a fat present, which he opens.

'A beach towel! Sure it's big enough to sleep in! I'll certainly use this at Hervey Bay,' Paddy exclaims.

'That's what I got too!' Father John says, displaying his large towel.

'This has the Irish colours, green white and gold…with a bit of blue like the Australian sky,' Paddy says, holding the towel at arms length.

'And these are from Niamh and me,' Barbie says, handing a parcel to each of the other men, and a combined gift to Olga and Aaron.

The men open their gifts. There's a razor, brush in a mug, aftershave, and small handtowel in each parcel. 'We'll get the sheilas with this stink,' Luigi says, grinning, his teeth flashing white in his tanned face.

'I think you're right Luigi!' Barney says, sniffing the aftershave lotion and pretending to faint.

'Wow, I might get a wife with all this paraphernalia!' Bob says, rubbing his stubbly chin.

'Look at this, Olga,' Aaron says, opening their presents. 'It's a painting of a cane fire. It's amazing!'

'Is it real?' Olga asks sticking her nose near the painted surface, sniffing. 'Who painted it?' She squints at the scrawl on the left hand bottom corner.

'Me,' I say, embarrassed she didn't realise that fact.

'No!' Olga is staring at the painting. 'It's so…professional! The flames look real. Where did you learn to paint like this?'

'Here…Barbie taught me.'

'Niamh, I only showed you how to mix the paint! Honestly, she's amazing. She can paint anything and it just turns out beaut…' Barbie interjects.

'Struth!' Aaron says, examining the painting in more detail. 'And I love the frame. Very neat!'

'I got the frame done at Bazza's…'

'He's done a nice job Niamh.'

Olga removes the wrapping from Barbie's present. 'Mmm…aboriginal art. Very nice!'

Barbie blushes under her deep brown skin. 'Niamh said you'd like it. Blame her!'

'We have two budding artists in our midst,' Father John states, his eyes big and bright. 'This seems very strange, all those dots everywhere.'

'It's got a story to it!' Barbie states.

'Has it now?'

'Go on, tell us the story Barbs!' Aaron says, handing the framed picture to her.

'Well, here we've got a family together, they're the different coloured hands. They're going on a journey through life. They're headed towards the sun…all the dotted lines are the roads. The animals are showing the way. That's the sun right there! It's a good reminder that we go to Jesus.'

'God Almighty!' Paddy states. 'I'd never have worked that one out!'

'If you really like it, I'll do you both one!'

'Would you now?'

'I would,' Barbie replies, laughing, 'Fair dinkum.'

'Sure she's a grand girl,' Paddy says encouragingly.

'Sure that would be grand,' Father John says, showing genuine gratitude. 'I've never seen the like in my life before. Very cultural if you ask me!' he adds conclusively.

'It's aboriginal art,' Paddy says knowingly. The pair stare into the painting, totally enraptured by the spots.

Barbie turns to me. 'Niamh, while the children are playing quietly, let's put these in our rooms.' She indicates our gifts.

'All right,' I reply.

We both pick up armfuls of presents and head in the direction of our rooms. We part at the hallway and she goes to the left. I head to the right.

'I'll come back to your room Niamh. I want to chat…,' she says, hurrying forward. A few minutes later she stands in the doorway of my room.

'Have you told Olga about… you know…?'

'I think she knows! I'm worried that she'll fire me.'

'She might. She doesn't like babies! How long have you got to go…?'

237

'I'm not sure. Probably three and a half months…'

'Struth Niamh, didn't you say anything…to anybody… the father?' She sits on the bed shaking her head.

My head is bowed. 'No.' I lie.

'Honesty is the best policy Niamh. I think you should come clean with Olga. You owe her that much.'

'I will…but what'll happen if she fires me? And Father John will kill me when he finds out,' I lament.

She leans forward with her face cupped in her hands. 'Maybe we could share a place? A flat or something like that?' she whispers softly.

'That sounds great!…When?'

'When I get back from holiday.'

'You're going away?'

'I always go home for the holidays. Don't worry, I'll be back!'

'But how can I manage without you…'

'Olga's got the Jensen girl, Nancy, coming to give a hand. You'll be right mate!' she assures me.

'So, just hang in there until I get back, ok?' She kisses my cheek and holds both my hands, then disappears leaving me with the stark memory of her bright white smile and compassionate eyes.

I stand in the doorway for some time, thinking. 'It's you and me against the world baby,' I say quietly.

…

Two weeks go by and I notice Olga hardly speaks to me. One hot evening I put James to bed and go for a stroll on the back patio where there's a breeze. I'm walking back and forth enjoying the freshness on my cheeks when I hear voices from below the patio. I move back and without thinking, listen in.

'You haven't noticed anything about her?'

'She's a good-looker that's for sure!'

'She's pregnant!'

'Struth, is that what she told you?'

'No, of course not.'

'You women amaze me. How can you know these things?'

'Fair dinkum! Sure as hell, she's up the duff…'

'Struth, you'd never know it.'

'Have you seen anything…going on Aaron?'

'No…but, I have noticed the way Bob's eyes follow her when she passes by!'

'And the others! No seriously, it can't be Bob.'

'Why not Olga?'

'He's past it! Do you know if she's gone out with anyone?'

'Nope.'

'She'll have to go, that's all!'

'Calm down Olga. I thought you made some work agreement.'

'A baby wasn't part of it. You know how I feel about babies…She's still under Father John's care.'

'Struth! D'you think he's the father?'

'No Aaron! He's just a Father, not a real one…Anyway, he's too ancient!'

'I've heard some of those Irish are virile…'

'Well, he's not the type…. They might take the baby off her, and put it up for adoption.'

'Well Olga, there's your answer.'

'But she can't stay here…'

'Where can she go to?'

'I don't know Aaron. I just want her to leave.'

'Why don't you just talk to her…?'

'No… She's deceitful…I don't trust her now…'

'What about your sister in Sydney? She's always complaining that she needs a housekeeper.'

'Maybe.'

'Why don't we sleep on it and work something out tomorrow. Struth, I'm tired…' Aaron yawns.

I don't want to hear any more so I'm creeping back to my room. I'm packing a few things. Tomorrow is my day off.

…

On the following morning I rise early. 'James, come on, we're going for a walk,' I say, waking the sleepy, hot child.

'Mammy…'

'Here, have your teddy bear that Santa gave you.' I give him his fluffy bear with a bright red jacket. He hugs it. I head out the door at the back and walk around the side of the house through the grass. A wisp of smoke tantalizes my nose. I cough.

'G'day!' It's Bob. He's sitting on an old beer keg having a smoke. 'Smoke bothering you?'

'Just a bit.'

'Struth girl, I apologize for that. You're the early bird today.'

'I'm just going to visit Father John and Uncle Paddy.'

'Haven't seen anybody coming for yis.'

'No, I was going to walk.'

'Are you stark raving mad girl. In this heat. It'll be a hundred today, if not more.'

'We've got all day.'

'Aw, what the heck, I'll take you there.' He throws his cigarette on the ground and stubs it out with the heel of his thong.

'But aren't you going to work…'

'Naw, RDO!'

'RDO?' I say.

'I'm not working today, and I need to see a mate about something in Ha'vey Bay.'

He lifts James into the middle seat in the Ute. 'You'll be right Mate,' he says to James.

James grins.

I climb up and sit beside James. 'You are here early yourself!' I mention casually.

'Need to see Aaron about something…but it can wait.'

After a few minutes on the road, Bob turns into his own driveway. 'I'll just grab a few cold ones,' he says, stopping the truck and leaping out. He comes back in a few minutes with a box of beer under his arm.

He puts it in the esky sitting on the tray in the back of the ute, behind the driver's side.

'You didn't get too hot?'

'No, we're fine!' I reply.

'Air conditioning,' he says, winding the window right down and allowing the soft warm breeze to blow through. We zoom along the almost deserted road in silence. James has fallen asleep on my lap.

'Nothing serious up?' Bob asks, breaking the uncomfortable silence.

'No!' I reply shortly.

'Well, if there's anything I can do…just ask!' He sounds like he means that.

'Thanks Bob,' I reply.

We drive to Hervey Bay and pull up outside Uncle Paddy's place.

'Pick you up in a few hours?'

'That's very kind of you. Yes please,' I reply.

'I'll see you later then?'

'Right!'

'Here, I'll take Jamie,' he says, lifting a sleepy boy from the cabin.

'Mammy…'

I clamber from the high cab.

'Come on James,' I say, holding him tightly by the hand as his wobbly legs find their balance. I open Paddy's gate and walk down the short driveway to the front door. The door is open.

'Hello! Father John. Paddy! Anyone home?' I call out.

I press the handle of the flyscreen door. It's unlocked.

I move into the family room. 'Hello, anybody home?' I call out again. There's no answer.

There's a door open in Father John's office on the room at the side of the sitting room. 'Hello!' I say softly.

I walk into the room and look around. There's just a desk with a lamp and a Barlock typewriter with an unfinished letter sticking out of it. Without even thinking I head towards it. James is following me, holding his teddy bear.

I read aloud: *Dear Mar…tin…*

…thank you for the photo…graph. You look…happy in your new… parish. The…weather here has been …very hot and…. Wind…y, not at all… like our dear… Erin…

'See James,' I say excitedly to James, who has crawled into an old armchair in one corner of the room, 'I can read a letter!' James stares at me for a moment, then his eyelids drop. Where's the photograph? I'm wondering. Of course, there's more than one Martin in the world… I rummage through some cards lying on the desk. 'Here's some…!' I'm shaking as I stare at a photograph of an old church building, then a photograph of a group of people, all smiling, in a very sunny place, under vines… 'It can't be Ireland…can it?' I whisper, frantically trying to grasp its meaning.

'Well, she's a fine woman…' I hear Father John and Paddy coming up the pathway, almost at the door.

With trembling hands I bundle the photos and step out of the room. I stand just outside the door as Paddy comes through the front door, and goes straight to the kitchen, not even seeing me. 'You have to watch your p's and q's with her John.'

Father John is wiping his feet at the front door. His head jerks upwards when he sees me. 'Niamh, what are you doing here?'

'…the door was unlocked.'

'Were you in my office?' Father John says fiercely.

I point to James, who's asleep on the soft armchair just inside the office door. 'James…fell asleep.'

Father John strides across to me and stares from the doorway into the room. He looks at James, glances at his desk, then turns back. 'We'll close the door, and let him have his rest,' he whispers, clicking the door shut.

'Niamh, come over here. What's the matter? You look like you've seen a ghost!'

'Here, sit down,' Paddy says, pulling the armchair towards me.

I sit.

'Get her a drink Paddy!' Father John orders. Paddy rushes into the kitchen.

Father John waits for me to speak, giving me the 'go ahead' nod.

'I'm expecting…'

'Holy Mother of God!'

'You didn't notice?'

'No. Not a bit of it. Did you notice Paddy?' Father John asks, as he looks away from me. I can see his side profile. His lips are firmly set, like a man going to war.

'What?'

'Niamh's condition?'

'No. What's the matter with her?' Paddy comes from the kitchen with eyes opened wide.

'She's expecting!'

'Holy Moses!' He almost drops the glass of water. 'Who done this to you? I'll have his guts for garters!'

'Paddy, calm down. I'm sure Niamh can give us a reasonable explanation?'

'You're not about…to give birth?' Paddy asks, his concern suddenly focussed on my lap.

I drink the water. Father John and Paddy stare, alert, expecting a baby to drop onto the lounge room floor.

'No, not for a few months yet. They want me to go…' I start crying.

'Get a fresh handkerchief Paddy. Step on it!'

'There now, there now!' Father John says soothingly patting the back of my hand.

Uncle Paddy returns with a large handkerchief. 'Here!'

I wipe my eyes and blow my nose. 'Thanks.'

'So, what's all this about them wanting you to go…?' Father John asks with a blank expression on his face.

'They don't want me there, not like this!'

'So, they've asked you to leave?' Father John continues his investigation.

'Not exactly…'

'They haven't!'

'No.'

'Well, why don't you cross that bridge when you come to it.'

'But they want me to go…I heard them…'

'They might have wanted you to go…to the shop, or the doctor! I'm sure everything will work out.'

'No! I have to go…'

'Paddy, what do you think?'

'Me?'

'You. You've lived here long enough. Where can Niamh go?'

'To a hospital. That's where….'

'So they don't use midwives here?' Father John seems serious now.

'No, not that I know of.'

'There's your answer Niamh!' He leans over and pats my hand.

'What's my answer?'

'Go to the hospital. That's what Australians do. Isn't that right Paddy?'

'What?' Paddy asks rushing in from the kitchen.

'The hospital. Where Australians go.'

'Too right!'

'You don't understand Father John. I'm not worried about where I'm having the baby…'

'Well, that's not a good attitude Niamh. You must think of…your unborn child. That's paramount.'

He stops talking. I wait a moment before I speak. 'I need someplace to live. Me and James, and the baby, when it arrives.'

'I see! That's a different kettle of fish.'

'I wondered if I could stay here…'

'Here? So that's what all this is about.' He stares at me disapprovingly. 'Sure now, what would people think. Two grown men living with a young woman of the female species?'

'But…you're o…' I nearly said 'old enough to be my father.' I don't say what I'm thinking.

'No buts. Decorum is the thing…we have to remain aloof from all appearances of evil…'

'I think of you as a father…'

'I am your spiritual father, and your guardian, I realize that.'

'So, you can't help me?'

'Not in the fashion you describe. It's out of the question! Paddy, make Niamh a cup of tea with lots of sugar. That should help.'

'I was trying to do that!' Paddy says, ambling back to the kitchen.

'How are you getting home?' Father John asks me.

'Bob's coming to get us in about an hour or so.'

'Well, you just take your time and have a wee rest on the sofa. As they say here, *'she'll be apples.'* I'll go and see what Paddy's doing with that cup of tea.'

I lie down and close my eyes. I can hear Paddy and John having a animated conversation.

'She's sleeping. She could give it up,' Father John's hushed voice says.

'For adoption you mean?' Paddy answers. 'That's an awful thing for a woman to have to do…'

'We can't have the Schmidts upset…'

I get up and quietly go outside. I walk across the road and stare at the waves churning restlessly.

Some time later I hear Bob's truck pulling up outside Paddy's place. I cross back over the road and head into the house to collect James.

I hear Father John call 'I'll get James.'

He scurries into the office and emerges with a sleepy James, who's sucking his thumb. 'Don't do that. Dirty,' Father John says, flicking James' hand. James curls his lip and is about to cry.

'Now now, off you go to your mother,' Father John says to James, pushing him towards me.

A few minutes after we leave Hervey Bay. Bob, looking straight ahead begins a conversation, 'So, everything ok?'

'Yes!' I reply briefly.

We jolt silently along the road. James is snoozing again. I recall the day I left Ireland, and a picture of Maeve disappearing through the fields is recaptured in my mind.

Chapter ten

That afternoon everyone seems to be helping themselves to leftovers from the fridge. I make James and me a sandwich and go to my room, with a tea bag in a cup of water and milk. James is playing with his toys. I can hear voices of the twins somewhere, probably out the back.

'Well James. We might get to count the stars in Australia yet.' I bite into my crab sandwich and have a sip of tea. 'Let's eat and drink James, for tomorrow…struth, who knows?'

The following morning I rise up early and tidy the kitchen, which I must say, is in a terrible mess since yesterday. 'I miss you Barbie,' I say aloud as I wipe the table down and set it up for breakfast. I go back to my room and pack my little bag with the few things I had when I came here. I pick up the sock with the rings in it. I tip the contents onto the ground. Four gold rings tinkle onto the shining floorboards. I stare at them, as they lie there, staring at me. 'Four empty spaces…Niall, my love, my heart. You gave me Kathleen and James, now you're gone forever. Jim, my husband, jealousy ruled your life. Did you drown in the water or the poteen? Sam…dear Sam, American to the core! My star of the ocean.

I hope you made it? Martin…pius Martin.' I laugh here thinking of Martin. He was such a paradox, like his rolled gold ring. But he was funny! 'You're going to be a real father!' I pause. 'You're a real child,' I say to the moving bundle inside me. 'There's a big hole in every ring, like the hole you all left in my world.' My melancholic mood diminishes as I finish packing my things. The thought of how much I might get for the rings suddenly crosses my mind. I find a pen and a piece of paper and write in my crude handwriting,

> *'Dear Olga and Aaron, Thank you for being kind to me. I have to go. I will always remember you Adam and Ben.*
> *Love from Niamh James and x.'*

…

I pluck James out of bed, take him to the toilet and then dress him while he's still half asleep. I pack his things, including his new toys.

'Here, eat some choco-pops,' I encourage him. He sits in a high chair at the kitchen table. He's in a daze dangling his spoon into the brown and white concoction in front of him, barely visible in the dawning light. 'Pop,' he says as he listens to the choco-pops having a fight. 'Hurry up and eat your breakfast. It'll make you strong.' Slowly he munches away. I can't hurry him at all.

By five o'clock in the morning we're ready to leave. 'Shh. This way,' I whisper, creeping out onto the back verandah and moving silently down the steps. The air is still and warm.

'We goin' Mammy?'

'Yes James!' I reply. 'Be really quiet, like a mouse.'

'Mouse!' he giggles.

The birds are beginning their morning halleluiah as the day filters through the darkness. We creep along the left side of the house. I know the blue heeler dog and the black cat are on the other side, hopefully sleeping. We move safely away from the house and get to the main road, which has a small amount of grassy area at the sides. I trudge along the road for around ten minutes.

'You can walk now,' I say breathlessly. James is heavier than I had realized. I slow down to keep in step with James. We're passing by the nearest house to the farm when a dog suddenly barks furtively at us. James clings on to my legs and I step back from the roadside, my heart pounding.

'Hello doggie,' I whisper breathlessly to the black and white sheepdog, barking and leaping up inside the gate. Suddenly a figure's footsteps can be heard crunching through the gravel driveway. A harsh voice calls out, 'Apollo, what's up?'

I quickly move into the shadow of some wayward cane plant, which has grown in a clump on the roadside.

'Mammy,' James says, suddenly breaking into an awesome cry.

I turn his face towards my cotton frock and try to soothe his trembling form. 'It's all right James…quiet now.'

'Anybody there?' A voice calls out as the gate is opened. I try to hold my tummy in as I hide myself behind the cane plant.

Suddenly the dog leaps up on us and I emit a scream, falling backwards with James at the same time.

I look into the face of a friendly dog, whose tongue is hanging out and perilously close to my face.

'Apollo, get back here,' a commanding voice rings out. The dog steps off and returns to his master, tail between his legs. A face stares into mine as a hand is extended to me. I take the hand and get on my feet. James is already on his small feet.

'Struth, Niamh! I'm sorry. Are you ok mate?'

I brush grass off me. 'I think so.'

'What are you doing snooping around at this time of the morning?' he asks bluntly.

'I'm not snooping. I'm off to Hervey Bay,' I reply.

'Struth that's a long way to walk…I'll give you a lift.'

'No thanks anyway. We have to go!' I say, leaning over to pick up my bag. As I lurch forward I lose my balance and almost fall over.

Luigi grabs me by the waist. 'You've had a fright. Come inside and take a seat…have a cuppa.'

'All right,' I reply.

Luigi takes my bag and puts James on his shoulders. I follow him inside the gate with Apollo brushing against my legs. He closes the gate and we walk along the semi-paved pathway towards the house. 'Sit' he commands as we reach the front entrance. Apollo immediately sits in front of the steps, his tongue dangling and his eyes staring in adoration at his master.

'Good dog,' Luigi says, rubbing its head. The dog flops down on his belly as we climb up the steps of the house. The house is a highset timber Queenslander, painted white and built-in on the lower part. The steps lead to a verandah and Luigi's living area.

'Sorry about the mess,' he says, picking up a bundle of newspapers and magazines, scrunching them and shoving them into a bin near a sink. 'Take a possie…'

'Thanks,' I say sitting on an old sofa that smells like Apollo. A few items of clothing hang over the back of the faded purple and green geometric design cover.

'I'm grateful,' I say, relaxing.

Luigi hurries to fill his electric jug. 'Tank water,' he says. 'Makes the best tea in the world.' He grins at me.

His muscular shoulders portray the fitness of a cane cutter. His hair is black, unruly and wavy. A moustache covers the perimeters of his top lip. The stubble on his tanned face is visible in the dim light. His hairy chest appears to be black in contrast to the whiteness of his singlet. He's wearing baggy shorts and thongs on his feet. His eyes are deepset and hidden by black bushy eyebrows, giving him a sinister look.

He glances at me for a moment as he searches for something. 'Tea pot should be right here,' he says, opening a series of cupboard doors above the sink. 'What about a teabag,' he finally asks.

'I don't mind teabags,' I reply.

Several minutes later he wipes the laminated round

kitchen table with a tea towel and places two mugs of tea on it. He takes a packet of chocolate biscuits from the large fridge that is sitting at the side of the kitchen. 'Do you want milk for James?' he asks.

'He loves milk,' I reply.

'I'll make him a strawberry milkshake,' Luigi says, prising open the lid on a tin with a pink label. He mixes a spoonful of pink sugary stuff, and then pours milk from a bottle into a glass. The milk turns bright pink. 'This is my favourite drink…' His shoulders shake as he laughs at himself. 'Sit over here,' he says, wiping the chair with a tea towel.

James and I sit on two steel chairs with grey plastic seats, and black legs, slightly torn in places. 'What about yourself?' I ask.

'There's one in the bedroom.' He hurries into the room in a short hallway and returns with a wooden chair. 'Got this for two bucks at a second-hand shop,' he explains happily, his shoulders shaking again as he guffaws.

'It looks like good value for money,' I comment.

He sits down and stares into his mug. His head jerks up at me, 'You need a saucer for the teabag!' He jumps up and places a chipped saucer on the table.

'I usually leave it in,' I say.

'Oh' he replies. 'Milk?' he asks, grabbing the bottle of milk off the sink.

'Yes please!'

He pours a little of the milk into our mugs. 'I always use gold tops,' he explains. 'More creamy!' We sip our tea in silence as James makes the most obnoxious slurping noises. 'So, what's going on?' he asks, finally.

'I'm just leaving my employment…'

'And heading to Hervey Bay?'

'I was really going to Bundaberg. I hear there are lots of jobs…' I say slowly, revealing my secret plan.

'That so?'

'It is,' I reply.

'Did you know you were going the long way to Bundy?'

'No!'

'It's quicker if you go through Apple Tree Creek…'

'Where's that?'

'He turns around in the chair. 'That way…North…' He stays quiet for a few moments, and then wipes his brow with the back of his hand. 'I should tell you, I know…'

'The way to Bundaberg?' I ask.

'No! You heard of the Bush Telegraph?'

I shake my head.

'Struth. It's how news travels around these parts.'

'What news?'

He licks his bottom lip and then stares into my face. 'The news that you're up the duff!'

'That's a quaint expression. I've heard it once before!'

'In the family way, that's what it means!'

My face is turning hot at this remark. 'I think I guessed that. So everybody knows about my condition?'

'Aaron mentioned it to us yesterday, in passing… Hey, I'm sorry for ya.' He takes a deep breath. 'I've been thinking, I might be able to help you.'

'Have the baby?'

'No! Well, not exactly… I heard that Olga's not happy about you staying on.'

'You heard right then. So how can you help?'

He clears his throat. 'I've got room here. You can stay as long as you want,' he says in a sudden gush of words.

'Here?' I look around at the mess.

'Not up here. Downstairs. C'me on, I'll show you if you like.'

He picks James up at that moment and I follow the pair of them down the steps. He opens a grey painted wooden door just under the steps and I follow him inside. He switches on a light.

'It looks…modern,' I say, surprised at what I see.

'It's not that old. Stuey had it built for his mother, but she passed on.' He looks at me. 'Then he sold the place. This has been used for storage and that…'

We walk straight into a living area that has a kitchen bench. The floor is tiled right through with white and green tiles. The kitchen cupboards are a bright green with a brown trim, and bright green knobs on the doors. The bench is finished in a wooden look. I run my hand along it.

'It's only veneer,' he says. 'Dusty! Sorry.'

A dusty orange light shade swings over a place where a table is meant to be. It has a homely feeling. 'It's nice.'

Luigi kicks some empty boxes aside, turning a dozen cockroaches from their pleasant home.

I let a sharp screech.

'I'm sorry about that,' Luigi apologizes for their presence. 'The roaches get into everything. Don't worry, I'll give them the flick before you…if you move in.'

I'm standing holding my heart with fright. James is busy chasing the cockroaches.

'No. Dirty!' I tell him.

'I won't move any more boxes. There's a servery through to here,' he explains, peering through at me from the wall dividing the kitchen and the living area.

'Very convenient,' I note, nodding in approval.

'And down here we have a bathroom, toilet and two bedrooms.'

The bathroom is tiled throughout, with a polished sink, bath and a separate shower with sliding glass doors.

'Mm,' I say approvingly.

'The bedrooms have built ins,' he says, pushing open a door on the left. 'This is the master,' he says, as we enter a large room with a big window on one side and louvred wardrobes on another. It's painted in a light green colour.

'The other one is a bit smaller. But you can still fit two single beds in here,' Luigi says.

It's also painted light green.

'Why don't you live down here?' I ask Luigi after we finish inspecting the place and start to climb back up the stairs. I stop halfway and breathe deeply.

'Look. It's beautiful,' I exclaim, watching the sun rising in the east and extending its rays across the canefields.

'That's why I like it up here. The view,' he says decisively. 'I was going to rent it out…'

'I'll pay,' I insist. 'I have some money.'

'Struth no! I don't need your money! Fair dinkum, I want to give you a hand.'

'I think the place is lovely, but how can I pay you?'

'That's the catch!' he says, suddenly laughing nervously. 'I'm a hopeless cook, so I need a cook…'

'I don't mind cooking,' I reply nonchalantly.

'And a housekeeper?'

'All right! You're on mate!' I say happily, confidently.

'It's a deal then?'

'Yes Luigi, it's a deal!'

He spits on his hand and holds it out.

I spit on mine and we shake hands. He suddenly looks less sinister to me, as his teeth and eyes shine, against the backdrop of the rising sun.

'So, when do I start?' I ask.

'As soon as you like!' He glances up to a clock on the wall. 'Look at the time,' he says. 'I need a showa…doing a bit of fencing today.' He pauses and looks at me. 'We're supposed to have an early start.'

'I'm sorry Luigi…'

'No worries Mate! Why don't you go and see Olga and give her the news?'

'I left her a letter…but, all right, I'll do that. Then can I come back here and tidy up a bit?'

'Ok. Here, I'll give you a couple of keys.' He takes his own keys off a nail in the wall and pulls off two keys. 'This one is for your front door, and the other is for mine.'

'You trust me then?'

'Can't think why not?' he says, giving me that big grin again. 'Fair dinkum, I have to fly.'

Fortunately for me Olga had not found my letter. I tear it up and head for the kitchen as though things are normal. I start to make breakfast for the children. A few minutes later Olga rushes in.

'Niamh, we've got some extra men doing some fencing. I promised them lunch. Can you handle six?'

'Certainly Olga.'

She looks at me. 'I need to have a chat with you soon,' she begins.

'I'm moving in with Luigi.'

She stops and stares at me with her mouth open. 'Struth, he's the father…we were wondering…'

'No…he's not. He offered me the flat…'

'Oh! My mistake. Sorry! Are you ok with that?'

'I am.'

'And you'll do the lunches for me?'

'I will. Sandwiches all right?'

'Sure! Nancy should be here shortly, so she can help out. Barbara is going to be away for a few more weeks…Well, I've got a CWCI meeting to get to…'

'Can I leave a bit early today. I want to tidy up Luigi's place.'

'Struth yes. Of course you can… Can you ask Nancy to look after the boys if I'm not back?'

Before I reply Olga's lavender fragrance is all that remains as she whizzes through the door.

'I will…'

In the following few days I spend all my spare time cleaning up both Luigi's place and the flat downstairs. I have a meal ready for Luigi on the first night, much to his surprise.

'Man, that smells great. What's cooking?' he asks as he enters the door.

'I found a good piece of roast meat, so I roasted it, I say, pulling down the oven door, allowing the aroma of roasted meat to fill the air.

'Want a hand?' he asks.

'You can carve…' I say, placing the hot dish on the shiny sink.

'I'll get the carving knife,' he hums happily.

'I've also roasted some spuds, and there's peas. I used the frozen ones.'

'I forgot I had those…'

'Well, we're almost there,' I say happily.

After our meal I take the plates and put them in the sink. 'Would you like your just desert?' I ask.

'You mean Sweets?'

'I do. I made an apple pie. And I know there's ice cream in the freezer.'

'Struth that sounds like heaven. How can I be so lucky when I'm not even Irish?'

I just smile as I hand him a large piece of apple pie and a pile of ice cream.

'Where did you learn to cook this good?'

I hand James a small portion and take my own dish and sit down. 'Well!' I correct him. 'Maeve taught me.'

'Maeve?' he asks. 'Who's she?'

'My sister. My step-sister really.'

'Where's she?'

'Ireland.'

'Is she as good looking as you?'

'She's married…'

'Right…what about you?'

'My husband is dead…he drowned.' At least one of them did!

'Sorry to hear that!'

'It's all right now.'

'Niamh, what about furniture?'

'Furniture?'

'Downstairs! You need somewhere to sit down.'

'I've still got my room at Olga's. I was thinking I could buy things gradually at the second hand shop in Maryborough…'

'I've got time tomorrow. We can pick out a few things if you like,' he suggests.

'I don't know. I already had time off today…' I say hesitatingly.

'No worries! I'll tee it up with Olga,' he says confidently.

The following day Luigi and I go shopping. It was a very

interesting and amazing event. As soon as I stopped at a piece of furniture and indicated I liked it, he insisted on calling the store salesman and proceeded to purchase the item. I found I had to restrain my opinion until I checked the price to retard his enthusiasm. In only two hours we return with a truck full of items, including two single beds, a cot, two rugs for the floor, four kitchen chairs with metal legs, a matching table, all in an obscure lemon and orange pattern, two orange bedside lamps and small veneered bedside tables. Luigi also pays for a purple and orange coloured sofa, which they call a lounge here, and can be used as a bed; two extra armchairs, a fridge and a washing machine.

'I think you should have a dryer too, especially with the baby and all,' he says.

'You've bought enough! I don't need a dryer, sure the sun is always shining here!'

'I was thinking of when the baby comes …nappies…'

'Begorrah I never saw a man so…domesticated…' I reply.

'I have three sisters, Jackie, Grace and Roxanne…I've helped them with their kids…up north.'

'There! You should be spending money on them, not on me! I'm causing you a lot of expense. I can pay you back.'

'No way mate,' he says. 'My sisters have plenty. I've been procrastinating for months about this place …now it's got furniture! I'm chuffed Niamh.'

'Are you sure now?'

'Struth, I'm Sure! I've got buckets of money…' he grins shamelessly.

The following day he leaves for Townsville. 'See y'u next week,' he says, as we wave goodbye.

'When?'

'Sometime, probably Thursday or Friday. I'll give you a buzz…' The truck lurches forward.

Apollo flies like a rocket to the front gate, following him down the gravel driveway. He sits and waits for Luigi to pass through the gate. Luigi hops out of the truck to close the gate and ruffles the dog's head. Apollo barks and wags his tail. I watch from the walkway. 'Call him' Luigi says, as the gate closes and Apollo begins to whine.

'Apollo!' I call. He turns and looks at me and then whines louder. I go inside and take a handful of his favourite dog food and place it in his shiny bowl. 'Here, brekkie,' I say. He rushes back to me and almost knocks the bowl from my hand. 'No. Stay!' I say.

He sits and gazes up at me. 'Here. Eat!' I say, placing the bowl beside him. Immediately his head is inside the bowl and the food is consumed.

'Greedy guts,' I say, shaking my head. 'Come on James, let's have our breakfast now!'

…

Several weeks go by and Barbie still hasn't returned. Nancy Jensen is helping full time at the Schmidts, and my bulge is suddenly protruding very obviously. Towards the end of February Olga insists that I visit her doctor, Janette Walker. She thinks the baby is due in about six weeks, so refers me to the resident gynaecologist at Maryborough Base Hospital, Doctor Johannes Schuster. He's a sympathetic, professional man, with confidence seeping through his smile and permanent furrow in his brows. He's middle-aged, tall and thin. I feel at ease in his presence. I'm booked in to have my confinement, and best of all, the doctor assures me there's only one baby, so that's a relief! Barbie returns from her extended holiday in the middle of March. She says she was helping with a special Summer School outreach in Mundubbera.

Everything's working out, I muse, as the month of April of seventy-two suddenly arrives. I trudge with James through the shortcut from Luigi's house to the farm when suddenly I can see Barbie out on the patio, busy. She's been a bit cool towards us since she returned, and I can't imagine why? Our warm friendship seems to have gotten lost at Mundubbera.

'G'day Niamh, James.' Barbie greets us civilly as we climb up the steps at the back. 'There's eight for lunch today, besides muggins, so if you can clean the cos, chop the tomatoes and set the table, that'll be all. Helen is doing the other stuff.'

'Certainly, I'll do that!' I reply, wondering who Helen is?

Immediately a young girl of about fifteen appears in the doorway leading to the Patio.

'Hello, I'm Niamh. You must be Helen…what's your surname? I think I've seen you before?' I say, recalling her familiarity.

'It's… Walker. I just live down the road.'

She's a big girl for her fifteen years or so, with dark hair tied back in a ponytail. Her mouth is so full of teeth they stick out when she smiles, which is quite often. Her shoulders are a bit stooped, making her arms look extra long as though she's been working too hard. She smiles and turns to follow Barbie's pathway to the kitchen. A few moments later I can hear the two females chatting and laughing. I bring James into the playroom where the twins are enjoying their toys. I suddenly have this feeling of being alone, totally alone. I watch the boys playing, utterly unaware of my presence, before I go into the kitchen to begin my day's work.

…

Three weeks later, on Monday 24th April, nineteen seventy-two, I wake up through the night with chronic pains in my lower stomach. I sit up, and then walk around the small bedroom, trying to get comfort. I flick the light on over the kitchen table and put the electric kettle on. I watch it boiling away. It's a grand kettle. I wish I had one of these back in Ireland! It makes this whistling sound and then goes 'pop' as the lid hops off. I try to stop it quickly, before it wakes the whole house up. It's a good distraction while I catch my breath. I'm wondering if I've eaten something poisonous today? The cramps go away and I sit down with a cup of tea.

This'll settle my stomach, I'm thinking. I turn the radio on softly. After half an hour I feel a bit calmer. The pains have definitely gone. It must be the oysters I had for lunch at the Schmidts? I yawn deeply as I head towards the bedroom, when suddenly there's a soft knock on the door.

'Who's that?' I call out from behind the latch.

'Me.'

'Come in Luigi,' I say, pulling the little chain over and opening the door wide. 'What are you wanting?' I ask.

He's never done this before. He's wearing just a singlet and shorts. His feet are bare.

'You ok?' he asks.

'I'm fine. I'm sorry about the noise. It's the kettle!'

'I just feel worried about you…you know…'

'I know…the baby…'

'Fair dinkum, it's making me nervous…are you sure you're ok mate?'

'I've had a few sharp pains. I think I might have eaten something that upset my stomach…oysters!'

'For lunch?'

'That's right. Aaron brought a whole esky full.'

'I had those. I'm fine!'

It might not be the oysters then, I'm thinking. 'Well, it might be the baby…can I get you a cup of tea?' I ask, heading for the kitchen.

'She's right mate. I don't drink tea this late. So have you still got them?'

'Got what? D'you mean the bowls I borrowed?'

'No. The pains! My sister had shocking pains when she had her first child…'

'They're gone. It's not my first child either, so don't worry, I'll know…'

'You're sure?'

'I'm very sure. Go and have your rest,' I assure him.

'Ok. Whatever you think. I'll be off…' Luigi shifts his feet, rubbing them against each other for a moment. He shuffles towards the door with his hands hooked in the top of his elasticised shorts, shoulders drooping. He's wobbling, or is it me seeing things.

'Oh…' I feel the pains coming back again.

'Lie down,' Luigi insists, as he rushes towards me and catches me before I fall in a heap. He helps me onto the bed.

I curl up on the bed for a few minutes. 'They're gone.'

'Shouldn't you be timing them? That's what the doctor said.'

'I should. But it's too much bother, and they're not that close yet! Look, I'm ok Luigi; I could be like this for hours. I'll take a headache pill. Off you go! Back to bed.'

'Sure?'

'Sure!' I say smiling. 'She'll be apples mate!' Crab apples more likely, I'm thinking.

'Call me as soon as you need to…promise?' Luigi reluctantly heads back up the steps to his own place. I can hear his footsteps in the still night, clomp, and clomp…

'I will,' I reply softly as the sound fades upwards.

Just as his door shuts with a soft thud, the pains come back. I double up with shock. There are beads of sweat on my forehead. I feel like I'm dying!

'It's definitely time up for you my little crab apple!'

Forty minutes later, I'm knocking softly on Luigi's door, carrying my old bag.

'I'm here,' he calls out, opening up. 'You ok?'

'They're getting close. Five minutes… I'll have to go soon, I'm thinking!'

'I'll just put a shirt on. I'll take you. What about James?'

'He's still sleeping. I can ask Barbie to check on him.'

He helps me to climb into the cattle truck and we almost fly towards the Schmidts. Luigi pulls up with a jerk at the side of the house. I'm hanging tightly onto the dashboard of the cattle truck.

'You want me to talk to her?' I ask, releasing my grip on the dusty vinyl. I think he's a bit shy with girls.

'No. I'll do it. Quicker…' Luigi says, pulling on the handbrake and leaping from the truck. He dashes around the back of the house. About two minutes later he's running back towards the truck. He jumps in and releases the handbrake, backing up, then turns around and goes forward through the open gates.

'You ok?' he asks as we turn into the main road.

'I'm fine. What did she say?'

'She'll look after him, no worries!'

'That's a relief. Thanks Luigi…' I say sincerely.

In the midst of another contraction about eight minutes later Luigi skids the truck to a halt outside the hospital. I can't help laughing as I almost slide off the seat.

'Sorry!' he says, yanking the handbrake. He jumps out and runs around to the passenger side.

'Come on,' he says, holding his arms out.

'You're not going to carry me?' I protest, breathing deeply. 'I'm too fat…'

'Sure am,' he says, lifting me easily into his arms and walking smartly towards the double doors.

'It's stopped again,' I say with relief as he places me on my feet at reception.

'She's having a baby!' he almost screams to the girl on the other side of the reception counter.

Twenty minutes later I'm lying in bed, huffing and puffing. A young nurse called Susan Jones is busy examining me. 'Doctor Schuster will be here shortly. Do you want hubby to stay with you?'

'Hubby?' It sounds like the name of a teddy bear.

'Him,' she says, flicking her head towards the waiting room.

'He's not my husband!'

'Boyfriend?'

'No!' I breathe deeply. The pains are getting strong.

I pause to catch my breath as pains subside. 'Just someone who's helping me out.'

'Just breathe slowly and deeply. There's a mask here if you want it. It'll help you relax.'

'No…' I close my eyes. A few seconds later I change my mind. 'Where's the mask that can help me?'

'Here.' Sister Jones places this thing over my mouth and nose. I breathe deeply.

'Thanks very much,' I mumble under the fogging plastic shield.

'Doc will be with you shortly,' she says, leaving me all alone with the 'mask'.

Ten minutes later the doctor examines me and looks at me with his dedicated smile. 'Shouldn't be long now.'

He leaves.

Sister Dianne Kruger, the nurse in charge enters the room a few minutes later holding a huge needle.

'Just a little jab…' she advises, turning down the cover and pulling up my hospital gown until she finds a good space on my thigh for a jab. 'It'll help calm you down.'

'Ouch!' I say in anticipation of the pain.

'I haven't done it yet!' She laughs. 'Hold still.' There, she says triumphantly, rubbing the spot.

I felt a little prick, but squeezed my eyes shut to avoid any more confrontation with the large needle.

Immediately I feel more relaxed, floppy. Three quarters of an hour later, Sister Kruger is instructing me in the art of birthing.

'Hold it. Push. Now!'

The doctor and two more nurses suddenly arrive on the scene as I give one final gasp.

Tears fill my eyes, and relief descends as my baby emerges, screaming, amid a flurry of nurses and a masked doctor whose only furrowed brow and greying eyebrows identifies him as Johannes Schuster. 'It's a boy! He's fine!' he says under his mask, his eyes directed towards me.

'Vitals seem good.' He addresses Susan Jones, the nurse standing by a tiny crib.

'You did well,' Sister Jones says from under her white mask. You'd think I'd won an Olympic medal.

I beam with happiness. I nod my head and smile. Such a relief. It's unbelievable!

'Thanks, Doctor, sisters…' I whisper.

Sister Jones places the wiggly pink morsel of humanity on my stomach for a swift moment. Then she picks him up and wraps him in a soft blanket. She places him in weighing scales and I can hear him crying heartily.

'Just a couple of stitches, …' I hear the doctor vaguely at the end of the bed. All I can see are green pieces of canvas covering me from my knees down, so I'm not sure what's going on. Stitches? I'm probably deformed now! Then Susan Jones places the tiny wrapped bundle into my arms.

Who cares? 'He's beautiful,' I say, tears shimmering in my eyes.

'Six pounds eleven ounces! He's our first Anzac baby today!'

'I thought that was a biscuit?' I say puzzled at the expression.

'It is. Mum used to make them after school…yum…' She sighs. Seriously, don't you know it's a day to remember when hundreds of Aussie and New Zealand soldiers were killed?'

'No, I didn't know that! It's not a good day to be born then!'

'Struth, of course it is! It's a very special day! They died so we could live! She helps us get settled for our first feed. 'He'll get the girls, that's for sure,' Susan says, her warm hazel eyes sparkling like gold.

'Just like his daddy,' I whisper sarcastically, as his tiny fingers fold themselves around one of mine.

'Feed him,' Sister Jones says abruptly. 'He's been waiting nine months for this…' She settles baby.

'Would you like a cup of tea?'

'I would love a cup of tea.'

'Won't be long…' She disappears behind the curtains.

'What would your Grandfather Sean say if he could see you?' I say softly, kissing his soft pink brow.

'Tea?' Susan announces, suddenly appearing between the curtains, holding a cup and saucer.

'Thank you.'

Half an hour later I hear the voice of my first visitor, Luigi. 'Are you decent?' he asks, holding back a moment.

'Yes! Come on in,' I say, inviting him from behind the curtained bed.

Luigi, with his mop of hair coming first, then his dark eyes and finally his bright smile, under his trimmed moustache appears. His hand looks almost black next to the faded green curtains.

'Have you been waiting all this time?' I ask, genuinely thankful for Luigi's presence.

'I made a few calls, to spread the good news.'

'Oh! Thanks. That was kind of you.'

'Struth, he's so…small,' Luigi says, his white smile brightening his dark countenance. A tiny pink hand soon holds his dark finger tightly.

'He'll grow,' I say laughing.

Sister Jones suddenly appears again. 'We're moving you to the general ward just down the hall.'

Busily she rearranges the bed so that it becomes a cot on one side. 'I'll need to take baby away now.'

'Why, what's wrong?'

'Nothing! Don't worry. It's normal procedure. He'll be in the nursery in a half hour or so.'

She removes the child from my arms and places him in a mobile cot.

'A wardsman should be here soon to shift you….'

'Thanks very much, Sister…' I say as she moves out of my sight.

Luigi stands by the bed staring at me. 'You did great mate!'

'I couldn't have done it without you Luigi.'

'I think you did actually,' he says, his teeth flashing into a huge smile. His shoulders shake with mirth.

'What do you mean?' I ask.

'It's nothing. Don't worry mate, she's apples.'

'Well, I appreciate what you did. Thanks very much…'

Were those tears I see in his eyes, I'm wondering? No, not Luigi!

A few hours later, after I'm moved to a general ward, Father John and Uncle Paddy arrive, bearing gifts. They're both wearing their best suits, Father John in sombre black and Uncle Paddy in a light grey.

Father John has his white collar on.

I've just had my first short walk, so I'm seated on the edge of the bed.

'You're not going to hear confessions?' I ask, jokingly.

'Not today. However, I want to remind you that this new member of the flock needs to be christened as soon as possible,' Father John says.

'Yes Father…'

'Where is he…?' Uncle Paddy asks, peering around the room, looking under the bed.

'He's a baby Paddy. He can't crawl under the bed yet! He's in the nursery. Just go down the hall and turn left.'

'So that's where they hide them? In the nursery. That's very clever!' he says light-heartedly, his eyes sparkling, disclosing their midnight blue colour.

'Before we go to the nursery, here, have these!' Father John says, shoving a bunch of roses near my face.

'They're beautiful,' I exclaim, sniffing deeply.

'Don't waste your whiff! They're plastic,' Uncle Paddy informs me, laughing his deep laugh.

'They're not. They're silk,' Father John declares.

'They're plastic,' Uncle Paddy insists. 'Artificial. Just feel them!'

'They feel like silk! I swear they're silk,' Father John says, his confidence shaken.

'The girl said they were plastic. Remember Christine! They look like plastic,' Paddy corrects, raising his voice a little.

'Well, if that honest Christian girl said so, you might be right Paddy!'

Father John turns to me. 'Sure they'll last longer than fresh flowers.'

'Have you brought a camera, Uncle Paddy?' I ask, noticing a little black bag in his hand.

'He did Niamh,' Father John interjects before Paddy can reply. 'He wants to take a snap, if that's all right?'

'It's fine with me,' I say.

'But are you sure it's all right?' Paddy asks. 'I wouldn't want to upset anyone.'

'I'm sure nobody will mind. Come on, I'll show you the way to the nursery.'

'I can't wait to see the little chap,' Uncle Paddy cries out, skipping for joy. The pair rush towards the nursery. I put my feet into my flip-flops and head after them, travelling a little more cautiously.

'That's him, the one over there,' I can hear Uncle Paddy say. He's aiming his camera through the glass.

'Begorrah it is,' Father John agrees.

'No. Don't,' I call out. They stop and stare at me.

'The one with the black hair. He looks as Irish as me father,' Father John declares.

'No, he's not. That's Dimitri! I met his mother just before you came. The one in the far crib belongs to us. I'll go and bring him over.'

I traipse into the nursery and take the crib to the viewing window, picking up the little bundle and holding him in my arms. Paddy is now taking pictures through the window. John is directing him.

'Can I take him out there and get a picture?' I ask Sister Rose, who's watching the pair with amusement.

'Sure, just don't let them cough on him.'

'I won't, I promise.'

I take the little cot on wheels out to the two animated men. 'You're not to cough on him,' I say sternly.

'Sure why would we do that? He looks like you John, small short-sized!' Paddy declares.

He peers into the crib. 'I was a large baby by all accounts,' he argues.

'You were a weeny little thing. I remember!' Paddy says in an all-knowing way.

'You were only five years old. How would you know the difference?' He stares into the crib. 'Sure now I wouldn't call him a weeny little thing!' Father John retorts. 'He's a fine child. He looks like his mother if you ask me.'

'Except there's one problem,' Paddy replies, fiddling with the buttons on his camera.

'What's that Paddy?'

'He's a boy and his mother is a girl.'

'God that's so true,' Father John agrees. 'You're right there!'

'Say cheese!' Paddy shouts, alerting Father John and me to look at the camera. After a quick flash Paddy looks around with a gleam in his eyes. 'I'll ask the nurse to take a photograph of the whole family, the four of us.'

'Sure that would be grand Paddy. You know we look like a real family, with a father a mother and an uncle.'

'And what am I?' Paddy asks.

'The uncle!' Father John states emphatically.

'Why can't you be the uncle for a change?' Paddy asks.

'No Paddy, that wouldn't be right. I have the title of Father already!'

'You're right. Now here's a proposition?' he adds. 'How about me being the grandfather? I've never had a grand-child, and I am nearly old enough for that now.' He puts the camera on the window ledge. 'Maybe I can get a snap of me with my grandchild?'

With only a slight hesitation I gently pass the wrapped child to Paddy, whose face beams like a beacon with happiness. 'Can you take the snap Niamh?' he asks, grinning from ear to ear.

'You're not used to holding children, so mind you don't squeeze him,' Father John advises his brother.

'Sure I used to change your nappies when you were a little fella! You probably don't remember?'

'I certainly don't and neither should you. Remember, you were only five years old Paddy!'

'I was a big lad, and bright as a button…' Paddy replies confidently.

Father John takes a deep breath. 'Did you know I christened five babies in the past few months alone. Now how many have you christened?'

'Will the pair of yous be quiet,' I call out. 'I'll ask Sister to take the snap of us all together!'

She willingly agrees, so we shuffle ourselves together at her directions, and smile cheesely. She clicks the button. Paddy is busy making funny little noises at the child in his arms.

'So what's his name?' Father John asks.

'Goochy, goochy goo!' Paddy says over and over.

'You're right there Paddy. He's a real goochy goo,' I say, taking the child from Paddy's arms and placing him back in his crib.

'Are you out of your mind? That's a dreadful name,' Father John exclaims, his eyes growing round and his eyebrows hopping.

'What are you talking about Father John?' I ask.

'I'll never understand the younger generation. I remember someone in our old class at school being called 'Little thing,' and he grew up to be over six feet tall. What sort of a name is Goochy Goo, a cartoon character or what?'

'That's not his name!' I exclaim, laughing voluntarily.

'Well, thank God for that!' Father John replies, relieved.

'I was thinking of John Patrick,' I say.

Father John is suddenly smiling brightly. 'Begorrah, that's a grand name. Yes, he looks like a little John Patrick.'

'That's a lovely name altogether, goochy goo!' Uncle Paddy agrees, his messed up hair and red face emerging from the baby's crib. 'But what about Patrick John? Now there's an even better name for you, me lad! The patron saint of Ireland and all!' His head flops back into the crib at this point. A grey strand touches the baby's nose. Baby awakes, kicking through its cocoon of blankets.

'It's in Niamh's hands Paddy. She knows what's best for the child,' Father John declares emphatically as I shove the crib and baby away from Paddy's advances.

'What about the father? Doesn't he have a say?' Paddy asks.

Father John stares at him.

'His father's gone Paddy…' I say, my face glowing with embarrassment.

'Why you're very indecorous Paddy!' Father John says. 'Come on, it's time to leave…I have an appointment about another christening.' He takes Paddy by the arm and shuffles him towards the door.

'I'm very sorry Niamh. I didn't know about the baby's father!' Paddy says, allowing himself to be moved along the corridor by his brother.

'It's all right Paddy! It's time for the baby's nap now anyway!'

I quickly wheel him back into the nursery, as he's supposed to sleep for another hour, after which time he's due for another feed. After settling John Patrick, I return to my ward. I relax on the bed for a little while. I must have dozed off as I'm suddenly awakened by voices.

'Barbie and James!' I say, sitting up. 'Come on, I'll take you to the nursery. John Patrick must be nearly due for a feed.'

'So, he's got a name already? John Patrick!' Barbie says civilly.

'He looks like a John Patrick,' I explain. 'It's good to see you Babs,' I say, changing the tone of the conversation.

'I can't stay long,' Barbie says as she follows me through the door. She's carrying James.

We head towards the nursery. James wants to walk, so Barbie puts him on his feet and we hold a hand each. Barbie stares ahead as though she's miles away.

I break the heavy silence. 'What's wrong?'

Barbie shrugs her shoulders. She's acting stubborn now! The steely silence returns. I have to confront the situation.

'It's me moving in with Luigi that's bothering you isn't it? You think I'm a slut don't you?'

Her face donnes an alarmed look. 'No!'

'No?' I thought I had hit the nail on the head!

'Niamh, I know you're not a mole! In fact I think it's great that Luigi gave you a home. It was a very Christian thing to do.'

'I don't believe it! So, what's the matter?'

'Well, seeing as you asked, I'll be honest with you… if you must know.'

'I must.'

'Struth Niamh. Well…I was a bit put out that you ran off to Luigi without telling me.'

'You were in Mundubbera.'

'I know Niamh, but you just didn't give me a chance to get back to you. I told you I'd try to get us a place together.'

'They said they didn't know if you were coming back! I had to go.'

'I thought you didn't want to share with me, that's all!'

'That's not true! I would have loved it!'

Barbie sighs and shakes her head. 'I should have contacted you!'

'Maybe you should! Maybe I should have tried harder to contact you too,' I suggest. I can feel tears rising in my eyes.

We stare at each other. We can't resist the love between us. Our arms wrap around each other and tears of sorry and joy mingle.

'I'm sorry Niamh.'

'Me too!'

'Mammy, Mammy,' I feel James pulling at my gown.

Barbie and I look into each other's eyes. 'Your lovely white collar's wet,' I exclaim.

'So's your lovely dressing gown!' Barbie smiles her heavenly smile. We laugh.

'Baby, baby!' James says excitedly, pointing to the cribs he can see through the nursery door, which has been left open.

'He's just by the window,' I tell them, wiping my tears with the hem of my dressing gown. 'The pink child with the baldy head,' I add by way of explanation.

'Struth he is so cute. Look James, your little brother,' Barbie says, lifting James up. James presses his hands and nose against the pane of glass. The glass fogs up.

'Can't see Mammy!' he says, banging the glass.

'I'll bring him out.' I move stiffly into the nursery and return with the crib on wheels.

'He is just perfect,' Barbie exclaims. 'He's not bald! I can see hair!' she says, laughing.

'You need a magnifying glass to see it,' I say, laughing.

'He's got bleached hair James,' she grins. 'Say hello to your brother.'

'Hello!' James says, leaning over from Barbie's strong grip to lay a squishy kiss on the face of the small huddled figure.

A week later Luigi arrives to take me home. Olga's given me a small baby basket, which fits neatly in the middle of the front seat of his cattle truck. With Luigi's help, I climb up into the passenger seat.

Life at the farm settles down nicely in a few days. Luigi filled both fridges and the kitchen pantry with food while I was in hospital, for which I thanked him profusely. John Patrick is sleeping a lot, but doesn't forget to scream for his food every four hours. Each morning James goes to the Schmidt's to play with the twins, supervised by Barbie. The three of us have a nap in the afternoon, which I really enjoy.

The inevitable christening of John Patrick arrives almost immediately.

...

On the following Sunday I'm picked up by the Godparents of Father John's choice, the Van de Boots.

'And how are you both, Mister and Missus Van de Boot? Are you prepared for this auspicious occasion?' Father John asks courteously as we pull up in the chapel car park at

Hervey Bay. He's wearing his full regalia, a gold and white robe with ties on the sides, like an apron, but very elegantly embroidered, with a white long sleeved frock under. He has a colourful scapular around his neck. He looks like the Pope! I feel really proud to know him.

'Ve are fine Father,' The Van de Boots reply.

'Vot a vonderful occasion!' Hank Van de Boot says, his eyes like bright blue beads.

'Tis true,' Father John replies.

'But I am also a vee bit nervous,' Hank Van de Boot says truthfully.

'That's understandable, but I assure you it will be a grand experience for you both,' Father John says as I emerge from the car, holding John Patrick in his long white embroidered gown and white blanket.

The robe has been given to me by the Van de Boots when they heard about their role in the christening. You can only just see the tiny pink face of the sleeping baby under the white knitted bonnet.

'We're all ready then?' Father John says, leading the way towards the front hallway of the church. 'Let's proceed.'

Two altar boys, dressed in white, with red gowns hanging down to their ankles and bare feet in thongs sticking out at the bottom, suddenly appear from behind the doorway. They are each holding a white, neatly arranged towel over their right arms.

I notice two more vehicles arriving. I turn around to see Olga, Aaron, Barbie and the twins emerging from their cream coloured Mercedes. Luigi is just arriving in Bob's ute. Barney and Nigel have come with them. A few minutes later they're all gathering around the large font.

'Give the child to the Godparents,' Father John instructs.

'Right, Father!' I say as I pass the baby to Thea Van de Boot, and the procedures continue.

John is as quiet as a lamb until the cold water is poured on his head. He screams noisily. Afterwards, Father John and the local priests, with the help of some ladies from the local Country Women's Association, have arranged to provide sandwiches, cakes and tea in a hall near the chapel. We all have an amiable time together.

In the following months I've been able to help Barbie with the twins a couple of days a week. This gives me a bit of extra cash in my pocket. Barbie and I have been painting pictures again. I've commenced an oil painting of the Schmidt's farm. Barbie is highly motivated to do Aboriginal art, coming up with amazing arrays of dots and tiny animal shapes, making wonderful displays. We usually paint for an hour or so every second day.

'I'm feeling a bit tired today,' I say to Barbie as the children lie on their mattress in the playroom.

'It's been hot for winter. Why don't you lie down with the kids, and I'll have a read,' Barbie suggests.

I yawn. It seems like a good idea. I fall asleep in around five minutes. Suddenly I wake up.

'Barbie…' I call out. I can just see her sitting on the verandah, reading her Bible. She gets up and comes into the playroom.

'What's the matter?' she whispers. 'The kids are still sleeping. John Patrick's fine.'

'I had a dream…I'll come out there,' I say, brushing my skirt and heading for the verandah. 'That was a short owld sleep,' I say, yawning again.

'What were you dreaming?' Barbie asks.

'I dreamed that you went away. I was calling you and you kept looking at me and moving away. Stupid dream,' I add.

'Struth! Want a drink?' Barbie asks, already heading towards the kitchen.

'Right.'

I sit and stare into the blackened canefields. Some of it has been burned lately, now that winter is here.

'Here.' Barbie places a glass of cold water on the table.

'Thanks Barbie.' We sit together in silence for a few minutes. 'I've just got this feeling that something's in the air… besides the burned cane smell,' I add, smiling.

Barbie remains silent for a few moments, then says. 'I'm thinking of going…' she says, still staring ahead.

'You're leaving?' I'm clutching my glass.

'God wants me to go back to my people.'

'God? Does he talk to you now?'

'I suppose you could say that…' She looks into the distance, as if God's out there somewhere.

'Where is he?'

'Who?'

'God? I wouldn't mind having a chat with him. Is he somewhere in the sky?'

'Niamh, don't mock! God is a spirit, so he's everywhere, but especially here,' she thumps her breast.

'In your heart you mean?'

'Yeah! My people need Jesus in their hearts,' she says seriously.

'Don't they know that the Jews killed him?'

'They know. They know that Jesus died, and rose again, remember, to give them life. They need hope right now! My sister wrote to me. Some of our people are in big trouble! Alcohol is the problem …fighting, kids sniffing cans…I can't talk about it, I'm too ashamed.'

'Can't the priest help?'

'Jesus is the only one that can really change things,' Barbie says.

'I'll come with you Barbie,' I say impulsively. 'You're the only real friend I have.'

'What about Father John?' she asks. 'I thought you told me that you're on probation for five years here?'

'I am! He might agree to let me go with you. I could ask him anyway,' I suggest to Barbie.

'You wouldn't want to see all the problems I'm hearing about. I think you're better off here.'

'You don't want me then?'

'Fair go Niamh! It's not that! The Lord's been eggin' me on. I need to do something for Him….' Barbie replies. She turns her face to me. It's glowing.

'I can't stop you!'

She shakes her head. 'I tell you what Niamh; I'll come back and bring you to meet my family one day…'

'When?' I ask, pushing back the lump in my throat.

'I don't know Niamh. When you're finished your probation.'

'That's another four years!'

'I can come back to see you before that!' she says. 'In a year maybe!'

'Will you promise you'll come back in a year!' I say. I don't know how I can survive even a year without her.

'I promise.' We hold each other for a long time and wet each other's collars.

'What about my driving lessons?' I ask, suddenly remembering Barbie has been teaching me how to drive her car.

'You're nearly ready.'

'Ready for what?'

'For a driving test.'

'No way! I don't feel ready.'

'How about I ask Luigi to give you a few lessons,' she says after pausing a moment.

'I'm not driving that cattle truck!'

'I'm sure Olga won't mind if you borrow her car. It's heaps better than my old bomb.'

'I like your little car…'

'Niamh, the gearbox sticks, smoke pours out of the back…you'll have to learn to drive a different car anyway.'

'I suppose…How will we keep in touch now?' I ask pensively.

'I'll write.'

'I'm not good at writing.'

'I'll give you a buzz sometimes!' she adds.

'Can I ring you too?'

'Yep. I'll give you my sister's number before I go.'

'You've taught me so much Barbie, how to read and write, how to paint and now how to drive. I owe you heaps.'

'Struth, it's nothin! You've got heaps of talent Niamh. I'll be happy if you use it.'

'I will. I promise,' I say. I wipe a stray tear from the side of my face, a few of them…

'Good. I'm going tomorrow, early! I'll say hooroo to James and John Patrick now,' she says.

'So soon!'

'Yep. So soon…'

That night Luigi brings up the matter of my driving during our late dinner. 'Barbie says you're learning to drive, huh?' he says, putting his knife and fork down.

'I'm still not very good at it,' I say, standing up and taking his plate.

'That's not what I heard. Come on, sit down,' he says quietly.

I sit back down. 'I don't feel right about asking Olga to borrow her car. It's so big…'

'I wasn't thinking of Olga. I'm arranging for you to have driving lessons. If that's ok with you?' he advises me seriously.

'But they cost money…'

'Everything costs something. Niamh.' He reaches out to take my hand and then stops. 'You have been doing so much for me, all this cooking and cleaning…'

'That's nothing! I'm glad I've got more than the stars over me head,' I reply, smiling at him.

'Well, I think I can afford to pay for a few driving lessons. And I think I should give you some cash as well.'

I'm flabbergasted! 'I don't want money!'

'Struth I know that.' Luigi takes his wallet, which is lying on the table, and pulls out a couple of notes. 'Here, take these,' he says in a straightforward voice.

'But…I get child assistance and Olga gives me…'

'No buts…!' He holds the notes out to me.

'I couldn't!' I protest.

'Please,' he begs. 'Ease my conscience?'

'All right.' Reluctantly, but happily, I take the money. Two months later, I'm still having weekly driving lessons. I still don't feel confident to pass my test, so Luigi pays for another learner's permit and twelve more lessons. It's nearly the end of September and Luigi has gone up north for the last week, but should be back tonight. I'm sitting down trying to read a letter from Barbie. I've had a bath and feel cold, so pull out my warmest nightie and fluffy pale green dressing gown that Olga gave me. John's just had a night feed and both children are tucked in bed. It's nearly ten o'clock, when I hear his truck pull up and then I hear his footsteps as he ascends the outer stairs.

I take Luigi's dinner from off the pot of water and head outside and up the stairs. It's turned cold for spring, with sudden westerly winds howling. I shiver as I meet the cool night air. I knock on Luigi's door.

'Niamh, you're right! Come on in.' I hear Luigi's voice. The door opens.

'Here's your dinner. You're running late?'

'I know. Had a few hold-ups. Thanks for the tucka.' Luigi is dressed in a huge towel. 'Excuse me. I was just heading for the showa. I haven't had one for yonks. Sorry Niamh, do you mind?'

'No, you go on and have your shower.' I know the Queenslanders are paranoid about having their showers, even if it's freezing cold.

'Can I make you a cup of tea while you're in there, or do you want me to go?' I ask.

He closes the door and turns towards me. 'Niamh, I'd love a cup of tea, but it's late. You go on to bed. I'll be right mate...' he says, his voice going croaky as he speaks.

God, he sounds sick. 'Is everything all right Luigi,' I ask.

He sits down on a chair near the table, and puts his face in his hands.

'What's the matter Luigi?' I sink down on a chair opposite.

'I probably need some sleep...' suddenly his shoulders starts shaking.

'Luigi, what happened, go on, tell me?' I ask, rushing around by him and placing my hand on his shoulders.

He stops and stares at me from behind his hand. His eyes are red.

'You look terrible. You haven't been drinking…'

'Not much….' He pauses and looks up at me. He looks like a little lost boy with all that hair over his watery eyes.

'Niamh,' he says, and then pauses. 'I just buried my mother!' He stares at me as though he's looking right through me into another world.

'I'm sorry. I didn't even know…you had a mother,' I say. 'I mean…'

'It's ok. Niamh, she was a very unhappy woman. It's my fault.' His shoulders shake from his sobbing again.

'I'll make you that tea,' I suggest.

'No.' Luigi touches my hand. I hold his hand with two of mine. He's trembling.

'You're cold. Do you want me to get you a jumper Luigi?'

'Naw! I'll be 'right in a minute. Haven't you heard about people like me?'

'No, what?' I ask.

He has an impish look now. 'I don't feel the cold. I'm a Queenslander, a banana bender! No sense, no senses!'

'Sounds true!' I smile. He's brightening up. 'Tell me, what happened?'

'I never told you about my family, did I?'

'No.'

'Well, we had a cane farm up north, near Innisfail. My father died about ten years ago. My mother remarried. To cut a long story short, we didn't get on… I had been the man of the house until he came along. I couldn't stand it, so I left…' He puts his hands over his face again.

'There, there, don't cry.' I don't know what else to say. I'm holding his head on my shoulder.

His head jerks away. 'He didn't even tell me she was crook!' He shakes his head in dismay.

'No! What did she do? Did she hold up a bank or rob a shop…what?'

'Why would she do that?'

'I thought she was a crook?'

'No.' He laughs and laughs until he's almost crying.

'No, I mean she was crook, y'know, not good!'

I just stare. 'It sounds like the same thing to me.'

'Sick! She was sick!'

'Of course. I'm sorry… You must think I'm an egit?'

'No way. Niamh! You're sweet and funny.' Luigi stares into my eyes and draws me closer. 'You're my only friend.'

I sit down beside him. Suddenly I look into his tear-stained face. Our eyes close as our lips meet in a gentle kiss. A moment later he pulls away.

'Thanks for listening,' he says.

'I'll go and make us both a cup of tea,' I say, quietly rising, and heading towards the sink.

'I'll go and have my showa. You go on and get to bed,' he says, exiting down the hallway to the shower.

I wait for the kettle to boil. I pour the hot water into the mugs and dangle the tea bags up and down as the liquid becomes darker and darker. I enjoyed being kissed again. 'No, Niamh Farrell, you're a bold girl, thinking that. He's just sad because his mother's died!' I say to myself, thinking aloud. I look in Luigi's cupboard and find a tin with a lump of fruitcake wrapped in plastic. All this emotional stuff is making me hungry. I find Luigi's sharp knife and cut a couple of pieces of cake and place them on a plate. I pick up a piece and nibble at it. It's sweet and moist, like a kiss. 'Luigi needs his dinner, not cake,' I'm saying aloud as I place the warm plate on top of a pot with a bit of hot water in it. I should get back to the children, I'm thinking, as I lift the lid off the stew I made with lamb chops, potatoes, carrots a bit of pumpkin and onion, with gravy.

'It smells lovely. God it makes me hungry,' I say aloud. 'Luigi,' I say, as suddenly I notice he's standing behind me, wearing a pair of shorts and a singlet. That must be his pyjamas, I'm thinking.

'That was quick!' I exclaim.

'I don't muck around,' he replies. He looks more cheerful and sparkling with his wet hair slicked back.

'It smells great Niamh.' He sits down.

I put the plate of food down on the table. 'You smell great too Niamh,' he says as I lean over.

'Luigi, I'm so sorry about your mother. I …should go,' I say, daring to look him in the eyes.

'Struth, I'm real grateful to you Niamh. I won't forget this.'

Somehow we can't stop looking into each other's eyes. I can feel the blood rushing to my face. I want him to kiss me again. Somehow he moves me forward and I end up on his lap. He has his arms around my back.

'Niamh….'

'What?' I whisper. I throw my arms around his neck. We kiss each other. A few passionate minutes later he picks me up like a feather and gently carries me into his room, in the midst of laughter.

The dinner is cold and the tea is still waiting to be drunk when I kiss a sleeping Luigi goodnight and race downstairs to John's urgent crying. My breasts are bulging with milk, which is seeping all over my nightie. John and I are good and ready for his next feed. I'm sitting here with John sucking almost deliriously, and I'm wondered what on earth I've just done!

'Luigi's nice!' I whisper to the small sucking child. 'He doesn't look so sinister when he's wet and his face is shining. He doesn't ask too many questions. He's hardworking. He needs someone to love him.'

I think I need someone like Luigi right now, I reason.

'Oh God, please forgive me,' I say aloud.

John burps again, spilling a bit of milk on my breast. I wipe it with the spare fluffy nappy. 'Good boy,' I say, as I place the warm child on my shoulder and pat his back. Then I suddenly get a cold creepy feeling all over. I wonder what Luigi will think in the light of a new day, which is fast approaching?

My instinct was right! We can hardly look each other in

the face the next day. A week goes by while he's working at the Schmidt's farm. I decide we need to talk, so I invite him to have a nightcap with me after the children are asleep.

'The other night…' I begin. 'Your mother…'

'Struth I was a bit of a mess. I'm sorry. I don't know what I was thinking…'

'Don't be sorry. I am lonely too with Barbie gone…'

'Niamh, I have to be honest with you! I really enjoyed the other night!'

'And I'll be honest with you.'

'I want you to be honest with me. Fair dinkum!' he says, looking me in the eyes, flinching a little.

'I enjoyed it very much!' I say coyly.

'Hey, that's good. Real good.'

He seems really relieved to hear that.

We enjoy our cup of tea and then he looks into my eyes. 'Even if we both enjoyed the other night I don't want to take advantage of you again.'

'I might have taken advantage of you!' I comment lightly.

His shoulders shake with laughter. 'Struth, maybe you did!'

'So, do you want me to go…to leave the flat downstairs?' I ask seriously.

'Leave!' He looks aghast, then grins. 'Struth no! Niamh, please stay here. I just love having you here when I come back. And you're great company.'

'So, you want things to be as they were before the other night!'

'No matter what you say, I know I took advantage of you. It won't happen again, I promise!' he says, staring resolutely into my eyes, taking the full blame for the event.

…

About a month later, in the first week of November and after a hard day's work, Luigi and I are sitting together in the orange and purple lounge chair. The children are sleeping.

'Niamh,' he says. He puts his face in his hand, pulls them down his cheeks and stares at me.

'What?' I reply tensely.

'I've been thinking. That night.'

'The one?'

'The one! Something happened since then.'

'What?'

'I've fallen in love with you,' he says in a rush.

'Don't be daft! You're still getting over your mother's death...'

'It's not that! I'll always remember my mother! But I can't stop thinking about you, all day long. I dream of you every night.'

'Stop it Luigi. You're joking!' I say in my broadest Irish accent.

'I never was more serious in my life.' His eyes are sparkling as he stares into mine. 'I love you. I really do!' he says, as our lips meet in a gentle kiss, that spontaneously turns into a more passionate event.

Later that night, as we lie in each other's arms, Luigi turns to look into my face.

'Marry me!' he says.

'I can't get married....' I say, rolling away from his piercing gaze.

'Why not?' he asks, his face the picture of a puzzle.

I shake my head. 'It's a long story. I need to check the children.'

'If it's the kids...I love James and John as if they were my own.'

'I know that,' I say, sitting on the edge of the bed, holding my dressing gown closely around me. 'I just can't marry you. Please don't ask me why.'

'I thought the Irish girls were always keen to get married. I don't understand Niamh!'

'I used to be like that when I was young,' I reply.

'Struth, how old are you?' he asks, suddenly sitting up, staring into my face.

'I turned twenty last week.'

Now he really sits up. 'Fair dinkum? Niamh, you never said a word! That's terrible.'

'To turn twenty is terrible!'

'Struth, I mean you should have had a party or something. I feel bad now.'

'Don't feel bad. I think I'm happier than I've been in ages.' I suddenly kiss his cheek. 'You make me feel…loved. That's all I want. I don't care about parties.'

'Struth,' he says, reaching out and touching my arm. 'Niamh, you're the best thing that's happened to me since the harvesters came in.'

'You're so romantic,' I say, turning to him and smiling.

'I try,' he retorts sarcastically. 'But, seriously, remember, it's a woman's prerogative to change her mind! If you do…just tell me…ok?'

'I'll remember that. But there's one thing….'

'What?' he asks, his eyes popping open a bit.

'Just don't tell Father John and Uncle Paddy, will you?'

'It was your birthday?'

'No! About us! They want me to marry a good Irish Catholic boy in Hervey Bay.'

'Only if you promise me one thing?' he says, smiling, relaxing. 'Move up here with me. There's more room for the kids. You can use downstairs as your studio…'

'Mm. Studio. I like the sound of that…But, I like having my own space downstairs.'

'Whatever! Sure!'

Luigi pays for another twelve driving lessons and finally nearly three months later, just after my second Christmas in Australia, I arrive home clutching my driver's license. That night when Luigi comes in from the farm around teatime, I run to meet him at the door, and throw my arms around his neck.

'Struth, what have I done right?' he says, his gruff laugh tickling my ear. He holds me slightly away from him, his brown hands on my freckled shoulders. 'Don't tell me darl' you did it?'

'I did indeed,' I'm saying, my face nearly breaking with my grin.

'Knew you would,' he says, picking me up and whirling me around the entry, nearly knocking a vase with tall flowers over.

'Watch the art…vase!'

'I'm not watching anything tonight except you!' He laughs again. 'I'm taking you out to dinner.'

'But what about the children?'

'No worries. I'll get one of me mates to come here with their tinnies.'

'You will not,' I'm saying, trying to be serious. 'I'll ask Helen if she'll come over for an hour or two.'

'Whatever you like darl. You're a bonzer sheila. You'll do me!'

'So, I'll call her?'

'Yeah. Give her a buzz. I'll go and take a showa' and get my good daks on.'

He hums Waltzing Matilda as he heads towards the shower, singing louder and louder as he runs the water over himself.

I'm off downstairs to my own bathroom. I turn the tap of the bath on. I suppose I've sweated a bit today, with all the nerves I used up on that driving test, I'm thinking as I mix some bubble bath into the warm water. What on earth would Maeve or me da think now? They couldn't imagine me as a driver, like a bus driver! And sitting in my own bathtub, what a life! I ring Helen while the bath fills up with bubbly water. Her mother answers.

'Hello Missus Walker, I got my license…

'Great darl', that's terrific news…' Missus Walker replies.

'…And I was wondering if Helen might look after the children for an hour or two. Luigi wants to take me out to dinner to celebrate,' I spurt out with excitement.

'Struth why not? Go for it love! I'll get Helen.'

I'm glad she knew who I was. I forgot to introduce myself, egit, I'm thinking. I can hear her shouting Helen's name…

'Hello!' It's Helen's voice.

'Guess what Helen?'

'You got your license?'

'How did you know?' I'm staring at the 'phone wondering.

'Mum just told me. What time do you want me?'

'In about half an hour or so. How does that suit yourself?'

'No worries mate, I'll be there. We've had dinner, and I was bored anyway. TV is boring…'

'Thanks very much Helen.' I put the 'phone down, just as Luigi comes down the stairs with a towel around him.

'Is that what you're wearing going to dinner.'

'No!' he laughs. 'I wanted to know what you want me to wear.'

'How about that bright yellow shirt I gave you?'

'Is it clean?' he asks, staring at me as though I know everything.

'It should be. It's in the drawers in the far cupboard! I'll wear my green shirt and white skirt. Then we'll look really Irish.'

James comes in from his little bed, just as I relax in the tub. 'I want a drink Mammy,' he says.

'Mammy's having a bath now.'

He starts crying. He knows when I'm going out because that's when I have a nice soak in the bath.

'Don't be a baby James. Mammy is going out with Luigi because I can drive now. Beep, beep!' I add.

James scowls at me. 'Me, me!' he cries.

I'm drying myself off, disgusted that my lovely soak is disturbed.

'Helen's coming around. She'll read you a bedtime story.' I know he loves that. With the towel wrapped around me I kneel down to James' height.

'But you have to be lying very quiet in bed, otherwise she won't read a story.'

James stares at me for a moment, then rushes off to his room.

'Good boy,' I call out after him.

We have a lovely night at Hervey Bay. We eat dinner at the Wharf Restaurant, which looks out over the ocean. I love to listen to the sound of the waves. Luigi insists I have a glass of wine.

'Barossa Pink Pearl,' he says. 'Struth, that's a great drop!'

Well, with the wine and the dinner I feel light headed, so Luigi takes me for a stroll on the beach. We splash our feet in the water until my white skirt is soaking. The ends of his trousers are wet too.

'I'd better get you home Niamh, before you're crook.'

'I know what that means,' I say, shaking my finger at Luigi. 'I know it doesn't mean I'm a crook. It means…what does it mean Luigi,' I can hardly think straight now.

'I'm sorry Niamh. I didn't know you'd react like this. Come on home now.'

'I'm fine,' I say, pulling his face to mine. He kisses me. I almost fall over. He catches me.

'You feel like a cardboard man,' I say, disgusted. I laugh.

'Look, I want to get you home to bed. You've had too much wine,' he says, tugging my hand.

'Catch me first,' I yell, running off into the darkness.

Within a minute he catches up and I collapse into the soft sand. I can feel its coolness under my neck. I can see the stars staring down at me. 'Look at the stars Luigi.'

Luigi stares at me.

'No! Up there,' I point to the sky.

'Struth, I know where the stars are.' He looks up.

'They're so beautiful, like diamonds on a black dress,' I say, my words coming out like a pot boiling over.

'Come on. Lie down here and look at them Luigi,' I say staring into the sky.

'You win,' he says, lying down and staring upwards.

'I think you have more stars in Australia than Ireland,' I say in a slurred whisper.

'That's because you're seeing double Niamh. Come on, I'm worried about you getting crook.'

'Stop worrying about me! It's summer! Let's just look at the stars, for a minute, please. They look so close. I'd love to sit on one of them.'

'They're millions of light years away Niamh. You'd be so old when you got there you'd be dead. Some say they're only gas bubbles, so they probably wouldn't hold you!'

'I'd be like humpty dumpty…!' My eyes close all by themselves and I flop back in the sand.

'Don't fall asleep! That's the sheila. Up…on your feet…'

He helps me up on my feet and then carries me in his arms as he trudges through the thick sand.

The next morning I wake up in the bed downstairs. My breasts are sore and wet with milk. Luigi has dressed me in my special maternity nightie and John is crying loudly.

Suddenly Luigi is standing next to the bed. 'Come on Niamh, John needs his feed.'

He helps me up and brings John over to the bed and places him in my arms.

'Will you be right?' he asks as I fumble with the buttons on my nightie.

'Here, let me do that,' he continues, undoing the last two. 'I'll get James ready for school,' he says as he places an extra pillow under my arm.

'It's only a summer play group…thanks… I wasn't going to bother today,' I mumble as I feel the grateful suction of John. 'I hope you won't be drunk after this lot,' I add, as John gulps his breakfast.

After I feed John I manage to put a nappy on him. Then I fall on the bed and the next thing I know Luigi is waking me up again.

'Are you still crook?' he asks.

'I feel awful. I'll never ever drink that pink lemonade again, I swear,' I mumble.

'It was sparkling wine, not lemonade…here, drink this,' Luigi says in a commanding voice.

'No! What is it?'

'The hair of the dog! You need to get your strength back for what you're about to do.'

'Not Apollo's? And what am I about to do?' I say, taking the glass and staring into the murky liquid.

Luigi laughs. 'It's not Apollo's hair. It's a fix-it drink. Come on, drink up!'

'You sound like a bossy Irishman now!' I reply. I obediently drink the liquid and hand the glass to Luigi, falling back on the bed.

'Get up. I want to show you something!' Luigi insists.

'I don't want to see your naked body! Maybe last night it was a possibility, but not now, please…' I say, closing my eyes and burying my head in the pillow. A picture of Luigi with only a towel wrapped around him visions itself in my mind.

'Ok. I'll give it to someone else then!'

'What, I ask,' forcing myself to sit up and open my eyes.

'Get dressed and come out the front,' Luigi says. 'James has to go shortly…'

I pull my legs out of the bed and place them on the floor. I attempt to stand up, but find myself sitting on the bed again.

'Come here. I'll help you. Put these on!' He takes my jeans off the back of a chair and helps me put my feet into them.

'Take your nightie off now. I'll find a top.' He goes to the cupboard drawer and rummages in it for a suitable top. I attempt to take my nightie off, and fail miserably. I sigh and sit on the bed with the rumpled gown around me.

'No worries. I'll give you a hand,' Luigi says, seeing my dilemma.

'Put your arms up,' he instructs.

I do that. He pulls the nightie off in one swift move.

'Here,' he says as he hands a tee shirt to me.

I fumble with it. 'Help,' I whisper, smiling.

'Struth Niamh!' he says, pulling the shirt over my head. 'You're in a bad state all right!'

'My hair…'

He hands me the silver comb that Paddy and Father John bought me. 'Gotta go…I've got to get something ready…' he says, rushing out the door.

I nod my head.

'What is going on?' I ask, running the comb through my tangled curls, groaning with every stroke. 'I wish I had straight hair,' I say, tugging at a resistant knot. I throw the comb on the dressing table and stumble to the front door. I peer outside. The light blazes at my eyes. I blink and stare out to where Luigi is standing, next to a yellow coloured car.

'Do you like it?' he exclaims as he sees me standing in the doorway. 'It's a nineteen sixty-six Mini…little beauty,' he says. 'Bought it for five hundred smackers.'

'Who's is it?' I ask, rubbing my eyes, and leaning on the doorpost.

'It's yours darl" he says, striding over to me with something sparkling in his hand.

'Mine! What's that?'

'Keys, car keys.'

'Why did you buy a new car?'

'For you,' Luigi adds, smiling from ear to ear, 'a belated birthday present.'

'For me?' I say, wondering if I'm just having a dream and about to wake up. 'Luigi!' I say. 'I don't believe it!'

'It's not new, but it's only done ten thousand clicks…an old lady owned it!'

'It's gorgeous!' Suddenly I feel absolutely sober. I walk steadily towards the car, Luigi by my side.

The bright yellow paintwork glistens as Luigi opens the driver's door.

I gape inside. It's all lined with a soft cloth fabric in a cream colour, with a baby seat for John Patrick, and a high padded seat for James.

'Get in and have a spin,' Luigi directs. 'Your zip. Here, let me…'

'What?'

'Your pants. The zip's undone!'

I fumble and it moves up about an inch.

'Struth, what are you doing? Come on, breath in!'

'They're too tight!' I mumble.

'I'll buy you a new pair, bigger ones!'

'Not on your nanny! I'll go on a diet!'

Luigi looks me in the face. 'Niamh, you're perfect whatever size you are!'

'Go on with you! You've got the gift of the gab, that's for sure!'

'Whatever! Can you get your perfect peaches into the car, please!' Luigi begs, holding my arm.

I slide into the driver's seat and close my eyes for a moment. My bottom may look like peaches, but my stomach feels like I've eaten too many… I close my eyes trying to relax my swirling brain. Luigi is doing something in the back, probably removing beer bottles! I take a deep breath and turn the key. The sound of the engine soothes my brain somehow. I can hear Luigi clicking something in the back and then he slides into the front passenger seat.

'Go…' he nods his head in the affirmative.

I move the gear stick into first gear and release the clutch, slow, simultaneously pressing the accelerator. 'It's so smooth, not like the truck,' I add, smiling from ear to ear, as we drift slowly down the driveway. I put the car into second gear…

'Glad you like it darl,' Luigi says, smiling from ear to ear in the front passenger seat. 'Don't forget your seat belt,' he adds, pulling the strap and clicking it shut over my hip.

'Where to?' I ask as we surge forward.

'You're the driver, you tell us!'

'Oh my God!' I slam on the brakes and skid to a halt on the gravel driveway.

'Struth, what's up?'

'I'm a ninny! James and John! I forgot them!' I cry out loud, shaking my head.

'Whee!' a small voice cries out from the back seat.

'Niamh darl, they're in the back. I strapped them in while you were mucking about …'

'Ops,' I say, feeling my face getting hot. 'I think I forgot an important instruction…'

'The mirror,' Luigi says, filling in the blank in my mind.

I twist the mirror until I can see two pairs of eyes happily staring back at me.

'Sorry. I'm in a bit of a flutter. I also forgot the shoulder check! Maybe you should be driving?'

'No. It's your car, and you should be sober from that brew I gave you.'

'I'm as sober as a judge,' I say confidently.

'I can see that! Keep going, you'll be right darl', James' play group is only down the road.'

'Right!' I say, moving forward, definitely sober. I don't want to miss one of the happiest days of my life.

Chapter eleven

As John's first birthday approaches, a letter arrives from Barbie. The post has come late, so I am busy preparing a meal when it arrives. After we've had our dinner and cleaned up the kitchen I sit down at the kitchen table with a cup of tea. Luigi is having a beer. I take a deep breath. The thrill of being able to read a letter is still an exciting experience for me.

'Barbie's coming,' I say.

'Uh-huh,' responds Luigi.

After we put the boys to bed, around seven thirty, Luigi flops down in the sofa and stares at the telly.

'I need to talk to you Luigi,' I say standing in front of the flashing screen.

'Aw, darl' let me see the end of *Number 96*. Luigi smiles. 'Struth, it's a shocker! But it's funny.' His shoulders shake with glee at his humour.

The music to signal the end of the show comes on just then. I push the button and the television flashes to a blank screen.

'She'll know. I know she'll know. I'm really worried,' I say.

'Niamh, who exactly will know that you know, that I don't know?'

'You do know.'

'Fair dinkum Niamh. I don't have a clue what you're on about!' Luigi says, sitting up straight and twisting his body to stare at me. He puts his hand on my leg as he says it.

'Keep your hands off me.'

He pulls his hands away. 'Is that what's wrong?'

'What?'

'You don't want me touching you. You got your rags on or something?'

I can feel myself blushing. 'Don't be rude! I don't wear rags any more Luigi,' I say quietly.

'So what's the matter darl'?' he asks sympathetically, folding his arms so that he can't touch me. 'Struth what have I done?'

'It's not you! It's Barbie. She'll know we're … I can't say it! I feel so cheap…'

'Now I'm tweaking!' His mouth pauses in an open position. 'I think. Is it because you don't want Barbie to know we're sh…'

'Don't say that,' I butt in.

'Bloody Hell! Let's call a spade a spade,' he insists. We both stare at each other for a moment. 'When's she comin' over exactly?' Luigi asks, his brows furrowed.

He's listening at last!

'Next week.'

'Not to worry then!'

'What do you mean? That's in a couple of day's time. We'll have to face her.'

'Look, she won't even see me for dust!'

'So, are you going to hide in the cane fields, and come out at night in the dark?' I ask.

'Hey, there's a bitch inside you darl'…Naw! Remember I'm going up north next week… so I won't be here when she comes,' Luigi says slowly.

I stare at him. 'I'm sorry. I forgot about that…'

'So you won't have to explain…me!'

I sigh. 'That's a relief!'

Luigi shakes his head. 'I really impress you…' He grins. 'My bird loves when I fly the coup…'struth…I'm a lucky man.'

'You are so, Luigi de Vinci!' I smile cheekily and kiss his rough lower face. 'Friends?' I hold my hands out towards him.

'Come here,' he says, drawing me close and placing his arm around my shoulders. 'Give's a good one.' He pouts his lips. We enjoy a solid kiss for a moment.

A little voice is suddenly beside us. 'Mammy…I'm hungry…'

I pull away from Luigi to see my tiny son holding his stomach.

Luigi stares at James. 'You didn't eat all your dinner, that's why you're hungry.'

'I'll give him a glass of milk,' I say, jumping up.

'Then you'll have to brush your choppers again, and go to the toilet,' Luigi informs James, leaning forward, gritting his teeth and staring into James' round, blue eyes.

'Not hungry Mammy,' he says suddenly.

'Right mate, off to bed and not another word, do you understand?'

James nods his head.

'If you go straight to sleep I might take you in the truck after school tomorrow.' Luigi's final offer sends James running to bed.

'Well, that's sorted that out. I think I'll make a cup of tea,' I say, taking the kettle and filling it from the tap. 'But you'll be back on Saturday, for John's birthday party, won't you?'

'I wouldn't miss it for the world darl.'

I feel a soft tingle in my heart for this lovely rough diamond.

On the following Monday Barbie arrives. 'Hello…it's me. Anyone home?' she calls at the front door. It's afternoon and I've just been giving John a relaxing, long feed.

'Barbie,' I say, rushing to meet her, holding John in my arms, and pulling my shirt down at the same time.

We three hug for a long moment.

'Struth you've grown,' she says to John, who responds by crying.

'Don't worry! He'll be all right after he gets to know you again. So, what's happening?' I ask as she comes into the family room. I pop John into his playpen. He pulls himself up and walks around the rails, staring at us and making funny noises.

'He'll escape from that thing soon, won't you mate?'

'He will. You're invited to his first birthday party on Saturday. We're going to have balloons and ice cream…'

'Struth, I wouldn't miss that for the world, would I John Patrick! Can I bring someone with me?'

'You can surely. Everyone is welcome Barbie. It's at three o'clock in the afternoon, after his nap!'

'You have a dinky-di nap and I'll be there!' Barbie speaks to John Patrick.

'So what's going on in your world?' I ask, drawing out a chair for Barbie. 'Sit down and tell me a story. Would you like a nice cool drink?'

'That'd be good, thanks. Well,' Barbie says, sitting down. 'Struth, have I got good news or what!'

'I'll get that cool drink. It's so hot!' I say, opening the fridge and taking out a plastic jug of cool water with a piece of lemon floating on top. 'When is this weather going to cool down…It's April…'

'You should be out west. Man that's a shocker!'

'So, what's been going on with your "ministry" stuff?' I pour two drinks.

'The Lord is really fab! He's just been blessing the socks off the coloured folk. Six people got saved on Sunday at the tent meeting. It was just awesome! Wow!'

'Wow!' I repeat. I can't imagine what she's all excited about. I spent so many long nights in makeshift tents. They are not exciting to me. But I want to feel excited for Barbie.

'And, I want to ask you something?'

She probably wants to know if I'm sleeping with Luigi! What am I going to say?

'John might need a nappy change,' I say, jumping up from my chair and pulling him out of the playpen.

She's staring at me. Her eyes are twinkling. I'll have to tell her, I'm thinking!

'Niamh, I've got a secret…' She flings her left hand out and wiggles her fingers.

I sit down and jiggle John on my knee. His soft skin feels damp to my touch, or are my hands sweating? I stare at the gold band with a tiny diamond in the centre.

'It's lovely. Congratulations Barbie. So, you've met Mister Right?'

'I have. He's the one,' she says, her eyes dancing, her face glowing. 'He gave me the ring a few months ago.'

'Well, you're a dark horse,' I say jokingly rebuking Barbie.

'Well,' she puts her head to one side the way she does when she's thinking hard. 'I had to pray about it, before I broadcast it to the bush telegraph around here.'

'But you took the ring?' I add, a bit vixen like, but with a smile.

'It's not everyday that happens! It's just that he's such a good catch Niamh. Fair dinkum, I can't really believe what's happening to me,' she says, her eyes misting over, as though her thoughts are filled to the brim by the man of her dreams.

'You're in love! And what's the name of the lucky lad?' I ask, wondering who on earth could have such an amazing effect on Barbie.

'Dale Freedman!'

'He doesn't sound Aboriginal.'

'No, he's not. He's the son of a Missionary. I think his grandparents were originally from Germany and England. Both his parents were born here. They run a fair dinkum Christian Mission Retirement centre out near Proston. Dale and I grew up together out west. Went to the same small school at Murgon,' Barbie says, her mind contemplating those childhood days at school.

'So, didn't you like him then?' I ask.

'Well, he was a bit older than me. I was just a skinny kid then. But all the girls were in love with him at some time. I remember one girl, Sue, who used to faint when he came near her.' Barbie laughs. 'It was so funny Niamh, she'd say, 'He's coming, he's noticed me,' then she's go all pale and slide to the ground before he even said 'Hello'. Then we'd all have to fan her and get her a drink and he'd just slink away.'

'Gosh. He must be gorgeous. Did he know she fainted because of him?'

'I don't know. She was a pale, tall thin girl who got sick a lot, so he might have thought she was just a sickly kid. She used to get so upset after that, she'd go home crying. Poor Sue!' Barbie sighs.

'Poor Sue! So he didn't marry her…?' I ask.

'No. He said he hasn't been ready until now. He's six years older than me. That suits me fine Niamh!' Barbie adds.

'He's a cradle snatcher!' I say grinning.

'I like being his baby! Truly, I think men don't mature until they're thirty…if ever,' she says with her wise look.

'You might be right! But you haven't told me how you know…the love thing happened,' I say, 'Excuse the smell,' I say, as John Patrick makes a joyful noise from his rear end.

'Phew,' Barbie says, holding her nose, turning her head away.

'I'll have to go and change him,' I explain as I head towards John's room where his change table is.

Barbie follows and leans on the doorpost as I place John Patrick on the table. 'Luigi bought me this. It's fabulous Babs; a lot better than the floor…' I remove his dirty nappy, clean his soft round bottom, hold his two legs together, lift them and place a nice triangle of folded fluffy dry nappy underneath, gingerly holding it together with two large blue safety pins. 'I'll just rinse this,' I say. 'Can you watch him a minute?'

'Sure,' Barbie says, coming over and talking to John Patrick whilst I head to the toilet and rinse the nappy. I place the nappy in a bucket near the toilet, cover it with a lid, wash my hands and return to John's room. Barbie has John in her arms by now. 'Have you seen those disposable nappies?' she asks.

'But you can't wash them,' I say.

'Struth Niamh, that's why they're disposable,' Barbie replies, throwing her head back, laughing.

'And what do you do with them when they're dirty?'

'Are you fair dinkum?'

I nod my head.

'Put a match to them…' She laughs again.

'What about the smell of all that plastic and stuff burning? I hate fires!' I add thoughtfully.

'Struth you might be right, but that's what I'm going to use…if I get a baby.' She kisses John Patrick's cheek. 'He's beautiful, like an angel. You should put him in one of those baby contests,' she suggests.

It's a nice compliment! 'Can you put him back in his playpen?' I ask rhetorically, tidying up the change area in John's room and then going back to the living room where John is in his pen, playing with some squeaky toys.

'He'll have a nap shortly,' I say briefly, as John Patrick flops onto his back, his head resting on his tiny blue, smiling face pillow. His eyes move into the half closed position as I place a dummy in his mouth. 'I hate these things, but he loves it, and they work.'

'I'll take that tip on board,' Barbie says, nodding her head.

'Let's sit on the sofa,' I say, relaxing, followed by Barbie. 'So, tell me your love story…'

Barbie sits up slightly as she begins happily. 'When I went

back to see my folks last year, he had just come from Bible college in Brisbane. The church was doing an outreach and we worked together. I got stuck in the mud and he helped free me. That was it! It was unreal Niamh. Providence I think… After we got the truck back on its four wheels again we were so happy we hugged each other. I was muddy, my hair was a mess, and my bare feet were covered in grease and dirt. It was the most wonderful moment of my life!'

'I knew some pigs in the old country who were like that!'

'Pigs?'

'They love rolling in mud, especially when you've just washed them! But never mind about the pigs, what happened?'

'He looked me in the eyes and said… no, I can't tell you.' Barbie suddenly stops.

'Did you find out what it was?' I ask, my eyes wide with wonder.

'What?'

'What he couldn't tell you?' I reply to her wondering face.

'No…he didn't say that that he couldn't tell me. I'm saying I can't …'

'Am I your friend or what?' I ask indignantly.

'Well, seeing as you put it that way, I guess I'll have to tell you.' She looks at me with such a prim and proper look on her face, like the cat that's fallen into the bucket of cream.

'This is what he said… Fair dinkum!' She clears her throat and puts on a deeper voice. 'Struth Barbie, I can't believe you're the little kid I teased at school. You're a knockout!"

'Knockout! Did he think you were a boxer? No wonder you didn't want to tell me!' I exclaim.

'No' she replies, throwing her head back and laughing heartily. 'He didn't think I was a boxer. He said knockout…' she blurts out.

I laugh heartily. I don't know what I'm laughing at?

She wipes her eyes. 'It's a really nice compliment.'

'So, it was a compliment?'

'It was the best compliment I ever had Niamh.'

'God you're a strange lot down under! So, where is Mister wonderful ring giver now?'

'He's busy. He's getting the music and lighting set up. He's a wonderful singer, and a guitarist. He's awesome! He's probably still talking to the Jorgensons. He's so friendly. He's perfect Niamh,' Barbie says, her eyes dancing.

'I never knew there was such a man in the whole world. Well, I'm truly delighted for you Barbie. I hope you have a great life together.'

'Thanks Niamh. Now for the next exciting piece of the story!'

'What?' I ask, wondering if she's pregnant!

'Do you remember I said I'd bring you to meet my folk a year ago?'

'I remember,'

'Well, you're going to meet them soon!'

'I am?'

'Too right mate. They're all coming here!'

I feel astonished. 'Just to see me?'

'Not exactly,' she laughs. 'There's going to be a wedding here in two weeks time! Will you be my Matron of Honour?'

'Matron of Honour! Sure what would I wear?'

'A hired dress! I've already picked my dress out. We won't have time to make anything, so I was wondering if you and Helen might agree to hire the same dress at the hire shop in Maryborough?'

'So, who'll wear the dress?' I ask. My mind envisions Helen running up the aisle, then disappearing out the back, and then me running up the aisle in the same dress.

'You and Helen,' Barbie says.

'How can we wear the same dress? She's a bit bigger than me too, begorrah.'

'Struth Niamh! I mean, hire the same style of dress!'

Barbie says, giggling. 'Niamh, sometimes I think you're still in the dreamtime.'

I find myself laughing at myself. 'I don't think I ever left it. To tell you the truth Barbie, my mind is not me own lately.' I excuse my stupidity.

'The main thing is, can you afford it Niamh? The dress I mean,' she explains clearly now.

'I've got tucks of money now.' I can feel the blood rushing up to my temples now as I recall Luigi giving me a fifty dollar note last week. I stare down at my knees.

'Fair dinkum? That's good, real good, 'cos I really want you to be right there Niamh!' Barbie says seriously.

'It's your day Barbie. As I said, money is no object. I'll wear whatever you want me to wear, even if it's a sack. I've got the money for anything you want!'

'No sackcloth and ashes at my wedding! But I did see a couple of purple dresses, which should fit you and Helen. You'll look great in purple, and it's my favourite colour! Can we go there tomorrow and 'ave a look? I'll take the car and pick you and Helen up. What do you say?'

'Wait on now. I have a car and I can please myself. If you like I'll pick you and Helen up and we can go together, what about that?' I ask.

'Struth Niamh, you've got your license!'

'I have, only got it by the skin of me teeth! But don't tell Luigi that! It's been great. He bought me a lovely car.'

'Luigi bought you a car. Fair dinkum? Very nice of him…' She says, nodding her head, and raising her eyebrows.

'…Well, you asked him to help me pay for my driving lessons, and he did! He's been very good to me.'

'You can say that again!'

'He's been very good to me!' I repeat for her benefit.

'Ok Niamh. You said that already!'

'I thought…never mind.'

'Well, if you're picking me up that means Dale can have our car if he needs it, so that's cool. We're at the Jorgensens.'

'The Jorgensens?' I say with a question in my voice.

'That young couple from church. They live in the old Queenslander down the road, near the service station,' Barbie explains.

'Is that the yellow house with the high roof and all that cake icing stuff around the edges?'

'That's not cake icing, that's wrought iron.' She throws her head back laughing. I join in and have a giggle.

'That's what it looks like to me!' I say, between breaths and laughs.

'Yes, it's the one Niamh. Yellow Queenslander. Struth, you're funny! I really miss you. We always had a good laugh together,' Barbie says, wiping her eyes with her skirt. 'So, do you want to pick me and Helen up around ten.'

'Ten in the morning?' I ask to clarify the matter.

'I think so Niamh. The shops don't open at night.' She laughs again.

'What is so funny Babs?' I ask, completely puzzled by what she's laughing at.

'Well, I've heard they do stay open in some places, like Melbourne.'

'We'll make it ten o'clock in the morning then. I'll have time to feed John Patrick, drop James off and tidy up a bit here. We can have a good time together again.'

'Too right! I'll be ready,' Barbie squeals. 'I'd better bring a pile of hankies, in case we can't stop laughing,' she adds, her face cracking into a big smile again.

Now is my chance to tell her about Luigi. I take a deep breath. My mouth opens. My palate feels too dry to speak. I gulp a drink of cold water.

'So what about you Niamh? How is James? Are you still helping with the twins?'

'I'm still with Olga, though only two afternoons a week. The boys are going to pre-school. James is going to play-group now - three mornings a week. He loves it!'

'Time flies. Niamh. You'll have to try and write to me...keep in touch. I brought you this.' She hands me a bookmark. 'That's the ten commandments.'

'Is that right? They all fit on this little piece of paper...'

'They're shortened a bit… 'Struth, I don't know how the Israelites did it. Obey God I mean.'

I cough and my face turns hot pink. I stare at the long strip of grey paper with a red tassel on the end.

'Is that supposed to be a whip?'

She laughs 'Struth no. It's so's you can find the page.'

'Of course. I'm an egit.'

'Don't run yourself down Niamh!'

'I won't if I'm driving,' I say jokingly.

After another long laugh, Barbie asks me the inevitable hard question. 'So are you still sweeping for Luigi?'

Did she say 'sleeping' with Luigi? My mouth drops open. She must know! 'What?'

'Sweeping, cleaning? I guess you must be, if you're still staying here.'

'I am…'I mumble, picking up a toy from the floor.

'Done any painting lately?'

'Yep. I have Babs. I started four paintings last week. I was in a painting frenzy! They're a bit of a muddle, but I'll get there,' I explain. 'There's a few finished over there on the floor along the wall in the hallway,' I explain, walking towards them.

'Hey, they look great. Let me have a closer look.' Barbie gets up and strolls over, then cocks her head from side to side as she studies each painting.

'They're great. I love them, especially that one with the cane blowing in the breeze, and the one with the cane fire,' Barbie says emphatically. 'I thought you didn't like fires?'

'I thought painting them might get it out of my system.'

'Fair dinkum? They're great. Masterpieces if you ask me.'

'Yerra, go on, you're just saying that!' I say, embarrassed.

'Struth I am not. I think you should have an art show!' Barbie says.

'Maybe I will. Go on, take the one you like.'

'Do you mean that?'

'I certainly do. You're my best friend and my teacher. I should give you something you like. You'll have to frame it though.'

'Well, if you're sure, can I take this one?'

She takes the large canvas with a cane fire and a man belting the flames with a sack in the foreground and holds it up, her arms spreading wide. 'He looks a bit like Luigi!'

'He might be. I was painting on the balcony, and I could see men banging the flames in the distance, and I was thinking of him that day.'

'It's great. Have you signed it?'

'There, like you taught me, in an obscure place.'

'Niamh' she reads.

'What about you? You do all those lovely designs, such fine work, all those dots everywhere, making beautiful Carlyle patterns… like Missus Connor's knitting, every stitch in its proper place,' I say, for an instant seeing Missus Connor knitting a great big jumper for Tom.

'Struth, I haven't had time. There are too many souls to be saved out there, like rocks on the highway, and Dale has been keeping me…busy,' Barbie says, blushing under her fine tanned skin.

'Well, you should get back to it one day,' I say suddenly feeling sad.

'I will, I promise.'

'I'll roll it up for you.' I take the canvas and quickly roll it into a long cylinder. 'I'll put an elastic band around it,' I say, reaching into my apron pocket and discovering a red elastic band. 'These are great,' I say. 'There.' I hand her the roll.

'Thanks! Now, will you come to one of our meetings? Just one night?' Barbie begs.

I knew she'd ask me that! 'I'll have to get someone to look after James and John Patrick,' I say as an excuse.

'What about Luigi, or Helen?' Barbie suggests.

'Luigi might, if he's back,' I explain.

'Where is he?'

'This week he's gone to Townsville, trucking, as he calls it. He'll be back Saturday.'

'Do you think you could come Sunday then?' Barbie asks. 'I know he doesn't usually work Sundays.'

'I might. I'll ask him…'

'He's a dinky-di Aussie! But he's still a man, so don't let him take advantage of you, will you?'

'No. I won't. He won't…' I'm wondering if I'm lying. The little bookmark with the Ten Commandments feels like it's going to burn my dress pocket.

'Struth I'd better head off. Dale will be worrying about me. He might need the car too!' Barbie sighs. 'Well, see you tomorrow, at ten.' She waves goodbye.

'I'll see you then,' I reply, returning her wave.

Luigi arrives back home at six am on Saturday morning. I hear his footsteps on the stairs outside, and I am suddenly wide awake, despite having fed John at four. I pull myself out of bed, deciding that it's too hot to wear a dressing gown. I shove my feet into my flip-flops; thongs, they call them, and head out the door and up the steps, just wearing my cotton nightie.

'Come in darl,' Luigi says before I'm at the top of the steps. I move inside the door and give him a big hug. He kisses my head, then my lips.

'How was your trip?' I ask, stepping back and looking him up and down.

'Not bad. Met a few kangas on the road, nearly had a buster, but otherwise everything went sweet.'

'That's grand. Will I make you some breakfast?' I ask, looking into his face.

'Naw. Had a burger from the Servo joint. I'm not hungry, just dead tired.'

'Well if you're sure. I was going to make myself a cup of tea before it gets too hot. Do you want one?'

'No. I'll be right. Listen darl, I brought you back something, and the kids,' he says, opening his backpack, which is lying on the floor.

'Here,' he hands me a brown bag with a little box in it.

'What is it?'

'Open it and see.'

I open the lid.

'Luigi, look at that!'

'You like it?'

'It's gorgeous!' I pull the bracelet out and he helps me clip it on my wrist.

'Look at the vibrant colours!' I exclaim. 'I've never seen the like before.'

'They're opals. Bought it from a miner. It's fair dinkum gold too! Hand made.'

'Must have cost a fortune.'

'Don't you worry about that. It suits you. The colours and that!' Luigi says with a satisfied smile on his face.

'You mean the red bits are the colour of my eyes, or the green?'

'Struth darl, I think you're right!' Luigi says, staring into my eyes for an instance, then smiling, showing his white teeth beneath his black moustache. 'I was thinking more of your art,' Luigi explains. 'I hope you're not running out of anything?'

'There's a few canvasses left and tucks of paint. Hey, thanks Luigi,' I say. We kiss each other. 'Well I missed you too. I ran out of washing and cleaning!'

'No worries matey!' He chuckles. 'I brought back a bagful of washing, so you can sing the Irish Washerwoman to your hearts content,' he says cheekily.

'You're the luckiest man in the world, Luigi DeVinci.'

'The luck of the Irish, 'struth that's what it is!' He yawns. 'You're my lucky charm…'

'I hope so…I'll go before the kids wake up. I've got a lot of things to do for the party. Don't forget that!'

'Can you give me a buzz when it's time?'

'All right. I'll do that! I'll see you a bit later then?'

'Right. I'll have a quick showa and then I'll hit the sack.'

I feel like a bird as I flip down the steps. I don't know what I'd do if anything happened to him.

At ten o'clock there's a knock on the door. It's Barbie.

'Hello there, what are you doing here so soon?' I ask, giving her a hug whilst holding my floured hands away from her. 'I'm hot!'

'Struth, It's too hot for baking Niamh! Thought you might need a hand, so I brought a few things.' She plonks a plastic bag on the table.

'What?' I ask, opening the bag up.

'Balloons with faces, noisy things. Lollies, paper hats, and a plate, compliments of the Jorgensens,' she says, placing a plastic container on the table. 'Lamingtons,' she says, lifting the lid, 'and chocolate slice,' she adds.

'That's not a plate, that's more like a plastic container.'

'It is, Niamh.'

'So why do you call it a plate? To me a plate is a white porcelain thing to eat off!'

'We always call it a plate. You'll just have to learn the lingo! Even a dingbat knows it means food!' Barbie explains.

'Dingbat? That sounds like a bat that sings! They look great anyway!' I exclaim. 'And this chocolate slice makes me drool!'

'Here, have one?' she says, holding the lamington container open.

'They smell lovely, chocolate and coconut! I forgot that I'm on a diet!'

'Today?'

'Well, maybe tomorrow,' I say, picking out a smallish one, and taking a big bite. 'It is John Patrick's birthday party. I'm sure he'd be disappointed if I didn't enjoy myself and eat something forbidden.'

'We're no better than Eve!' she giggles. 'I might have one too! Mind you my wedding dress is very fitted Niamh, so I have to be careful.'

'Mmm,' I say, enjoying the mixture of soft sponge cake, creamy chocolate and slightly toasted coconut.

'Food from heaven,' I mumble between bites. 'I've been doing fairy cakes and sandwiches. Trying to get them done before it gets too hot.'

'Looks great Niamh. Do you want me to do the balloons?' She takes the plastic packet with colourful balloons inside.

'Would you? I was going to get Luigi to blow them up. He has this pump… thing.'

'Where is he?'

'In bed!' I say. 'Probably still sleeping. He didn't get back until six this morning.'

'Fair dinkum! So is he coming to John's party?'

'He said he would.'

'Dale will come over after he sorts some of the electronic stuff with the guys. I told him it's this 'av'y. What else has to be done?'

'I got some bright plastic table cloths, which I'll put on the tables Luigi set up for me last week…in the car port.'

'Sure Niamh. I'll handle that. What about drinks?' Barbie says, looking around, noticing my one jug of cold water dripping moisture onto the plastic tablecloth.

'I've got some cordial and bottles of soft drink. Some are in Olga's fridge.'

'Want me to go over there and get them?' Barbie asks.

'God that'd be great. But maybe a bit later. I'll need some way of keeping them cool.'

'No worries. I'll give you a hand for a while then I'll see if I can borrow an esky and get some ice as well. So, where's James?' Barbie asks, as though she's satisfied that the domestic side of the duties are sorted out. Her eyes are big and bright with anticipation of James' arrival around the corner.

'Sorry Babs!' I say, apologizing for what I've done with James. 'I brought him over to Olga's this morning to play with the twins. I should go and get him back soon.'

'Hows about I get him to come back with me?'

'Righto! They'll probably be giving each other black eyes

by now! He'll be seeing them later anyway. Thanks Babs,' I say, feeling honestly grateful for her help.

'Is Helen coming?' Barbie asks, pouring herself a glass of water.

'She is at that. She said she'd come early and give me a hand. She might be on her way by now?' I add, looking out the window, half expecting to see Helen strolling through the narrow pathway between the high cane blowing in the wind. Helen never hurries for anyone, so I'm not surprised she's still on her way. I don't say this to Barbie.

'Don't hold your breath for Helen. She'll come when she comes,' Barbie says insightfully.

I burst into song. 'She'll be coming round the mountains when she comes…Singing I, I, yippee, yippee I'

'What?'

'It's a song me da used to sing…'

'Is it Gaelic?'

'I don't think so….'

'I'll have to learn that…' She laughs. 'Thanks for the cold water. I'll get James,' she says, rinsing the glass and placing it upside down on the draining board. She skips out the door.

Helen comes over around two, with a plate of pikelets and jam.

'Mum sent these,' she says, holding the plate out to me.

'Here, I'll take them,' Barbie says, whisking them away.

Helen immediately has several children hanging on her leg. They seem to flock to her side like a fly-to-fly paper.

By three o'clock the whole place seemed filled with people, balloons, streamers, fairy cakes, lemonade and a lot of noisy chatter.

Barbie brings Ben, Adam, and James. The twins are running around like chooks with their heads off, except they're screaming their heads off. James tags along after them. 'Here's Uncle Paddy and Father John!' Barbie says as she brings out a pile of plastic cups for the children's drinks.

'Right! I'll come out there,' I say, piling a plate with fairy cakes, dotted with hundreds and thousands.

'Good afternoon. I hope we're not too late!' Father John says as he hurries from the car. Uncle Paddy is hot on his heels.

'No! You're not. How are you Father John, Uncle Paddy?' I ask, peering over the plate of fairy cakes.

'I'm very well, and how's yourself? And how is our favourite grandchild?'

'We're all fine. I think little John is more interested in the wrapping on everything than what's inside,' I add.

'And I'm well too. Here y'are,' Uncle Paddy says, handing me a gift with blue wrapping, held together with a few rolls of sticky tape.

'Paddy wrapped it!' Father John says.

'It's not the best,' Paddy says, straightening up a corner and tearing the paper a bit more.

'I'm sure John won't worry at all,' I assure Paddy. His face brightens.

'Why don't you give it to John yourself?' I say. 'I've got my hands full…'

'Here, give it to me Paddy,' Father John says, taking the parcel.

I place the cakes on a small table. Paddy limps a little as he follows me.

'What is it?' I ask Paddy.

'It's the leg.'

'You bought a leg for John?'

'I thought you meant my limp. It's the old arthritis coming back. Winter must be around the corner.'

'I don't know how you can call it winter. So, what did you get John?'

'A set of golf clubs!'

'I mean little John, who's one year old Paddy,' I say, bursting out into laughter.

Paddy's eyes light up and his smile fills his face with a hundred lines. 'It's true. You see, Father John and meself love to play golf, so I thought it was a good idea for John Patrick, our namesake!' Paddy explains.

'You're joking!' I exclaim.

'They're only plastic!' Paddy assures me, 'They're not real at all.' He winks at me.

The Van de Boots arrive just then.

'Hallo Niamh,' Thea Van de Boot says in her distinctly Dutch accent. 'This is Kimberley, our neighbour's little kinder. Kimberley, say 'hallo' to Missus…what vill I call you Niamh?' Thea Van de Boot says edging the child forward by the shoulders.

'Niamh will be grand.'

'Say hallo to Niamh, Kimberley,' Thea instructs.

'Hello Knee…' Kimberley says shyly. She's a cute blonde haired little girl with hazel coloured eyes and a huge red ribbon in her hair, to match her red and white dress, white socks with red lace and black patent shoes with a little bow on front.

'Hello there yourself! You're a beautiful little girl, Kimberley,' I say, bending down to her level.

She smiles, lighting up her chubby face, and holding her dress on its skirting. 'That's a sweet name. And that's a very pretty dress. Would you like a fairy cake?' I offer her the plate.

She stares for a moment, then nervously picks up a cake from the centre of the plate.

'Say thank you,' Thea instructs sharply.

My attention is suddenly drawn to a ripping sound. John, sitting on his plump bottom in the middle of the concrete floor seems oblivious of what's going on, tearing up paper and putting it in his mouth instead of playing with his new presents. I hurry over, bending down to remove all the paper from around him and from within the confines of his sloppy mouth. 'Yuk!' I exclaim. As I rise up again I notice Barbie standing at the brightly covered table pouring drinks into plastic cups. 'I promised to wake Luigi up. Can you look after this lot?'

'Struth sure! Go on, get him out of the sack.'

'Thanks Babs.'

'No worries mate,' she says, continuing to pour cool drinks into plastic cups, attracting a crowd of small people.

I run up the stairs. His front door is ajar. 'Luigi,' I call out.

'I'm in here darl,' his voice rings back.

'Party time!' I yell from the door. 'Just making sure you're coming down.'

Luigi's unshaven face with his black knotty locks peers around the corner near the bathroom. 'Got no gear on darl'. 'Aving a showa!' he informs me, his white teeth contrasting vividly with its hairy surrounds.

'Right. See you later then!' I say, hurrying back down the stairs.

Twenty minutes later he turns up looking refreshed. He's wearing the latest body hugging open neck shirt of bright lime green colour, patterned with white hibiscuses. The colours heighten the deep tan on his neck arms and face. His pants are also the latest body hugging type, with flattened tummy and sailor styled bottoms, in a mild green hue. His face is shining from scrubbing with soap, and except for his moustache, clean-shaven. His mullet hairstyle is wet and slicked down, just touching the nape of his neck. To me he suddenly appears deliriously handsome! He has a big parcel in his arms.

He looks around and calls out 'Where's me old mate John Patrick?'

'He's over here,' I say, beckoning Luigi towards John and me.

Luigi wriggles through the crowd, holding the parcel over his head.

'Da, da,' John Patrick says, grasping at the colourful wrapping.

'Mammy will help you take the paper off,' I say, taking my eyes off Luigi's attractive appearance and focussing on John Patrick, who gets so excited he's bouncing up and down on his bottom.

'It's a…car!' I exclaim. A little red and yellow plastic car! There's no floor, therefore John can run his feet along the ground. There are also pedals a bit further along, for when his little legs grow a bit more. Luigi lifts John Patrick into the driver's seat.

John bangs on the steering wheel. 'Press this,' Luigi says, pressing John's hand on a rubber ball sticking out near the steering wheel. It goes *beep*. John topples over with excitement. Luigi and I laugh and our eyes connect deeply for an instant. Suddenly the small crowd is gathering around us, including James, who puts his foot into the driver's seat.

'You're too big for this. It's John's!' I say.

'I've got something for you James!' Luigi says. 'Come on mate, I'll show you!'

James immediately holds out his hand to Luigi and they both head towards the back of the building. A couple of minutes later I hear siren noises and a bell ringing.

'What's wrong?' I say, rushing out.

'It's his new fire engine!' Luigi states.

'God it's gorgeous. It's bigger than himself!'

James sits proudly inside the red fire engine. He's pulling a little cord with a bell. On the roof there's a little ladder, and underneath there are eight black and silver wheels.

'It must have cost a small fortune!' I exclaim as the guests come over to investigate the noise. 'It's not his birthday!' I whisper to Luigi.

'I didn't want him to feel left out.'

'Is that right?' I'm not sure it's such a good idea, but at least James is happy.

'It's mine Mammy. My fire engine!' James screams happily.

The following evening, I'm relaxing on the sofa when I remember something. 'Luigi, I promised Barbie I'd go to her meeting tonight, but I'm jaded after John's party yesterday, and getting up for Mass this morning.'

'Give yourself a break darl,' Luigi suggests, sitting next to me, placing his arm around my shoulders.

'I'd love that, but I'd better keep my word.'

'Sure darl'. Whatever you want. Hows about I grab some fish and chips for the kids.'

'I'd like that,' I say, yawning. 'I'll feed John before I leave.'

Luigi stares at me with his dark brows furling, indicating that he's really thinking things through. 'It's five o'clock now, so why don't I go and get some dinner and you can have a nap?'

'That sounds luxurious. I will then.'

'I'll take James with me in the truck,' Luigi says, picking James up and wiping his filthy face. 'He's been eating chocolate again.'

'Mmm,' James says, licking his lips.

'Have you been in the fridge again mate?' Luigi asks James.

James' face turns into a pre-crying state. 'No crying matey. No more chocolate today, otherwise you won't eat your dinner. Understood?' Luigi asks James.

James nods his head.

'Right James. We're going for a ride to the chippo, ok?'

'Ok!' James nods his head again.

'Come on. Up you get!' Luigi swings James onto his shoulders. James' face is glowing as he hangs gingerly onto Luigi's thick mullet haircut.

Off they go, making noises, Luigi saying, 'Get your head down matey…,' as he crouches and they move through the doorway. 'Oh… don't rip my hair mate….'

James laughs. They look like they belong together, I reflect as I flop down on the nice cool sheets. I close my eyes gratefully and sprawl out for comfort as I wait for them to return with our meal. John is still having his afternoon nap and is asleep lying on his tummy in his cot. He's wearing a thin vest and a nappy, so he can be as cool as possible. The ceiling fan is drumming away taking me into the land of sweet dreams.

The smell of deep-fried chips wafts under my nose.

'Something's burning!' I say, leaping up.

'Chippies,' James yells, sticking a long thin brown hot chip in my mouth.

I chew on it as Luigi heads into the kitchen. I can hear him tearing up pieces of butcher paper. I can just imagine what our plates will be. 'Come and get it!' he yells out.

John stirs. 'Shh, be quiet you two. John Patrick's waking up.'

I sneak into the kitchen and just as I'm about to sit down John starts bawling.

'I'll get him,' Luigi says, shoving a handful of fish pieces into his mouth. 'It's hot!'

Five minutes later Luigi returns with John Patrick in his arms.

'Here Mum,' he says, dropping him into my arms. 'I gave him a fresh nappy. He was nearly dry.'

'You smell nice,' I say, kissing John Patrick's soft shoulders.

'Here, you can have a feed while I have mine.'

I lift my top and John Patrick greedily attaches his mouth to my nipple.

An hour later I drive off in my yellow Mini and head towards the chapel hall. I feel relieved to see several cars parked and people cluttered around the door, happily chatting to one another. I don't want people taking too much notice of me, so I slip past the people and head inside. This is the first time I've been inside a protestant church. What would Father John think if he could see me now, I wonder. He'd probably excommunicate me…I smile at the thought. The place looks very bare; there's nothing on the walls except a poster of a sunset with the words, which I can easily read: 'I am the Light of the World.' Something is written under that but I can't make it out. In the front of the church there is no altar, just a small wooden cross on the wall with fancy looking words 'He has Risen!' above it. A few steps lead up to a slightly raised platform on which there are a lectern and a table with a white cloth on it, with a dove embroidered on it. There are no stained glass windows or statues, which makes the place feel a bit chilly. I sit down on a plastic chair under a swirling fan and the breeze fans my bare shoulders. I am just wearing a thin cotton frock with no sleeves, and a pair of sandals on my feet. I hug my bare arms for a moment, enjoying the crisp coolness.

I'm interrupted by a soft female voice. 'Are you cold?' A lady wearing a floral cotton frock and a badge saying *officer* stands nearby.

'I'm all right thanks!'

'We thought it would get very hot in here tonight with the crowds, so we put them all on, full boar.'

'It's been such a very hot day!' I reply.

'My name is Edith Waldron, are you visiting?'

'No. I live here. I'm Niamh,' I say, putting my hand out to shake her outstretched right hand.

'No, I mean a visitor to church?'

'Oh no! I go to the Catholic Church at Hervey Bay. My…friend is Father John Hurley,' I say.

She suddenly smiles very broadly. 'I don't know him personally, but I have met Father Cahill from down there. Lovely man. Does Religious Instruction! So you're just visiting us tonight? Are you with someone Niamh?'

'I'm a friend of Barbie's.'

'Oh, that's right. You're the Irish lass? Yes, I've heard about you. Let me see now, you work at the Schmidt's farm. You live with the wog…cane cutter I mean. I heard you had a baby?' Her eyes open wide as she questions me to see if the information is correct. Sure she knows a lot more about me than I know about her.

'He's been christened. He's just had his first birthday!'

'That's wonderful Niamh. So, do you know the Lord?' She asks, surprising me.

'Lord who?' I ask. She must mean the Lord of this piece of land, like in Ireland.

'Jesus,' she whispers.

'Oh.'

Her eyes scrutinize my face.

'Not very well,' I say, avoiding her stare. She reminds me of Martin, looking right through me like that, reading my mind.

'Well, we all need to get to know him better. Would you like a programme?' she asks, moving closer to let someone pass into the next seat.

'Yes, please!' I reply. She leaves and I breathe a sigh of relief. I look behind into the crowd, searching for Barbie. I turn back around and suddenly she's right there. She and Dale are on the stage, sorting out some wires. She immediately spots me and uses her hand to beckon me up there. I move into the aisle and climb onto the platform.

'Dale, this is me good mate Niamh,' Barbie says.

'Hello there,' I say.

He turns around looking a bit startled, but his hand reaches out immediately. 'G'day! Sorry I missed the party.'

Wow! I think, what a gorgeous looking lad! He's fair-haired, with a tanned complexion and a rugged look with broad shoulders. He's tall, probably well over six feet. He's wearing a cowboy vest with jewels decorating it. He looks like a film star. 'We missed you,' I reply, smiling.

'Barbie's told me heaps about you. Excuse me. I'll catch you later?' He removes his grip.

'Certainly,' I reply.

He heads back to some plugs and wire. Barbie is smiling. She looks great in a cowgirl hat and bright purple jewelled vest and long skirt.

'He's gorgeous,' I whisper.

'Wait until you hear him sing!' she says, leaning over.

People start coming up and asking questions about the music and sound.

'I'll go back down there!' I say, catching Barbie's eye as another tall man who sports an American accent approaches her. I sit down where I was before and relax. The stage is filling up with personnel carrying things like guitars and drums and others just walking about. They all wear cowboy outfits. Suddenly it's quiet, then I hear 'one, two three' echoing from the stage. The lights are low and they start playing hymns. The songs are displayed on a big overhead screen. People join in, singing and clapping. I join in. After several songs, the pastor comes onto the stage, with a flurry of clapping surrounding his entrance.

'Welcome folks. My name is Wesley Bridges; I'm the pastor of this church. God bless you all,' he says. 'Let's pray.' After an astonishing prayer where he just seemed to talk to God as if He was right in the room, he suddenly stops and stares into the crowd again. 'Tonight we have a special guest speaker, William Westfield. He was born in Australia but grew up in the United States of America, and now he's returned with a new life! The life of Jesus Christ!'

People clap and cheer at this. I cheer as well. 'Slainte!' I yell.

'Praise the Lord,' a woman who is sitting next to me says. She stares at me for a moment.

I nod my head. 'Praise the Lord!' I say quietly.

William Westfield comes onto the platform. The music tones down, fading into the background. The lights rise up on stage. There is a hush. He opens a bible and lays it before him. I find that this man fascinates me. I can't stop watching his mouth moving. I think I can almost see the words as they come out. Then something happens that I can only describe as supernatural, but it was as if he was just speaking to me, alone.

William Westfield is quoting the bible and raising the open book over his head and pointing into the crowd. 'Jesus said, 'If you asked me for a drink I would have given you water. Real water. Water that would quench your thirst forever!'' He pauses. 'You have had five husbands, and the one you now have is not your husband.'

He must know all about me. It's probably that woman, Edith Waldron…

Westfield continues, 'Jesus knows every thought in your mind. He knows about your life. He knows your hardships, your trials, your sins!' he says. He's staring at me again. 'Come unto me…'

I'm longing to go up there, to be free, to stop clinging on to the chair. Barbie is calling me. As I stand up and move forward it's like a wonderful dream and I'm going to heaven. I look into a man's face. It's so full of compassion that I can't help crying. Tears are streaming down my face.

'Jesus loves you!'

I close my eyes and enjoy the moment of bliss. It feels like I'm in a soft, invisible shower. I look up. A woman is standing next to me with her eyes closed. She's got her hand on my shoulders and is praying for me.

'Come and sit down,' she says, leading me towards a partitioned area.

I sit down.

'Did you want to accept Jesus as your Saviour?'

'Definitely. I do!' I say, tears welling in my eyes.

'Here,' the woman hands me a clean white hankerchief.

'Thank you,' I say, taking the hankie and blowing my nose.

'Would you like to pray?' she asks me.

'I know the Our Father, Hail Mary and Glory Be…'

'You can just say what's on your mind. God loves that.'

'I don't know how to do that,' I say.

'You can repeat what I say if you like…'

I nod my head.

'Dear Father,' she says, 'thank you for sending this lovely woman here today. What's your name?'

'Niamh,' I reply.

She continues. 'We know that you love Niamh very much, Jesus, because you died for her sins. Please help her to understand how much you can do for her. How much you want her to live for you. You are the way the truth and the life.'

Suddenly I find myself talking to God as if he's right here. 'Dear God, I want my life to be right with you. Please help me to understand what you want.'

'That's a beautiful prayer,' the woman says, her face aglow.

I return home to my sleeping boys and a tired Luigi who's lying on the sofa watching television.

'Hi darl" he greets me as I come inside.

I just smile and stare at him. 'Hi Luigi.'

'What have they done to you?' he asks, his face concerned.

'I'm clean!' I say happily.

Luigi asks. 'You had a good soak before you left.' He sits up looking alarmed. 'Did they get you to drink something?'

'No. Just a cup of tea at the end.'

'They probably laced it with something,' Luigi says.

'No. It wasn't like that. It's spiritual,' I say, smiling from ear to ear.

'Well, it's sure done you good darl. You look radiant,' Luigi says, staring at me.

'Luigi, I want to ask you something?'

'No way! I'm not going there…'

'That's not what I was going to say.' I pause and stare into his rugged face. 'Do you still want to marry me?'

'I don't follow you Niamh.'

'You still want me?'

Luigi gets up and hugs me. 'Of course I do. Possibly more than anything else in the world!' He looks down into my eyes.

'Possibly? Is there another?'

'There is!' he replies, grinning from ear to ear. 'A new harvester.' Then he turns to me and kisses me on the mouth. 'Struth, you're soft. Yep, that kiss is worth more than a harvester, a new one!'

'So, do you love me?'

'Well, I'd even give up the footy on a Saturday for you, so I must love you.' He catches my face in his hands and pulls my lips to his. After a few minutes we both need to come up for air.

'Niamh, I need you darl, now!' Luigi says, his hands moving across my neck and onto my buttons.

'Slow down Mister Harvester, the cane's not ready yet.'

'Come on darl, what's up?'

'You have to marry me first!'

'Holy Moses, what are you coming at?'

'We should try to build up our friendship before we hit the sack thing…'

'Friendship! We are great mates, and we have had a good time in the hay. What have they put into your pretty head?'

'Nobody's told me anything. It's me conscience. It's what I know we should do.'

'You know I'll marry you tonight if that's the case!'

'We have to organize a few things first,' I say. 'It's not every day a girl gets married.'

'Struth! I never heard you say this before! Now you probably want the whole caboodle, limos, church service, flowers, everything!'

'No. I just want a few friends and afternoon tea, something like that,' I assure Luigi.

'Struth darl', make it as quick as possible. I'm randy as a bear…'

'I'll go and see Father John tomorrow,' I say. 'I'll tell him you have an unquenched passion for me that can't wait.'

'Slow down Niamh. I can wait you know! But not too long!' We kiss again. After a few minutes, we separate.

'This is going to be hard, but with God nothing is impossible,' I say.

'Please, don't preach Niamh! I'm going to have a showa.'

John Patrick cries loudly from his room.

'Well, me buttons are all undone and ready for you John Patrick,' I call out to the crying child.

'Lucky John Patrick!' Luigi says sombrely.

John Patrick wails loudly. James calls out, 'Mammy, Mammy.'

'Now all Hell's broke loose,' I say.

'Come on matey, let's have a bedtime story, then I'll have a nice freezing cold showa.' Luigi goes towards James' bedroom.

The next day I visit Father John and Uncle Paddy. I have the children with me as Luigi is busy helping Olga and Aaron prepare a field for planting.

'Hello there,' Father John says, as we stand outside his screened door.

'Come on in. What's the pleasure of your visit? And how are my two favourite children?'

'They're fine,' I reply on behalf of James and John. James runs over to Paddy and I put John Patrick down on the floor.

'Hello there James, me boy,' Paddy says. 'You're looking great Niamh,' he adds, looking up from his newspaper reading. Paddy is relaxing in a pair of scruffy faded blue pants, which has been cut off just around knee height. Bits of thread dangle around his knobbly knees. He's wearing a stained white shirt with an open neck, the sleeves untidily open. His feet are bare. A pair of flip-flops lie beside his chair.

'Thanks Paddy,' I say, coming over to him and giving him a kiss on the cheek.

'Would you like a cup of tea,' he asks.

'That'd be lovely,' I say.

Paddy hurries around the corner into the kitchen.

'Sit down Niamh,' Father John says, busily removing some books from an armchair. He's wearing his black long trousers and a clean white shirt, opened at the neckline. He dabs a handkerchief on his forehead, where beads of sweat have risen. ''Tis very hot these last few days.'

'It is. It's the black trousers you're wearing,' I reply.

Father John leans towards me and says, 'I've been very tempted to cut my trouser legs off, like my delinquent brother here.' Then he leans even closer as if he's telling me a secret, 'But God is helping me to resist that sinful action, and pour coals on the Devil's head!' he mumbles.

'You're a tower of strength Father John,' I say encouragingly.

'Well, I've always had that strength of character inside myself. It's been a great blessing to my soul,' he says with a lilt in his voice.

'That's grand,' I say agreeably. I sit on the sofa and watch John Patrick crawling around the floor.

'You didn't come here to give me compliments no doubt, did you?' Father John asks, sinking back into his old armchair.

''Tis true. I'll come to the point.' I pause for one moment, and then continue. 'Luigi and I want to get married.'

'Married?' Father John's eyebrows rise up to his balding head. 'I didn't even know you had such a serious friendship.'

'Very serious Father John. I…we want to get married as soon as possible,' I mutter.

'You're not in the family way again, are you?'

'No. It's nothing like that.'

'Well now, I think you shouldn't be in so much of a hurry. Remember the proverb, Hurry Murray, rushing mother dies!' He suddenly stops and looks at me over his reading glasses. 'Why not wait until next year, it will give this man a chance to build his faith up!'

'A year! I think Jesus wants me to get married now!'

'Jesus?' Father John exclaims. He leaps up. 'Jesus is gone back to heaven, His Holiness the Pope is his Vicar on earth. Have you been talking privately to His Holiness then?'

'No!'

'Niamh, I might warn you about hearing voices. Many have been led astray by such notions.'

'It's my conscience! We've been living together Father!' There, I'm in hot water now, I'm thinking!

Father John stares at me, speechless. 'Mother of God, you're a wicked sinner!'

'I know Father, that's why I want to get married quickly. To put things right.'

'Well,' he sighs. 'Even if that's your plight, I can't marry you for around twelve months.'

The noise of a rattling cup and saucer interrupts us. 'Here's your tea,' Paddy says. 'Just the thing for a hot day. It helps you get up a good sweat!' he advises.

'Thanks Paddy, It's just what I need.' Gingerly I sip the hot tea.

'So, what's this I hear John? Are you trying to hinder this girl getting married?' Paddy asks, standing up straight with his hands on his hips.

'Big ears,' Father John says roughly.

'All the better to hear you,' Paddy replies. 'So why can't they get married sooner than a year?'

'The answer is very simple, if only I was allowed to explain the situation, you would have known by now!'

Paddy and I stare at Father John, waiting for his explanation.

'I was talking to Father Cahill the other day, and he advised me that people are now booking up to twelve months for weddings. Every Saturday is gone!'

'So, what about all the other days?' Paddy asks.

'They're reserved for funerals and the like. I'm an honoured guest here, I don't run things,' Father John explains.

'So, couldn't some other celebrant marry her?'

'Well, it can't be in our chapel. We could try another parish, but I'm not fully acquainted with their procedures.'

'Father John, could I get married in a non-Catholic church?'

'Of course, if that's your choice.'

'There you are Niamh, why don't you ask at another church?'

'If Father John doesn't object…'

'No, sure I can't stop you, and I wouldn't want to.' He removes his glasses and cleans them with a handkerchief.

'Well, I might do that then! Thanks again Paddy and John! If I do find someone to marry us shortly, would one of ye give me away? You know you're the closest relatives I have in Australia?'

'Sure now, that's probably the truth,' Paddy says happily.

'He wouldn't give tuppence away!' Father John says sarcastically. 'I'm your guardian, so I could possibly do that for you.'

'And I'm your Australian connection, so I'd love to give you away,' Paddy says, glaring at his brother.

'I'm grateful to ye both. I'll get back to you as soon as I can. Now I must be off. James, John Patrick, wave goodbye to Father John and Uncle Paddy!' We get in the car and we're back home in under half an hour. I'm just turning in the driveway when Barbie comes walking, her hands strained with several shopping bags. 'Want to hop in and save your legs?' I ask, stopping beside her and winding the window down.

'Ta,' Barbie replies. I open the passenger side door for her and she clambers inside, placing the bags on the floor around her.

'So, have you been doing a bit of shopping?' I ask Barbie as we drive up the short distance to the house.

'Just some things for the big day. I found a great under-skirt for you and Helen, I mean one each by the way.'

I smile. I get the picture.

'It's nearly here Niamh. I'm getting so nervous.'

'I'm sure everything will work itself out…,' I reply. I sigh.

'Hey what's up?' she asks me suddenly.

'Well, I do want to have a chat with you.'

'Struth, you sound so serious. Is it something to do with the other night?' Barbie asks, her face a picture of concern.

'Sort of. I'll just get the boys inside and we can sit down with a nice cool drink, and I'll explain,' I say, pulling the car to a stop.

After I give the boys a drink and some of the left over

cakes from the party, Barbie and I sit down with a cool drink and a couple of lamingtons.

'Well, come on, what's the story?' Barbie asks, placing the plastic bags on the sofa.

'It all started the other night at the chapel. I thought the preacher was talking to me personally.'.

'So, what do you think that means?' Barbie asks.

'God knows about Luigi and me,' I blurt out.

'You mean that you're living together?' Barbie says.

'God Almighty! How do you know?' I say in alarm.

'Struth Niamh, I'm not blind, but I never judge or con-demn anybody,' Barbie says, reaching for my hand.

'Well, I think you deserve to hear the truth about us. It's all my fault. You see Luigi has asked me to marry him…many times. I swore I'd never marry again. Until now I've been too scared. Every time I get involved with a man he dies or disappears. I feel like I've been cursed,' I confess to Barbie.

'Struth Niamh, that is so sad! Y'know Jesus said, 'If the son sets you free, you will be free indeed," Barbie prat-tles.

'I think that's exactly what's happened to me Barbie!' I sit down. 'I've been set free to marry Luigi.'

'Niamh, that's a miracle.' Barbie sits beside me.

'It is! I want to get married straight away, but Father John says the church is booked up for a whole year on Saturdays, so he can't do it.'

'Does it have to be Father John who marries you, and does it have to be Saturday?'

'No, although I would have liked that. The most impor-tant thing is that I get married legally. Any day is fine with me. Beggars can't be choosers. I also know that!'

'What about my Pastor, Wesley? He's a marriage cel-ebrant.'

'Do you really think he'd do it? Can I see him now?' I ask.

'You are in a rush. Give him a ring and ask him. Here, I've

got his number written down in my book.' She rummages through her beaded bag. 'Struth, it's here, somewhere. Yes! Here y'are…'

After a quick call, I arrange to meet him at seven.

'See, I told you he was nice,' Barbie says.

'There's a snag!' I say.

'What's that Niamh?'

'He wants Luigi to come too! I didn't want him to have to be too involved in this bit.'

'Niamh, Luigi is involved. Struth you're marrying each other! You're supposed to do everything together, that's the whole idea!'

'I'll ask him after dinner. He's always in a good mood then. Oh, Barbie, we should be talking about your wedding. You've been buying stuff, working so hard. You wanted to show me what you bought!'

'Well, Dale and I have been doing everything together, except buying dresses!' She pulls a wrapped item from the plastic bag. 'Try this. It's the underskirt.'

'Looks stiff,' I say, as the layers of tulle springs into shape next to my body.

'You'll have to try it on with the purple dress tomorrow,' Barbie says. 'It's all coming together. I got the flowers organized, and all the ladies are bringing a plate, so the whole church can join in after the ceremony. It's so cool. God is so good to us,' Barbie says.

'He is,' I agree, much to my own amazement.

'And they've been painting the outside of the building all this week,' Barbie notes happily. 'They said it was already planned last year. Coincidence or providence?' she asks coyly, looking upwards.

The following Saturday, the fifth of May, nineteen seventy three, at ten o'clock in the morning, Helen and I are waiting at the front of the Chapel. We stand in the porch trying to keep as cool as possible. The bright sun is reflecting on the newly painted walls, helping to keep the internal parts cooler.

'She's here!' Helen says, peeping around the corner. 'Come on,' she calls as she hurries towards the halting white Humber sedan. Barbie waits patiently inside as we wait beside the car. Marty, a friend of Luigi's, who is the driver, hurries around to the passenger rear door and opens it wide. Barbie's be-splendid billowing concoction of lace and tulle, springs out of the car door firstly. A satin court and a shapely ankle follow this mass of white. Barbie's white gloved hands and veiled face complete the bridal picture. Barbie's sister, Maisie, is coming towards us, with her small daughter in tow. The girl is Susie, who's having trouble keeping up with her mother, and has the appearance of having being dragged through the grass. Susie's left hand clutches a white basket with white rose petals, which are tumbling to the ground as she skids forward. She is decked in a ankle length, shimmering purple dress, with circles of white flowers pinned on the hemline. Her dark hair is adorned with tiny white dots, which appear as flower-buds as she comes closer. They are arranged in consecutive circles around her head, giving her hair the likeness of aboriginal art. Dale is waiting inside the chapel with Barney. They are dressed in white shirts and black waistcoats with purple bow ties and dusty pink trousers flared at the bottoms. Dale, with his tanned good looks and sun bleached hair, contrasts with Barney's ebony coloured skin. Luigi is holding John and James and sits quietly next to them on the back row of seats. The chapel is filled with parishioners and there's a sense of excitement in the air. Black and white are joined in one hubbub of picturesque, colourful joy.

'You look grand!' I say to Barbie as I pick some of the billowing tulle off the dusty ground.

'I'm so nervous I can't stop praying, *let him be here Lord!*" she says.

I grin mischievously 'I heard that he forgot and he's still in bed!'

'No!' she retorts. Her face turns a shade lighter under the veil.

'Only joking! He looks more nervous than yourself!' I say quickly before she faints.

Maisie suddenly drags little Susie forward, followed by Helen and then me. Barbie comes last, with Michael Belamy, her stepfather. Barbie's natural mother died soon after she was born, and her father died a few years later. Her stepmother Julie Belamy is already in the front seat of the chapel.

We all traipse after Maisie and Susie until we reach the portico. The music begins with the tune, 'Here comes the Bride.' Then we begin our bridal walk down the short aisle. Today it seems longer than it was last night at the dress rehearsal. I notice Barbie's older sister and brother are at the wedding today, plus four nephews. Susie is taking long steps and throwing the petals as she goes, giggling. 'Keep moving,' I hear Helen say as Susie stops suddenly. 'Flowers all gone!' she says loudly, tipping her basket upside down. This extracts spontaneous laughter from some of the congregation. We eventually get to where Pastor Wesley Bridges is waiting, dressed in a dark coloured suit, white shirt and tie. After the ceremony we all move to a marquee where tables are decorated in bridal array. A central table is laden with a smorgasbord of all types of wonderful salads and meats. The party goes on until around two in the afternoon, when Barbie and Dale leave in their pale blue Morris 1100, with several pairs of old boots banging on the street as they move into second gear. The words 'just married' have been painted in whitewash on the boot of the car, to announce their grand decision to all. They're off for a couple of days honeymoon in Pialba, Hervey Bay.

Chapter twelve

A few days later, I'm wondering what I'm going to wear for my own wedding. Barbie offered me her dress, but it's not what I want, this being my third wedding…! I tell her I don't want a white dress. I would feel like a hypocrite! So, now, I have no dress to wear. I'm praying night and day about it.

I visit the Schmidts to take care of the boys on Tuesday afternoon. Olga isn't feeling well, so sits in a chair with us.

'I thought I'd better take it easy today Niamh. I think I got a tummy bug…How is everything shaping up for the big day?' she asks politely as I hand her a cool fizzy drink.

'Grand. Luigi's had a chat with the pastor. Barbie and Helen have agreed to be my bridesmaids…'

'Fair dinkum? You know if you need help with anything, just ask.'

'I will,' I reply.

She suddenly smiles. 'I remember when I got married, I had so much trouble with my dress. It had to be taken out three times and back in twice before the big day…' She looks at me. 'You've got such a great shape Niamh, I don't suppose you'll have that problem?'

'No. I don't even have a dress,' I say before I have time to think about it.

'What?'

'I've been looking in all the shops on my days off. I've not seen anything I want. I'm thinking of going to Hervey Bay to look for something there,' I confide to her.

'Niamh, the wedding is what? In two weeks?'

'It is…'

'It's not the cost, is it?'

'No. I have money. It's just that I'm not sure what to wear.'

'The Bride Shop in Pialba has some nice bridal dresses…'

'I don't want to wear a white dress,' I exclaim.

'Struth why not?' she says back, very surprised indeed.

'I want to wear something different… It's my third wedding!'

'Your third?'

'It is!' I say soberly.

She's obviously very surprised now. 'I thought you had one husband who drowned…'

'I did. The other one fell off a horse and died.'

'Fair dinkum? Struth, that's terrible. I am very sorry.'

'Don't worry. It's water under the bridge now.'

'Niamh, I might be able to help you. Wait here,' Olga hurries away.

She must need to visit the lav, I'm thinking.

A few minutes later she returns with a wrapped package in her arms. 'Move the blocks,' she says.

I quickly run my arm along the wooden table and send the blocks to the floor. The three boys respond by scrabbling for them. Olga looks disapprovingly at me for an instant, then places the package on the table.

'This has never been worn,' she says, undoing the wrapping.

I'm mesmerized as the wrapping unfolds to reveal the most beautiful dress I have ever laid my eyes on.

It's a pale bone coloured lacy dress, with a high waistline and pearl buttons, with lacy, bell shaped sleeves. The dress skirt falls in uneven layers to ankle length. It's lined with antique white satin.

'Olga, it's gorgeous'. I ask, forgetting my manners, 'Where did you get it?'

'I bought it in America before I was married. That's nearly seven years ago now.'

I'm wondering how Olga ever fitted into it. She is about the same height as myself, but a good bit broader.

'I was going to wear it to a special gala night in Brisbane, but I just could not get myself to fit into it after the holiday. It was two sizes too small when I bought it. I thought I would help me to lose weight! I tried it on and I had to force the zip which literally burst open just when Aaron walked in on me. He said I looked like a stripper.'

'What a horrible thing to say!' I exclaim.

'It was! He said he didn't mean it, but we almost broke up after that. I just packed it away after that, hoping I'd magically lose weight, and show him I could look great in it!'

'And did you?' I ask, genuinely interested.

'It never happened! I went up two sizes instead of down! Aaron was very kind about that, saying there was more of me to love…'

'That was some consolation.' I nod my head in agreeance.

'Just before the big event he took me shopping in Brisbane and bought me a beautiful royal blue evening gown, which I wore once.'

'That sounds lovely.'

'It was. I've got a photo. Come and have a look.' We both walk into the lounge and there on the wall over a dark cupboard is a lovely photo of Olga and Aaron. 'This is a photo of the big night,' she says, leading me through.

I admire the picture of Olga with her hair in curls, piled high on her head. Her face emits a light pink blush, which looks painted on. The royal blue dress reveals a large white triangle of skin. Aaron's black gloved hand is timidly arranged behind her, holding her left arm at the elbow. His black suit is contrasted by a white shirt and royal blue bow tie. His shiny hair cascades forward in a wave on his forehead. They are both smiling nervously. 'You both look like royalty,' I remark.

'It's the dress I think.'

'It looks great.'

'Aaron still knows what looks right on me.'

We return to the rumpus room and I stare at the lacy frock. 'It looks a bit small.'

'Struth Niamh, you're half my size. Go on, try it on.'

'Well, all right…' I take the dress into my old room and return with the zip undone at the back. 'I'm a bit worried about the ripped zip. I might do more damage.'

'Let me see. The zip needs replacing, but there's plenty of room, at least an inch!' Olga says. 'Fair dinkum, it was made for you Niamh,' she says, stepping back in amazement. 'The high waistline is back in now too! '

I stare into the long mirror. 'It looks great. But I'm not good at sewing zips.'

'No worries mate. I'll ask Jan Walker, Helen's mum. She's a professional seamstress. And I'll get her to shorten it a bit. The latest look is either the mini or the midi, so what would you prefer?'

'It would be different to wear a mini…not too mini mind you!'

'Just above the knee? And you can wear some of those shiny stockings. They're the latest fashion craze!'

'All right. Why not?' I ask, 'But Olga, please let me pay for the dress, and the alterations.'

'Struth, no way! It can be part of my contribution to the wedding. To tell you the truth, I'm thrilled you can wear it on such a special occasion.'

John Patrick cries out just then. He's playing on the verandah, banging a toy on the ground. I rush out and pick him up.

'Well, I'd better get this beautiful gown off before John Patrick vomits on me, or something worse,' I say, putting John Patrick down and handing him a colourful ball to play with. 'There you are now. Bounce that!' I instruct my child.

Helen is borrowing a 'shocking pink' coloured gown with a high waistline. Her mother is adjusting it so it fits perfectly. It's a floor length dress, which is being shortened to just above the knee. Barbie is back from her honeymoon and asks me to approve a lemon coloured frock from what she calls her 'formal days'. It's being dry cleaned and expanded slightly for the occasion. They both have a high waistline and choker neckline, with slightly cutaway sleeves. I think the same pattern was used for both of these! Olga manages to get some cream coloured lace, which we've stitched around the necklines of Barbie and Helen's dress, so they blend in with mine, and make them more 'bridal'.

We're getting married on Saturday afternoon the 26th May, at four o'clock. The Pastor fitted us in after another wedding that finished around twelve.

'I just hope they clean the joint up before we walk in there,' I hear Barbie say as we get ourselves dressed.

The three girls, Olga and a friend of hers, Rachel Kingdom have all gathered at my flat in Luigi's house. The hairdresser did a roaring trade today with the lot of us. I wanted to leave my hair down around my shoulders, which is the fashion now, so the hairdresser said it would suit me better with some up and some down, like some of the latest singers wear their hair. She fitted the big straw coloured sunhat, which has a lacy look and a long satin ribbon tied around the crown, which hangs down slightly at the back.

'Well girls, this is the moment of truth,' Olga says as she helps Helen pull up her zip.

'I had such a lot of Kentucky Fried Chicken last night I hope it still fits…' she confesses.

'She's right mate,' Olga says, 'Zip's up!'

'Thank God,' Helen says.

By quarter to four we're all ready in our mini bridal gowns, rearing to go! Father John and Paddy couldn't agree as to who would give me away, so they're both coming to do the job!

Colin and Marty, two of Luigi's friends own Triumph 2000's. One car is white; the other is a yellow, the same colour as Barbie's dress. Paddy, Father John and I will travel in the white car, Helen and Barbie in the yellow one. Colin and Marty have polished up both cars and we've tied ribbons on the front of the cars, pink and yellow on the girls' car and cream on mine. Paddy and John have just turned up.

'Come on in Father John and Paddy,' I say, inviting the pair inside. Paddy looks great in his grey suit with a fresh white shirt and a bright green tie. Father John is wearing a black suit with a white shirt. 'Would you like a cup of tea then?' I ask.

'That would be nice.' They both agree.

'Sorry Niamh. No tea please,' Barbie says, rushing over to me and taking the jug from my hand. She looks at the clock on the wall. 'We're supposed to be there in ten minutes.'

'Well, Father John and Paddy are having a cup of tea. We need to steady our nerves,' I say adamantly, picking up the jug and filling it with water.

'Sure we're all right Niamh. We had a cup just before we left the bay,' Father John says.

'Well, have one with me then, just for the road.'

'I will then Niamh. That'll be grand,' Paddy replies.

'Well, all right, I have a small cup,' Father John says.

Barbie shrugs her shoulders. 'Struth! Well I may as well have one too,' she says, taking a cup out of the cupboard.

'And me,' Helen says, flopping down in the sofa. 'Well, Olga and Rachel have gone, so they won't know!' she says, throwing her sturdy, shimmering, stockinged legs over the edge of the couch.

'That's so true. Why not girls?' I ask. 'Let's have a cuppa together. Cheers,' I say.

'Cheers,' the others reply. We all sit in silence for a moment, drinking tea.

'What about Colin and Marty?' Barbie asks. 'They're sitting out in the hot car, waiting.'

'They'd probably prefer a beer,' I suggest. 'Here, have a couple of Luigi's. He won't mind,' I say, taking two brown bottles from the fridge.

'No Niamh, they shouldn't be drinking and driving,' Barbie protests.

'Just one?' I question her wisdom.

'I'll give it to them,' Helen says, suddenly rousing herself from her relaxed state. She places a bottle opener on the cap of two bottles. A slight burst of gas and she stomps outside with one in each hand.

'Wanna beer guys?' she calls to Marty and Colin.

'Thanks. Great stuff,' is the resounding reply. She smiles, wiggles her body and gazes at the two as they enjoy their cool drink.

Barbie shakes her head, 'Struth Helen needs Jesus, before she finds herself in deep trouble.'

Suddenly there's a beeping of car horns.

'Come on, we're going to be late for sure,' Barbie says. 'Oh my lipstick is all gone.'

'Mine too,' I say.

'And mine,' Helen says, coming back into the family room. The three of us rush into the bathroom and reapply our lipstick. The three of us smack our lips together at the same time and burst out laughing. 'One day they'll invent a lipstick that lasts a bit longer!' Barbie states.

'If we're still alive?' I reply.

We stare happily at our lipsticked mouths and then head back into the living room.

'Sure you all look like the Rose of Tralee,' Paddy says encouragingly.

'They do indeed!' Father John says agreeably.

'Don't forget your flowers, and the horseshoe,' Barbie reminds me as she and Helen get into the yellow car. 'See you shortly?' she says as Father John, Paddy and I wave goodbye.

'Well Paddy, this is our one opportunity to travel in a bride's car. Come on Niamh, it's time to go.'

So, with Father John on my right and Uncle Paddy on my left, with my flowers and horseshoe in front, we head towards the glisteningly polished car. Colin, our driver, who's wearing his best white shirt, black bow-tie and black trousers, is leaning on its bonnet, smoking. As we approach, he quickly stubs out his cigarettes with his shoe, grinding the ashes into the gravel. He scratches the back of his neck and shakes his head. 'Struth…you're a sight for sore eyes! The three of you!' he exclaims, helping us into the car.

Colin shuts the doors and climbs into the driver's seat. He gives us a final glance in his rear vision mirror and turns the key. Father John and Paddy pat one of my hands instinctively at that precise moment.

…

We arrive at the chapel ten minutes later. The recently painted cream coloured timber building with its tiny cross on its pointy pinnacle and long arched windows on each side of the front porch exudes a warm friendliness in the soft sunlit day. The area immediately surrounding it is dotted with brightly adorned people, waiting anxiously for the moment of the bride's arrival. Barbie and Helen are standing on the shady side of the building as I emerge from the car. They immediately hurry towards me. Both girls look stunning and very girlish in their pink and lemon mini dresses with bright flowers in their hands to match.

Olga and Rachel are looking after James and John and are waiting outside the chapel. Olga is holding a golden cushion, which James will carry, bearing the ring.

James looks almost comical in his tiny black suit, cream coloured shirt and black bow-tie. His ginger curls simply refused to be tamed by the hairdresser who finally allows them to twist into their natural course. He runs towards me, followed by Rachel, who's carrying John. John reaches his small hand out to me. 'Mam…mam…'

I take them both in my arms for a moment.

'Hold it there,' a voice says. It's the photographer, Peter Hewitt. 'That's nice. Say cheese,' he says.

'Smile for the picture,' I tell James, who grins artificially at the camera. John leans his head on my shoulder.

'And who's got the most important part in this, but the boy with the ring!' Paddy says as I place James on the ground and Rachel takes John in her arms.

James sticks his chest out proudly. 'You have to be good boys now. You'll get ice cream and cake later,' I explain. James licks his lips and runs to where Olga and the twins are standing. John cries.

'I'll take him,' Rachel says, holding her arms out. 'Here, have this,' Rachel says, she says, luring him with a biscuit.

Paddy and John are waiting for me. I stand between them and the photographer immediately takes a picture of us.

Peter the photographer takes charge. 'Inside now, please,' he directs, then hurries ahead of us.

I take Father John and Paddy's arm and the music begins to play 'Here comes the bride.'

A flash makes me blink. Others keen to get a snap of us join the photographer. I smile willingly, happily.

My heart races as I see Luigi looking spruced up in a cream coloured suit with a cream coloured tie to match, and his trimmed mullet hairstyle. He is standing next to his best friends, Barney and Nigel, who are both wearing the same cream coloured flared leg suits with yellow and pink ties to match up with the girls. And so I become Missus Niamh de Vinci, wife of Luigi de Vinci.

Afterwards, we all trot off to the hall. There the ladies have prepared a great feast. People are coming through holding dishes and plates, and some have brightly wrapped gifts in their hands. The table is heavy laden with gifts already! The room has been decorated with cream, yellow and pink balloons.

After we all eat to our hearts content, Barney gives a speech, thanking the beautiful bridesmaids. Barbie and

Helen. Luigi thanks Barney and Nigel, and everyone for coming.

After that we're asked to have a dance, so Luigi and I get up and do a bit of a waltz. Others join in.

Rachel comes over with John. 'Sorry, he wants you Niamh,' she says.

My breasts are beginning to feel sore.

'I'll feed him,' I tell her.

'You go on darl' Luigi says, ushering me off with John.

I head outside behind a bougainvillea bush where there's an old wooden bench. I sit down and undo the buttons at the top of my dress. I begin to feed my hungry baby. As I begin to relax, voices come in our direction. After a moment I see Luigi talking to Marjorie Travers who is a friend of his sister Jackie. Luigi said he hardly knew her, but she was a good friend of Jackie's and was driving down with her from Cairns.

'So, you're finally caught in the net?'

'What's it to you Marj?'

'What about us?' she asks Luigi in a low tone.

Luigi shrugs his shoulders, 'What we had is over Marj. I'm a married man now!'

'Struth you sound so smug! I didn't even know you had a serious relationship, let alone that you were getting married. It's lucky I rang Jackie the other day and I found out.'

'So, why did you bother to come if you're so cheesed off?'

'I wanted to tell you this Luigi. You're a creep, and a yobbo!'

She swirls around in her floral cotton frock and high-heeled shoes, stamping off into the grass, her caramel coloured permed hair bobbing hysterically.

I can hardly believe what I've just overheard! Later that day, Luigi, myself and the two children climb into my own car and head off to Hervey Bay with the children. The short three day holiday is Father John and Paddy's wedding gift to us. We have a grand time in a unit near Urangan, where sea and sand are only a few metres away. The breezes are fresh and the view of the blue sea stretches as far as the eye can see. Luigi organizes a boat trip to Fraser Island, with two-night stop over, making our holiday a bit longer. On the first day on Fraser Island we appear to be one of only two families at the hotel in Eurong, opposite seventy-five mile beach. To wake up on Frazer Island is like waking up in Heaven. We have a self-contained unit, with our own kitchen and bathroom, and an extra room for the children. Luigi decides to cook breakfast, while I'm still in bed, basking in sleep. After a few moments of concern when the smell of burning floats past my nose and around the room, Luigi announces breakfast is ready. We all sit outside the unit on a verandah overlooking the sea, the breeze blowing slightly. Luigi happily opens a bottle of champagne to serve with my tea and toast.

'I only burned four pieces,' he says grinning, pouring the sparkling liquid. The toast is soggy and cold, but it doesn't matter, I'm so happy to be married.

Luigi hires a four-wheel drive vehicle and takes us to unbelievably beautiful spots, such as Lake McKenzie, where the sapphire blue of the water is encompassed by glistening sand, which looks like fine icing sugar. Colourful birds fly hither and thither, making sweet tunes for us. Well, our holiday comes to an end and we pack our things and head back to our home just outside the city of Maryborough.

…

Our life falls into an enjoyable domestic routine. The only real difference is that the children and I move upstairs with Luigi, and we use downstairs for lunchtime meals and John's nap times, and for storing my artwork. Luigi is thinking of building the stairs inside, so we can go up and down without having to go outside, and I can use the internal verandah as my studio, even on windy days! He's busy helping to get the Schmidt's cane fields ready for planting. He wants to get his own paddock done as well, so he's flat out all day, presently. I've been spending more time painting. I feel relaxed and somehow my artwork reflects my moods. I am presently working on a seascape, with the sun rising just on the horizon, inspired I reckon by our trip to Frazer Island. I'm also working on a painting of Luigi and two boys clambering over him. He's got his head back and appears to be in ecstasy. Another one I'm working on is James lying on the grass, chewing on a piece of cane, totally absorbed in his own world. Another painting is one of some blue flowers I found among the cane. I placed them in the jar of water this morning and I'm trying to capture their beauty before they fade away and die. With the cooler weather coming now, I am painting more and more. I still, almost reluctantly, help Olga with the boys on a couple of afternoons. Sometimes they come over here after school, and sometimes James goes over to their place. This gives me a bit of extra money to spend in whatever way I want.

Around August, three months after we've been married, I get an unexpected visit from Father John in the middle of the week, mid-morning. James has been dropped off to pre-school for the morning, John Patrick is having his morning nap, which he has shortened to half an hour. Luigi has left since early this morning. I feel a surge of surprise to see Father John suddenly appearing, walking up the driveway.

'Come on in Father John,' I say, wiping my brushes quickly with a bit of turps.

'So, what have we got here?' he asks, viewing my present work.

'It's just a few flowers I found growing among the cane. They looked so pretty I decided to paint them,' I say. 'They remind me of Ireland,' I add.

'Is it for sale?' he replies.

'You don't want to buy it now do you?'

'I do.'

'Well, when it's finished I'll offer you a special price.'

'So, you'll put it aside for me then?' he asks. He sounds so serious.

'I will,' I reply. 'So, what are you doing in this neck of the woods?' I ask, taking off my painter's apron and heading to the kitchen. 'I'll put the kettle on…' I say.

'Grand, that's grand Niamh,' Father John replies, wiping his feet and coming inside. 'So, how's married life treating you?' he asks as I click on the electric jug.

'It's wonderful. Luigi is a really good provider. Every time he goes away he brings me back tubes of paint. It's like Christmas every few weeks. The kids adore him too,' I add, taking down a couple of cups out of the cupboard and a packet of Nice biscuits. I rinse the teapot with hot water and place three spoons of tea on the bottom, then burst their aroma with the boiling water.

'That's great news. So, where's the lad, John Patrick?' he asks.

'Shh. He's still has a nap at this time of day, even though he's sixteen months old now.'

We sit down and I pour out a cuppa for Father John. I pass the small jug of milk and bowl of sugar across the table.

'So, are you going to tell me or not?' I ask.

'What?'

'Why you are here? I know it's not your regular routine,' I say, tearing the biscuit wrapping and tipping the biscuits onto a plate. 'Help yourself!' I offer.

'Don't mind if I do.' He sits and munches for a moment, contemplating what to tell me no doubt.

'I got a lift with a parishioner. He's picking me up in an hour!' He leans towards me and whispers.

'I'm going away…'

It sounds like he's sharing a huge secret with me. 'Away…Where to?'

'To Spain, and perhaps Ireland.'

He looks so serious now. 'Is it a holiday?' I ask.

'Not exactly. It's more of a humanitarian exercise,' he says, sipping his hot tea.

'That sounds very intriguing! Whereabouts in Spain might you be going to?

'Jumilla! You've probably never heard of it?'

'No Father.'

'Neither had I until recently…'

'So why are you going there?'

He pauses and his eyes drift into a distant place. 'I hear that the wine is particularly good…'

'So, you're going all the way to Spain for a drop of red?' I say, quite amazed.

'Not at all,' he tut tuts me. 'But I hear it's superb wine made from the legendary monastrell grapes.'

'legendary grapes,' that's a new one to me. 'Is that all?'

'No, that is not all, at all. They have wonderful religious festivals. In fact there's one coming up, a annual parade through the streets… I hope to participate in it!'

'So, what's brought this on Father?'

'I'm not sure I should divulge the issue to you.'

'Well, don't tell me then. What I never knew never hurt me.'

'However, I think it is my duty to tell you…'

I just stare at him, waiting. 'Sure I'm not stopping you. Go on then.'

He coughs. 'There was an accident…a young curate was involved.'

'So, what has that to do with you Father?'

'I was his mentor in Ireland for a time…'

'I see!' I say, sipping my tea, feeling drawn into the issue.

'No you don't see at all. The important thing is that I give the support he needs now.'

'So what happened? The curate in the accident…?'

'I'm not sure of the details. He's in a coma…'

'A coma? Me da was always worried about being hit by a bus…'

'A fist by all accounts…'

I gasp. 'A fist! That's even worse. So, whose fist was it?'

'Some larrikin.'

'Why?'

'I can't exactly work that out. He was simply doing his priestly duty…counselling a parishioner. I hope to find out more when I get there.'

'I see. When will you be back?' I ask.

'I'm not sure. Paddy is expecting me for Christmas, but I might spend that time with my friends in Dublin. I'll decide my itinerary after I visit Spain, and I know how I'm fixed.'

'You mean money?'

'I do.'

'Do you want me to give you some monetary support?'

'Not at all. Sure I've been saving since I arrived here. I appreciate your kind gesture. You're like a real daughter to me.'

'That's a fine compliment. Well, I wish you journeying mercies as they say.'

'Thank you Niamh. I'm sure I'll need it. Can I say good-bye to John Patrick?' he asks as he pushes the chair back to stand up.

'Come on in.'

We tiptoe into John Patrick's room and he's sleeping soundly. After a light kiss on his cheek, Father John and I sneak back out.

'Jason should be waiting for me by now…'

'Sure you should have asked him to come in…' I chide quietly as I walk a few yards down the driveway with him. Jason hasn't arrived yet.

'I'll just wait at the gate. I need time for reflection,' he says.

'Keep in the shade of the old gum tree,' I suggest. I suddenly give him a kiss on the cheek. He stares at me. There are tears in his eyes. I turn and head back to the house, waving goodbye three times.

…

On the following Sunday I meet Paddy and have lunch with him after Mass. Now that I have my own car, the de Boots don't bother to pick me up. I'm sitting in Paddy's kitchen and he's getting a couple of mugs out of his cupboard. The boys are playing with Paddy's train set in his room.

'They love that train!' I remark. 'You've really done a lot of work on the scenery. It looks real!'

'It's just a hobby. It helps me pass the time away. And I've made some good friends at the club…'

We leave James happily operating the switches whilst John watches excitedly from the distance of his portable play pen.

'Did he get off all right?' I ask as we reach the kitchen.

'Indeed he did. He rang me on our neighbour's 'phone when he got to Spain. He said it was a long flight to Rome, but the connection worked out well. He was impressed with Qantas…'

'So, he arrived safely, so to speak?'

'He did, thank God. You know Niamh, I'm seriously thinking of installing a telephone…my brother John could ring me directly then…' He sits in the chair beside me. I look at him before I speak, gaining his attention.

'You miss him, don't you?'

He stares into his cup. 'After all these years of being by meself, I thought I'd never get used to having him around, telling me off all the time…and now I…' he stops and removes his glasses. His head is lowered, but I can tell there are tears in his eyes.

'Sure if you got a telephone I could give you a ring when I'm coming, and not give you a fright.'

He rubs his glasses with his large handkerchief. 'I might yet. I'm just a bit wary of the cost of all that new technology…'

'It's not that expensive. I think it's worth having one. It's very handy in an emergency too.'

'You're convincing me to get one…'

'What about when Father John returns. Maybe you could share the cost?'

'Sure I wouldn't need one then. Seeing he'll be back here.'

'Never mind about that now Paddy, tell me about the Spanish curate that got belted up Paddy?'

Paddy's lips mesh into a straight line. 'He's not Spanish…
Anyway I'm not at leave to tell anyone…'

'So, you don't know the lad?' I ask.

'No.'

'His name's not Martin is it?'

Paddy's eyes nearly pop out of his glasses. 'Begorrah, you
must be a detective! How did you find that out?'

'It's just that I knew a priest called Martin. I can't divulge
any more than that,' I answer.

'So be it! He might not be the same fellow, so there,'
Paddy says.

'But he might!' I reply.

'How much do you know about him?'

'I saw a picture of him. Martin O'Reardon is his name,'
I say emphatically.

'The name's right. Martin O'Reardon. God help us all!'
he smiles at me now. 'What else do you know?'

'He's John's father!' I add.

'You're wrong there, begorrah! He's much younger than
me brother John.'

I laugh. 'Paddy, I'm talking about John Patrick, my
son.'

'Oh!' Paddy stands with a butter knife held in his hand,
looking like he just got off a train at the wrong station. He
sits down, puts the knife on the table and scratches his
head. 'Now, come here. What are you telling me?' he asks,
his eyebrows furled.

'Well, it's a long story, but would you believe, Father
Martin O'Reardon and I were nearly married!'

'Is that when he went to be a priest?' Paddy asks.

'No. He was a priest already. He was going to leave the
priesthood and marry me. He said he loved me! …but he
left me when he found out I was going to have his child,' I
add, almost sarcastically.

'The cur!' Paddy says fiercely, staring at me, his face grim.
'If he wasn't my own flesh and blood I'd have his guts for
garters!' he stammers.

'So, are you saying you're also related to Martin O'Reardon?'

'I think I've let the cat out of the bag, but to hell with it. I'll tell you the truth. Did you know that my own brother John is his father?'

'I thought he might be, but I wasn't really sure until right this minute. Now I know who Father John reminds me of, Martin O'Reardon!'

'There is a resemblance there,' Paddy agrees.

'So, how come his surname is O'Reardon and not Hurley?'

'Well now, as far as I know there was a grand young nun at the local convent, Sister Marian O'Reardon…can you work out the rest of the picture?'

'Begorrah, I can!'

'It's such an upside-down world. Sure we're probably all related somewhere down the line…'

'You might be right Paddy. So, what happened in Spain?'

'It has a grand history, sometimes bloody mind…'

'No, I mean what happened to Martin in Spain.'

'Of course. I'll tell you now.' Paddy sits down and stares into his cup. If there was no tea in it I'd swear he's reading the tea leaves. He finally opens his mouth, and says, 'It started when Martin fell in love with a young woman. She was already married, or engaged to a rich plantation owner. Her brother threatened Martin, then the word got out that they were running off together to Ireland. Then one day he just came in, found them together and beat the hell out of Martin. Almost killed him.'

'That's terrible Paddy. So what about the woman, was she all right?'

'She ran off to her parents place. It was then discovered she was going to have a child. She claims it's Martin's, but he can't speak for himself now.'

'That poor family, how terrible!'

'I know. And the brother has been arrested and will be charged with manslaughter if Martin dies.'

He looks up. 'What's the world coming to at all?'

'It's a very crazy, mixed up world all right. So, what's Father John's role in all that?'

'Well, I think they're looking for spiritual support. John was the one who recommended he go to Spain, so he feels somewhat responsible. He wants to be able to pray with the family in their time of need I suppose.'

'Do they know Father John is Martin's father then?'

'Begorrah, I doubt that, and don't you say a word to them!'

'I won't I promise.'

Paddy looks suddenly pensive. 'I knew a lovely Spanish lady in Dublin, once.' His eyes mist over with visions of his Spanish dancing lady. 'Maria Questa. She went off and married another!' He smiles as he says that.

'I'm very sorry Paddy. Did you meet the one who stole her heart?'

'No. It wasn't a human. It was God! She became a nun. I saw her once after she left me, and she fainted right on the spot in the chapel.'

'What did you do Paddy?'

'I was a coward. I ran out the door as fast as I could.'

'Thanks for telling me the whole truth Paddy.' I take Paddy's mug and place it in the sink automatically turning the tap on and rinsing it. 'That was a gorgeous cup of tea Paddy,' I say.

'Where's me tea?' I hear Paddy ask as I place the rinsed cup on the sink. 'Did I drink it all already?'

'Yes Paddy, you've had your tea,' I remark.

Chapter thirteen

Five months later, at the beginning of nineteen seventy four, Father John arrives back in Hervey Bay. We have a grand barbeque at our place in Maryborough, to celebrate his homecoming.

'So what's the news about Father Martin?' I ask immediately. The question has been on my mind since I said goodbye.

'Well, it's like this...'

Suddenly Paddy is standing with his mouth open and two glasses of drink in his hand. Since Father John arrived there's a new bounce in Paddy's step.

'It's grand that you're back. Here's one for the road,' Paddy says, handing Father John a large lemonade.

'Just what the doctor ordered. I missed the warm Australian weather, especially in Hervey Bay.'

'It's a bit hot right now but I don't mind. It's better than the cold, I always say,' Paddy says, humming to himself, 'Roses are red my love...'

'So, what happened?' I ask Father John again.

'When?'

'When you went to Spain,' I say, feeling rather anxious now.

'The weather was nice and warm there, but it's cold enough in winter. It's a grand place though, with grapes growing by the buckets. They make beautiful wines you know,' he explains. 'I brought you back a bottle by the way,' he says.

'That's kind of you Father. So what happened to Father Martin?' I ask, staring Father John in the face.

'It's a sad story Niamh. Very sad indeed!'

'Hallo Father,' the Van de Boots say as they march over and give him a big handshake.

'It's vonderful, you come back,' Thea Van de Boot says, her mouth wide with a smile. Her head is nodding continually as if she agrees with herself in everything.

'Prost!' Hank Van de Boot says, raising his glass.

'Prost! And Slainte!' Father John replies.

It takes me a good hour to get Father John on his own again.

'Did Father Martin die?' I ask him straight out.

'How did you know?' he asks, a puzzled look appearing on his face. 'I haven't even told Paddy!'

'I only guessed. That's terrible…when?'

'It is Niamh. Very sad indeed! But, to tell the truth, the poor lad was just a vegetable. It was God's mercy to take him off to his eternal abode,' Father John says solemnly. 'Two weeks ago, on the first of January, they took him off life support. We buried him a week later…'

'I'm sorry Father…. Was there a big funeral?'

'There was. He was very popular with the girls…all the people in that town. You should have seen the flowers, and the beautiful young girls! You'd think it was the Pope that died,' he says, smiling to himself. 'You should have tasted the wine that flowed afterwards to quench our sorrows…it was unbelievable.' He suddenly looks at me, his eyes bright. 'It reminded me of the wedding at Cana – where Jesus' first miracle took place. All those vats of wine…' He licks his lips as though he's tasting them all.

'So, he's buried over there?' I ask.

'Yes. He's resting among the green hills, overlooking a great vineyard. Even I'd be happy there,' he says. 'He was treated like their own son.'

'What about the fellow that hit him. Did they get him?'

'He's been incarcerated but he's appealed his case and now there will probably be another court case. I may have to return to Spain…'

'For the court case?'

'No, no, not at all. For the people Niamh! They're lovely people, very like the Irish! If I wasn't Irish meself I'd say they were even friendlier. The woman he was counselling has a little child now, Rosa! She is so docile, so beautiful!' he says absendmindedly.

'God love her!' I say, remembering my baby girl. A lump comes into my throat.

'Thank God she's gone back to live with her parents. They are very supportive.'

'That's good news. Well, I'll get you another drink, to wet your whistle,' I say, taking Father John's almost empty glass and heading towards the kitchen. I return to the car-port area with two glasses of lemonade and hand one to Father John.

'Thank you Niamh,' he says absendmindedly. 'What a grand boy John Patrick is. He's grown so fast.'

'He has. He gets around in his car already. And he's started playing golf.'

'Good, good!'

Father John watches intently as John Patrick kicks a big black and white ball and falls over. Luigi suddenly appears beside him. He picks the boy up, wipes his knees and taps him on his padded bottom. He sees Father John and comes over, his hand outstretched.

'Welcome back to Oz?'

'Thank you! And what about yourselves, you and Niamh? You wouldn't be planning another offspring by any chance?'

'Struth nothing's sacred any more! We're working on it,' Luigi says, grinning, placing his arm around my shoulders. 'Aren't we darl?'

I try to smile.

'That's good. We need to keep the Australian population growing,' Father John says loudly.

'We're Fair dinkum about it, Father John!' Luigi says, 'We're trying hard, aren't we darl?'

'I've got to find James,' I say, rushing off with my face as red as a ripe tomato.

…

Four months later, around the time of our first anniversary, I feel sick one morning.

'Luigi, I think we're going to have a baby,' I say, returning from the lavatory. 'Father John's wish is coming true!'

'Have you been to the doctor?' he asks.

'No, just the lav. I'm sick. I'm going back to bed, I say, climbing under the sheets. 'Can you look after the kids,' I ask lethargically. 'I feel awful.'

'Are you sure you're not crook?'

'No. It's morning sickness.'

'Hows about I make you some toast. Will that help?' Luigi asks kindly.

'No, I don't feel like anything,' I reply, closing my eyes.

Two weeks later I receive a pregnancy test from the local doctor. As soon as Luigi comes home I meet him at the door. 'Luigi, the doc rang.'

'So what's the news of the day?'

'Positive!'

'Gee that's great darl. I'm going to be a dad! '

'And I'm going to be a Mammy again! Great!' I say, with nearly as much happiness as Luigi. It's what it's all about, isn't it?

'This is the best news,' he says, jumping around the hallway.

'Well, at least someone's over the moon, and fit,' I say,

'but I still feel sick…' I hurry away to the bathroom to be sick.

In October, nineteen seventy-four when I turn twenty-two Luigi is up north. I actually forget about my birthday until the 'phone rings.

'Hello, Niamh speaking…'

'Happy birthday,' comes the voice on the other end.

'Barbie!' I scream.

'Hey, don't shout, it hurts. I just remembered what day it is, the thirty-first! What are you doing?'

'Nothing. I forgot what day it was…are you ringing long distance?'

There's a silence for a moment, then laughter. 'Nope! I'm here. I'll come and see you lata…'

'Hey that fantastic. When?'

A couple of hours later Barbie introduces me to her olive skinned baby daughter, Carly.

'She's eight months old already,' Barbie says. 'She's been a blessing to our family….'

'She's so beautiful. She looks like you, I think.'

'I think she's prettier,' Barbie says. 'She's got a bit of her dad in her!'

'Mmm.' She does look much fairer than Barbie. Even her hair is nearly blonde. 'She has your big, beautiful, brown eyes.'

'Well, she's truly ours! She was born on 10th February, almost exactly nine months after our honeymoon!'

'You worked that out well,' I say, laughing.

'Not really! It happened because it was meant to be! And look at you!' she says, noticing my expanding tummy. 'When's it due, how've you been?'

'January. I've been really well this time. I think it's because Luigi and I are very happy…'

'Here, I brought you this,' she says, handing me a gift wrapped in colourful paper, with a big bunch of red, green and white ribbons cascading on top.

'Did you wrap this?'

'Yep!'

'You're a genius!'

'Open it! I can't wait!'

Carefully, I remove the wrapping. 'It's some of your art work?' I say, admiring the wooden carving. 'It looks like a turtle.'

'A tortoise, see his toes? My Aunty engraved it.'

'It's lovely. Thank you Barbie.'

'She also engraved it on the back.' She flips it over. '*To Niamh. Happy 22nd 31-10-'74. B, D & C.*. Seeing as I missed your twenty-first last year, I thought I'd give something special.'

'That's grand. Does the B, D and C stand Barbie, Dale and Carly?'

'That's right.'

'So, where's Dale now?'

'He's still at Bible College in Sydney. Getting another degree! He's got brains! Did I tell you I went for a while, but I just couldn't hack it.'

'But you're so bright, what was wrong with it?'

'Nothing. It was me! I was pregnant. I decided to go back to my sister at Murgon to have Carly, and I've been staying there ever since.'

'So when is Dale finishing?'

'He's still got a year and a half to go. It seems like a long time Niamh. I really miss him.'

'Well, when you see him, please thank Dale for this beautiful gift. I'll always treasure it!' We hug.

John Patrick suddenly appears, running from his bedroom. He stops when he sees Barbie and the baby.

'Come and see Baby Carly,' I say, beckoning him towards us.

Two months later, on Sunday evening, the 22nd December nineteen seventy four, just before Christmas day, our baby decides to come along rather suddenly. Luigi has just managed to get me to Maryborough Base Hospital half an hour before baby arrives. The staff allow Luigi to be with me for the birth.

'Come on darl, push,' he's saying to me. Suddenly he disappears from sight, and a nurse lets a loud scream. I sit up. Luigi's lying on the floor.

The nurses are trying to get him back on his feet. They drag him to his feet and he wanders off in a half daze to a nearby chair. After that I have to go it alone with my little girl.

Nicole and I are sitting up in bed when Luigi pokes his dark head through the curtain. 'Sorry darl. I must have eaten something strange,' he says, excusing his fainting spell.

'Well, Nicole made it without anyone's help. She's a real battler, this one,' I say, pulling the corner of the pink blanket off her pink face.

'She's a beauty, just like her mum, our little Nicole Barbara,' Luigi says happily.

Suddenly a nurse comes in from behind the curtain, with a vase holding a bunch of bright red roses.

'For my little ladies,' Luigi says, his eyes like stars shining brightly.

'Thanks Luigi.' I whisper. 'They smell gorgeous. I think Nicole loves them.'

…

'Darl,' Luigi says one day just after our second anniversary in May seventy-five, after spending a bit of time looking through my paintings.

'What?' I ask.

'I think I should take a few of these with me when I go up north. I could sell them for you.'

'Well, I am getting a mountain of them, I reply. I can hardly move in the house without tripping over one.

'I'm off to Cairns this week. If you pile them up I can work out how I'm going to carry them in the truck.'

'What about some of the framed ones?' I ask. 'Downstairs there's a whole pile of them, flowers, beach scenes, the lot...'

Wiping the paint off my hands as we go, we head downstairs

and eventually decide on selling about a dozen of my older works of which I have seen enough.

'These are so good Niamh. You are a genius,' Luigi compliments me. 'Do you think it might be a good idea to put a sign up near the roadway. People could come and have a look,' Luigi suggests.

'No! Please Luigi. What if I'm feeding Nicole, or worse still, in the middle of a painting? No, I'd hate that. I'd rather sell the ones I'm fed up looking at.'

'It was just an idea. It's just that if you continue at the rate you're going, we'll all have to move out and leave the paintings here!' He grins.

'Babs suggested I hold an art show some time ago. Why don't I ask the pastor if I can use the hall?'

'Niamh, that's a bonzer idea. I'll give him a ring now!'

'No, wait. He might think that's a bit rude. Let me think about it!'

'Sure darl,' he says, kissing me on the nose. 'But we'll have to find a regular outlet for you. 'Struth, it's a shame to keep your talent under cover.'

...

One hot January day in seventy-six, I receive a belated birthday card for Nicole's first birthday and a letter from Barbie. I sit down with a nice cool iced water and have a read. By the time I finish reading the letter, I know there's something seriously wrong. I decide to ring Barbie that evening.

'Got your card and letter Babs, thanks!'

'That's ok. I'll have to come and see her. My Carly is nearly two. I have been thinking of coming to Maryborough...'

'I'd really love to see you and Carly!' I say. 'So when are you coming?' I ask impatiently.

There's a pause for a moment. 'I can drive down next week, when I get Carly's allowance.'

'That's great Babs. I can't wait!'

Four days later, I'm in the middle of washing nappies when a car beeps in the driveway.

'Barbie!' I scream, leaving the basket of wet clothes and running towards her little blue Morris 1100.

We hug each other for a few minutes.

'It's so good to see you Babs!' I say, tears coming in me eyes.

'You too! I'll get Carly out. She's been so good, sleeping most of the way,' she says, undoing Carly's safety strap from her baby chair.

'She's grown so much. You are so beautiful,' I say sincerely. 'Come on inside. I'll put the kettle on!'

'I'd love a cool one Niamh!'

'Sure, you can have as many cool ones as you want.'

John and Nicole are playing together on the floor rug. Nicole stands up and runs towards me.

'She's stunning; and running!' Barbie's eyes open wide at the sight.

Nicole hugs my leg and stares at Barbie and Carly. 'She walked at nine months!'

'Hello there,' Babs says, bending down. 'This is Carly.'

Carly reaches out and touches Nicky. Nicky ducks behind my leg.

'Come on, Carly's our friend,' I say encouragingly. Nicky comes around and throws her arms around Carly, hugging her.

'She's got Luigi's thick curly dark hair. I always wanted dark hair,' I say. 'Now I'm nearly a blonde. I … can't understand my own thinking half of the time…' I laugh

Barbie laughs. 'You can have my dark hair any time.' Barbie smiles her huge bright smile. Her eyes are not smiling though.

'Here, I'll get the children some biscuits and a drink. That'll keep them happy while we catch up on things,' I say, taking a fresh packet of biscuits from the cupboard. John, Carly and Nicky sit on the tiny chairs at the low table Luigi bought for the boys. 'Here you are, biscuits.' I place them in a plastic dish, two for each child, alongside a drink of pineapple cordial.

We sit down at the kitchen table.

'It's like old times,' I say happily.

'Yeah, nearly.'

'I suppose things have changed when you think of it!' I suggest.

'Yep. Niamh, could you have dreamed that we'd both be married and have daughters in a few years?'

'It's great. Luigi is such a good father…'

I stop and look at Barbie. 'What's wrong…?'

Barbara looks at me with such hurt and sorrow in her eyes, I reach out and touch her hand. 'Has it got something to do with Dale?'

'He's left me,' she says, her lips quivering. 'I think!' she adds.

'No! How dare he do that to you!' I say angrily. I'm surprised how angry I feel for Barbie.

'No. It was my fault Niamh.'

'I don't believe that. It takes two to tango they say,' I retort.

'Fair dinkum. He's not to blame.'

'So what in the world happened?'

She takes a sip of her drink and a deep breath. 'He hasn't seen us for over six months, not since last mid-term break.'

'Didn't he come for Christmas?'

'Naw! He just sent us a card and some money!'

'Did he explain why?'

'He said he that he could make extra money working over Christmas.'

'Do you think he's telling the truth or what Babs?'

'I don't know what to think. I didn't want to tell you this, but he hasn't rung me for two months!'

'Is that right now! Tell me Babs, have you rung him?'

'I have, twice, and each time he's cut me short. There's something coming between us and for the life of me I can't work it out Niamh. Not since he came back from America!'

'He's been to America!'

'Last year.'

'So, what about money? How are you fixed?'

'I'm ok Niamh. I live pretty cheaply at Murgon. Dale sends me a little bit of money every forthnight, but other than that, he seems to have cut us out of his life. I've prayed and prayed…God still hasn't answered my prayers.'

'Babs, why don't you just turn up at the Bible college and discuss it. Find out what's going on.'

'I couldn't do that Niamh…'

'I'll come with you! Why don't we drive down in my car with all the childers and…give him a surprise!' I suggest ecstatically.

'Have you got any idea how far it is?' Babs asks, her eyes widening with awe at her own thoughts.

'It know it's far away, round and round the corner, I suppose you might say?'

'It'd take days for us to get there!'

'Even in a car?'

'Yes Niamh, even in a car…'

'So what are you going to do?'

'Struth I don't know! I'm trying to be patient.' She sighs as she says this.

'Why don't I give you some money to fly down?'

'No. I couldn't take your hard earned dollars! Besides, I really believe it's his move. He's got to want to see us Niamh.'

'Sure why wouldn't he want to see you, you're his family?'

She screws up her face. 'I wasn't going to bring this up, but you may as well know. Look!' She delves into her bag and pulls out a out a crumpled photo'

'It's a great snap, just a bit crushed. What are you getting at?' I ask, staring at the photo of Dale with two young women and another fellow, standing under a tree in dappled sunlight.

'He's got his arm around the two blondes.'

'So, are you telling me that's he's got two girlfriends?'

'Fair dinkum, that's what I think!' she replies.

'He's a Christian! He wouldn't do that!'

'He shouldn't, that's the truth. I'm just not sure that our marriage is rock solid…!' Barbara says, her lips beginning to quiver.

'Has he told you that?' I ask.

'He hasn't said anything…'

I stare into Barbara's face. 'You know Barbie, I remember you saying that we shouldn't judge each other too much, but now you're judging Dale by a photo he sent you…'

'And the fact that he hasn't visited us in over six months…'

'That a point. But even so, you're conclusions might just be incorrect!'

'I dunno! Maybe you're right. He sent me the photo, so I suppose he wasn't worried. But I thought he wanted me to know that he had his own friends now…His letters seem so short and cold…'

'You're probably going loony being on your own with a child! I think you just need to get out of the rut. So do I! Why don't we let our hair down and go off to Hervey Bay for the day, seeing as we can't go to Sydney? We can run on the beach, watch the waves…visit Paddy's for a cup of tea…'

'But what about your washing?' she asks, noticing the pile of wet nappies lying in the basket.

'Two shakes of a lamb's tail and they'll be on the line, blowing themselves dry,' I say, picking up the basket and heading outside.

'Here, I'll give you a hand Niamh,' Barbara says, following me with a bucket of pegs.

We both enjoy the rest of the day at Hervey Bay. We call in to see Paddy but the two brothers aren't at home. 'They're probably at the Spanish club?' I suggest. We toddle off to the nearest shop and buy ourselves ice creams instead.

Luigi is away, so I take the initiative to invite Barbara and Carly to stay with us for a while. After we come back from Hervey Bay we tidy up a mountain of paintings downstairs and the place is all ready for her before tea.

'There's a bed and I can give you the fold up cot!'

'Sounds great Niamh.'

'Now I'm going to make a suggestion. Give Dale a ring and tell him we'd love to pay for him to come and visit you. That way he'll have no excuse, and you'll find out the truth of the matter!'

'But you should talk about it to Luigi first!'

'He's away for a few more days, so I'll make the decision that I know he would make if he was here! We both love you so much, we want you and Dale to be together!'

After several minutes of discussion, I win and she agrees to my offer.

'Struth, ok!'

'There's the 'phone, go ahead, ring your husband now!' I say, trying to be serious.

'He's still my husband isn't he! Thanks heaps Niamh. 'Oh God help me!'

Twenty minutes later she comes into the family room, emotional, smiling. 'Your plan worked Niamh. He's coming!'

'That grand news! So what was the problem?' I ask inquisitively.

'He's broke! He said that since I left, most of our supporters have stopped giving him money, and he's just making ends meet. He's been trying to stop me finding out.'

'So, what about his trip to America?'

'I asked him about that. He said the college paid from their funds. He hasn't even told his lecturers that he's got hardly any money. When I said you and Luigi insisted on paying for his trip up here, he agreed to come instantly! He was crying Niamh. He's been longing to see me and Carly…'

'When's he coming?' I ask excitedly.

'He's got holidays for another four weeks. He's been working at a supermarket, filling shelves, so he's going to try and get a train trip here on Monday. Oh Niamh…' suddenly she bursts out crying.

'There there, have a good cry Babs. Luigi and I have buckets of money now. I'll get some cash from the bank tomorrow and you can send it down to him.'

She suddenly looks brighter. 'You're a bonzer sheila Niamh. God bless you! I know what I can do. I can put it straight into our student account. God, why didn't I check that account. I didn't even think of it! I might have found out there's nothing in it!' Barbara laments.

'How about I make you a nice cup of tea?' I suggest.

A few days later Luigi arrives home, and is completely in agreeance to helping Dale, Barbara and Carly.

He confirms his approval immediately.

'Here Babs, Niamh and I want to give you something extra,' Luigi says, opening his wallet and handing Barbie a roll of notes.

'No way,' she says. 'You've done enough already. I can't!'

'Struth, Babs, if we can't help each other, there's no hope in life!' He grins as he says that.

'Fair dinkum? Ok! Thank you both so much darls,' Barbara says. 'I'll pay you back one day, I promise.'

'No. This is a gift,' Luigi says proudly. 'Isn't your religion based on God's gift sort of caper?'

'True! 'Struth, you're right again Luigi,' Barbara says happily.

...

Well, Dale does manage to come up about a week later and stays for two weeks. Luigi surprises them again by booking them into a hotel in Hervey Bay. Dale is overjoyed at seeing his wife and daughter, and after seeing them together I have no doubt that they truly do belong to each other. I offer to go with Barbie to the station to say goodbye to Dale.

'Niamh, thank you so much for this, I don't know how to repay you. I'm honestly sorry for the misunderstandings I caused, but I thought I was doing the right thing by not telling Babs. How wrong can someone be? Now I know the truth of the saying, *The heart is deceitful and very wicked, and we just can't know it!* Now I know my family is more important than money or secrets. God has shown me that through you and Luigi.'

'Sure you're a great preacher and all! 'Tis our duty, and our joy to help our friends! You're back together again, that's all that matters. Luigi and I are very happy for the both of you!'

'We're blessed to have such faithful friends Niamh.'

'Sure it's not very hard to be friends with you both. Remember that Barbie has been my closest girlfriend.

'Struth, thanks again Niamh,' Dale says. He grips my hand so firmly I think it's nearly broken.

I stand back as Barbie and Dale kiss each other goodbye and then he hugs his daughter Carly, who locks her hands around his neck.

'Daddy has to go now Carly,' Barbie says. 'Come on, I'll get you a lolly.'

Carly's hands loosen and she leans over to her mother.

'Bye hon', write soon,' Barbie says as Dale steps on the train and moves through the carriages, waving from the window.

A few minutes later the train chuffs its way out of sight. Barbie puts Carly into the baby seat of the car, and then blows her nose. We get back in my car and drive down the road.

'Babs, there's a corner shop open. Do you want to get Carly that lolly you promised. And I need to get some fags for Luigi. He'll never give them up. And he wants a paper.'

'I'll get them,' Barbie says, getting ready to open the passenger side door.

'All right. Here's five dollars,' I say, opening my purse.

She takes the money and heads into the shop. A few minutes later she returns with a paper, cigarettes and a small bag of assorted lollies for Carly, and another bag.

'For your lot,' Barbie says.

'The boys are probably still in bed, but you never know.

I wouldn't want a war at this hour of the morning,' I say as I start the engine and head home. After a few minutes I open my mouth, 'So, you and Dale have made up all right?'

'It was wonderful. Like another honeymoon!' Barbie says.

'That's great. So what about the blondes?' I ask

'I did mention that photo. He told me they are both married now!'

'So, you did all that worrying for nothing!' I say as we turn in the driveway.

'Struth I don't really know, maybe I'm just too sensitive Niamh, but I think there might have been something going on. But he didn't say too much on that issue, so I left it at that. I have my husband back and I intend to keep him this time.'

'That's great. You know what?'

'What Niamh?'

'I think you should pay him a visit in the next holidays, just to you know…be a good wife, that's what Maeve used to say to me!' I put the brakes on and stop the car. 'And Maeve was a very wise woman.'

Barbie nods her head. 'I'll pray about that Niamh.'

'Come on in and I'll make you that cup of hot tea before the sun is scorching.'

James, John and Luigi holding Nicole, who's crying her eyes out, meet the three of us at the door.

'Glad you're back darl,' Luigi says, handing over the precious child to me.

'Thanks darl,' I say as I take the squealing child into my arms. 'Look what Barbie bought you lot. Lollies.'

'Yeah!' the boys echo.

…

Barbie has had another child, a little boy, whom she calls Charles, and Dale returns to Murgon when Charles arrives in October, seventy-six. The whole family are now back in Sydney for his graduation early in nineteen seventy-seven. They are staying at the Bible college residential area for a week.

Luigi has been heading up north again and the Summer is back with a fierce vengeance. Nicole has had her second birthday and is a very active little child with a mind of her own. John Patrick is nearly five now and starting school. He loves playing with his little train set and the red fire engine that James is too big to fit into now. James is nearly eight and he's in grade four at the local school.

I'm still helping Olga out with the boys after school some days. Helen has gone and married Nigel, the man from our Australian Capital, Canberra. They both still work at the Schmidt's cane farm. Helen helps Olga after school with the boys on two days. James often goes over to play with them though lately I've been making him have a rest, as he gets overactive, and needs to do his homework before playing all evening.

Luigi keeps encouraging me to paint pictures, and tries to sell them when he goes away. I think I'm addicted to painting, as I wake up every day thinking of painting. I find that I can talk to God really well while I'm painting. We often seem to be having a great conversation. I ask questions and then I get the answers. I think nearly every question has been answered in one way or another. I wonder sometimes if people saw me talking they'd think I was talking to my paintings and they'd probably label me as being mad! Maybe I am? I'm still breast-feeding Nicole in the morning and at bedtime. I often sit with her and read the Bible aloud at night, while I'm feeding her. She seems to fall asleep better that way! Luigi says it's time to give up breastfeeding and to let her grow up, but I think there's a bit of jealousy there. I have taken one step in that matter and have bought her a new cup with a picture of a duck on it. She calls it her ducky cup.

The Summer passed quickly with the hot days turning into cooler nights. Luigi is very concerned about the lack of rain this year, because he says it reduces the cane harvest ratio or something like that. I told him to pray for rain.

'Sorry darl, I don't see the point!' he says. 'You pray.'

'All right, I will,' I reply. 'Dear Jesus, please send rain because otherwise Luigi doesn't believe in your wonderful powers.'

'Hey, don't say that!' he says.

'It's true though, isn't it?' I say seriously.

'It's just that I don't know if all this prayer stuff works. Sometimes it rains when you pray and sometimes it doesn't. Why is that?'

'I'll ask Him,' I say. 'Dear Jesus, please tell Luigi why it sometimes doesn't rain and sometimes it does, because I don't know why, Amen.'

Luigi buries his head under the bed sheet.

I jump under with him. 'Are you afraid of God?' I ask.

'Not as much as you!' he replies.

I kiss him. I remember what Maeve used to say about being a good wife.

The next morning we wake up to pouring rain.

'How's that for an answer to our prayers?'

Luigi just stares at the rain falling like sheets from heaven. 'Struth!' he exclaims.

…

The months pass quickly with three children and canvasses selling like hot cakes. It's nearly June, the start of harvest and the worst time of year around here as far as I'm concerned. Everywhere there's smoke and fire and burning cane already. This year it's like a burning frenzy. Everywhere you look there's black smoke filling the skies and bits of charred cane are falling like black snow all over the place.

'I've got to get an early start tomorrow darl. Cane's being burned,' he adds as he slips under the sheets beside me.

'I hate that. Can you be really careful Luigi?'

'I always am darl,' is his glib reply. 'I'll be gone by six, so don't get up. I'll be right. You need your rest darl,' he says, hugging me.

'I am tired. The kids seem to have so much energy lately, or maybe I'm just wearing out.' I turn around to face Luigi.

'Darl, you know what I've been thinking?'

'No,' I reply smiling. 'I'm not a clairvoyant.'

'You don't have an engagement ring, do you?'

'I have five golden rings, sure that's enough.'

'No, it's not good enough! I never gave you an engagement ring. I'd like to get you one soon!' he says.

'I don't need it now. I'm married already!'

'Please darl' I want to!' he pleas.

'All right, for my birthday.'

'That's nearly November! I want to get you one as soon as we've got a break from this work here. Maybe in a couple of weeks?'

'What reason can we have to buy such an expensive thing for me?' I ask.

'Our fourth wedding anniversary,' he suggests excitedly.

'It's gone!'

'Shucks, I missed it!' He smiles sheepishly at me.

'No you didn't! You can't remember giving me those opal earrings, which I love?'

'Oh yeah, I forgot.' He brings his face close to mind. 'I want you to come and help me chose a ring. That's a command!' he laughs. 'Six more weeks of this and then we shop. I might take you to Brisbane...'

'How can I argue with you?' I say, feeling like I lost this argument, which really means I won a ring. Luigi's eyes close and within sixty seconds he's snoring happily.

It's the school holidays, mid term break now, July of seventy-seven. I've got the two boys under me feet, so I'm thinking that a nice bit of shopping in Brisbane to look for a ring will be good therapy.

Well, it's a nice sunny winter's day here, so Luigi and the fellows have gotten an early start. I can see the flames in the distance rising into the blue sky, making it all black and shadowy.

It's ten o'clock and I notice that the wind has come up strongly.

'Me nappies!' I say, looking out at the washing line.

'James, you look after John and Nicole for Mammy. I'm going to move the nappies to the other side of the house.'

'Ok!' is the unhurried reply.

'And remember to stay in the house until the smoke dies down,' I add.

'Ok Mum,' James says, speaking for all three children playing on the living room floor. Luigi has bought the boys a couple of jig saw puzzles and they are happy doing them for now.

I head out the back where we had an extension built, and I actually catch some of the large pieces of black ash falling like black snow.

I unpeg the washing and notice that the flames are getting so high I can feel the heat from here.

I'm wondering if I shouldn't put these in the clothes dryer that Luigi bought me for rainy days. I head into the laundry with the wet nappies and set up the dryer.

'Mum, the flames are getting close,' James says. He's standing in the doorway with his binoculars. 'Wow, it looks great!' he exclaims.

'It's very dangerous. Don't you go near it,' I chide as I walk past him into the living room.

John Patrick is lying on his tummy on the floor absorbed by a jigsaw puzzle.

'Where's Nicole?' I ask John.

'Dunno!' John shakes his head.

I head into the bedrooms and look under the beds. Sometimes she goes for a nap in a quiet place like a cupboard or even in the laundry basket.

'Nicky, Nicky,' I call. No answer. My heart-beat is rising as I search in nooks and crannies.

'James, where's Nicole,' I ask. My heart is beginning to beat a little heavily by now.

'Dunno Mum. Look at this!' he exclaims.

I snap the binoculars from his hands.

'Hey, why did you do that?'

'Because I can't find Nicole. You are supposed to keep an eye on her. Now help me look for her, please?' I know my face must look awesome, for James just nods his head.

'She might be under the bed,' he says, heading for the bedrooms.

'No. She's not there… She didn't go out the back steps, did she?' I ask.

'Don't know Mum.'

'John, go and look in all the cupboards for Nicky.' I shout. John ignores me. 'I'm doing the jigsaw,' he says.

'John,' I say, standing over him. 'Your sister is missing. We have to find her before she gets burnt in the flames.'

John stares at me with his mouth open.

'Now, go and look in the cupboards and call me loudly if you find her,' I shout.

He runs off to look in his room first.

I head out the back and look around. Old Apollo is lying just under the steps in the shade. He looks up and wags his tail for a moment, panting with his tongue hanging out.

'Nicky, Nicky,' I call loudly. I walk around the house peering underneath where the gaps in the wood are.

James comes out to me, shaking his head. His face is white.

'Can't find her Mum,' he says.

'God Almighty! Where can she have gone?' I ask him, feeling near to tears by now. 'You didn't open the screen door, did you?'

'Maybe…,' he replies, licking his dry lips.

'Which one?' I ask, holding his shoulders.

'You're hurting me!' he yells.

'Sorry! Which door?' I ask again my voice tense and getting louder.

'The front door,' he replies, then adds, 'Mum, I think I remember something going past me. I thought it was Apollo.'

By now I'm running down the track that leads to the field. James is following me.

'Nicky, Nicky,' I'm calling. We're getting awfully close to the flames.

I see Luigi. He comes over. He's carrying a wet sack and he's black with soot.

'What's up?'

'Nicky, I can't find her,' I shout.

'My God!' he says staring into the burning cane.

'Stay here, it's too dangerous. I'll look for her,' he says.

James stands next to me. We both stare at the flames roaring through the dry cane, like a giant fire dragon hurrying through a field, devouring everything in its path.

'Oh God!' I cry aloud. I turn to James. I don't want him getting hurt. 'James, go back and stay with John. Come back here only if you find Nicky, ok?'

'Yes Mum,' he says and runs back along the track, flakes of black ash following him.

I move a bit nearer to the flames. 'Surely she wouldn't go in there? Then I hear a child's cry between the roaring of the fire. 'Nicky,' Nicky,' I shout. 'Mammy's here!'

By now Nigel, Barney and Bob are close by, all looking for Nicky. Luigi comes over from the direction of the child crying.

'Over there, I think I hear her,' I say, pointing to where the flames haven't burned yet.

'Nicky,' Luigi shouts as he races towards the noise.

'The wind's turning,' Bob says. 'Come on boys, let's beat this thing before it gets there.'

The three men rush over towards where Luigi has gone, beating out the flames as they go.

'Oh God, help. Please don't let my baby die,' I yell out to God.

Suddenly I see Luigi running towards me. He's carrying something wrapped in his sack. As he reaches me I see a small hand. 'Nicky, Nicky,' I roar as I run towards them. Flames seem to be everywhere. Even as I see Luigi getting closer and closer, something is wrong. 'Nicky, Nicky, Oh

God no!' I cry aloud. I rush towards them realizing before we meet that Luigi is on fire!

I take Nicky from his arms and he rolls on the ground. I grab the sack with one hand and belt Luigi as I'm screaming, 'Help! Luigi's on fire!'

I scream so loudly that Bob, Barney and Nigel all appear simultaneously and throw their sacks on Luigi, putting out the fire.

'I'll get an ambulance,' Bob says, running as fast as he can towards the house. I'm kneeling next to Luigi. He's shivering and his eyes are closed.

'Get him out of this hell,' I command Barney and Nigel. They immediately try to lift Luigi and carry him away from the flames.

I run along the pathway in front of them, with Nicky in my arms. Her breathing is very shallow. 'It's all right love, Mammy's here,' I repeat over and over as I run towards the house. My heart is pounding like thunder. This is a nightmare! I'm thinking. It can't be real. Oh God no, don't let it be real, I cry aloud as I run, my legs moving automatically. By the time we reach the house I can hear the siren of the ambulance coming up the driveway. 'Thank God,' I say, wrapping Nicky in a warm blanket. Her face is white. James and John stand looking, their mouths flopping open, their eyes fearful.

'I'm taking Nicky to the hospital. You two come with us,' I say, heading out the door.

'I'll look after the boys,' I hear Nigel say as I move along, my eyes filling with tears.

'Thanks Nigel. James and John, be good for Nigel. We'll come back later,' I say. It feels like someone else is talking, not me.

The medical people are already tending to Luigi. They lift him on to a stretcher and place an oxygen mask over his face. They give him some sort of needle and then wrap him in aluminium foil and move him inside the ambulance.

'Come on, inside the ambulance,' a tall young man says as I hurry towards them carrying Nicky. 'Is she all right?'

'I don't know,' I say, handing over the child.

'Oxygen,' he says, placing a mask over her face.

By the time we reach the hospital Nicky is sitting up.

I look at Luigi. His eyes are closed.

'Oh God,' I whisper. To see him like this makes my heart feel like a stone.

Nicky comes home from hospital the following day. She had minor burns and smoke inhalation. She proudly displays her two bandaged fingers. Luigi is another story. Nigel and Helen are looking after James, John and Nicky while I spend most of the day sitting next to Luigi.

On the third day Luigi wakes up. My prayers are being answered, I'm thinking.

'Nicky? How's Nicky?' These are his first words in three days.

'She's well. She's back home, bright as a button,' I assure him.

'How are you darl?'

'I'm fine, and how about yourself?'

'I'm fine, just fine,' he says. His eyes are brightening and he's smiling.

He just looks at me. He has tears in his eyes. 'Love you darl,' he says.

'And I love you too my darling,' I reply.

'Tell my daughter and the boys, I love them. We'll get that ring darl. A big diamond!'

'Sure, we will! I'll tell the children you love them. They know you love them…' I say automatically, desperately willing him to say more. We just stare at each other after that. A nurse comes in briskly. 'He needs his meds,' she says.

'Do you want me to leave?' I ask politely.

She nods her head and says quietly, 'He's still critical. He'll be asleep in a few minutes.'

'I'll go darling,' I say, leaning over and ever so gently brushing his forehead with a soft kiss.

He tries to lift his hand again. 'She'll be apples darl,' he says, his eyes closing even as I'm speaking.

I rush out the door of the hospital and rummage for the car keys in my bag. The tears are just blowing in the wind as I hurry along in the cold night air. I have this awful feeling in the pit of my stomach.

'God, please, she said he's critical! Please don't let him die! I can't live without him now! I mumble through my tears and runny nose.' I get in the car and blow my nose. Then I just burst out crying, sobbing until I think my heart is going to break from crying. I lay my head on the steering wheel. I must have fallen asleep, because I wake up cold and shivering. It's black dark outside. I switch on the internal car light and stare at the blurry dial on the clock in the dash. 'Three o'clock!' I start the car up and head for home. The next day I go to the hospital to find Luigi is worse.

'When is he going to get better?' I ask the young doctor with the thin nose who's rushing past.

He stops abruptly and stares at me. 'He's still on the critical list. His vitals are affected, now. There's not much hope… I'm sorry.'

'What do you mean? You're a doctor, you're supposed to help him get better,' I wail. My voice sounds croaky.

The doctor looks me in the eye. 'We can only do our best!'

'I know that. I'm grateful. Is he in much pain?'

'He's been deteriorating, but he's on morphine… Perhaps you should think about saying goodbye,' he remarks. 'We can't guarantee anything now…'

'Goodbye?' I repeat his words. The doctor hurries off, his coat flapping in the breeze.

Just then Barbie turns up. 'Babs…' I call out as she comes running towards me.

'I'm so sorry Niamh. How is he?'

'Not good. Oh Babs…He's worse!' Somehow she's holding me and I'm just crying on her shoulder.

I don't know how long we were there, standing in the cold hallway. It didn't matter, there was no time any more. 'Can't Jesus help him?' I whisper.

'He can!' Barbie says softly. 'Can we see him?'

'I suppose,' I say, blowing my nose with Barbie's tissues. 'Thanks Babs.' I burst out crying again. 'I'm sorry, he's your friend too! Come on Babs, we'll go in together.'

'Ok!'

We creep into the room and the only sound is a machine working away like a mini factory, going hush, hush. There's another machine going beep, beep. They seem so loud. We stand by the bed. Luigi has his eyes shut. He's motionless.

'He looks peaceful,' Barbie says, smiling at me.

'He does begorrah,' I say. 'Very peaceful. I should bring the children in…?' my voice breaks. I take a deep breath as Barbie hands me another wad of tissues.

'Niamh,' a voice whispers.

'Luigi,' you're awake. I feel elated.

'Forgive me…Jesus…'

'I forgive you for anything you ever done!'

Barbie doesn't want to miss out. She brings her face close to Luigi. 'Jesus died for you. He's got your seat ready in Heaven…'

'No Babs, not yet!' I whisper. 'Please Jesus, let Luigi get better.'

Even as I speak, Luigi's face turns a paler shade of white. His lips are smiling.

'Luigi!' I whisper close to his ear. He doesn't response.

'Excuse me….' A voice rings out behind me.

I jump in fright and stare over my shoulder. It's doctor Farrington, the one with the thin nose. 'Sorry Doctor, I didn't see you creeping in….'

He goes over to the machines and takes a look. His face is so serious it would make a clock stop.

'What's the verdict doctor,' I ask. My hands are trembling as I twist them together.

'He's deteriorating rapidly…

The following day while I'm standing by the bed, gazing at a sleeping Luigi, the doctor comes in and stands next to me at the bedside. 'He's having a sound sleep!' I whisper.

'He's not sleeping. He's in a coma. He's been totally on

life support equipment since last night,' he adds. 'Would you like some time with your husband?'

'Please!'

He dashes past me, his stethoscope flapping.

I stare at Luigi and pretend he's able to hear me. I speak in a low voice, so he knows it's important to listen. 'Well, Luigi de Vinci, you've been a really good husband to me. You've been a great father and provider. I know God must love you because I do.' I pause here and stare. I could have sworn he moved. I continue my soliloquy: 'Jesus loves you Luigi. Remember what Barbie said. He died for you. His blood washes all your sins away. I want to say goodbye, but I'll just say, see you. Till we meet again at Jesus feet, that's what the song says! James, John and Nicky love you. I love you too...' I bend over and kiss the top of his forehead, which is the only piece of skin not damaged by the fire. It was where his hat hung down. I move back from the bed. I'm sure I saw his eyelids flicker, but then again, maybe not. The doctors take him off the machines the following day, Saturday, the 16th July. He died almost immediately, they inform me.

...

Barbie, Olga and Aaron are wonderful. They've organized all the funeral arrangements, so I don't have to worry about it. James and John are very upset about the whole thing. I'm not sure I'm able to comfort them. Nicky keeps calling for her daddy, and I just don't know what to say to her. Barbie is staying with me until Dale and the children arrive for the funeral. After the children are in bed I sit at the kitchen table, having a cup of tea with Barbie. 'It's all my fault Barbie,' I say.

'Don't say that Niamh. It was an accident. Struth he wasn't the first you know. I wish they'd find a different way to process the cane!'

'Babs, I know if I had been a good mother and looked after my children none of this would have happened. I was worried about a bit of washing getting sooty, now Luigi's gone forever.'

'Niamh, you have to forgive yourself. You'll have to move on, for the kids sakes.'

'I can't. I feel so upset about the whole thing. I know how dangerous the fires are. I shouldn't have trusted James to look after my baby. Babs, I could have lost her too!'

Barbie holds my hand. It feels warm and comforting. 'Remember this, Luigi died saving his child. He loved her so much he died to save her. He's like Jesus,' she says, suddenly realizing the parable.

'Except Jesus came back alive,' I say sarcastically.

'But Luigi will rise again one day. We know that!'

'I need him now Barbie, not in some far distant place.'

Dale and Barbie stay at the church manse for a few days after the funeral.

Barbie comes up to see me in the morning. 'Niamh,' I've made you a nice cuppa and a bit of crumpet and honey,' she says.

I come from the bedroom where I've been getting dressed. I come out with Nicole in my arms. 'Thanks Babs. The kids have had breakfast already though,' I say. 'Nicky, you go and play in your room.'

'Me, for me!' she says, reaching for the crumpets.

'All right. Can I give her some?'

'Sure, they're for yous,' Barbie says.

I break off a piece and hand it to Nicole. She chews it greedily.

'Good girl. Now go and play with the train set. Mammy set it up for you.'

She runs off to her room.

'Come on, sit down and eat something,' Barbie says, sitting on a kitchen chair.

'All right. I've not been very hungry lately,' I say, 'but this smells great.'

'Where's Dale?' I ask.

'He's taking the children for a walk. It'll do him good to spend some time with his kids,' she says.

'James and John are in the bedroom playing with the

games Luigi bought them. The worst thing about them is the batteries.'

'Why doesn't someone invent a battery that doesn't wear out?'

'That's a great idea Babs, why don't we do it?'

She laughs. I laugh.

'So, how are your batteries going?' she asks as we wipe the tears from our eyes.

'Very low Babs!' I reply.

'Is there anything I can do for you Niamh?'

'You can't bring him back. That's all I want really,' I say in my mournful voice.

'Niamh,' Barbie pauses and reaches for my cold hand. I pull it away. 'You have to bite the bullet and pick up the pieces now.' She pauses.

'It's easy for you to say that. I've lost three husbands! I'm jinxed, that's what!'

'Jesus says, if the Son sets you free, you will be free indeed!' Barbie says, trying to comfort me.

'Please Babs, don't preach at me. It's the truth, I'm jinxed.'

'You're not jinxed Niamh. Don't say that!'

'So, why has this happened to me? Because I'm an egit, stupid, or jinxed. Take your pick, but pick one of them,' I say, standing up, despite the fact that I'm shaking all over.

'Niamh, sit down, you're as white as a Cockatoo!' Barbie says reaching out as though I'm going to fall over.

I sit down. I hide my face in my hands. 'If God brought Luigi to me why did he take him away again?'

'Niamh, I don't know the answer. Some things are bigger than us. We're like little ants running around an ant mound. We can't see the big picture, that's what,' Barbie blurts out.

'Babs, I feel empty inside, like someone's ripped out my guts,' I express myself vehemently as I stare into Barbie's face.

'Niamh, nobody can really share your pain, I know that.

But I know that Luigi found love with you. Real love. He died to save the child he loved because he loved you all,' Barbie says adamantly.

I just keep sitting, staring into the distance. Maybe if I look hard I can see Luigi somewhere, somehow, some day?

Luigi had been handling our accounts. I am relieved to find that the house and Luigi's small piece of cane farming land has been paid for, and he owned the truck. I find that there is also a few thousand dollars in the bank.

…

It's the year nineteen eighty, three years down the track. My art sales are slowing down, the money Luigi left is gone and I've sold his truck. One good thing is that Nicky is enjoying her first year of school.

To improve my artwork I've joined up with a local art group and we go off to special scenic places to do natural painting once a forthnight. I'm really enjoying their company, learning heaps. At night I do feel lonely without Luigi, but I am usually so tired I don't have much time to feel sorry for myself.

I've stopped going to Hervey Bay every week to Mass. I usually go to the little chapel up the road, which is more convenient, and I don't need money for petrol. The people there are very friendly and often invite me and the kids over for lunch on Sundays. I sometimes invite them back here as well. Uncle Paddy comes here once a week now and I make a meal for him. He's nearly seventy now but looks sprightly for his age. He looks forward to seeing the children. Father John comes when he can. He's back in Spain for a few months at the moment, visiting little Rosa and her family again. He's been going over there about once a year for up to six months, and having a great time by the sounds of it.

I've got one problem at the moment. That is, I have so many paintings I can hardly move in this place. I've literally done hundreds of paintings over the years. Paddy has been taking a few down to Hervey Bay from time to time, which is a great help. I've also started selling paintings at a Flea Market on Saturdays. I'm wondering how I can sell more, so I ring Barbie and talk to her about it.

'Why don't you put a sign up outside the gateway?' she asks.

'You know what, Luigi said the same thing…' I exclaim, gasping.

'Struth, do it Niamh,' she urges me.

Well, that was Saturday. James, John, Nicky and I design a sign together, and nail it to the gum tree at the entrance to the driveway. We're very pleased with our efforts. On Monday morning, after I drop the children at school I'm sitting in my studio staring out over the fields, painting a scene with white fluffy clouds and small people sitting in a field below. I'm trying to give the impression of a big world from my own perspective. I'm mixing up a nice shade of blue when I see a car pulling up in the driveway.

'It worked!' I squeal. 'Thank you Lord,' I whisper. I put my brush down and take off my painting apron. By then the man is knocking on the door downstairs.

I trip down the stairs and open the door.

He looks like a friendly man, with grey eyes, light brown hair going a bit thin in top, and when he smiles his eyes crinkle at the edges. He's average build. When he speaks it seems like he's very familiar.

'The top of the morning to you,' he says in a 'put on' Irish accent. Not a very convincing accent, I'm thinking.

'I'm Jerry O'Donnell, entrepreneur,' he says, extending his right hand.

'Niamh de Vinci,' I say, smiling coolly.

'de Vince?' he says. 'Sure that's Italian! I thought you might be Irish!' he says, stepping back.

'What if I am?'

'There you are now. I'm right!'

'And you are Irish too?'

'I am begorrah!' he replies, his accent getting thicker

381

by the moment. 'How come you've got an Italian name?' he says, his eyes twinkling.

'Wedlock!' I reply, smiling despite myself.

'Ah, ha, the dreaded wedlock thing!' he says.

'Now, would there be a bit of tae in the pot for a weary traveller?' he asks cheekily.

'There might,' I say just as cheekily. 'Step inside and I'll see if the hob's warm.'

We go inside, up the stairs to the kitchen. I'm wiping my hands with my oily rag as I go. I wash my hands in the kitchen sink, and switch the kettle on.

'God don't tell me you've got an electric kettle.'

'We're very advanced in Queensland,' I admit.

'I can see that. May I take a seat?' he asks.

'Yes, but bring it back,' I reply.

He laughs.

'Well now, would you like tea or coffee?' I ask pleasantly.

'Tea would be nice, I think.'

'Whatever you want! For you I'll make a whole pot,' I say, dusting the old teapot on the shelf and rinsing it with the boiling water.

After a few minutes we're sitting down at the kitchen table with our pot of tea and packet of biscuits.

'If I knew you were coming I would have made you a cake,' I say, pouring the hot tea.

'This is grand,' he says, sighing with delight.

After a few moments silence as we stir our tea, he asks the inevitable question.

'So, where is he?'

'Who?'

'Your husband?'

'He's gone.'

'Not to glory?'

I nod. 'He is.' Suddenly there's a lump in my throat.

'Whist now, I'm sorry to hear that…' he says.

'He died in a cane fire over three years ago now,' I say as explanation.

'Sure now you don't have to explain anything. But I thank you for telling me,' he says politely.

'So, why did you come here?' I ask, feeling suddenly weary.

'Well, I don't know if I should tell you that,' he replies.

I turn back to him and sit down. 'No, I insist, please tell me. You have me intrigued now.'

'There's a problem…' he says.

'A problem,' I repeat. 'What has James done?'

'James?' he asks.

'My son. He's been causing me trouble since his father died…he suddenly throws a tantrum…'

'No. It's not that at all at all. You are the artist Niamh?' he asks, sniffing the air.

'I am.'

'That's where the problems lie.'

'My paintings?'

He nods his head and his eyes open wide.

'What's the matter with them?' I ask.

He leans forward, then sits up. 'Is that one you're working on now?' He indicates my easel with the picture of an old house surrounded by palm trees.

I walk over to the easel. 'It's for one of the women at church. She asked me to do three of these. It's her home…'

'How much is she paying you for these?'

I shrug my shoulders. 'She already gave me twenty dollars…'

'For this one?'

'No, that's to cover my cost for the three. She will frame them herself…'

'Now I see where one problem lies,' he says categorically.

'What problem?' I shake my head.

'It's your thinking,' he advises me.

I can feel the hairs rising on the back on my neck now as I suffer his rudeness. 'My thinking… What are you saying?'

'It's the size of your thinking. Come and sit down Alanna...'

We return to our seats in the kitchen. I stare at him. I'm beginning to feel like throwing him out the door.

'People like my paintings. Some have said I paint masterpieces,' I say, remembering Barbie's words.

'They are. Small masterpieces,' he says.

'What?'

'Missus de Vinci.' He licks his lips and leans forward. 'I purchased one of your paintings down the road...

'Hervey Bay...' I add.

'That's the place. The price of the small masterpiece was wrong in the first place.'

'Sometimes they put the wrong price on, that's all. I'll give you back your money if you're not satisfied...'

'No. I don't want my money back.' He suddenly pulls his wallet from his hip pocket. 'Here,' he says, holding out a fifty dollar note.

'What's that for?'

'The painting I bought. It was far too cheap. Take it. Go on! But there is something else.'

'Honestly I can't make head or tail of you Jerry.' I take the fifty.

'You're a very talented woman. I think that sort of talent is in the genetics. Were your parents artistic?

'Me da was.' I think of my father designing tin spoons, beautiful in every detail.

'The second problem is...'

'Second problem?'

'You need to display your work on larger canvasses... These are far too small.'

'But it's what people want.' I defend my position.

'They think they want a small painting at a small price, but you need to think big. Bigger canvas, bigger dollars!' He leans forward again.

'I can't do that. I'm used to small picture size paintings. I'd take ages to finish a great big picture. Now I can complete a painting in a couple of weeks, sometimes a day, when it's warm…'

'Would you be willing to take me on then?'

'Take you on. What in God's name do you mean?'

'Your new manager,' he says.

'I don't have any manager, so I don't know why I need a new one,' I explain. 'I can't pay you.' Ha, that'll put an end to this fellow's remarks. He obviously wants money!

'Not to worry!' he replies. 'I'll work on commission. Go on, give us a go?'

'Commission?' I'm flabbergasted now. Maybe I should give him a try. I desperately need to get rid of paintings lying around the room. 'Before I say yes, can you agree to selling the paintings I have already done?'

He shrugs his shoulders. 'No worries at all. But only if you promise to start painting on a big canvas?'

'Well, Luigi bought me so many large rolls of canvas… I've been cutting them down to size. I could try.'

He grins happily, showing his uneven teeth. His eyes light up like a lighthouse and his eyes crinkle at the edges again, giving him a mature appearance.

'Good. That's very good. Now about the terms of the contract…I'll sell the paintings and give myself a commission. How does ten percent suit yourself?'

'You mean I don't have to pay you if you don't sell anything?'

'That's what I mean.'

'What about twenty percent?' I argue.

'Twenty percent is too much. Ten would be fine,' he argues back. 'I intend to get a great price for your work, at least double what you're getting now.'

He's so optimistic and he hardly knows me. 'How about fifteen?' I ask.

'I might agree to twelve.'

'Twelve then,' I say. We shake hands. We're both grinning from ear to ear.

'You're a smart business woman by all accounts,' he says.

Nobody ever called me a smart businesswoman before! Maybe I am!

The following day Jerry stretches out a roll of canvas and cuts a piece about one and a half metres by one and a half metres. For two days I just stare at the white canvas and shake my head. I'm overwhelmed by the sheer size of the white mass. A whole week goes by and I just sit and stare at the canvas every day, then get up and leave it. I'm tidying up through the intervals and come across a small photo of Fraser Island, with its bright blue sky and white beach. I try to imagine it as a huge scene, and so I finally begin my first big picture…The painting takes six months to complete. Jerry frames it with a golden coloured frame that he's constructed himself, and sells it to a local hotel within two days of its completion.

'They loved it,' he says happily, rubbing his hands together.

'How much did you sell it for?' I ask as a matter of interest.

'Five.'

'Five hundred dollars!' I exclaim.

'Yes.'

'That's great.'

'That was for the frame. The picture cost a lot more than that.'

'You can't rob people!'

'No. I can't. But it was worth every cent.'

'How much?'

'Five thousand.'

I slump into the chair. 'I don't want to be a get rich quick artist,' I say.

'I'm telling you it was worth every bit of that. I've already set up your next canvas downstairs…'

The following morning I find a huge stretched canvas sitting on a specially constructed easel.

'This is twice as big…too big Jerry…I can't do it.'

He looks at me with a gleam in his eye. 'I know you can.'

Six months later I put the final touches to a scene of a long, winding road with deep cane fields hugging its sides. An occasional roofline dots the landscape.

Every time Jerry comes over he just shakes his head in amazement. A week after completion, Jerry frames it with a blonde wood frame. It's sold to a local retired cane farmer the following day.

Jerry comes in that afternoon and holds out the cheque. 'Twenty…thousand dollars'

Now I shake my head. 'Jerry…it's too dear…'

'Never say that Niamh. He's lucky I sold it to him at that price. I nearly asked for twenty five thousand!'

I just laugh. 'What's next Jerry, a canvas that won't fit into the house?'

'You'll see,' he says. 'Right now you need a break to carry on with your other work.'

'My small masterpieces?'

'All right! Just a few,' he says. 'Just for a little while.'

Two weeks later Jerry has erected another large canvas. Within six months I complete a painting of the Mary River, with houses sprinkled on the shore's edges, a few fishing boats and several pelicans. The emphasis is on the vastness of the river, its sparkling surface, and the light blue of the sky with wispy clouds, reflected in the water. The whole picture gives the feeling of tranquillity underscored with expectancy.

Jerry's renting a small shop with living quarters above, in Maryborough. He comes over one morning after the children have gone to school.

'G'day,' he says, pulling up in his new van.

'Begorrah, you must be doing well. Is that new?' I ask as I peg the clothes on the line.

'Tis indeed! Come here and have a look Niamh.'

I come over and Jerry rolls up the door at the back of the van. I stare into the interior of the van. There are velvet lined trays like in the back of a bakers van. 'You're not selling cakes now are you?' I ask, surprised at the ingenuity of the outfitting.

'No. You don't put cakes on velvet! They're so that I can transport your paintings without damaging them. It's me own invention,' he adds.

'You're a genius, no doubt about it!' I exclaim admiringly.

'Well, I'm a jack-of-all-trades. Jerry of all trades I should say,' he remarks.

'That deserves a cup of tea!' I say, feeling very happy right now.

'I would love to have the pleasure of your company over a nice hot cuppa, but on this occasion, no, I won't.'

'Don't you like my company?

'You're great company. A ball. But I'm keen to be on my way. I'm heading off to Brisbane to try our luck there. I just wanted to steal a few more paintings while I'm up this way.' He whispers softly, like it's a secret.

'You're incorrigible! There's plenty lying around. I'll help you,' I say, abandoning my washing.

'Can I take all these with lovely cane fields blowing in the wind,' he asks.

'Except for that one there,' I point to one with a small child sitting in the foreground of the cane field.

'That's the one that'll sell,' he says, sighing.

'So, are you saying the others won't?' I ask.

'No. Not at all. They'll probably all sell. But you have to give me your best work. Even if I don't sell it, I can use it as an example,' he explains to me. 'How about if someone wants one, you'll paint one exactly like that for them.'

I think about that for a minute. 'All right,' I say, nodding my head.

'Right, I'll take it then,' he says, lifting the large painting and holding it above his head.

I just watch, wondering if I'm doing the right thing. What if he sells it on me?

As if he hears my thoughts he says, 'I promise I won't sell it, so don't worry!'

'I won't,' I reply, relieved.

'Well,' I'm off now,' he calls out as he closes over the back door of the van.

'You're the best thing that's happened around these parts since sliced bread,' I say encouragingly.

'That's my girl,' he says, reaching out to shake my hand. My heart leaps with surprise as he touches the back of my hand to his lips.

'What's all this?' I ask, smiling happily.

'Trying to be a gentleman, that's all.'

He's too charming!

He stares up at me with those twinkling eyes. 'Keep the art active,' he says. 'We don't want to run out of paintings!'

'Don't worry, we won't', I reply.

Chapter fourteen

Somehow our relationship continues in this vein for the next extraordinary ten years. Jerry is happy with the money he's making. He bought himself a little house with a workroom closer to Maryborough. He makes all sorts of little gadgets to enhance my paintings. For me, it's a time of recovery, as I move on with my life. I might add, it's a time of artistic contentment. I keep painting and he sells. One day, in the middle of a sunny but windy winters day, he turns up at the house. His expression tells me there's something wrong. I have just returned after dropping Nicole at her high school. She's sixteen now and this will be her last year, year twelve, so she's quickly growing into a young woman. John is nineteen now, and is working this year with Jerry. He's doing a computer course part time and helping Jerry with the picture framing at the shop. James is mad about horses, so works on a stud farm in Tinana, a small township five kilometres from here. He spends most of his spare time horse riding, and has even entered gymkhanas, and won a few cups no less.

'You're early,' I say, strolling over to his van as he grinds to a halt. 'I've just got back from the school...what's wrong?'

'Nothing Niamh.' He fiddles with his hands. 'Well, how about that cup of tea you're always promising me?'

'Right, come on in and I'll put the kettle on,' I say, leading the way up the stairs. As he follows me, I suddenly become conscious of the size of my bottom, which has grown a bit over the years. I blush at the thought that he might be watching me. I glance back. Thankfully Jerry's busy staring at the stairs, not my bottom.

'So, what's going on?' I ask as we sit down at the kitchen table, and I pour the tea.

Jerry leans his elbows on the table and puts his hands near his chin. 'Sales are dropping Niamh. I think I'm loosing my touch…'

'Don't blame yourself. Maybe I'm loosing my touch. I have been feeling a bit uninspired lately.'

'I have an idea to stir the old flame…'

'What?'

'You know how you've talked about Ireland and how you'd like to go back one day?'

'One day… not right now! I don't know anybody there now, except Father John, and he's not there at all. He's in Spain…'

'Yes, I know that. But what would you think if I told you that you could have an exhibition in Dublin?'

'You mean a painting exhibition?'

'Yes, that's what I mean!' he replies, a little sarcastically.

'No Jerry, if they find out I was born a tinceard, they'd be mad,' I reply.

'Niamh that was a long time ago! Times have changed. What matters is that you're are a gifted artist! How many years has it been since you were there?'

'Oh God, twenty years or so…' I reply. 'The years have flown so quickly,' I add.

'Well, I think it's time for you to return to Ireland.'

'Maybe. So how will we work out the right paintings to bring?'

'I still have a few of the first paintings you did. They're on me walls. They have a real Irish touch to them, sort of Irish Australian. They'd sell well over there.'

'But they're old hat now…haven't I improved?'

'Your style has changed. They're still incredible…We will bring some of your more modern works, those large paintings of outdoor scenes, just for contrast. I have to tell you… I've already sent photos of some to a friend who is a director in the Dublin Art Gallery. He's very impressed!'

'So, when are you intending to have this exhibition?'

'Just after Christmas.'

'It's so cold there then!' I exclaim, shivering at the thought of the rain, wind and snow.

'We could make it March, or April?' he says. 'It's up to you, and the gallery of course,' he says, leaning back and staring at me as thought I started all this. 'We can only ask.'

'What about the money?' I ask.

'Money?' he asks.

'The cost of all this,' I say, trying to explain.

'Niamh, have you looked at your bank statement lately?'

I shake my head. 'You know I hate figures. I'm sorry, I've been a bit slack…'

'You're a millionaire!' he says with a puzzled look in his face. 'You're amazing!'

'Have you been gambling?' I ask, suspiciously.

'No, I don't gamble any more! You've earned the money, and I've got the commission.'

'I don't believe it!' I say.

'Have a look next time! I've been thinking about investing in shares, or gold, something like that,' he says.

'What for?' I ask.

'That's what you're supposed to do with money, invest it!' he declares.

'But what about all the starving children around the world?' I say, suddenly thinking of all the things I could do with that money. 'We could send some to Africa, or to Missionaries…'

'Look, Niamh, you can send money to those things, in fact I would love you to take an interest in writing out a cheque or two… but right now I need your say so about a trip to Ireland. It's a golden opportunity,' he adds, nodding his head.

'Nicole leaves school at the end of the year. It's a turning point in their life. I don't want to be too far away'

'It'll only be for a short time, not for ever.'

'How long?'

'Six at the most,' he says.

'Months?'

'No! Weeks.'

'Weeks? That's all right then! Can it be April,' I say. 'That's my favourite month!'

He suddenly places his hand out and I take it. 'April it is then, provided the gallery agrees!'

'Shake,' he says, almost knocking the milk carton over.

'Done,' I reply.

'Well, I must be off then.'

…

April 1992 comes around as quickly as anything. I'm still finishing one painting of a sunrise over the cane fields. Jerry wants us to bring it to Ireland.

'So, have you packed yet?' Olga asks me as she spots me on a trip from the shops.

'I haven't even finished all the paintings I'm taking, let alone packed my bags.'

'Well, if there's anything I can do love, I'm here,' she says. 'In fact, how would you like me to pack your things for you?'

I sigh. 'That would be fantastic!'

'I'll pop over tomorrow morning after breakfast…around eight-thirty be ok?'

'Ok' I nod my head.

Suddenly, a few weeks later, we're ready to head to

Brisbane Airport. Jerry has decided to bring the van to Brisbane Airport and leave it in secured parking until we return.

'Well Niamh, this is it!' Jerry says, taking the last of the suitcases and placing them in the van with the rest of the luggage. Most of the paintings have already been sent on ahead.

'Thanks Jerry. Did you get the last painting?' I ask. I've only just finished it a week ago and we needed it to dry out a bit before transporting it.

'It's packed and ready to go. I'm still a bit worried about the paint being dry enough. I've brought a small emergency kit in case you might be doing a few touch ups when we get there,' he says.

'Right! Jerry, did you pack travel sickness pills?' I ask.

'We can get some at the airport,' he explains. 'We have to get going.'

'I'm ready then,' I say hoping to God I am really ready to return to Ireland.

Barbie, Carly, Charles and her youngest child Abigale, come to see us off. They now live at the manse near the chapel. 'Niamh, I always knew you were a genius,' Barbie says, giving me a huge hug as we get into the van. 'I'll keep an eye on your lot. Make sure they behave.'

'I don't need her to look after us,' Nicky whispers in my ear.

'I know! But John does,' I whisper back. That makes Nicole happy.

'Thanks Barbie,' I call out as I get in the passenger side of the car.

'Just remember to send us a card!' she yells out.

Everyone looks so happy, I wonder why!

Four hours later we arrive at Brisbane Airport and check in at the long counter. Our bags are whisked away and all I'm left with is my handbag and my 'beauty case'.

As we board the Qantas jumbo jet, a feeling that can only be described as fear mingled with excitement, fills my chest. Once we're in the air, the feeling of fear disappears, and I enjoy the spectacular view from on high. The airhostesses are very diligent, checking us every few minutes, and feeding us so much food, I wonder if I might still fit the nice clothes I bought. We have a stopover in Hong Kong and then London, where we board an Aer Lingus 'plane. A few hours after that we're on Irish soil.

It is refreshing to hear the Irish accents on the last airplane. My own accent seems to be returning within an hour.

After going through customs we enter the foyer area.

'Would you look at that!' Jerry says, indicating a large placard with "DeVinci and O'Donnell" on it. You're famous already.

We introduce ourselves to the man in a uniform. 'Robert Watters at your service. We have a taxi waiting for you Sir, Mam.'

After a half hour ride in the taxi we are ushered into a hotel in O'Connell Street, Dublin.

'Not bad,' I say to Jerry as young men in blue uniforms take our baggage and escort us to our rooms.

'Here you are now. Two rooms, with room service on request,' the young man says, opening the door and placing our bags inside. He's standing, smiling at us.

'I think we can manage now,' I say. The young man's chin drops to his chest.

'What's going on?' I whisper to Jerry as he comes into the room.

'A tip. Give the lad a tip,' he whispers back.

'I don't have any Irish money,' I say.

'Here,' Jerry says, handing the lad a pound note.

'Oh…right,' I answer. I might have known he'd be over-organized. I've never met anyone quite like Jerry for being able to organize me and lift me out of my constant muddle.

'Tomorrow we have a special opening at the Gallery, so I want you to be nice and fresh,' Jerry says after a sumptuous meal that night in the hotel.

That night I slept like a log and wake up very early in the morning.

I'm sitting at the window, gazing into the streets below. It's a hazy, cold day, with a little drizzle, but to me it looks like paradise. Everything moves as in a dream. Crowds of people are already surging along the footpaths, with umbrellas of every conceivable colour. Lights peep through shop windows, and reflect spectacular patterns on the otherwise dark river Liffey, as it winds its way to the sea. I hear a knock on the door, and rush to open it, tying my dressing-gown belt. 'Jerry' I say, slipping into the corridor. Jerry is all dressed up in a suit, with his hair slicked back and clean-shaven.

'I want to tell you about the day's programme. Can I get you a coffee? There's a little morning coffee place on this floor.'

'I'm not dressed…'

'You look grand. Come on, I saw a couple in their slippers in there,' he says, ushering me along the corridor.

The smell of roasting coffee and the moist Dublin air mingles in my head, making me want to cry.

'Here, sit down, and I'll get you something,' Jerry says, indicating a softly padded corner seat.

The mood is hushed. A couple are talking softly to each other, whispering secrets no doubt, I'm thinking.

'Here y'are,' Jerry says, placing a tray on the table. 'Coffee,' he says, placing a pot of coffee and a jug of cream on the table. 'And bacon and eggs,' he says, placing a plate of food in front of my nose.

'Thanks!' I whisper.

Jerry puts the tray away and returns with his own plate of food and some utensils. 'So, what's up?' he asks without even looking at me.

'Oh Jerry, I can't believe I'm here, that's all. It's like a dream,' I add.

'Thanks to me,' he says, sitting down and taking my hand in his. 'Now, eat up, like a good girl. You've got a very big day ahead.'

'I just want to thank the Lord,' I say, closing my eyes.

'Whatever you want to do…' Jerry says, waiting for a moment, his fork poised for attack on his two sunny side up fried eggs.

'Thanks Lord for all your blessings,' I whisper.

'Thank Him for me too, won't you?' Jerry says.

'Thank Him yourself!' I reply.

We're both quiet for the next few minutes.

'Now,' Jerry says between gulps of hot coffee, munched eggs, bacon and black pudding, 'the thing is, the show gets off the ground at ten.'

'Today?'

'That right! I want you to be there for the first couple of hours. The Gallery have organized morning tea and sandwiches for the patrons. The press will be there.'

'I feel so dowdy,' I say, suddenly realizing I've not even combed my hair.

'Niamh, you always look lovely. You're a very beautiful woman,' Jerry says factually. 'But, I've found a hairdresser downstairs and booked you in for the rolls royce treatment – in half an hour,' he adds.

'Well, you are the organizer,' I say, slightly startled that Jerry would think of such feminine procedures. 'You're certainly on the ball. Thanks Jerry!' I say, almost reluctantly, wishing I'd thought of booking into the hairdresser myself. 'So, what am I going to wear?' I ask, almost talking to myself.

'Your green suit and apricot coloured thing under it,' Jerry says before I can even think of what I've got hanging up in the cupboard.

'It might need a bit of an iron,' I remark.

'There's an iron in the room, in the cupboard,' he says. And an ironing board,' he adds. 'I'll do that for you if you like. Well, we've got a long day ahead. Let's get moving,' Jerry says, standing up.

By six o'clock that evening I'm only too happy to kick off my high heels and flop on the covers of the bed.

'God what a day,' I moan, yawning. 'I'll sleep well tonight, I surely will.'

'You did very well!' Jerry says, sitting on the bed, and taking out a little notepad and a pen from his pocket. 'We didn't make too many sales though,' he adds. 'Still, things should pick up once the newspapers print your story.'

'If they print it!' I say. 'I think that photographer was more interested in the angles of my face than my art,' I tell Jerry.

'I noticed that! That's a bit of a concern.'

'How do you mean Jerry?'

'Your beauty is a distraction from the sales. It's a bit of a worry.'

'Oh Jerry, don't!' I say, closing my eyes. 'I'm not a young girleen any more.'

'It's a fact Niamh. But we need to sell a few paintings, otherwise we might not have the fare back to Australia.'

I sit up straight at that. 'You're joking,' I exclaim.

'Of course I am,' he says seriously.

'I'm a flop. That's what!'

After dinner we go for a walk along O'Connell Bridge, looking into the shimmering reflections in the water. 'It's cold,' I say, as a shiver runs up my spine.

'Got a coin Mam?' a small face peers up at me behind dark eyes, unkempt hair and bedraggled clothes.

'Jerry, have you got something to give this child?'

'Here,' Jerry says, passing a handful of coins to me.

'Is that all?'

'How much do you want?'

'Have you got a pound?' I ask.

'No, only a fiver!'

'Well, that'll do!' I say, almost snatching the note from his hand and passing it to the boy.

He stares at it and for a minute I see the fading light reflects tears in his eyes.

'Thanks very much Sir, Mam!' he whispers as he runs into the darkness of the back streets.

'You can't give these people all your money!' Jerry rebukes me.

'Why not?'

Jerry doesn't reply.

The next day I awake to a knock on the door, early. It's barely light. I quickly pull on my dressing gown and stumble to the door. 'Who is it at this hour?'

'Me!' The voice is Jerry's.

'What are you doing Jerry? It's only five, and its freezing cold!' I say, stepping into the corridor.

'Come over to my room,' he says, marching away. I follow like a little puppy.

'I'll make you a cup of something. Tea?'

'Right!' I sit in the little armchair next to a table, where the daily paper is lying.

'What's going on?' I ask.

'This,' Jerry says, his face beaming. He turns the front page to me.

'My God!' I exclaim. There I am as big and bold as you like, sitting on the front page, against the backdrop of two paintings, in full colour. 'You'd think I was a celebrity!' I say, almost feeling faint with the shock.

'Just read it! I know you don't like reading too much, but this is all about you…'

'What? You read it to me Jerry…I'm too nervous…'

He lifts the paper and folds it. 'Right!' he reads 'Niamh de Vinci is a renowned artist in Australia and throughout the world. Through an unfortunate accident, her husband, Luigi was killed while trying to save their daughter Nicole in a cane fire, in Queensland. Following this tragedy Niamh's artwork found new impetus.'

'What!' I exclaim, standing up. 'How did they get that?' I ask.

'Wait, there's more…' Jerry says, continuing. 'Her Irish heritage has been retained in her artistic expressions, with fine emphasis on pertinent details. Her earlier works express a sombre reality…. Niamh is visiting Dublin for a week long exhibition, accompanied by her long time manager, Jerry O'Donnell, who grew up in Glasnevin.'

'Did you tell them all this? Jerry…'

'It's the truth. You're always on about truth! It's a good line…' Jerry says, looking awfully guilty.

'It's just a publicity stunt, Jerry! I loved Luigi, he was a great father, and…I miss him so much. I don't want my life plastered all over the paper…' I'm suddenly shaking all over. Jerry puts his arm around me. I brush it off. 'Go away,' I say roughly.

'Hey, I'm sorry. I'm just trying to do my job, that's all,' he says sharply. 'I'm a salesman, remember?'

I sit down. 'I know. You're doing your best. I'm sorry,' I say, slumping into the chair.

'Look Niamh, you left this whole thing up to me. I'm very sorry if this upsets you, but it got the front page, and that's great news!'

'I know Jerry,' I say, '…but I only wish you'd asked me.'

'And you would have said 'No', wouldn't you?'

'I would!'

We both laugh.

'Friends again?' Jerry asks comfortingly. 'Now you go and wash your face…we have a very big day again. I need you to look as good as your photos. Hows about I meet you in half an hour for breakfast!'

'All right.' I stand up and let Jerry put his arm around my shoulders. He leans over and kisses my forehead.

'That's my girl!' he says, squeezing my shoulder gently. 'I think we're going to meet some very important customers today. Wear your cream coloured suit today…nice and fresh.'

The day proves to be very hectic, with many people coming to the gallery out of curiosity, I'm sure.

Emer, Jerry's sister, joins us for an evening meal at the hotel.

After Emer's taxi takes her home, Jerry and I sit in a quiet corner, sipping our coffee.

'We did well today. Ten paintings were earmarked for sale,' Jerry advises me.

'Is that so? Who bought them?'

'There's a list at the Gallery. They're your fans now! They'll pick the paintings up at the end of the exhibition. I have a feeling we'll be bringing most home again…unless…'

'Unless what?'

'We could leave some of the paintings here, with the art gallery? They can sell them at a later date perhaps.'

'So, how many did we bring? I ask.'

'Eighty two …' Jerry advises.

'I hope we don't sell them all,' I exclaim.

Jerry looks surprised. 'Why not? That's the reason we're here.'

'Well, I was looking at them today. I really don't want to sell the one of Finn McCool, or that one of Luigi in the cane fire!'

'Niamh, that's preposterous! You can do another one whenever you want.'

'They're never the same again…' I stop talking and stare into my coffee cup, stirring the spoon around the edges. I don't want to argue with Jerry again. Suddenly I feel a sense of loss.

'Niamh, they're paintings, not people…' Jerry says quietly. 'You have to be more business like. You have to shake off that emotional attachment to your work if you want to grow…'

I shrug my shoulders.

His hand reaches for mine in an odd moment of compassion. 'I know it's hard, but you can do it girl!'

By the end of the week nearly fifty of the paintings are sold or have deposits on them.

Jerry and I are sitting in the lounge room of the hotel and Jerry is working out his sums with his calculator. He looks so happy! 'Boy, we've made a bloody fortune this week!' he states, suddenly realizing I'm here, sitting next to him.

'Don't swear! How much?' I ask dryly. I'm thinking that he certainly loves money!

'Sorry! Well, after all our expenses, and the cost of shipping the paintings, and the insurance, probably over a million!'

'So, we've made a million dollars in one week. I can't believe my paintings are worth that much!'

'Niamh, we've made a million pounds, that's nearly two million dollars!'

'What do we want with all that money?'

'Niamh, that's business. I tell you what, why don't we spend a bit in Ireland. We'll take the next week off and head for the hills?'

'Can we go south?'

'Wherever you want, my dear, wherever you want. We can even take a trip to Europe while we're here.'

'I'd like to visit Cork, and Galway,' I say before he gets too carried away. 'And maybe Spain.'

'Why not? We'll head off tomorrow. Leave all to me, my friend!' He kisses my hand.

'Oh Jerry,' I say, staring into his sparkling eyes. He looks so happy.

'Niamh…' his face seems so close to mine. He's squeezing my hand too tightly, but I daren't look away.

Suddenly he kisses me on the cheek. He releases the pressure on my hand.

'You're worth your weight in gold…' he says, 'literally!'

The next day we head off to Galway in a large hired Mercedes. Emer joins us for the trip.

'Cork?' I say, settling into the comfortable seat.

It is late afternoon when we finally hit the city of Cork, and the wind is blowing fiercely.

'Well, here's the hub of Cork,' Jerry says, pulling up in Grand Parade.

'Come on outside and I'll take a snap,' Jerry says.

Emer and I huddle together, our backs to the wind.

'You'd make a grand sister in law,' Emer says, surprising me.

I laugh lightly. 'Jerry! He's my manager, nothing more!'

'Say cheese,' Jerry's instructing as our teeth chatter away.

'Let's get out of here into the warmth,' Jerry suggests as the rain comes pouring down.

'There's a little café over there,' I say, hurrying to get inside.

We sit down and a girl comes over immediately with a pencil and notebook.

'What are you having'?' she asks.

'Sandwiches…' I suggest. The other two nod their heads in agreement.

Twenty minutes later the wiatress, Violet, comes bearing a tray.

We wait as she places the food and drinks on the table, sighing all the time.

'Do you know any Flynns around these parts?' I ask after she unburdens herself.

'There's a few, bedad!' she says. 'One not far away, and there's another crowd up the road, past the Garda sign,' she waves her pencil in the direction. 'Oh, and there's the tourist place along the road on the way to Galway, near Lisdoonuarna. They're Flynns. The place is called…*Maeve Flynn's Shamrock Fall de dahls.*'

I nearly fall off the chair, 'Is that right?'

'It is bedad! Very dear stuff,' she says, scowling.'You can't miss it. It's got a large green sheep on the roof… who ever heard of a green sheep? Stupid!' she adds.

'Can we go there?' I beg Jerry.

'To see a green sheep? It's too late now. We'll have to find lodgings first,' he says, looking at his watch.

'I've always wanted to see Blarney Castle,' Emer says quietly.

'No worries! We can do that! We're nearly there,' Jerry says immediately.

'He sounds so Australian now,' Emer comments sadly as we leave the café.

For the next hour we roam around up and down Blarney Castle. We even kiss the stone wall at the top.

'I've never been so ashamed in my life,' Emer says as she pushes her skirt down.

'You should have worn jeans or something like that!'

Emer shakes her head. 'Never! I'm a lady, remember!'

'I can see that!' I remark, wondering if she felt ladylike when her frock blew over her head while she was lying on her back kissing the Blarney stone. We head off for Killarney and end up staying the night at Muckross, in an old castle. 'It's the first time I've ever stayed in a castle,' I remark agreeably as we climb up the stone, carpeted stairway to beautifully modernized rooms, with a jacuzzi nearby.

The following day we leave Killarney early and arrive in Galway and have mornong tea at a nice little café called Walsh's.

It starts to rain just as we go to leave. 'Wouldn't you know, it's raining cats and dogs,' I lament as we rush to the car.

'It's only a spit,' Jerry says. 'So where to now?'

'Scriob!' I say, pointing to the spot on the map.

'Scriob here we come,' Jerry says, backing the car into the traffic.

After driving around the whole area, all we find is an old shop, with boarded up windows, a faded name over the door, and a broken sign.

'That's the shop I used to go to!' I say excitedly.

'It's probably got ghosts in there now!' Jerry says, pulling up, then driving away immediately.

I'm beginning to feel this part of our trip has been a waste of time. 'It's so different, not like I remember at all,' I say sadly.

'What about the green sheep shop Jerry,' Emer asks. 'The one Niamh asked about yesterday?'

'Two against one now is it?' he asks, grinning. 'All right, we'll look for the green sheep,' Jerry says as we return towards Galway and then speed down winding roads for over an hour.

'Don't go so fast Jerry, or we might miss it!' Emer says, holding onto the back of the seat to stay steady.

'It's the winding roads that make you feel like you're going fast. All right, I'll slow down a bit.'

'The girl said it was at the crossroads. It might be near here,' I remind Jerry, peering out into the rolling countryside.

'There's a turn coming up. It might be that,' he adds.

We do a sharp left and skid on the wet roads. We drive slowly down the street to the next crossroad sign.

'There it is, *'Maeve Flynn's Shamrock Fall de dahls'*, that's what it's called,' I remark, noticing s fluffy green sheep on a pole tied to a large shiny green shamrock.

Jerry pulls up with a jerk.

'It's a bit out of the way down here. God Almighty, I never saw a shamrock that big!' Emer muses gazing upwards.

'I think it's plastic Emer,' I say. I open the door and leap out. This place is just lovely. There's a big shop window with a paved walkway, hedged on each side with flowers of every kind. Gnomes peer out from everywhere as though they're guarding the place.

'Come on, these places have lovely things,' Emer says, joining me as I head for the shop door.

'It's shut,' I say, pushing on the door.

'She's gone for lunch,' Emer says drearily. 'Back at 2: 00 pm.'

Jerry joins us. 'You're out of luck again Niamh. It's only one, so do you want to come back in an hour?'

'What about that gate over there?' I suggest, heading towards a small picket fence as I speak. It meanders around the side of the building.

'I'll come with you, in case there's a mad dog,' Jerry suggests, hurrying to catch up with me.

'I'm going back to wait in the car. It's freezing,' Emer advises, trudging off.

I peer over the gate. 'There's a woman in the back garden…' I say, 'and a small child.'

'Hello there!' Jerry calls out. The woman looks up and stares at us. 'At least there's no dog,' he says sarcastically.

I open the gate and walk towards the woman. She's standing still, flowers in one hand and a small fork in the other. She's wearing a very ornate blouse, calf-length skirt and a big hat with flowers all over it. On her feet are rubber boots. Even from here I know that it's Maeve. My heart races as I hurry towards her.

She moves towards me. The little child sits in the grass and stares. She must be around two, I reckon, like Kathleen was when I last saw her.

'Maeve,' I call out, my voice is just a whisper. This is a moment I have wanted to experience for so many years. A great love for my only sister fills my heart. I can feel the tears running down my face. Thank you Lord, I cry in my heart. As we come face to face, I know I'm bursting with happiness. I see Maeve's face. She doesn't recognize me.

'It's me, Niamh,' I call out.

She suddenly strides towards me wielding the fork. 'Niamh, it's yourself? I thought I saw a ghost,' she says.

'I'm back,' I say lamely.

She stares at me through thick glasses. She suddenly comes towards me and throws her arms around me.

'After all these years. Yerra, give us a look at you?' She holds me by the shoulders. 'You've grown.'

I seem to be staring down at her from a great height. She must have shrunk!

'I've come all the way from Australia.'

'Australia? To see me?'

'I'm having an art exhibition.'

'I don't believe it. Sure you were never any good at sewing or knitting.'

'No, but I like art, oil painting!'

'Did you see the notice in the newspapers?' Jerry asks.

'Not at all! Now who might you be?' she asks Jerry.

'I'm Niamh's business manager.'

'I see. So, you're in the papers now?'

'I am!' I reply, feeling guilty for being in the papers.

'So, you don't want to know us now, I suppose?'

'I do Maeve. I want to find out about everyone, Paid, yourself, Moiré, me da, Aunty Maura…'

She suddenly hangs her head. 'Your da died two weeks ago.'

'Oh Maeve, I'm sorry! Is Aunty Maura all right?'

'No, she died a few years ago.' She looks me in the eye with her bifocals. 'She never got over the disgrace you brought on her. It drove her to drink.'

'That's terrible,' I reply.

'Yes, we heard you ran off with a priest no less.'

'He went to Spain and I was sent to Australia. He's dead now!'

'So, you admit it then. We were right! Well, it killed my dear mother. She wore herself out praying for you to be redeemed.'

'So, you met Father Martin did you?'

'We did.'

'He said he couldn't find you because you had all left this part.'

'Sure he got it all mixed up. I told him you were drowned.'

'But I was rescued, you know that!'

'Well, I felt it was for the good. If you were drowned you couldn't bring us any more trouble and shame!'

'So, you lied to him, and he lied to me,' I say, abruptly.

'I did what I thought was best for the family name! Me and Paid have our honour. We're respectable citizens in this part now. We have our own business and we employ locals from time to time.'

'So, do you know what happened to my little girl?'

'I heard she went back to be with her rightful parents, the Connors. Tom died about five years after that, probably from all the upset he had to endure with garda and the like. The place got sold up. Jacinta took the child and went to God knows where. We haven't seen hide not hair of them since.'

I can see we're not being invited into the house. 'Maeve, if ever you come to Australia, please come and see me.'

'Australia! Sure that's no man's land.'

'I'd send you the fare. I...we've got tucks of money now,' I say quickly.

'Niamh's right. We can afford to have her family over.'

'I couldn't accept that. Sure we've got our own money.'

'Here's our card. It's got our address. If you change your mind, please visit us, and Paid,' Jerry says lightly.

She takes the card and stares at it, then pops it into her apron pocket. I notice the small child crawling towards us.

'Whose child is it?' I ask.

She picks the baby up. 'This is Rhona, Moira's little one.'

'Rhona! G'day,' I say.

'After Rhonan.' She stares at me. 'He married Nora. Begorrah you missed a good fellow there...'

'Do they live around here then?'

'No, he found enough money to buy their fares to America. Sure they're probably millionaires by now.'

'I'm very happy for them. So, who did Moiré marry?' I ask.

'She married a fine fellow, Eamon Tiernan, grand lad. 'They live in Thurles. I'm looking after the child for a week. She's expecting her second and needs a break. She's a great girl, a credit to our family.'

'That's grand news. I wish them good luck!'

We pause and stare at each other. Jerry twitches restlessly. 'My sister is waiting for us in the car.'

'It was grand seeing you again Maeve,' I say, wondering whether to go or stay.

'Well, I have my shop to run. Are you staying in these parts?'

'No, we're doing a quick tour you might say,' Jerry explains. 'We need to be heading back to Dublin for the final day of the art exhibition.'

'Well, if you visit these parts again, and you're not in a hurry, come and see me,' Maeve says.

'We will,' I reply. 'Well, goodbye Maeve,' I say, 'goodbye Rhona.'

I give Maeve a quick hug. She relaxed for a few moments then pulls away as Rhona starts to wiggle.

'Slean leat!' she says, heading towards the back door of the shop.

'I thought we were finished with the art exhibition?' I whisper to Jerry as we close the gate.

'I rang the gallery last night and they would love one extra day's exhibition, so I said Friday would suit.'

'That's tomorrow!' I exclaim as we get into the car.

'That's right,' Jerry replies. 'It's great isn't it?'

…

A week later we return to Australia and I am plummeted into a deep depression. Jerry thinks it's jet lag.

I find the only relief to my heaviness of heart is my art. I paint all day and all night too, if Jerry or Nicole don't insist I go to bed. A couple of weeks later, I'm busy painting a picture of a sleeping cat when Barbie turns up at the door, with a plastic container.

'Come in Babs. I need a break, and I see you brought a plate!' I say, placing my brush into a jar of turps and wiping the bits of paint off my hands.

'I did indeed! I had the morning off. Thought you might need a chat,' she says, slipping into the chair at the kitchen table. 'Here, freshly made lammies,' she says, pulling open the lid and releasing the chocolate and coconut aroma.

'Smells delicious,' I say, pouring her tea.

After a few minutes of general conversation, Barbie stares at me.

'What?' I ask before she says anything.

'Struth you look skinny, and white,' she says. 'What's the matter?'

'I am white!'

'Whiter than white!'

'It's probably the trip to Ireland. They hardly ever see the sun there. One day the sun did shine…but only for a moment,' I say, remembering the brief glimpse of sunlight outside Maeve's gate.

'Fair dinkum, so why are you so despondent since you came back?' Barbie asks.

'I think I feel really disappointed that I left it so late to visit. It seems that most of the folk I knew were gone. Just seeing Maeve brought old memories back. And I didn't find out what happened to Kathleen…'

'But you did meet your sister Maeve?'

'I did, and I think she's softened a bit. I suppose I did find out a few things, but it just leaves a bad taste in my mouth to think I just missed seeing my dad. I would give anything for a single hug from him now.'

'Well, it sounds to me like you've forgiven your father.'

'I have actually. I remember some of the good things about him now, like him bringing home a pound of sweets when we were kids. I thought it was worth a pound in value, but he meant a pound in weight! It took me years to figure that out!'

'Sounds like a fair dinkum Irish story.' She laughs. 'I think you did well. You did make a reconnection with your family, struth that's important!'

'It is. I could have done worse I suppose. I might not have gone back at all if it wasn't for Jerry, and I was lucky to find Maeve,' I reply, suddenly smiling, feeling a little lighter in my heart.

…

One evening, while I am painting, Jerry turns up with a bunch of flowers in his hand.

'Who died?' I ask.

'These are for you my dear,' he says grandly.

'What do you want?' I ask bluntly.

'A moment of your time?'

I put the brushes away and put the kettle on, while Jerry finds a vase for the flowers.

'No sense in letting them die…Don't make tea for me. I

brought a bottle of wine,' he says, pulling a bottle of Moselle from his jacket pocket.

'You'll ruin that jacket,' I admonish him.

We both sit down with a glass and I wait for him to speak. I notice he has shaved and he smells strongly of after shave. This must be serious, I'm thinking.

Jerry looks down then into my face. 'Marriage,' he says.

'What about marriage?' I ask, curious.

'I'm thinking of getting married,' he says coolly.

'You?' I never thought of Jerry as a married person. He's always been so free. 'What about your freedom?' I ask.

'I'm serious.' He leans towards me. 'You know you're my very best friend in all the world, despite our differences,' he says, staring into my eyes.

This is very strange, I'm thinking. 'What about, you know…managing my affairs, and all that?' I blurt out.

'Don't worry, I'll still manage your finances and your tours,' he says. 'Nothing will change in that area. Not on my account,' he says. 'In fact things are going very well right now and that's why I'm thinking about marriage.' He stares at me with a blank face.

'Jerry, I'm feeling a bit funny…' I whisper.

'I'm sorry Niamh,' he says, suddenly coming around to my side of the table .

'You'd better lie down. I thought you got over that shock you had in Ireland,' he says seriously.

'I have,' I mumble. The room is spinning.

Suddenly I'm in his arms and he's carrying me towards the bedroom. I feel so weak, like all my strength has suddenly vanished into thin air. He places me gently on the bed and stands up.

'Maybe I should call a doctor,' he says.

'No. I'll be all right in a minute.'

'Do you want a hand getting undressed?' he asks next.

'No thanks Jerry. I'll just lie here. I need a shower,' I say. 'I'm probably too hot,' I add lamely.

'You're hot stuff all right,' he jokes, then stares at my

serious expression and my pallor. 'I hope it wasn't me that upset you?' he asks, his face suddenly darkened by a frown.

I don't want to answer that. I close my eyes. Go away Jerry, please!

I hear a whisper close to my ear, 'I'll come back tomorrow,' and as if he can hear my thoughts, he tiptoes out of the room.

The next day I ask Barbie to come over if she can. By lunchtime she's pulling up in her old Morris 1100 at the back door. Her happy laughter precedes her into my kitchen.

'I'm just having a bite. Would you like a sandwich?' I ask, standing up.

'Struth no! I've just had lunch. Sit down, eat your lunch. I'll watch,' she says authoritatively.

She looks at me. 'You're not depressed again?' she asks as I butter a piece of bread. I shake my head.

I put down the butter knife. 'It's Jerry,' I say.

'What's he done?'

'He hasn't done anything. That's the strange thing,' I say, feeling weak all over again.

'You're gone pale again. Struth, he must have done something bad,' she concludes.

'No. I think he wants me to marry him,' I blurt out.

Barbie's eyes widen. Her mouth opens and stays that way for a full ten seconds. Then she says, 'No?'

'Yes!' I say.

She shakes her head. 'What'd you say?'

'I nearly fainted. He said he'd come back tomorrow. Barbie, I don't know what to say to him. I never even knew he felt this way.'

'Fair dinkum? Has he been romantic before?'

'No, not at all, but last night he brought me those flowers,' I say, waving towards the vase with the colourful array of orchids and other flowers.

'Very expensive flowers! So does he love you?'

'He loves the kids. He even said so,' I say.

'He's not marrying the kids. He's marrying you. He has to say he loves you before he can do that,' she states.

I smile. 'He'd make a good father, but he's been doing that for years…why now?'

'He's after your money?'

'Mm. He does love money, but he has access to all the money now.'

'Well, you need a husband, not a gold digger. And another thing, Jerry is an atheist,' she adds, then takes a deep breath.

'So, you're saying I shouldn't marry him?'

'I'm not saying nothing. But it doesn't add up Niamh. He didn't tell you he loves you, that's enough not to say *I do*. Do you love him? 'cos that's the third most important thing!'

'Third?'

'Yes. One, he should say he loves you, and mean it! Two he should love God, and three, you should love him. Everything else will fall into place after that.'

'Mmm,' I mumble. 'You're right Barbie! It was a strange kind of proposal. Maybe he means something else, perhaps living together or something. He did say the word marriage though.'

'Well, you make up your own mind. I have to fly Niamh. Got to meet the teacher. Trouble with Charles. We just want him to finish his education and make something of himself!' she says. 'Pray for him will you?'

I nod my head.

'And I'll pray for you and Jerry,' she says as she hurries to her car.

That afternoon Jerry rings me and asks me out to dinner.

At six thirty he turns up in a suit, his face and car shining.

Jerry has booked a table for two at a restaurant in Hervey Bay. As we sit down, he looks at me. 'You look great tonight,' he says meaningfully.

I smile, 'Thanks Jerry. You scrubbed up well yourself,' I reply.

After a pleasant meal I wait for him to bring up the subject of marriage.

'So, have you thought about it?' he says at last, after finishing a whole bottle of red wine, I might add.

'I have,' I reply shortly.

'Should I get married then?' he asks passionately.

'You have to be in love to get married,' Jerry, I reply, sipping my first glass of wine. I want to keep my wits about me now.

'I am. Madly!' he says.

'You are?' I ask. 'I haven't noticed it Jerry,' I say quietly.

'No. How could you? I never told anyone,' he blurts out. His eyes look into mine. I can see pain and tension, and red rims from the wine.

'Why didn't you tell me before?'

He pauses and thinks. 'I wanted to be sure. Niamh, I can't live without her,' he says emotionally. 'I never thought I'd say such words! There, now you know everything!'

'Wow…Who are you talking about?' I ask.

'Deirdre Page.'

I'm almost choking on the mouthful of wine. 'Deirdre Page? Who's she, when she's at home?'

'She's me old flame in Ireland. I met her again, once, when we were there. Now I know I love her,' he says, tears welling in his eyes.

'Have I met her?' I manage to ask.

'You must have! You couldn't miss her. She came into the gallery in Dublin one day. She's such a fine woman, looks after herself very well. We had coffee together that evening.'

Somehow the jigsaw is all fitting together now. I lean forward. 'You're a dark horse Jerry O'Donnell. The important thing is though, does she love you?'

He suddenly blesses himself. 'Oh God I hope so!'

'Jerry, why don't you invite her on a holiday in Australia and find out how she feels about you?'

'God, that's a great idea Niamh. But it'll cost a bit of money.'

'So, how are our finances?'

'In good shape,' he says confidently. 'You know we made good money in Ireland. I am very pleased with the financial outcome of that,' he adds. 'And we have further orders since then...'

'Well, pay for her ticket. Give her something. Buy her a nice ring,' I add. I laugh.

'What are you laughing at?' he asks me, his own face brightening by my laughter. 'I'm very serious, you know!' he smiles nevertheless.

'I thought you wanted to marry me!' I exclaim.

'You?'

'Me!'

He throws his head back and laughs so heartily I feel infuriated.

'That's not that funny,' I say as he paused between breaths.

'Oh, it is!' He takes the napkin and wipes his teary face. 'No wonder you fainted,' he says, laughing again.

'No wonder,' I reply, remembering last night. I laugh. We both laugh so much the other patrons in the restaurant stare at us.

'Let's get out of here,' Jerry suggests, calling for the bill. The young waiter hurries over. They are glad to see the back of us.

About a month later Jerry comes to see me. He's holding a letter in his hand. An opened letter.

'She's coming!' he yells as he comes into the family room.

'Who's coming Jerry?' Nicky asks, looking up from her cosy perch on a beanbag, watching telly.

'She's an old friend from Ireland,' he adds.

'When?' I ask

'The first of September,' he replies.

'Where's she going to stay?'

'She can stay at my place. Don't worry Niamh, I've got a spare room.'

…

Jerry drives down to meet her and stays the night in Brisbane, in a motel. The next day they arrive in Maryborough. I have never seen Jerry so nervous, or so happy. Deirdre is probably the same age as Jerry, forty something. She's very professional looking, with permed brown hair, delicate white skin and a strong Dublin accent. She's solid in stature and almost as tall as Jerry.

'It's lovely to meet you,' I say, extending my hand.

'It's grand to be here,' she replies, looking at Jerry with eyes full of Irish mist.

That's a good sign. She loves him, I'm thinking. A month later, the day before Deirdre returns to Ireland, she and Jerry announce their engagement. We have an impromptu engagement party. During the evening I have a few moments alone with Jerry.

'What do you think now?' he asks. His smile says it all.

'She's perfect for you Jerry,' I assure him.

'I know. It's a miracle. I never saw it before. Thank God I'm not too late,' he exclaims.

'Too late?'

'Nobody's realized what a prize she is. She could have been snatched away from me just like that,' he clicks his fingers to explain what he means. 'I've the luck of the Irish, for sure!'

'So, when's the wedding day?' I dare to ask.

'We haven't decided. We don't know whether to have it here, or in Ireland. She wants to talk to her family about it,' Jerry tells me. His face looks disturbed.

'Well, all her family are over there. It might be easier that way,' I suggest.

'Do you think so?'

'I do.'

'I could sell a few paintings while I'm there.'

'Jerry, try to forget the salesman thing for once in your life!'

'It's in me blood Niamh. It's not me fault,' he replies, grinning happily.

'Only a few then. You have to spend time with your lovely bride.'

'I've known her for years Niamh.'

'But being married is a bit different to just courting?'

'I hope not!' Jerry's face looks alarmed.

'I'm sure all the surprises will be good ones,' I quickly respond.

'God I hope so. I hope I'm not getting into deep waters here?'

'Yerra Jerry go on. You're ripe for love and marriage!'

'Niamh, you're my best friend. I wanted you and the kids to be at the wedding...'

'Jerry, the most important thing is Deirdre and her family and yours. Maybe we could have a second wedding celebration when you come back?'

'That's a brilliant idea Niamh.'

'You are coming back here then?'

'We've talked about that. Deirdre loves Australia. She's itching to come and live here. Her mother and father died a few years ago, so she's been very lonely. She's got one sister, and a couple of aunts who will miss her...She's happy to work with me in the business. We could do with a helping hand.'

'Oh,' I reply spontaneously. 'That's news to me.'

'Sure it's not news to me. I've been needing help for over a year.'

'Why didn't you say so?'

'I was just too busy...'

'I would have helped you...'

'No way Niamh. You are an artist. You have to keep the brush moving on the canvas. That's where the rubber meets the road as they say.'

'So, can we afford an employee?' I ask.

'We can.'

'Your word is good enough for me Jerry. So, what does Deirdre do in Ireland?

'She's a shop assistant in a very grand store in Dublin, Cleary's! She loves sales. Not that I want my wife to be working, mind. But if she wants to do that, it's fine with me,' he concludes.

'Wife?' I say, looking at Jerry. I never thought I'd hear him say that word.

'Oh God, I'm getting a wife!'

'Jerry, you're getting the prize Jerry.'

'You're right. The prize. A wife!'

'Jerry, you'll be very happy. I know it. I only wish I could be as happy!'

Jerry leaves for Ireland a month later and they have a wonderful Christmas wedding in Ballymun, Dublin. Well, Jerry and his blushing bride return with all sorts of gifts from Ireland.

'Would you believe there were orders for some of your paintings at the gallery,' Jerry states. 'I don't think they would have told us if I hadn't asked,' he adds.

'Which paintings?' I ask.

'The ones you didn't want to sell, remember? I brought the bits of paper with me. Here, there they are.'

'There are six here,' I say.

'Three for each order, so we've got two orders. That's how it works. You take one, send one back and give the last one when the painting is paid for,' he explains.

'What's the name?' I ask, 'The writing's terrible!'

'The cane fire is for …Richard Ramsbottom.' Jerry looks up. 'I know him. He visited the gallery and I talked to him while you were out.'

'And, the other one is for…a couple called Niall and Bernadette Dempsey, I think,' Jerry says, squinting as he tries to decipher the writing.

'There's a small note stuck to the back with sticky tape,' Jerry adds. 'Here,' he says.

I unfold the single piece of notepaper. 'Can you read it Jerry?'

Jerry reads: 'Niall will be arriving in Australia next July. He will pick up the painting then, if convenient. It's signed "Bernadette".' Jerry pauses and shakes his head. 'They must really love your work!' Jerry stares at me. 'Not that I blame them. Would you have it ready by then?' Jerry asks.

'I hope so,' I reply absendmindedly.

'Is something wrong Niamh?' Jerry asks, staring at me.

'I feel a bit funny. I need to sit down,' I say.

Jerry brings the chair over. 'Here, sit.'

'Thanks.' I sit.

'Are you all right now?' he asks.

I look up at Jerry from my chair. 'I think so. You're sure that's the right name?'

Jerry reads the pieces of paper again. He nods his head. 'I'm certain. Why?'

'It's the same name as someone I used to know,' I say.

'Sure there are probably thousands of Irish names that are the same,' Jerry says jokingly.

He looks anxious to leave. 'You can go Jerry. It's probably the heat. I might have a cup of tea,' I say.

'I'll be on my way then. The builders are making a mess of things at the house. I want to sort them out. I don't want Deirdre getting anxious…' He turns to go, then turns back. 'Do you want me to answer this?' he asks, holding up the letter.

I nod my head.

…

Just before the end of June, a caller comes to the door. It's a breezy cool day, but the sun is shining, which makes it feel warm, especially with the windows closed. I open the door and the wind howls through. It's a man I haven't met before. He's a thin, short man of around forty or fifty. He's got a long face and is wearing a cap. He's dressed in a dark grey suit.

'G'day,' I say.

'The top of the morning to yourself. Is this the home of Jerry O'Donnell? He removes his cap and holds it to his chest. His wispy hair blows across his bony skull. He has a strong Irish accent, I notice. 'He lives down the road,' I explain.

'I have to collect a painting. This is the address,' he says as he holds up a piece of paper to verify himself.

'Are you Niall Dempsey?' I ask, almost relieved to think I was so mistaken. If ever a man looked different to my Niall, it's this man.

'No. My name is Joe Smith.'

I almost feel disappointed now. If this had been Niall Dempsey, all my longings would have gone. Now I have another problem. I can't remember painting anything for Joe Smith. I try to smile at the man.

'I'm sorry, I don't remember your name? What painting did you order?' I ask politely.

'A horse!' he answers abruptly.

'I'm sorry! I only have one painting on order, but it's for a Mister Niall and Bernadette Dempsey!' I say slowly.

'That's it!' he says, his grey eyes sparkling, his mouth almost drooling with delight.

'But you said you were Joe Smith? I don't understand,' I say taking a deep breath.

'He's in the car,' Joe says.

'Who?' I ask.

'Mister Dempsey.' He says that almost with contempt at my ignorance. 'I'll get him!'

'Come in and have a cup of tea!'

'I will!' He hurries back to the car, his coat tails flapping in the breeze.

I fly up the steps two at a time and put the kettle on, taking deep breaths as I go. My Niall died, it can't be him. I take a packet of biscuits from the cupboard, fix the cushions on the lounge chair and pick up a bunch of papers from the floor. I wish I kept this place a bit tidier! I can hear noises on the stairway as they make their way up...

'One more,' I hear Joe's voice say as a clattering noise proceeds the visitors.

What are they doing? I wonder. I hang over the rail on the top of the stairs. I can see the top of a head with dark hair and a pair of hefty shoulders. The man is banging a stick on the steps, as though he's killing a cockroach. As they climb the stairs, I quickly rush back into the kitchen and make a pot of tea. I take the cups and saucers down and place them on the table. I'm shaking so much I nearly drop them. Spoons, I think, rummaging in the cutlery drawer with my shaking hand.

'Good morning,' a voice says at the living room entrance. I turn around and I look into the man's face. I can't speak. It's as if a spell has come over me. I stare at him as though I'm seeing a ghost. His face is blank. Joe introduces us. 'This is Niall Dempsey,' he says.

'I'm Niamh de Vinci,' I say, walking over to meet him. It is him! I know it. His hand is shaking as our fingers touch.

'Niall…' I say.

'Niamh,' he replies. He just holds my hand in his and stares at my face. It's as if he's looking right through me. He doesn't recognize me, I can see that. He's probably looking for a redhead! My hairdresser insists the blonde look is more attractive, and I believed her. Maybe it's all the wrinkles, and I've put on so much weight, and my hair is short now…'Come and sit down,' I say.

'Will we leave the stick here,' Joe asks, placing the stick against the top rail.

'The stick?' I notice it now, it's got a white part on one end. 'I'm sorry. I didn't realize that - you're blind?' I say. Niall wasn't blind. What's going on?

'I am,' Niall states, smiling.

'Blind?' Of course! Oh my God, what am I saying? I have so many questions now. I swallow and take a breath. 'I've made the tea?' My hand is stuck in his.

'I'll show him where the chair is,' Joe interrupts.

'Of course. Sit down, over here.' My hand is immediately free. I rush towards the table as though I'm an actor in a play. This is the last act, the finale, and I'm messing the lines up. Joe takes Niall's arm and leads him to the chair. They both sit down. My knees feel weak. I sit.

'I'm sure you make a lovely cup Mam!' Joe says, staring at the pot.

'Thank you. Will I pour?' I ask. I almost drop the shaking teapot. 'Sorry. I think it's too heavy,' I say breathlessly.

'I'll be Mammy?' Joe suggests, taking the pot in his hand and tipping it into the three cups.

It gives me a chance to look at Niall's face, but I daren't stare. He's much older than my Niall. Of course he is stupid, it's been over twenty years! There's a tinge of grey here and there. Is it him? I'm almost certain. Or did he have a twin brother? 'Did you have a nice trip?' I ask, mechanically.

'We did indeed,' Joe replies, taking the packet of biscuits and piling half a dozen on the small plate next to his cup. Then he stirs his tea frantically, making clinking noises with the spoon. The noises reverberate in the kitchen, culling the silence.

Has Niall come to see me, I wonder. 'Are you staying around here?' I ask.

'We are!' Joe replies.

'Whereabouts?' I ask breathlessly. My voice sounds squeaky, like a mouses'.

Niall speaks. 'A place called Tinana.'

'So you have accommodation then?' I say stiffly.

'We have!' Joe says, staring at a biscuit that's fallen into his cup.

'We called in there, and made a booking,' Niall explains, gingerly holding his cup of tea in his hand, not drinking it yet.

'Are you staying long?' I ask.

'A while,' Joe replies.

'Just touring?' I ask.

'I'm going to have eye surgery in a Brisbane hospital. What's the name of it Joe?' Niall asks.

Oh my God, he's having surgery! He could die! But he's supposed to be dead already…

'The Princess Alexandra,' Joe says.

'I hope everything goes well for you then,' I say politely.

Niall sips his tea at last. I know it must be him. His hands. I know the hands are the same!

'It will!' Joe says, finishing the last biscuit on his plate.

'I have a good surgeon. The best in the world I believe,' Niall says, placing his cup on the saucer with a slight clink.

'Who's that?' I venture to ask.

'Doctor Readwell,' he says.

'It's an appropriate name anyway,' I say, laughing lightly.

The two men smile. 'I never thought of that before,' Joe says, his eyes brightening like shiny buttons on a dark jacket. He laughs heartily now. 'You're a bright one!' He stops laughing. 'We have to be going now,' Joe suddenly gets up. 'We need to pick up the painting,' he adds.

'I haven't packed it... Can Jerry come around to the hotel with it this evening?' I ask, suddenly feeling flustered.

'He can,' Joe replies, turning on the spot and marching over to where Niall's cane is leaning.

'Niamh, thank you very much for the tea. It was lovely,' Niall says, standing up.

Joe places the cane in his hand. 'Come on, it's this way…' They head towards the stairs.

Niall turns to me for a moment. 'Can I meet you again?' he asks.

'Certainly. Would you want me to come with Jerry to the hotel this evening?'

'That would be grand,' Niall replies. His voice is like music.

I can hardly breathe. As they leave, my heart pounds. I sit down and try to get my wits about me again. I immediately give Barbie a ring and invite her over. 'Barbie, come on over. I need to talk to you.'

Twenty minutes later Barbie is coming through the door.

'Come in Barbie. You won't believe what happened today,' I say. 'I still don't believe it myself.'

I already have the coffee made. 'I think I need a cup of coffee right now,' I say, sitting down opposite Barbie at the kitchen table. 'Niall sat at this table today!' My voice blurts this out.

'Struth? Your dead husband?'

'It was almost definitely him,' I reply.

'Niamh, you've either been on the booze or off in the spirit?' Barbie states, reaching over and placing the back of her hand on my forehead. 'You haven't been taking anything?'

'No, not even aspro,' I reply. 'He's real! He ordered a painting, and now he's come to pick it up!'

'That's amazing. Did he know it was you?'

'I'm almost certain he did! But the fact that he couldn't see me makes me wonder if he did recognize me,' I reply.

She looks up at me inquisitively. 'So, how come he didn't see you?'

'He's blind. He's come for an operation and they're staying in Tinana,' I say.

'Hold it mate! Did you say 'blind?''

'Yes.'

She looks into her cup and swirls the coffee around. 'So, he's not dead, just blind!'

'He might die. He's having an operation?' I blurt out my feelings.

'Jesus could make him see properly!' she interjects this comment. 'So, did you find out where he's having the op?'

'I did! Princess Alexandra Hospital,' I reply.

'So! Is he trying to reconnect or what?' she asks pointedly.

'All I know Barbie is that he ordered the painting, and he came all the way here to collect it.'

'So, is he married or available?' she asks.

'I don't know Babs. I just talked to him for a few minutes. But there might be a wife. Bernadette. Her name is on the docket,' I say. 'Jerry had the docket with the name Bernadette and Niall Dempsey.' Suddenly it hits me like a ton of bricks. 'He must be married!'

'Well, I wonder what he's up to? You know the rules. You shall not commit adultery!'

'She might have died,' I say promptly.

'How old is the docket?'

I sigh deeply. 'Not very old. Oh Barbie…'

'I know how you still feel about him, but life goes on…'

My heart suddenly lurches in my breast. 'When we shook hands, it was like an electric shock. We had a connection…'

'Remember, he's married! Don't let feelings make you sin,' she admonishes, getting up from her chair.

'Ok, if he's married to her, why didn't she come here with him?' I'm challenging Barbie's theory now.

'Struth, I thought you said she did,' Barbie says, sitting down again. 'Give me the facts girl!'

'No. It was a man called Joe Smith.'

'Joe. My God he's not a homosexual?'

'No, they're not like that.'

'How would you know? You don't know what he's been up to for twenty years. Be real Niamh!'

'Honestly Babs, he was a sort of carer.'

'All I know is that you need to be careful. We live in a crazy mixed up world now. God's word is being thrashed!'

'Barbie, he invited me to visit them at the hotel.'

'Well, don't go alone!' Barbie advises, standing up and holding the back of the chair. 'Niamh, I have to go. I just popped in while I was passing by. I'm helping at the op shop,' she says, brushing her crinkled skirt. 'I'll pray for you Niamh. I honestly would love to see you happy again, but this sounds sus…' These were her last words for now.

After tea that evening Jerry and I visit the hotel at Tinana. The two men are staying in a self-contained unit at the back of the hotel.

'Come in,' Joe says, opening the door widely. 'We're just watching the box,' he says, rushing over to the television set and turning the sound down.

'This is Jerry O'Donnell,' I say introducing Jerry to Niall and Joe.

Both men stand up. 'Please to meet you Sir,' Joe states proudly.

'How do you do?' They shake hands.

'We brought the painting with us. You should see if you like it before you take it away,' Jerry suggests. He uses his business voice now.

Joe looks at Niall. 'Do you want me to have a look?'

Niall nods his head. 'You can describe it to me.'

I take this moment to ask about the wife thing. 'What about Bernadette?'

'Sure Bernadette is back in Ireland,' Joe explains, as though I should know that.

'Won't she want to see it too?' I ask.

'It's Niall who wants the painting,' Joe explains. 'Bernadette was the first to notice the likeness,' he says thoughtfully.

'Likeness?' I ask.

'The likeness of the rider on the horse to Niall and the horse looks like one we knew a long time ago. Niall's horse,' he says.

'So, do you want to send something to your wife?' Jerry asks now. 'I can send her a photo.'

Thank you Jerry for bringing up the wife topic!

'No. She's not his wife!' Joe says, his eyes widening with amusement. 'She's his sister.' He laughs, as though we should have known that too.

'Sister?' I say. He never told me about a sister, or any of his family for that matter!

'He never married another,' Joe replies on behalf of Niall as though Niall can't speak for himself. He's blind, not dumb! 'Not after what happened…' He makes a sour face at this.

'Joe, would you like to go and bring us a drink from the hotel?' Niall suddenly asks Joe.

'We have some here!' He rushes over to the fridge and opens it. 'Beer, and wine,' he says triumphantly, adding, 'and nuts!'

'Maybe Niamh would prefer something lighter?' Niall says.

'Orange juice would be lovely,' I say.

'Can you get Niamh some orange juice,' Niall asks. 'And what's your pleasure Jerry?'

'A beer,' Jerry replies.

'Get Jerry a beer,' Niall says, taking a wallet from his trouser pocket and giving it to Joe.

Joe looks back at the fridge. 'Are you sure you don't want some of this stuff here?'

'It's much more expensive from there,' Jerry says.

'Is that right?' Joe asks, his shoulders suddenly straightening. 'Right, I'm off to the pub to get a drink. 'Would you like something too?' he asks Niall.

'A light beer.' He coughs, then asks, 'Jerry, can you go with Joe to help carry them?'

'Why not?' Jerry says, giving me a wink as he leaves.

I stand and stare at Niall.

'Sit down Niamh,' Niall says, sitting on the couch. He pats the seat next to him.

I sit down. We're both quiet for a moment, then both begin to speak at the same time.

'What…?' we say together.

'Go on Niamh?'

'So, you know who I am?' my heart pounds with each syllable.

'Kathleen Mary… my wife.'

He knows who I am.

'Niamh Murphy…' he adds.

I nod my head, then remember that he can't see me. 'Tis so…'

I feel so overcome I just sit, stunned. He waits on me, then becomes a bit restless.

'I've got a crow to pluck with you. Why did you run away from me, Niamh?'

I bite my lip and take a deep breath before I answer. 'They took me away…honest to God!'

He emits a deep sigh. 'I was wondering if that was the case. I believe you Niamh,' he replies quietly. There are tears in his eyes.

I pause. 'They said you were killed! That you fell off a horse…'

'I nearly was, begorrah. I was only coming to ask about you when my horse reared unexpectedly…'

'So, you did come looking for me at Scriob?'

'I did.'

'So, can you remember what happened?'

'I can see it as if it was yesterday. We galloped through the field, and then jumped the small stone wall. It was then the horse reared up. I was thrown off and I hit some rocks. I was unconscious for some time. Apparently Finn McCool bolted back home without me, and Tom Connor came looking for me. They found me the next day. They took me to Dublin.'

'I heard something like that. I think the tinceards put out a tripwire because they wanted the horse. They wouldn't harm you…' I explain.

'I was wondering why the horse reared up like that…It was unusual for Finn McCool.'

'Was that when you became…' I can hardly say the words.

'Blind?'

'Yes,' I nod my head even though he can't see me.

Niall sits up straighter now, his eyes turned away from me. 'They said I had concussion and the eye haemorrhaged and the retina detached.'

I gasp at all this. 'That sounds horrible!'

'It was! Especially when they said I wouldn't see again.'

'So, why are you having an operation now?'

'I did actually regain some sight, ten percent...'

'So can you see me?'

'Not really. It's like looking at someone through a painted window,' he states, looking at me. 'It's because of that they recommend the operation.'

'So, you'll be able to see again?'

'There's no guarantee. It's been a long time, so they've given me a fifty-fifty chance. It's worth it.' He nods his head.

'I hope so,' I exclaim.

He stares at me blankly. 'When I began to regain my sight about a month after the accident, I felt hopeful, so Joe took me to find you.'

'Oh God, so you came looking for me a second time?'

'I did. They told me you were married to another and didn't want to see me again. They said your life would not be worth living if I turned up again.'

'Who said that?'

'Some women at the campsite.'

'That's terrible, you must have felt like washing your hands of the lot of us! So, what happened then?'

'Well I didn't want to cause any more trouble to you, so I returned to Dublin and stayed in the old home with Joe, my sister and her child.'

'Now about Bernadette, is she your only sister?' I say the name.

'That's right.'

'And what's her child's name?'

'Fiona.'

'You sound like a very close family. That brings me to another subject,' I say.

'What's that Niamh?' he asks in such a soft lilting voice that it makes my heart flutter.

'I've got a crow to pluck with you Niall. You never told me about your family.

'I'm sorry Niamh. I didn't think I needed to?'

'Well, I'd just like to know, that's all,' I say persisting.

'I'll tell you then. My mother and father died about ten years before I met you. They were older parents. Mam was forty when she had me, and forty three when she had Bernadette. After they died, Joe became our guardian, and he had control of the property.'

'So, how did you get to be at the Connor's farm?'

'Well, Joe knew Mister Connor, and my dad for years, because of the horses. He offered me a job when I finished school and Joe insisted that I take it.'

'So, what about your sister?'

'She was a black sheep I suppose, for a while.' He stops for a moment, as though wondering if he should tell me this.

'Go on,' I say.

'Well, she ran away to England at seventeen, five years after Da passed away. We lost contact until a few months after you and I were married. She suddenly appeared at the house, with a small child, homeless, penniless.'

'That's terrible,' I comment.

'Joe and I took her in and we've been together until recently. She's met a nice man and they've gotten married now. Only six months ago. Fiona is living with them in Dunlaoghaire.'

'You could have taken me to your house in Dublin. Why didn't you?'

'You're right! And you're wrong! You see, the property could not be mine until I turned thirty. That was my parent's last wish. They wanted to know I was of responsible age.'

'Thirty!'

'I know. They were going to say forty, but Joe persuaded them to change it. When I met you I was twenty-five. I thought we could work with the Connors until I turned thirty, and then I'd give you a lovely surprise, a beautiful home and a horse stud. When I left you and promised I'd bring you to Dublin, I was going to tee it up with Joe because he didn't even know I'd married you at all.'

'Then the tinceards came and changed all that… It all seems so long ago now,' I lament.

'It does. But I want to know a bit about yourself. Joe did read something about you in the papers, so I know you lost your husband tragically, and you visited Ireland, with your manager, and I felt had to come and find out if it was yourself after all. We also read about your manager's wedding in Dublin, so I was compelled to come and meet you.'

'That's all correct. Since Luigi died in a cane fire, I've been on me own…'

Suddenly the door bursts open. Jerry follows Joe. Joe hands me an orange juice with a straw.

'Thanks.' I sip the cool juice.

'Very warm out there,' Joe says, mopping his brow.

'It's winter here,' I mention, smiling. I turn to Niall. 'When is your operation?'

'Next Friday. We'll be heading there on Monday,' Niall replies.

'What about the painting?' Jerry asks. 'Did you want to take it with you?'

'Yes,' Joe replies immediately.

'No!' Niall speaks. Niall's word is more powerful.

Joe looks at Niall in surprise.

'Can we leave it with you until the operation is finalized?' Niall asks.

'That's a grand idea,' Joe interrupts.

'That's fine. You've paid me, so it's yours now,' Jerry reminds him.

I didn't know that. I look at Jerry.

'I meant to tell you Niamh. Niall sent me a cheque six weeks ago. Did you want to see the painting? I can assure you it's amazing,' Jerry declares.

'No. I'll wait…' Niall replies.

Jerry, he's blind! I say with my eyes to Jerry.

'Right. Niamh, we have to head back now,' Jerry reminds me. 'She's got her family waiting,' he adds, grinning. 'Maybe we could all go out to dinner before you leave,' he says, noting my reluctance to leave.

'Come over for lunch tomorrow,' I invite them. 'It's Saturday and you can meet the kids.' I smile.

'Maybe Cindy and Katie can come with us. We'd like you to meet them,' Niall proposes.

'Cindy and Katie?' I repeat.

'They're coming to visit us tomorrow morning,' Joe says in an exasperated tone.

'Of course. They're more than welcome. We can have a barbie!' I say.

'More work,' Jerry comments.

'Jerry's really good at cooking a steak on the barbie,' I compliment Jerry.

'Around twelve then?' I inquire.

'That would be delightful,' Niall responds heartily. 'Would you like us to bring something?'

'No. You're our guests,' I say quickly. 'We've got tonnes of food.'

Joe nods his head in approval. 'I don't eat red meat,' he says. 'Mad cow disease…'

'You've no worries here mate, but I'll cook you pork sausages instead,' Jerry suggests.

The next day Joe and Niall arrive in their hired car. 'Come on in,' I say, 'and meet the family.' I usher them through into the barbeque area that Luigi built.

'Nicky, John, James, come and meet our guests,' I call to the three young adults. 'Where's Cindy and Katie?' I ask, looking around, wondering if I had somehow missed their coming.

'They couldn't come,' Joe says bluntly. 'I never saw so much food in me life.' He stares at the table arrayed with all sorts of food we normally eat.

Nicky suddenly rushes in, carrying two glasses. 'This is Nicole,' I introduce her to Joe and Niall. Joe is staring at the table laden with food.

'Hello,' Niall says, smiling at her.

'He's staring at me Mum?' she whispers to me.

'He's blind…'

'Blind,' she says loudly enough for Niall to hear..

He jerks his head back with a big smile. 'I can see enough to know that you're a very bright, happy young woman,' he replies.

She grins, then rushes off to join Carly and Abigale, Barbie's two girls, who are playing with some boys at the pool table. At this point John arrives holding a large bottle of coke.

'Where's James?'

'He's showing Charles his motor bike…'

I address Niall. 'Come and sit down,' I say as I lead him towards a wooden chair. He sits down.

'It's a grand day,' he says, looking into my face.

'First, let me get you a drink…' I hand him a cool beer. 'Now, tell me about this operation, will you?' I ask, dragging over a chair and sitting down next to him.

…

The following Wednesday night I can't sleep. I get up through the night and begin a painting of Niall from memory. The next morning, Barbie comes around. 'I want to be with him now,' I moan.

'Go for it matey, he's free. Don't let the opportunity pass. Struth, I know what happens when you do, so what are you waiting for?'

'I don't know. I'll go tomorrow.'

On Friday afternoon I arrive at the hospital. After a short enquiry I'm directed to the sixth floor, ward B3.

A smiling nurse greets me at a desk.

'Is it all right if I go in?'

The 'phone rings…She picks it up as she continues talking to me. 'I think there's someone with him…Go on…' She waves me through.

As I enter the room I notice a woman seated by his bed. She's leaning towards him as though she's sharing a secret. I stop and wait. Niall looks towards the entrance where I'm standing. 'Come on in Niamh,' he calls out.

I walk towards the bed. I wonder if he's had the operation already?

'Niamh, this is Ja… I mean Cindy,' he says.

'Cindy Casey.' She reiterates the name.

'G'day Cindy,' I reply. 'So, how do you two know each other?' I ask innocently.

'Cindy lives down here. She visited us in Tinana for Katie's sake,' Niall explains.

'There's a special Gymkhana training for a month,' Cindy explains further. 'I like to give my girl every opportunity. But I did know Niall back in Ireland. We were very good friends, especially after Tom died.'

She smiles momentarily and then cocks her head and stares at me. I look at her from the corner of my eye, concluding that she's probably around my age, getting to the top of the hill, touching forty! Her face is highly camouflaged with makeup. Her lashes are long, black and false. Her hair is an ash blonde, short. Her mouth is a tight orange line, which is extended beyond the shape of her lips, giving her lips the appearance of having a ridge around the outside.

Cindy wriggles restlessly on her chair. 'Take this chair. I'll just go and grab a fag,' she says, leaping up.

'You're not allowed to smoke in here,' Niall reminds her.

'I know that,' she says agitatedly. She moves swiftly out the door, giving Niall a backward glance of annoyance as she leaves.

'So, what's happening in this neck of the woods?' I ask, placing my bottom on the plastic chair.

'I'm still waiting. There's been some sort of delay.'

'I thought you could see. You knew it was me at the door...'

'I just knew it was you.'

I look at him. I don't know what to say. 'Where's Joe?' I ask, trying to think of something.

'He's gone for a bit of a walk. He doesn't like being cooped up.'

We sit in silence. 'I enjoyed the barbeque,' he says finally.

'It was a good day.'

'You have a lovely family,' he says seriously.

I don't even hear Cindy approaching until I detect a whiff of cigarette smoke.

'I'm back. Can I get you something Niall?' she asks, stepping in between Niall and me.

She has the curious ability to make me feel uneasy. 'I'll go…' I whisper.

Just then a nurse comes in. 'Excuse me,' she mutters, sliding the curtains around the bed.

'We can see when we're not wanted!' Cindy remarks, tipping her head sideways and stepping outside the curtained parameters. Niall's smile disappears as the curtains swirl and then close, like the end of act one.

'He's needs his pre-meds,' Cindy whispers to me as we slip outside and wait for the lift.

'I used to be a nurse…' she informs me as we wait for the lift to arrive.

'Were you?'

She nods her head. 'I was.' She scowls. 'It didn't suit me, so I gave up after a year.'

'That was quick!'

She keeps glancing at me and then looking away. 'You know, I keep thinking I've seen you before.'

'You might be right,' I reply, wondering if she's seen my picture in the papers in Ireland. I don't say that.

'You remind me of someone … I just can't put my finger on it.' She exhales abruptly, and then stubs out her cigarette in an ashtray standing nearby. The lift arrives and the door opens. A man engrossed in his own worries steps out. We step in and press the button.

'I live near Maryborough. Maybe you've seen me when you visit Tinana?'

'No, I've only been there once, a few days ago. I need another fag,' she says as the lift comes to a halt on the ground floor and we step out. As we walk towards the car park, she suddenly stops to light her cigarette. She inhales and then blows smoke upwards. 'I have to run,' she declares, looking at her wristwatch.

'Goodbye then,' I say, turning and heading towards my car.

...

That evening I stay at a motel close by. I ring Barbie to see how the kids are, and how she's coping. They're all going out for pizza, she tells me. The following morning I find out that Niall had his operation in the afternoon. He's in intensive care now. I notice a small chapel, so duck inside. I kneel down and lean on the back of the bench in front. 'Dear Lord, please help Niall see again. You caused the blind to see…at least don't let him die.' I pour my heart out to God. As I rest there, my heart is suddenly filled to the brim with a great peace. Afterwards, I stroll to a café and sit down. I'm feeling hungry. I notice a familiar figure strutting towards the café. I call out, 'Joe?'

Joe looks startled for a moment and then his lean face breaks into a large brown smile. He strides towards me.

'G'day Joe,' I say, giving him a bright smile.

'The top of the morning to yourself,' he replies, taking his cap off.

'Have you seen Niall yet Joe?'

'No. They told me he's not allowed visitors till tomorrow!'

We sit in silence. 'Would you like something to eat Joe?' I ask after a few moments.

'I would!'

'Sandwiches?' I suggest.

He nods his head and sits down. I place an order for two plates of mixed sandwiches.

'I'll bring them over,' the bright young sandy haired waitress says, smiling broadly.

'Thanks.' I return and sit down next to Joe.

'Nice day,' I say spontaneously.

'It is. Warm!' he says, mopping his brow. He's dressed in a suit, shirt and tie, with long pants and laced shoes. No wonder he's hot.

'Would you like to take your jacket off?' I venture to ask.

He looks at me as though I've asked him to jump off a bridge. 'They said it was winter.'

'You'd feel better!'

'To hell with it.' He suddenly rises and pulls off his jacket, hanging it carefully on the back of the chair.

He sits down, smiling happily.

'That's better,' I say, smiling in response.

'Sandwiches, and two pots of tea.' The waitress suddenly appears at the table bearing a tray.

'Thanks,' I reply.

After we relax in each other's company, I venture into the subject of relationships.

'Do you know much about Cindy?' I ask.

'How do you mean?' Joe's eyes express alarm.

'What happened with herself and Niall?'

'He nearly married her,' he says, glancing around to make sure nobody heard.

'Is that right?'

'After her husband died she was penniless. I think she might have squandered a bit of the money herself by all accounts, but it's not for me to judge.'

'So, how did Niall come to know her in the first place?' I ask curiously.

'The horses! She was working at the track.'

'With Niall?'

'Niall and Tom,' he says in an exasperated voice.

'Tom Connor?' I ask.

'The same,' he replies abruptly.

'I thought she was a nurse?'

'She never made it. Hadn't the brains! But she hooked Tom good and proper,' he adds.

'So Tom married her?' I ask.

'He did.'

'So, how many wives did he have? I know there was Kathleen, then Jacinta, and then Cindy!'

'No, you're wrong there! Jacinta…Cindy are the same

person,' Joe says, grinning. 'She didn't like the name Jacinta. Wanted a posh name,' he says.

'And the girl, Katie, is she her daughter?'

'Cindy is her stepmother!'

'Right, that's clear now. But I don't know why Niall still has so much to do with them?'

'Katie is like his own. He's been paying for her education since her father died,' he explains sitting back.

'You mean Tom?'

'I do. That's the man, Tom Connor!' he says triumphantly. 'God but you're a terror for questions. Are you one of the garda now?'

'No. I just need to get a few facts together. It's been a long time since I saw Niall!'

'I know all about you Missus de Vinci,' he says, nodding his head. 'I read it in the papers.'

'Can I ask one more question?' I say.

'Go ahead. I can see you need to get something off your chest.'

'Why didn't Niall and Cindy marry?' I ask

'Yerra woman! She didn't love him. She wanted the money, but she couldn't wait!'

'What money?'

He bows his head and then lifts it, as though he's in despair. 'Katie's. She got Tom's, but says there were too many bills. Then she put her claws into Niall. She thought he was going to get his sight back, but when the doctors said it was impossible she was a lot cooler. But she felt he owed her something...'

'Why was that?'

'Because of his friendship with the Connors. They were like family, and she wanted help raising the child. Niall didn't want the child to have any more dramas in her life.... that's another story! He agreed to send Cindy an allowance for Katie. She was happy with that.'

'Didn't Tom provide for his child himself?' I ask.

'Cindy denies that! He left her the property, but she blew

everything in bills! When she came to us about six months after Tom's death she claimed she couldn't afford to bring up the child, and wanted to put her in an orphanage. At that point, Tom's solicitor advised us that there was a trust account put by for Katie which she could access when she was thirty, or gets married.'

I shake my head. 'That's strange!'

'Not at all. It's precaution. I think it was a good move by the Connors, otherwise Cindy would have been able to get the money, and Katie would have been an orphan altogether.' He leans towards me. 'She's after the inheritance, and the horses too by all accounts, otherwise she'd be gone like the wind!'

'Horses?'

'Tom left a couple of champion horses in his will. One was to myself and there was another one…'

He shakes his head. 'That's what I think she's after. She makes my blood boil, that woman!' Joe excuses himself at this point and leaves abruptly.

I head along the hospital pathway where I almost collide with Cindy, who's hurrying towards me from another direction.

'Hello,' I say.

'It's you again!' she says, blowing smoke in my face.

I cough lightly. 'He's not allowed visitors till tomorrow,' I explain.

'Damn! I've come all the way for nothing. I could be making money, not spending it,' she says, looking at her watch.

'Would you like a coffee? There's a shopping centre just down the road. We can walk that far,' I suggest, having discovered it yesterday. 'They have lovely cakes.'

'Well, I've come all this way. I could do with a boost.'

We sit down in the comfortable café, looking out on a busy street, and place an order for coffee and cake.

Cindy stares at me, and puts her cup down. 'You know your name rings a bell with me!'

I act surprised. 'Does it? Actually I wanted to ask about you know, what you said yesterday.'

'What was that?'

'You and Niall being close. Why didn't you get married?'

'He's blind! And I felt we weren't compatible. I found someone else. But we've remained the best of friends…'

'Someone else?' I say, relieved for a moment. 'Joe?'

'No.' She laughs heartily. 'He's to old, and weird! Luke Dunne.'

'I don't know him,' I admit.

'The Dunnes of Dublin are a very grand family.'

'I didn't know Dublin that well…'

'Obviously. Where did you come from, the bog?'

'The west,' I reply briefly.

'There's something about you. I won't rest until I work it out.'

'I'd like to know about you and Luke Dunne, for it sounds like an interesting story?'

'I need a fag.' She lights one up.

I cough from the smoke. 'Sorry! I'm not used to it.'

'That's why I've come to Australia,' she says after an interval.

'To have a smoke?'

'No. To see Luke Dunne. He asked me to come. He's doing very well for himself. He owns three hotels now.' She places her cigarette on the ashtray, allowing the smoke to rise upwards.

'I don't see how this is your business at all. You're a very nosey woman! You're like a ghost from my past and you give me the creeps!' She suddenly holds her own arms and shivers. 'I'm meeting someone at twelve.' She pushes her chair away and leaves without saying goodbye.

…

Finally the day arrives when Niall's bandages can be removed and he's allowed visitors. I'm waiting in the foyer when Cindy arrives.

'Can we finally see him?' she asks

'The doctor's in there… '

'So, what have you been getting up to?' she asks me, sitting down as she speaks.

'Just having a look around the city. It's a great place, and the weather's been grand,' I reply.

'Brisbane is a great city all right. I love living here, there's more opportunities, and the air is fresh!' She suddenly lights up a cigarette as Joe comes through the ward doorway. His face looks white.

'What's the matter Joe? Sit down,' I urge him.

He sits. We both stare at his snow coloured cheeks. 'He's worse,' he gasps at last.

'He's still blind?' Cindy asks. 'After all that,' she adds fiercely.

'That's terrible. Who told you Joe?' I ask.

'I overheard the doctor talking. He said he's lost his sight completely.' He almost bursts into tears at that.

Cindy stands up. 'I hope Katie's support continues.'

We both stare at her in unbelief.

'Please, no smoking allowed,' a nurse says, hurrying past with a trolley.

'Sorry.' Cindy squeezes the tip of the burning cigarette, and snuffs the tiny fire.

'I'm going outside. I can't stand all these rules,' she states, popping her cigarette in her purse and heading towards the lifts.

Joe and I look at each other. 'How's Niall taking it?' I resume his concerns.

'I haven't seen him.'

'Joe, no matter what happens, we have to stand by him, you know that.'

'I do.'

We sit and wait, stunned by the news. The ward door opens, and a nurse followed by a doctor come through. We stare at them. The doctor is smiling. 'You must be Mister Dempsey's relatives?'

Joe nods. 'We are!' he says.

'Everything's fine.'

'He can see?' I ask, amazed.

'It will take some time for him to recover completely, but I'm optimistic.'

We continue to stare. 'He wants to see you both.'

We rise up like zombies and walk through the door. The curtains on the windows are drawn and the room is almost in darkness. Niall is sitting up and the bandages are removed. 'Niamh, Joe, come in.'

We move as in a dream until we stop at his bedside. 'You can see?' Joe asks.

'Things are a bit hazy. But I can make out your face Joe.'

'Begorrah!' Joe exclaims, grinning from ear to ear.

'Niamh, you're as beautiful as ever,' he suddenly says to me.

I stare at him. I lean forward and he hugs my shoulders, and kisses my cheek. I kiss his cheek gently.

Joe just stares, smiling happily.

'Take a seat,' Niall suggests. We find two chairs and sit down in the dim room.

'Tell us about the operation,' I say excitedly.

'Sure I was asleep all the time. I had a wonderful dream. I'll tell you about it some time.'

The following day, having visited Niall briefly once more, and enjoyed a shopping spree, I drive back to Maryborough. I bring back some new clothes for Nicky, Carly, Abigale, and Barbie, and videos for James, John and Charles.

'He'll be there for another week, then he's coming back here,' I explain to Barbie.

Two weeks later I visit Niall in his hotel at Tinana where he's recovering before returning to Ireland.

Niall suddenly turns to me. 'Would you like to go for a walk?'

'Before we do Niall, there is another crow I need to pluck with you.'

He looks concerned. 'I'm right here. Go ahead.'

'Do you remember we were having a conversation about

why you came to Australia? I mean I know you've had an operation and you've got responsibilities to Katie and Cindy, and you picked up the painting. Now I think you said you wanted to see if it was me or not?'

'That's true'

'Well, what I wanted to know was, why you wanted to see me.'

'Well, you have the facts right about all those things. I came for all those reasons you mentioned.' He stops and looks into my face. 'Niamh, the most important reason I came here is because I have been longing for you since the day I last kissed you goodbye.'

'So, when did you know it was me?'

'When we shook hands in Australia! When you had the write-up in the paper in Ireland, I had a wonderful hunch it was. I tried to get to the exhibition but I missed you as you had left already and returned to Australia. After that I had to follow my hunch, so I decided to buy a painting and arrange for my operation to be in Australia. I could have gone to Canada for that, so I found another reason to come here.' He pauses. 'But not only was there the consideration of Cindy and Katie, who lived in Australia, I also had some business to sort out... As you can see, there were many reasons, but you were the catalyst, you might say! If I found out it wasn't you I would have been sadly disappointed, but truly satisfied that I did everything in my heart to find you. Do you believe me?'

I stare at him, swallow the lump in my throat and laugh nervously. 'Sounds fair dinkum to me!'

'Fair dinkum?' He says. 'What sort of language is that?'

'True blue Aussie language.' I look into his face. 'The honest to God truth!'

We look at each other and suddenly we hug.

'I'd love to go for a walk with you,' I say as we reluctantly release our hold on each other.

He offers me the crook of his arm and I link it in mine.

Together we walk down the narrow road. 'This is where James works,' I comment as we move along a fenced property.

'That's the one.' He suddenly stops. 'Niamh, do you like diamonds?' he asks.

I feel startled and the thought that he might be proposing to me crosses my mind like an arrow. This is not the right time…too soon! I hesitate as he speaks and shrug my shoulders.

'Come over here,' he says, picking up the pace again and taking me to the right.

'There she is!' he indicates a beautiful chestnut filly that's grazing contentedly. As if she knows, she tosses her head and trots over.

'What do you think?'

'She is beautiful,' I say, patting her velvety nose.

'She's yours,' Niall says.

'How's that?'

'The Connors gave Finn McCool to me as a dowry when we were wedded. She is also that other business I was telling you about. We intended to match her up with a thoroughbred stallion, but she's yours.'

'A dowry? But you never told me about that? A dowry!'

'No, they asked me not to tell you.'

'Why not?' I ask, suddenly feeling offended.

'Well, they didn't want you to think they were selling you to me, or that you were worth a horse.'

'I would never have thought that!' I exclaim.

'Well, you had that bang on the head and they didn't know how you'd react.'

'I suppose they were only thinking of my welfare, as they always did!' I touch the beautiful animal on its white smooth nose. It snorts gently. 'So, what's your name?' I ask her.

'Diamond,' Niall says in response.

I laugh. 'She's the most beautiful diamond I've ever set my eyes on…'

'I don't think so,' Niall says.

'No?'

'Your eyes are the most beautiful diamonds I've ever seen.'

As I look towards Niall, I see two young people in the distance. 'Who's that with James?'

'That's Katie,' Niall says. 'She's not finished the special course until this weekend. She loves horses.'

'I've been looking forward to meeting Katie. I think I know her!'

'Well, why don't we go over there,' he suggests, as we watch the slim girl laughing, enrapturing James.

I knew this already, but it's a real shock to see her again. 'It's Kathleen.'

'No, it's Katie,' he contradicts me, opening a gate so that we can take a short cut.

I stop. 'You don't know the whole story. We…I had twins, Kathleen and James. I persuaded my sister to give Kathleen to Missus Connor.'

'My God Niamh, you gave your own child away? Why in God's name would you do that?'

'Not my child, *our* child! I thought she would have a better life. I knew the Connors would give her the chance she needed to be educated, and she'd have plenty of food and clothing…remember I was a tinceard with no home, few clothes and sometimes no food.'

His face is a mask of shock as he turns towards me. 'Niamh, are you saying that these are our children? And all this time I have cared for my own daughter?'

I feel the tears warming my cheeks. 'I am. I have no excuse for what I did. But I had good intentions, truly! God's forgiven me, I hope you can, then I can forgive myself!'

He automatically places his arms around my shoulders. 'Niamh, it's your heart I love. Whatever you tried to do for your child, you did it from the goodness of your heart. That's what's important. There's nothing to forgive.'

I look into his wonderful blurred face through my tears.

'Don't cry,' he says. 'This is the happiest day of my life, and I don't want another minute to be lost with crying.' He pulls a large handkerchief from his pocket. 'Take it, wipe your eyes, *mo vhoirneen.*'

I wipe my eyes and blow my nose, looking over the handkerchief to the two young people who are obviously smitten with each other. 'Do you think children follow their parents with the same mistakes?'

'Well now, I suppose they probably will, because as humans beings we all hurry to make our own mistakes; but then again maybe if they are warned and they listen, they might avoid a lot of trouble.'

I laugh. 'Well, just watching those two young people over there makes me feel so good, and also really bad.'

'You're a paradox. Why is that Niamh?' he asks, staring where I am looking.

'I can't tell you how much I've wanted to see my daughter again, but now that I'm here, I honestly don't know what to say to her…She was just a baby and now…'

'She's a beautiful young woman!'

'That's so true. And there's another problem looming already!' I continue.

'What's that now?'

'They seem to be too attached to each other.'

'Begorrah, I think you might be right!' He gazes at the two and then turns back to me. 'They say two heads are better than one!'

I look into his face, puzzled. 'What do you mean?'

'We'll work this out together. Would you like that?'

'I would,' I reply.

I take a deep breath, reach for his outstretched hand, and we walk together across the paddock.

The End

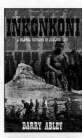   

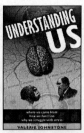

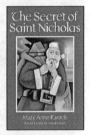

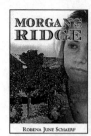   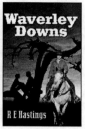

Best-selling titles by Kerry B. Collison

Readers are invited to visit our publishing websites at:

http://www.sidharta.com.au

http://www.publisher-guidelines.com/

http://temple-house.com/

Kerry B. Collison's home pages:

http://www.authorsden.com/visit/uthor.asp?AuthorID=2239

http://www.expat.or.id/sponsors/collison.html

http://clubs.yahoo.com/clubs/asianintelligencesresources

email: author@sidharta.com.au